NOT OUT OF HATE

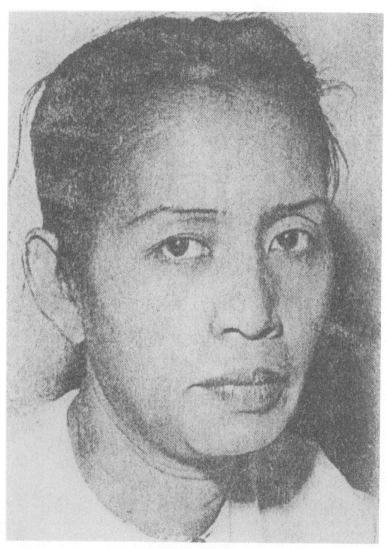

Ma Ma Lay in about 1962. (Photograph from: Minn Latt, "A dawn that went astray," *New Orient* 5 (1962), p. 175.)

NOT OUT OF HATE

A Novel of Burma by

Ma Ma Lay

Translated by Margaret Aung-Thwin
Introduced by Anna Allott
Afterword by Robert E. Vore

Edited by William H. Frederick

Ohio University Center for International Studies
Monographs in International Studies

Southeast Asia Series Number 88
Athens, Ohio 1991

Library of Congress Cataloging-in-Publication Data

Ma Ma Le , 1917-1982
    [Muin   r* ma hu. English].
    Not out of hate: a novel of Burma / by Ma Ma Lay; edited by
William H. Frederick ; translated by Margaret Aung-Thwin ;
introduced by Anna Allott
    p. cm. – Monographs in international studies. Southeast
Asia series ; no. 88
    Translation of : Muin   r* ma hu.
    Includes bibliographical references
    ISBN : 0-89680-167-5
    1. Burmese fiction–20th century–Translations into English.
2. English fiction–Translations from Burmese 3 Interpersonal
relations–Fiction. 4. Burma–Social life and customs–Fiction.
5. Burma–History–1824-1948–Fiction   I. Frederick, William H.
II Aung-Thwin, Margaret. III. Title IV. Series.
PL3986.5.E5M3 1991
895'.833–dc20   90-28553
                                       CIP

CONTENTS

MAP

A NOTE ON
NAMES AND SPELLING IN BURMESE

Names in Burmese, as in many other Southeast Asian languages, present something of a problem in English translation. The use of honorifics such as "U," for example is difficult to understand for speakers of a language in which such formalities are dispensed with and everyone is generally called by their first name, or as "you." Also the fact that the type of honorific used may depend on the relative social positions of the speaker, the person being spoken to, and even persons present (Ko Nay U and Maung Nay U) is confusing to English speakers accustomed to individuals retaining the same name in all occasions. In this translation we have decided to modify somewhat the Burmese system, using "I" and "you" when the flow of the text seemed to demand it, but not to Anglicize entirely. We think that approach, though not consistent, allows us to retain a Burmese flavor without getting in the way of the sense or the pace of the work.

The spelling of Burmese in English has not been standardized and there are several systems in use. Here too we have adopted an eclectic approach designed for the general reader rather than the linguist or the Burma specialist. That is, in the case of well-known names of places, objects, or individuals, we have retained the most common Anglicized spelling; for the rest, we have opted for renditions which are likely to be acceptable to the eye and ear of the average English speaker or reader, regardless of whether the rules of any one system are followed consistently. Well-eductaed Burmese frequently do the same. We have also eliminated hyphens. The result will undoubtedly not please some Burma experts, but seems to be less of a distraction to others attempting to appreciate this work.

Finally, although the official name of the nation of Burma was changed in 1989 to Myanmar, and Rangoon to Yangon, we have retained the older terms because they are familiar to the general reader and the subject is colonial Burma.

M. A-T. and W. H. F.

vii

CONTRIBUTORS

Ma Ma Lay, the author of the novel translated here, was one of Burma's most prominent literary figures. She died in 1982. For more information on Ma Ma Lay, see the Introduction, below.

Margaret Aung-Thwin grew up in British Burma, finishing her college education after World War II. She taught high school English in Rangoon and received a Fulbright grant to visit the United States. Dissatisfied with her country's educational system, she left Burma, lived for a time in India, and later settled in the United States with her children. She has taught Burmese at Cornell University, and later basic adult education skills to native Americans. Now retired and living in New York City, she teaches adult illiterates and translates Burmese literature.

Anna Allott teaches Burmese at the University of London's School for Oriental and African Studies. She is widely recognized as an authority on Burmese literature, especially of the modern period, and is the author of a number of articles and book chapters on the subject.

Robert E. Vore recently completed his master's degree in Southeast Asian Studies at Ohio University. A returned Peace Corps volunteer from the Philippines, he is presently a student in the doctoral program of English and American literature at Washington State University.

William H. Frederick is associate professor of history at Ohio University. A specialist in modern Indonesia, he has long had an interest in bringing translations of modern Southeast Asian literature to the English-speaking public.

TRANSLATOR'S PREFACE

Margaret Aung-Thwin

The idea of translating *Monywei Mahu* (Not Out of Hate) began
with hearing Mrs. Anna Allott's paper on the Burmese novel given
at an Association for Asian Studies conference in Chicago in 1982.
I was very excited as I listened to her discuss various Burmese
authors and their works, none of which had been translated into
English. I was amazed, also, that an English lady knew so much
about Burmese literature while I knew next to nothing. Very
impressed by her talk, I felt I wanted to try translating so that
Burmese literature could be better known outside of Burma.

I went up to her after the panel discussion was over and told
her how much her talk had affected me and that I wanted to try
translating one of the novels she had mentioned. We soon
decided I should do *Monywei Mahu*. I was attracted to this
particular work because it was written by a woman, and also
because I was intrigued with the story of a Burmese woman who
leaves her home and family to become a nun, in contrast to the
Western version, in which the nun leaves the convent to live in the
outside world; I thought there might be some interesting cultural
and social implications. I later discovered, of course, that the nun
was not the central character, and that in fact her role belonged
more to the background of the story.

When I was ready to begin, I could not find a copy of the novel, which at that time was next to impossible to get from Burma. So we arranged for Anna to xerox the first few chapters and mail them to me from England, and we would go on from there. Then I found a copy of the novel in Cornell University's Echols Collection.

Having never attempted such a project before, I just sat down in the kitchen, which had the best light, and day after day worked on the translation. I did not anticipate some of the difficulties I encountered. Sometimes I would take all day just to cover half a page. I could not help being overly conscientious, treating the material as if it were Holy Writ or Shakespeare and looking up the meaning of every single word. At day's end I felt like a little hen who had pecked and pecked at a kernel of corn all day and was still unable to crack it. I used to call up a Burmese housewife who lived in Manhattan to discuss Burmese medicine just so I could get the feel of it, but she herself was now more interested in Western medicine and had lost touch with the Burmese side of things. I felt culturally isolated working in a foreign milieu.

Another difficulty was that I did not have adequate dictionaries. The one I leaned on heavily was compiled by Adoniram Judson, the famous American Baptist missionary and scholar, who lived about the time of the British annexation of Burma. So the vocabulary was limited to words used in the nineteenth century, which presented a major problem. Just using Judson's scholarly work excited me, however, and I feel a personal debt to him.

One of the first problems was to make up my mind who I was translating for. I decided that the high school boys of Government High School in Rangoon, to whom I had taught English in my first teaching assignment, would be my audience. I thought that it would be a change if they read a Burmese novel they already knew, in an English version. (This was when I started treating the material like Shakespeare.) However, the novel did not seem to hold up at all to this sort of English. At this time I met a friend who was teaching comparative literature at an American college, and she encouraged me to translate the novel for her students, an approach that was better.

I ran into another problem when I worried about the wrong interpretation of actions set in a different social situation, and became defensive of Burmese culture. I kept explaining the action in parentheses (which got to be tiresome reading), but later these were skillfully turned into footnotes by my able editor. I also had problems with Burmese honorific terms, which if translated would puzzle and confuse readers. For example, a Mr. Joe Brown is addressed in English as "Mr." by people outside his family, "Joe" by his wife, and "Dad" by his children. His friends would also call him "Joe," while he would refer to himself as "I." In Burmese, however, Mr. Brown would refer to himself in the third person, as "Your Dad," "Your Uncle," or even "Joe." The precise usage of these "I" forms would change depending on the age of the person speaking and whether a younger or older person was being addressed. My editor convinced me to stick for the most part to English personal pronouns to facilitate matters.

I also made some problems for myself by not agreeing with what the author was doing to the characters. I wanted to make them over and change the plot, but had to restrain myself. I became unable to identify with the book and actually stopped working on it for over a year. These and many other similar difficulties delayed me further from completing my self-imposed task.

But for the kind encouragement of friends and family I would not have come to completion. Thanks to my daughter Maureen, for her gadfly goading, and to my son Michael, for his help and encouragement in getting the first chapters typed. The friends I would like to thank are many, among them Anna Allott, for inspiring me in the first place and then being generous with her time and knowledge whenever I sought her counsel. I would also like to thank John Ferguson, the unflagging and hard-working secretary-treasurer of the Burma Studies Group, who encouraged this humble project from its infancy and got it on its way by taking the time to read many chapters. My gratitude to Euan Bagshawe, an Englishman who had to help me with the nun's letter in chapter three, with its Pali and Buddhist exhortations. I felt that, although I blame the British colonial educational system for my knowing Jane Austen but not Ma Ma Lay, things have been evened up a bit in this small project with the help I received from my two British friends.

Finally, I was fortunate to find my very able editor, William Frederick of Ohio University, who offered to get the translation published virtually sight unseen after he read a short story of Ma Ma Lay's that I had translated. Bill finally managed to see the project through with his consummate editorial skills and warm encouragement, so that the elephant did not "get stuck at its tail."

To all my friends who were enthusiastic and patient all along and who finally, tactfully, did not ask how the translation was going—many thanks. You can ask. It's all over now.

New York
May 1990

INTRODUCTION

Anna Allott

Although the accounts of her life do not record when the young Burmese girl, Ma Tin Hlaing, first showed a talent for writing, they all without exception mention that the work she wrote when she was 37 years of age, already widowed and with three small children, won a government-sponsored literary prize, having been chosen as the best novel published in Burma in 1955. In spite of its heroine's tragic end, the novel was also very popular with the reading public, going into at least five editions during the 1950s and 1960s.[1] This introduction will attempt to suggest some of the reasons for the success of *Not Out of Hate* (Monywei Mahu), a novel which seems to reflect aspects of her own life more directly than her other works of fiction.

Ma Tin Hlaing was born on 13 April 1917, in a village near the small town of Bogalei in the district of Hpyapon, a rice-growing area of Lower Burma. This is the same area in which *Not*

---

1. After 1964 the military government instituted a series of National Literary Prizes for different categories of work. Increasingly, political rather than literary criteria have come to determine the choice of prize-winners, with the result that some prize-winning novels have not been popular with the reading public and have not sold well.

Out of Hate is set. She was the fourth of five children born to the manager of the local branch of Dawson's Bank, U Pya Cho, and his wife, Daw Hswi.[2] She first went to the American Baptist Mission School in Hpyapon, perhaps as a weekly boarder as it was some distance from her home. By the age of ten she had passed the seventh standard examination at the government school in nearby Bogalei, after which she was sent to continue her schooling in Rangoon at the Girls' Myoma High School (Myoma Amyothami Kyaung). Before she was able to complete her tenth standard (graduation) exam, the sudden breakdown of her mother's mental health obliged her to return home to take over the running of the household; she was just fifteen years old. (In *Not Out of Hate*, the young heroine's mother abandons her home and family, when her daughter is only thirteen, to enter a convent.)

Ma Tin Hlaing, clearly exceptionally intelligent, was now also politically aware, having been influenced in Rangoon by the tide of nationalist feeling that was gathering strength in Burma in the early 1930s. Back in Bogalei she joined the local branch of the Dobama organization when it was formed in 1936, and became its secretary. She met the organizations' leaders when they visited the town, attended their meetings, and joined them in writing articles and making speeches against the British. Being a keen follower of the Burmese press, she happened to read an article mocking Burmese girls for spending their time playing badminton, which provoked her into writing a spirited reply urging women to be as active and enterprising as men. This piece was published, with her photograph, in the leading Burmese daily of the time, *Myanma Alin* (The New Light of Burma), the chief editor of which, U Chit Maung, was a fervent nationalist—and also a confirmed bachelor. He was impressed by the article; they met and, to his fellow journalists' amazement, were married about a year later in 1938, when Ma Tin Hlaing was twenty. (The heroine of the novel marries an older man of 37 when she is still in her early twenties.)

The following year U Chit Maung started his own paper called *Gyanegyaw* (The Weekly Thunderer) and Ma Tin Hlaing took on the management of the finances. Without her business

---

2. The name Hswi is not Burmese and suggests that Ma Tin Hlaing's mother was partly of Chinese descent.

ability and competence the paper would not have survived. It was from this time that she began to write under the pen name Gyanegyaw Ma Ma Lay (Ma Ma Lay of *The Thunderer*).[3]

The war years from 1940-1945 must have been extremely full for Ma Ma Lay. She continued writing as a journalist; she began writing short stories, the first one appearing in *The Thunderer* in 1941; she wrote a first novel (*Ahpyu*, only published later, in 1947), and a second one as well (*Thuma* [She], published in 1944); and she had three children. Although she had wrought a transformation in the day-to-day life-style of her bachelor husband, the one area in which she could not and did not try to influence him was that of politics. Like most of Burma's leading nationalist politicians, U Chit Maung was greatly influenced by Marxism, a circumstance which helped to determine the political philosophy of his paper, *Gyanegyaw*. At the beginning of World War II, U Chit Maung and his wife moved from the center of Rangoon to a village outside the city, where it happened that their next door neighbor was Thakin Than Tun, later to become Burma's leading communist. Hence many of Ma Ma Lay's close friendships were with nationalist leaders, some of whom later became communists or supporters of very left-wing, anti-government policies. This led some people to think that Ma Ma Lay herself was a communist, and undoubtedly contributed to her arrest in 1963 and subsequent three-year detention.

---

3. The use of pen names is long-established and widespread in Burma; there are several reasons for this. Burmese names are short and often shared by many persons, hence writers customarily identified themselves by adding their place of birth to their given name. When novels and short stories were becoming established as new genres on the literary scene at the beginning of the twentieth century, certain writers of scholarly or religious works did not wish to reveal that they were also writing fiction. Later in the 1920s some young authors, keen to increase the number and readership of periodicals, would submit material under several different names at the same time. Other writers wanted to conceal their identity from rival publishers or from the authorities. In addition to identifying themselves by place of birth, writers frequently used the name of a magazine, such as *Dagon* (in the 1920s), or the words *theikpan* (college) or *teggatho* (university) before their own name or their chosen pen name.

In mid-1945, the Japanese having surrendered and the British colonial government having returned, the family moved back from the village to a northern suburb of Rangoon. Unexpectedly, when life should have become easier, U Chit Maung was taken to the hospital and died there on 2 April 1946; they had been married only nine years. This could have been a tragic turning point in the story of Ma Ma Lay's life and the end of a brilliant career, but it was not. Though heart-broken at the loss of the man she loved, the person who had been her inspiration and guide in this early stage of her career, she drove herself to continue writing. She poured her love and grief into a moving account of her husband and their brief time together, entitled *Thulo Lu* (A Man Like Him). This work, one of her longest books, appeared in 1947. It has been praised as her best work, standing as a landmark in the development of Burmese prose writing and displaying all the narrative skill, tension, and passion of a good novel.

At the same time, she continued to bring out the *Gyanegyaw* every week, even managing most weeks to write the leading articles herself. The hazards facing journalists in Burma during that turbulent postwar period (though not yet the arbitrary censorship that came in the 1960s) are well illustrated by the fact that an unwelcome mention in her paper of an item of news about the politician Thakin Tin led to an attack on the paper's office. In spite of the serious damage caused by this attack, she managed to continue publication. In December of that year she took on the job of editing the magazine *Kalaungshin*, a periodical started by the newly formed League of Women Writers, in line with her firm belief in the importance of the equal participation of women in all walks of life.

The failure of Western medicine to save her husband's life, together with the fact that her daughter had developed rickets during the war years, set Ma Ma Lay searching for alternative ways of treating disease, and she began to take a serious interest in traditional Burmese medicine. This interest was to remain with her for the rest of her life; indeed, in her later years treating and advising patients, as well as writing guides to medical treatments based on traditional diets, came to take precedence over fiction writing and journalism. In the opinion of some who knew her then, she developed a quite unjustified faith in the power of special diets coupled with cold showers to cure all ills. But we are jumping too far ahead.

In June 1947 a publication appeared on the Rangoon literary scene which was to be the main vehicle for bringing Ma Ma Lay's writing regularly, quickly, and cheaply to a wide readership for the next thirty years. *Shumawa* was a new monthly literary magazine which included short stories and serial novels, poetry, cartoons, and serious articles on literature and culture, together with plenty of advertisements, all aimed at a wide readership. Her work, both fiction and journalism, which continued to appear in *Gyanegyaw* between 1947 and 1952, was also featured in this new magazine after 1952, thus greatly increasing her popularity as a writer.[4]

The internal politics of newly independent Burma do not seem to have attracted Ma Ma Lay, but after 1948 she began to participate in international activities. In that year she toured India; she was also elected to the chairmanship of the National Writers' Association, a singular honor for a woman. In 1950 she made her first visit to Japan, and in 1952 she was part of a cultural delegation that toured China and the Soviet Union. Later in the 1950s Ma Ma Lay became caught up in the Soviet-led international peace movement, as can be seen from her articles with titles such as "The Flag of Peace." In 1958 she went as a delegate to the World Anti-nuclear Rearmament Congress in Japan, and on her return wrote a very powerful piece about Hiroshima. In December 1956 she was again in India, this time with two other Burmese

---

4. *Shumawa* is difficult to translate with a single English expression. Literally it means "not to be able to have one's fill of looking at," "something one cannot look at enough." This type of monthly fiction magazine, more than just a vehicle for short stories but not really a news magazine, had become well established in the 1920s; one of the best-known titles was *Dagon*. In the 100th issue of *Shumawa*, a special number published in September 1955, there is a list of the most regular contributors. Ma Ma Lay comes fourth in the list of 29, having contributed 31 pieces in all since the magazine's inception in 1947. Of the 29 listed, only 4 are women; the two women with a greater total of contributions that Ma Ma Lay are both poets, which leads us to the realization that Ma Ma Lay was indeed exceptional in being almost the only serious, influential woman prose writer in Burma during the early years of independence.

writers (Dagon Taya and Paragu) to attend the first Asian Writers' Conference. We get a glimpse of her physical appearance at that date from a memoir, written at the time of her death in 1982, by the writer Paragu. He tells us that during the conference a telegram arrived from Rangoon announcing that she had won the Translation Society (Sarpay Beikman) prize for her novel *Not Out of Hate*. Paragu arranged for the organizer of the conference, K. Anand (author of the English-language novel *Coolie*), to announce the news to the full session of writers. Dr. Anand, a Punjabi by birth, expressed his pleasure that the conference should be marked by having such a nationally honored Burmese author as a delegate, and finished by saying, "Please will the Burmese lady writer who resembles a beautiful Punjabi woman be so kind as to stand up." Paragu confessed that he was taken aback; he had not realized that this competent, hard-working, outspoken journalist and fellow writer was also, in the eyes of certain foreigners, a strikingly attractive woman. (In 1959 she married her second husband, the writer U Aung Zeiya.)

During the 1950s in Burma, for writers such as Ma Ma Lay who were concerned about the future of their country and the way society and the economy were developing, it was no longer as clear as it had been before independence who was to play the villain in works of fiction. In fact literature and culture were increasingly politicized, and disagreements over the role of literature in society became more bitter and more frequent. Many left-wing writers proclaimed that literature should follow the path of socialist realism, should aid in building a new socialist society, and should be of benefit to the working people.[5] One of the reasons for the popularity of *Not Out of Hate* may have been that it took the Burmese reader back to the immediate prewar period, when the population was reassuringly united in its political aspirations; the work could be enjoyed by right and left wings alike.

At the beginning of the 1960s a considerable number of writers decided that they would form a separate organization, outside the National Writers' Association, to be called the Writers'

---

5. In Burmese this is known as *pyeithu akyobyu sapei*. Such slogans were adopted by the military government after 1962 as part of the official policy toward literature.

Literary Club (*sayeihsaya sapei kalat*) for the pursuit of purely literary activities. The club was established on 26 February 1961; Ma Ma Lay was among the 38 writers present who signed their names in agreement with the aims of the group, and it was she who was chosen to be the general secretary, evidence of the respect and prestige she continued to enjoy as a writer at the time.[6]

However, within a year the political situation in the country was to change in a way that eventually left very little freedom of action to those writers who were not in favor of using their literary talents to support the building of the "Burmese Way to Socialism." In a coup in March 1962, a military government led by General Ne Win seized power and confined leading politicians to prison. Writers and journalists were at first wooed and encouraged to put their talents at the service of the "revolution"; a nation-wide literary conference was organized by the government in November 1962, at which the chair was taken by the writer Thein Pe Myint, a former communist. As chairman of the reception committee, Ma Ma Lay should have had the right to speak first, but Thein Pe Myint negotiated to prevent this from happening. Certain younger writers, unaware of the difficult position in which Ma Ma Lay found herself, criticized her behavior, at which point she decided she had had enough and resigned from all official positions.

Although an advocate of socialism, Ma Ma Lay soon came into conflict with the policies of the military regime. She had never hesitated to criticize injustice, corruption, inhumanity, pretentiousness, or hypocrisy, especially in her short stories. Despite her resignation from literary office, such was her reputation as an influential writer and outspoken critic of government corruption and inefficiency that she was not to be left in peace. On 14 December 1963 she was arrested at her home by officers of the Military Intelligence Service, on the pretext of having assisted Bo Let-ya, a former minister of defence and close comrade of Aung San, escape capture by the government. She was taken to prison and detained for a total of three years and two months before

---

6. It is interesting to note that one of the first activities to be organized by Ma Ma Lay for the members of the club was a series of lectures on the contemporary literary scene in countries outside Burma, starting with Great Britain followed by China and the Soviet Union.

being released on 5 February 1967. Happily, she was allowed pen and paper in prison, with the result that she had a long novel ready for publication when she emerged.

In the last fifteen years of her life, while devoting an increasing proportion of her time to medicine and healing, Ma Ma Lay wrote two more novels, a biography of a famous Burmese actress, and numerous articles for newspapers and magazines. In one of these novels, *Thwei* (Blood), published in 1973, she used the story of a Japanese girl's search for her Burmese half-brother to examine Burmese attitudes toward Japanese. The work was so effective that when it was translated into Japanese it was voted the best foreign novel of the year. An invitation by the Japanese government to visit Japan and receive the prize enabled Ma Ma Lay to make one last trip abroad in October 1980. Ma Ma Lay died peacefully at her home on 6 April 1982, but because of the general fear that she was still out of favor with the Ne Win regime, the death of Burma's most important modern woman writer passed virtually unnoted by the official literary establishment.

The first question that a would-be reader of *Not Out of Hate* will likely ask is, "What is it about?" The second may well be, "Why has it been chosen for translation?" To a certain extent, the two questions can be answered together. The story is set in Lower Burma, in the town of Moulmeingyun, in the years 1939 to 1942, just before the outbreak of World War II. It tells how an intelligent but naive young girl from an ordinary Burmese Buddhist family is attracted to an older, completely Westernized Burmese man; of their marriage and her unhappiness at the gulf she discovers between her own way of life and that of her husband; and of her illness and death. It is not primarily a novel about politics, though the main political events of the period play an important part in the development of the story. Rather, it is perhaps first a study of different types of love: unselfish love, which can allow the loved one to go free; selfish, suffocating love, which in seeking to hold tight only destroys the loved one; caring love of an elder sister; and anxious love of a daughter for a sick father. The novel's underlying ideological issue is the threat which the Western way of life poses to Burmese culture and traditional family relationships. It is for the insight that it offers into a Burmese view of all these topics that *Not Out of Hate* has been translated into English.

The story is comparatively simple in outline. In the early chapters we are given a detailed picture of an extended Burmese family. The younger daughter, in her twenties, lives at home running the household and helping her father with his business accounts. The father, aged about sixty and in poor health, is a rice-broker dealing with British firms. An older daughter, close to her sister, is married to a government doctor. Their brother, the oldest child, is aggressively anti-British and is involved in the nationalist movement. The mother left the family several years earlier to become a Buddhist nun, but keeps in touch periodically. The principal household also includes an older sister of the father who has been like a mother to the youngest daughter, and a servant girl.

At the same time as we learn of the complex relationships among the member of this Burmese family, we also see how they react to the arrival of a new neighbor, whom everyone is surprised to discover, given the gossip and furniture that has preceded him, is Burmese and not English as had been supposed. Sent by a British firm to handle their rice-purchasing, he is a bachelor with Western education and tastes; he lives more in the style of a colonial official than of a Burmese. There is extensive treatment of the ways in which the life and ideals of the newcomer and the family differ. The youngest daughter is much impressed with the bachelor, and they eventually marry despite the misgivings of her family. This is the beginning of a series of events which end in tragic conflict and misunderstandings, and in the death of the daughter, a victim not of hate but, ironically and in a number of ways, love and caring.

If it were simply the story of an unsuitable marriage ending in disaster, *Not Out of Hate* would almost certainly not have made such an impression on the Burmese reading public. They must have felt that the daughter in some way symbolized Burma itself, struggling to maintain its own culture in the face of the many attractions of the Western way of life as glimpsed in the colonial setting. Here, after all, was an intelligent, competent young woman led to bring about her own destruction by abandoning the Burmese way of life, against the advice of her family. Further strengthening the symbolic aspect of the story is the theme of conflict between Western and traditional types of medicine that is present throughout. The daughter dies of tuberculosis, contracted from her father (who also dies), which Western medical methods cannot cure. Her husband has totally rejected the idea that Burmese medicine might be effective, and she is condemned to rely on painful and, in the end, ineffective Western doctoring. But here again the condemnation has been made—and submitted to—not out of hate, but love.[7]

All of this human drama is intertwined with events on the national scene: in 1942, with Pearl Harbor and Singapore fallen to the Japanese, the Burma Independence Army advances on Rangoon but soon young nationalists are at risk and are being jailed by the Japanese military government. That these forces tear people apart only worsens the existing family and personal difficulties, and the poignancy of the final tragedy is increased by the juxtaposition of political and human circumstances.

It is interesting that Ma Ma Lay chose to write a novel about the years 1939-1942 rather than the period in which she was then living (the mid-1950s). Clearly her mother's mental illness, her own return at a young age from school, her involvement in political activities, and her marriage to U Chit Maung, all during the years in which *Not Out of Hate* is set, were experiences on which she was able to draw. It is also very likely that, in order to provide an appropriate political context for the personal story, she felt compelled to choose the most recent point in Burmese history when the country was united behind a single goal—in this case, independence—rather than attempt to deal with the confused period of the mid-1950s, when disagreement was in the air and there was a certain nostalgia for the atmosphere in which all pulled together in the struggle for freedom from British colonial rule.

---

7. The title *Not Out of Hate* is particularly interesting because it can describe much else in the novel besides the colonial relationship and the principal love relationship. Clearly, if somewhat more subtly, it may for example refer to the relationship Westernized Burmese have with traditional Burmese culture and society, or the relationship which the Buddhist nun in this story has with her family.

Not Out of Hate is Ma Ma Lay's fifth novel. Unlike her previous ones, it was published by the Shumawa Press, not by her own Gyanegyaw Press. We learn from the foreword to the book how this came about. Ma Ma Lay had begun to contribute regularly to *Shumawa* the magazine, for which she soon became one of the most popular writers of short stories and articles. The editor, U Kyaw, asked her to write a *long* short story which was to appear in two installments in the issues of May and June, 1955. (This type of serialization encouraged continuing sales from month to month.) He was printing the second, and he thought final, installment; when he came to the end of chapter fifteen, he sent an urgent message to Ma Ma Lay to tell her that she had two more pages in which to finish off the story! At this point, Ma Ma Lay tells us, she exploded in frustration. All through the writing she had been pressured to hurry up, yet at the same time asked to keep the work as short as possible; how could a person write under such conditions? She told U Kyaw that she bitterly regretted having agreed to write the story for *Shumawa* instead of doing in as a complete novel in the first place and publishing it with her own company. Finally there was an amicable settlement; it was agreed that there would be no further installments, that she would complete the book as soon as possible, and that it would be published by the Shu-mawa Press as a complete novel with all the parts restored that she had been forced to cut out. The reader will notice that the events of chapters 16 to 21 move more slowly and lack some of the dramatic tension of the earlier ones. Elsewhere Ma Ma Lay tells us that she needed to be under pressure in order to write effectively.[8]

---

8. It is worth noting that the Russian "translation" of *Monywei Mahu* is a drastically shortened version—119 pages as opposed to 364 pages in the original Burmese edition. Even if one calculates two pages of Burmese as equal in length to one page of Russian, some 126 pages of Burmese have been cut to produce the Russian version. The resulting "novella" reads well enough, but it is not a translation of Ma Ma Lay's novel, and was done without any reference to her.

❖   ❖   ❖

The novel in Burma has a relatively recent history; the first appeared in 1904. Short stories, published in daily and weekly newspapers, began to make their appearance in the following decade, and by the 1920s both genres were firmly established in the favor of the largely urban reading public. Almost from the beginning—and certainly from 1914, when U Lat wrote a famous work called *Shweipyizo*—most important Burmese novels had a political message, or at least political theme, which was that it was essential to maintain the dignity and integrity of Burmese Buddhist culture against the advance of Western education and technology, and that the best way to do this was to regain Burma's independence from Britain. During the 1930s many historical novels were written, many of them with nationalist heroes. It is sufficient for us to examine in detail the foreword written by U Chit Maung for his wife's first novel, *Thuma* (She), in 1944, to realize the extent to which the Burmese expected serious fiction to contribute to education and nation-building. The first point U Chit Maung makes is that the heroine of *Thuma*, Thet Thet, like the hero of his own prewar novel *Thu* (He), is a model character, the sort of person needed to set a good example to readers. Second, he says that a nation is made up of numerous households and families; if the families prosper then the nation will prosper, but quarrels at home lead to trouble, unhappiness, and inefficiency at work. Third, and for us most interestingly, he says that in building a new nation men and women are equally important.

> If both work together in harmony they will soon build the nation upon a firm foundation. But at the present time there are many who look down on women, who pour scorn on their ability and refuse to give them a part to play. Recently I have noticed that the writer Ma Ma Lay has written several articles in *Gya-ne-Gyaw* about how women's special capabilities could be used in national affairs, but these are little more than occasional flashes of lightning in the utterly black sky of the minds of those who believe that men are the masters of the world. With few exceptions, in films, novels, and plays women are shown as always turning

in tears to men for help in time of trouble; a plot in which a woman finds a way out of difficulty by applying her own effort and intelligence, her own practical common sense, is very rare. So I welcome this novel as being just what is needed. If it had been written by a man, one or both heroines would have ended up in Rangoon, weeping. But as it was written by a woman of exceptional imagination, the two heroines are shown overcoming their difficulties honorably and in a most unexpected manner. This novel shows not only a woman writer's intellectual ability, but also women's hidden strength. We are shown that a woman can find a way of surmounting difficulties in a dignified and respectable manner [that is, without resorting to prostitution]. If women such as are portrayed in this novel would display their abilities in real life, then the tasks of nation-building and world-building would be easier and lighter. When the country produces more people like the heroes of these two books [that is, his own and his wife's], Burma will enter the ranks of the leading nations of the world.

Quite apart from showing that U Chit Maung was an admiring husband, even an early feminist, this extract illustrates well the attitude of social responsibility which has characterized serious Burmese fiction from the beginning. Stories were designed to educate and set an example, as well as to entertain. It was not too much out of character, therefore, for left-wing writers to expect them also to help build a new socialist society.

From Ma Ma Lay's own introduction to her third novel, *Sheik* (Mind), published in 1951, we learn something more of her reasons for embarking on the writing of a novel. The work is about a young woman doctor, intelligent but not a good judge of character, who falls in love with and then is raped by a fellow doctor whom she trusts. Her life is shattered by the ensuing pregnancy. Ma Ma Lay tells us that she got the idea from seeing the film *Johnny Belinda*, in which a deaf and dumb girl is raped, becomes pregnant, and then is helped by a kind doctor. What struck her about the motion picture was the injustice of the situation in which it is the man who commits the rape and the woman who suffers afterwards. She decided to write a novel on this theme, a novel in which she would examine character and motive rather than simply tell a story. She confesses to being uncertain of her ability to portray and analyze character and emotion with sufficient skill. Although she had been writing fiction for some time, she had never written a love scene, let alone one in which a girl was forced to submit to a man; she feared that she would be unable to write it realistically.

Here we see how Ma Ma Lay was setting herself new goals, striving to bring the modern Burmese novel to the level of Western fiction. By the time she wrote *Not Out of Hate*, she had clearly gained confidence in herself. We also see that she was a committed feminist. Indeed, she always expected and demanded complete equality of treatment with men, and got it even when imprisoned. She also demanded that woman show equal effort and initiative. She did not believe that a woman should ever admit that she was inferior on account of her gender. As she says in *A Man Like Him*, she paid no attention to whether a person was male or female; she only took notice of their mind.

By September 1952, Ma Ma Lay already had written a fourth novel, this time not about a well-educated, middle class woman, but about the life of an ordinary peasant girl who worked in the paddy fields. Again we learn a great deal from her introduction to the work, entitled *Kabamyeiwe* (On This Earth). She tells us that her father was the manager of a large European-owned agricultural bank for which he was responsible for the management of 60,000 acres of paddy land. Although she was familiar with the details of the land-holding system, fixed interest rates, rules for delivering paddy, and so on from the regular meetings with paddy farmers who came to the bank to draw money, she realized when she decided to write about a peasant woman that she had no experience at all working in the paddy fields. Recalling a visit she had made to Thahton at paddy planting time a year earlier, she felt it would not be good enough merely to describe the young girls stooping over the young rice plants in the rain; she wanted to write so as to give a full picture of their living conditions and of the problems and hardships they faced in everyday life. She tells us that by describing the present difficult circumstances of the peasants she hoped to help bring about for them, as soon as possible, a new and just era, in the interest of peace and true independence for Burma. (Now, nearly forty years later, after all that has happened in Burma, there is a sad irony in such a statement.) The journalist in her wanted the novel to be authentic, based on actual peasant lives, reflecting the way peasants really spoke and what they really did. How could a person who had never in her life walked in a flooded paddy field write such a novel? She decided to make a close study of the subject.

As with her previous novel, she was constantly being pressed by the editor of *Shumawa* to give him something to publish for his readers. First she promised a story, then a long story, but as she wrote the work became longer and longer, exceeding the permitted length of a long serial, until the editor told her that they would publish it as a separate book. This enabled her to take her time and to accumulate background material. Even though she had been told that she was now free to write as long a work as she wished, she tried to keep the number of pages, and thus the price, down. Finally, she says, she left out passages dealing with new methods for farmers to pay land tax, and details of attempts to nationalize paddy land near Syriam! However well told the story might be, a novel loaded with such ambitious social purpose and such heavy educational content was not likely to win a popular literary prize.

Whether because of a lesson learned or natural development as a writer, however, when it came to Ma Ma Lay's fifth novel, the one translated here as *Not Out of Hate*, creative inspiration seems to have taken over from, though not supplanted, social concern. There is no explanatory foreword of any kind, and the story and the characters are left by the author to speak entirely for themselves.

Perhaps the final words of introduction should be given to a fellow Burmese writer, Daw Saw Mon Nyin, writing soon after Ma Ma Lay's death:

> Her seat was empty at the general meeting of Burmese writers; at this meeting she was no longer able to attend as the delegate from Yangin district—Gya-ne-gyaw Ma Ma Lay, who is held in such great respect by everyone for the clarity and excellence of her writing, and for her ability to give artistic expression to her

thoughts and feeling. Her books were serious in intent, thought-provoking, informative, and have been accorded an important place in the history of Burmese literature. Anyone can write so as to produce a book. But not everyone has the courage to lay open their own life and recount it just as it is, or has the ability to portray it in its full reality. Her reader is carried away by the outstanding quality of her writing.[9]

We hope that something of this quality shines through in this version, the first Burmese novel to be translated into English outside of Burma.[10]

---

9. From a memorial number of *Shumawa*, June 1982, pp. 163-68.
10. There have been at least two novels, or works resembling novels, translated into English in Burma, but they were intended for audiences there and not distributed elsewhere. The first was U Nu's *Man, the Wolf of Man*, written originally in Burmese in 1941 while he was under house arrest, then translated and serialized in *The Guardian Magazine* (Rangoon) I (June - October, 1954) and II (November 1954 - January 1955). Also worth mention is the work by Lu-du U Hla, really a series of portraits of prisoners, translated and published a number of years ago by Kathleen Forbes and her husband, the botanist Than Htun.

NOT OUT OF HATE

THE PRINCIPAL CHARACTERS

Way Way. A young Burmese girl, about seventeen years of age when the story opens, who lives at home and helps her father with his business.

U Po Thein. Way Way's father, aged about sixty, a rice-broker dealing with British firms. He is in poor health and suffers from tuberculosis.

Daw Thet. Way Way's aunt, sister of U Po Thein, who lives with the family.

Hta Hta. Way Way's older sister.

U Thet Hnan. Hta Hta's husband; a government medical doctor.

Ko Nay U. Way Way's older brother. He is involved in anti-British nationalist politics.

Than Than. Wife of Ko Nay U.

Daw Mya Thet. Way Way's mother, who has become a Buddhist nun in Upper Burma. She also is known by the ecclestiastical name *Thila Sari.*

Meh Aye. A servant girl in the household of U Po Thein.

U Saw Han. An Anglophile Burmese bachelor, 37 years old, who works for Bullock Brothers, a British rice-trading firm.

Maung Mya. U Saw Han's butler.

Way Way stood looking intently at the house next door. From her upstairs window she could look directly into the front room on the ground floor. It was different from anything she had ever seen. The house was being prepared for the new tenant's arrival. She could see that a smoke-colored carpet had been laid on the floor, and a greyish blue sofa and matching chairs had been arranged around it. Alongside the sofa and each chair were small low tables holding ashtrays. The tables were polished to a shine and were the reddish brown color of ripe *thabyei* fruit. In the middle of the carpet stood a rectangular coffee table that had no legs but seemed to be held up by solid piece of wood. Its black, polished surface gleamed with points of light. On the table sat a red porcelain vase shaped like a monk's begging bowl filled with a profusion of small, white *kalamet* flowers, like lilies of the valley, spraying out from all sides onto the table.

Way Way was delighted at the sight. The white of the flowers in the cherry-red bowl made an arresting picture on the dark, glass-like surface of the coffee table. She thought to herself, How lovely! . . . I could go on looking at it forever. She shifted her gaze to the upper end of the room, and against the wall she saw a piece of furniture that looked like a couch with six legs and a woven cane seat and back. It was the size of a single bed and rose a little at one end to form a kind of headrest. It had dark blue cushions of brand-new Mandalay Shwedaung silk arranged on it. At the lower end of the room, two crossed Burmese swords hung on the wall, red tassels dangling from their handles. A small Shan bag with seashells sewn on it was placed decoratively beneath the swords. Not a sound came from the house. The whole place was quiet and orderly, with an air of elegance and distinction.

Way Way looked over the room and was pleased with everything she saw. Glancing at the ceiling, she was enchanted with the pretty lampshade made from a small painted parasol from Bassein. Then she began to compare what she had seen with her own front sitting room downstairs.

Way Way lived in an old half-brick, half-timbered house built during her grandfather's time. Because he had become prosperous only after the house was built, it was very ordinary. Quite a public figure in his time, he had set up a rice mill on the river bank opposite Moulmein-gyun. He had been well known for buying a two-deck passenger steamboat and setting up a service between Moulmein-gyun and Rangoon in competition with the British-owned Irrawaddy Flotilla Company. The boat was called *Maekala*.[1] After her grandfather died, business declined and the rice mill and steamboat were lost, but about 500 acres of paddy lands remained. Way Way's father, U Po Thein, became the rice broker in Moulmeingyun who dealt with foreign firms. He lived his entire life in the same house his father had built.

Only when Way Way started comparing the two front rooms did she realize how very different they were. In her own sitting room downstairs there was a round marble-topped table with chairs around it. White cotton cloth covers were slipped over the backs of the chairs. These were decorated with multicolored parrots and peacocks, machine embroidered by Way Way herself. When she made them she had admired her handiwork lovingly and had looked at the room again and again, thinking it very elegant . . . until she saw the room next door.

Now, all of a sudden, the large betel box of woven bamboo, with its set of little silver bowls,[2] looked so provincial sitting on the marble-topped table. The plate-sized clay ashtray with painted flowers, kept handy nearby, looked common and ugly. The aluminum spittoon under the table, with its dark red betel stains, suddenly seemed almost revolting. The old long wooden settle near the table now was an awful eyesore.

---

1. Maekala is the name of a goddess who saved the embyro Buddha Mahazanaka from drowning.
2. The traditional set of containers for the condiments used in chewing betel.

As she stood there she recalled the floor of the room downstairs, always soiled with the footprints of the farmers who came from dawn till dusk to do business, and the desire to live in the elegant style of the house next door welled up powerfully inside her. That house appealed to her so much that it was becoming an obsession. It was to be occupied by an agent of Bullock Brothers, a British trading company in Rangoon that did business with U Po Thein. The news that a white man was going to live in the small town had spread excitedly all over the place.

It had started when Bullock Brothers had asked U Po Thein to help them locate a suitable house for their agent, who would open a rice-trading center for their company in Moulmeingyun. U Po Thein had looked all over town but had not found a suitable house; finally he had to ask his son, Ko Nay U, who lived next door, to give up his house for the Englishman.

The house had been duly cleaned and painted. Carpenters had been called in and renovations made. The bathroom had been made over to include an indoor toilet of the Western type. Way Way had teasingly said to her father, busy supervising the finishing touches on the house, "And you still don't even know when your Englishman is coming, Daddy."

"Yes, that's true, daughter. I guess when he hears from me that the preparations have been completed, he will show up," replied U Po Thein, trying to imagine what the white man looked like.

Way Way had never in her life seen an Englishman up close. Walking on the street during an occasional visit to Rangoon she had seen English men and women, but only from a distance. As she recalled their blue eyes, pointed noses, and reddish complexions, her heart palpitated with fear, just from the thought that one of them was going to be living so close.

A telegram arrived ahead of the Englishman. Because U Po Thein did not know English, Way Way had to read it to him. She had studied up to the seventh standard[3] at Moulmeingyun Middle School. Her brother, Ko Nay U, and her sister, Hta Hta, had completed high school. Her brother had gone to college, but quit

---

3. In the British colonial education system, the seventh standard marked the end of middle school.

in the first year because he got married. Soon after finishing high school, her sister had married a doctor who worked for the government; she now lived wherever her husband was posted, moving from one town to another. Way Way's mother had gone on a pilgrimage to a religious center in the Sagaing hills[4] when Way Way was just a child and had not returned. She had, at the time, dutifully written for and received permission from her husband, U Po Thein, to remain there and become a nun. From then on, Way Way had been brought up by her father's older sister, Daw Thet.

Although Way Way had wanted to go on to high school at Myaungmya, she had been obliged to end her schooling in order to look after her father, who was alone, since her older brother and sister had by then left home. She helped her father take care of the family business, keeping the records and accounts and handling the money.

It had now been about five years since she had studied English, so she read the telegram carefully to grasp its meaning. "The telegram is from Bullock Brothers in Rangoon, Daddy. They are asking you to meet the boat tomorrow morning when the servants and household furniture of their agent arrive."

U Po Thein pulled the telegram from Way Way's hands and looked at it with a frown, as though at a loss to know what to think. "No, daughter, . . . Isn't the agent coming as well? You'd better go ask your brother to read it . . . what does it mean?" he puzzled.

Way Way took the telegram from her father's hands and after reading it over again said, "There is no mention of the agent's coming, Daddy. It just asks you to meet the boat for the things and the servants."

"Who sent the telegram?" queried her father.

Looking down at the telegram again, Way Way said, "There isn't any name. It is a message from the office. There is only the name of the firm."

The next day U Po Thein rose early, before it was light, and went down to the dock to wait. The Rangoon Express steamer

---

4. Located in the north near Mandalay, the Sagaing hills area is the site of numerous monasteries, temples, caves, and retreats. Since ancient times it has been known as a center of the Buddhist faith.

drew up at exactly 6 A.M. Way Way was at home, spending the morning looking in the direction of the road that led from the dock. Her heart had jumped at the sound of the boat from Rangoon's steam whistle. She was very excited. It was not the excited anticipation one felt waiting for family members one has not seen for a long time, but a vague, restless feeling that made her keep straining her neck towards the road. Because of her burning curiosity to see the Englishman's household things and servants, now and then she stood at the front of the house to look down the street.

It was fully two hours after the sound of the steamer's arrival that the belongings began to appear in front of the house next door. There was an unbelievable amount of furniture. Indian coolies were pushing handcarts stacked high, and more coolies, strung out in a long line over the length of the main paved road, were carrying loads on their heads and on their shoulders.

Way Way stood watching the coolies take crates and boxes of all sizes into the house, wondering what on earth could be in them and feeling quite overwhelmed at how much of it there was. She noticed that household furniture such as dressers and chairs had been carefully wrapped and stitched in gunny sacking. Then Way Way saw a refrigerator for the first time in her life. She cried out to her aunt, "Auntie, Auntie Thet, look, look; come out and look at this huge white box thing!"

Daw Thet came running to the front door. She was startled. "Oh my goodness, what in the world is that extraordinary thing! So huge and so white!" she said as she stared at it.

Way Way's aunt was one of those people who thought very highly of the British and only just fell short of worshipping them. As befitted a British colonial subject, she had a servile attitude; she thought that everything English was superior and every English person her better. "That lot in the bazaar are all asking whether the Englishman next door has arrived yet," she said to Way Way. Daw Thet thought that an Englishman coming to live next door would enhance her importance in the eyes of the world.

Way Way listened on and off to her aunt's chatter but devoted her real attention to what was happening next door. Not only did she find the household effects amazing, but the two servants were even more astonishing. One was a short, dark-complexioned Burman about thirty years of age, and the other an

7

older Indian man of about fifty who wore gold rimmed spectacles and a dhoti.

"The servants of the English house are Burmese and Indian," announced Daw Thet, tapping Way Way's arm for attention. She went on with her observation, "They may be servants, but they certainly are smart-looking."

A long while after the furniture had been taken into the house, U Po Thein returned, smiling and shaking his head. He called out, "Daughter! The agent who is coming is Burmese! Not English!" A loud cry of surprise came out of Daw Thet's throat; Way Way was struck dumb. Open-mouthed and speechless, she stood dazed as U Po Thein continued, "After the steamer docked and the young servant, Maung Mya, came up to me and said, 'Sir, my *thakin*[5] will not be arriving until tomorrow evening, by motorboat,' I was still under the impression that he was English and, seeing so much furniture, I asked, 'Is your master's "English lady"[6] also coming?' He replied, 'Oh no, sir, my master is not English; he is Burmese.'" So saying, U Po Thein began to laugh uproariously.

Daw Thet, who had been unable to conceal her utter surprise and disappointment, said abruptly, "Who is he, then?" Way Way, thoroughly taken aback at the news, asked herself in bewilderment, With all those household belongings, what kind of a Burman could he be?

"U Saw Han is his name," said U Po Thein. "He's about thirty-seven years of age. It seems we won't get to see him until tomorrow evening."

So Way Way wondered all day long about what kind of man was coming to live next door. She had been in houses of high Burmese government officials where the servants had answered "your reverence" to their masters, but never before in her life had

---

5. The word "thakin" means "master," and was originally used only to refer to Englishmen in colonial Burma. In the 1930s, however, young, Western-educated Burmese nationalists appropriated the term. Using it with a fine sense of irony and pride, they insisted on calling themselves thakin, placed the word as an honorific before their names in order to identify themselves in a particularly dramatic way, and proceeded to build an independence movement around their leadership.

6. That is, an Englishwoman, the (white) wife of an Englishman.

she heard one Burman call another thakin. It was all thoroughly confusing and unprecedented.

Due to engine trouble, the agent U Saw Han did not arrive until very late the next night, and Way Way, who had been asleep, learned about it only when Daw Thet informed her the next morning. It took the servants all day to put the house next door in order, and only in the early morning light was Way Way really able to see it properly. So there she stood, looking intently at it from her upstairs window. As she watched, she heard what sounded like a gong from the back room of the house next door. She ran quickly into her aunt's room, where she could see better, and continued her observations.

❖ 2 ❖

Way Way looked out the window, hidden from view except for her head. She saw Maung Mya, the Burmese servant, standing near a table. He had a red silk *gaung-baung*[7] wrapped over his Western-style haircut, with one end sticking up jauntily a few inches. He wore a stiff-collared shirt with a spotless white cotton jacket over it. Around his waist was a washed dark blue silk *longyi*, a kind of Burmese sarong, worn short.[8] Over one shoulder was a white napkin. Maung Mya's jacket was fastened with buttons so as not to get in his way while he worked. He stood straight, chest out, legs together, and hands behind him. A gleaming white cloth covered the table, with napkins folded to resemble water lily buds, starched and white like Maung Mya's jacket.

Way Way looked at the white china teapot, the polished silver cream and sugar bowls, the biscuit tin of crackers imported from England, the jam jar and butter dish, the bananas, eggs and bread. She noted them all, item by item. This morning Way Way had awakened, gone downstairs for a bath, talked with her aunt about U Saw Han's arrival, and had forgotten to eat her breakfast. Looking at the meal on the neighbor's table, she started to feel hungry. The food reminded her of the sweets that people offered to monks on special occasions.

In Way Way's household people did not use a table and chairs but sat on the floor on finely woven mats placed around a low, round table in the kitchen. Maung Mya's straight stance near the nicely appointed table with chairs in the house next door seemed to enhance its elegance. A silver gong mounted on two

---

7. Traditional turban-like headgear worn by men.
8. The length of the longyi, and the fact that it was not brand-new, indicates the wearer's servant status.

elephant tusks on a sideboard made Way Way surmise that the sound she had heard earlier was to announce the meal.

The sound of boots was heard from the upstairs of the house. Way Way started and quickly withdrew her head from the window. She stood, shoulders flat against the wall. Footsteps—now clear, now faint—came down the stairs. Her heart started beating rapidly. Not daring to look out, she concentrated on listening to the sounds. Only when she heard the footsteps stop, a chair being drawn up, and then silence, did she dare peer out again. She could see the back and shoulders of U San Han, who was dark complexioned and well built. His hair was cut short, European style, and he wore a white long-sleeved shirt and khaki shorts. He was sitting up straight in his chair and pouring himself some tea.

As U San Han had his back to her, Way Way could observe him well. She was glad he was not facing her, for now she could study him to her heart's content. He ate his meal in silence. Standing motionless near the table was the waiting Maung Mya. She noticed that U Saw Han did not speak one word to him all during the meal. Having finished one cup of tea, U Saw Han poured himself another. As she watched him leisurely enjoying his meal, her own hunger seemed to be appeased.

Her initial reaction to the sight of Maung Mya, a Burmese, dressed as a butler and employed by U Saw Han, also a Burmese, made Way Way think, My goodness, U Saw Han certainly is Westernized! She recalled having seen men in red gaung-baungs in Rangoon who had been pointed out to her by her father as chauffeurs hired to drive Europeans' cars. Now that she observed Maung Mya's subservient mein and his red gaung-baung, she could only think of his master, U Saw Han, as European and not Burmese.

Having finished his meal, U Saw Han stood up from the table and started talking to Maung Mya, who had suddenly come to life from his statue-like position and was humbly listening to his master, nodding his head in acquiescence. U Saw Han's form then disappeared from view as he went into another part of the house, and Way Way returned from her aunt's room to her own.

Everything she had seen this morning had been so different from anything she was accustomed to that she realized that indeed there were two cultures involved, two cultures very different from each other. Way Way looked around her bedroom, and everything that met her eye seemed old and shabby. She felt she would like to live in the manner of the other house, which was worlds apart from her present surroundings. She suddenly felt insecure and full of self-doubt. Feeling awkward and ill at ease, Way Way walked over and stood in front of her dressing table. She had not done a thing since coming back upstairs from her morning bath, and began to worry that her aunt would notice and start scolding. She used a little water to thin her *thanaka* paste, a fragrant cosmetic made of freshly stone-ground sandalwood, before putting it on her face. Lifting her bangs from her forehead, she stared at herself in the mirror. The face she saw was young, fresh, and innocent, with clear eyes, a nice nose in profile, smiling lips, and a little beauty mark on her right cheek. She possessed a natural dignity and grace. Only when she saw her reflection in the mirror did she feel reassured and like herself again.

She rubbed a thin coating of thanaka paste on her face and pressed some pink Pompeii powder over it with a *toba*, a type of powder puff made from a piece of old soft fabric, a toiletry item favored by many traditional ladies. Way Way's toilet was finished very quickly. She did not need much makeup and knew that she looked all right with just a little face powder. With a small brush she brushed her eyebrows, which were prominently but naturally etched on her face, starting out thick and tapering off into a thin line at the ends. After combing and oiling her hair, she tied it with a black satin ribbon; gathering all the short strands as well, she wound it into a knot around a comb at the back of her head. She chose a pretty pink printed voile blouse with wide sleeves and a short bodice, a style that was very much in vogue. She picked a red Inle longyi in preference to a Chinese satin one because it did not have to be tucked in and showed the traditional black waist-band, which was very stylish to display. She looked into the full-length mirror on the wardrobe door and examined herself from various angles, turning this way and that. She took a roll of red crepe paper from the dresser drawer, tore off a small piece, wet it with her tongue, and rubbed it on her lips. Then Way Way went downstairs.

Her father, U Po Thein, was seated in the cane armchair, his legs crossed lotus fashion, with the betel box on his lap, chewing a wad of betel and talking to some farmers. On the wooden settle

12

near the marble-topped table sat two farmers, U Tha Kyu and the Indian Gaw Naw, neighbors who grew rice in adjoining fields. U Tha Kyu suffered from leukoderma, and his face and arms were covered with white patches. He always wore his "town" clothes: a dark serge jacket and a pink gaung-baung.

When she saw U Tha Kyu, Way Way smilingly greeted him and asked across the room, "Did you bring any *mohn-san*[9] with you?"

"Oh yes indeed," he replied in his polite country way, "and the missus sent some special fishballs and *ngapi*[10] as well."

Way Way was glad to hear that he had brought mohn-san. It was a family custom, when once a year this special treat came from the farmers, to mix it with a lot of sugar and coconut and share it with the neighbors. Going to the green, felt-covered office table, she sat down and opened the account books. The Indian, Gaw Naw, came up to her and asked her to total his accounts, reminding her to subtract from his wages the amount he borrowed in seed money during the rains. Way Way took a leather-bound ledger, looked for Gaw Naw's account, and started calculating.

"Judging from the prices this year, it doesn't look like the market will be too good . . . Steele Brother's and Arakan[11] have really kept the prices low . . . ," U Po Thein, his mouth full of betel, called across to U Tha Kyu.

"The *babu*[12] who owns the Chotari rice mill says that the wholesale price of paddy will be about a hundred and eighty," said U Tha Kyu. "I am thinking of selling the paddy I have left over at the going price, after paying for the seed rice and keeping aside the portion we will consume this year. I want to *shinpyu*[13] my son, Ngatauk, this February. What will be the yield of the field?"

"Pretty good, I think," U Po Thein replied to the younger man. Of all his tenant farmers, U Tha Kyu had the longest

---

9. A dessert made from a special kind of rice.
10. A pungent, anchovy-like fish paste used widely in Burmese cooking and also served as an accompaniment to rice and raw or cooked vegetables.
11. Names of large British trading firms.
12. A polite term referring to Indians, also used as a form of address.
13. The ceremony initiating a young boy into the Buddhist monkhood. It is always celebrated as lavishly as the family's means permit.

connection with him and was held in the highest regard. He was a farmer who lived by the sweat of his brow. At the time of World War I he had once worked a hundred acres of land and produced up to ten tons of rice a year. Then he was able to grow all the rice he could consume, and had all the bullocks and buffaloes he needed to till the ground. Later he fell on bad times, incurring debts and being forced to sell his animals. Consequently he could now only work fifty acres of paddy land.

"Take off half of what Gaw Naw owes us as payment for constructing the threshing floor, daughter," said U Po Thein.

Way Way had so much work that she sometimes had no time for meals. Being the daughter of a good rice broker, she had learned all the ways money was used to produce profit in the paddy business. She knew all about the different strains of rice and measurement by the basketful, by weight, and by yardstick. She kept separate books for paddy transplanting and harvesting, for income and expenditure. In addition, she kept account of the weight of the gold pieces given by tenant farmers as security against money they borrowed. She was knowledgeable and efficient in dealing with the various business transactions in which landowners had to engage.

U Kya Ngan, the Chinese rice broker, came into the house. U Po Thein stood up, left his cane armchair, and came to sit at the table. They started off talking about Bullock Brothers opening up the rice center and then went on to discuss the rise and fall of paddy prices.

Way Way was so engrossed in Gaw Naw's and U Tha Kyu's accounts that she did not notice another arrival at the door.

Starting up from his seat, U Po Thein welcomed the newcomer in a fluster. "Come on in, come on in," he cried. "Did you get any sleep at all last night?" Only when Way Way heard him say this did she raise her head from the account books and look up. U Saw Han had come, with two companions behind him. Remaining at the door was a watchman dressed in a dhoti and a long white turban wound around his head, the end of the turban falling behind him over his shoulders and halfway down his thighs. Accompanying him inside the door was a young man with a light complexion and gold teeth.

U Saw Han, who had been walking along with both hands in the pockets of his khaki shorts, took them out as he entered the

14

house and, removing his pith helmet, glanced in Way Way's direction before replying to her father. Way Way caught his calm, steady smile and blushed furiously, feeling suddenly vulnerable and defenseless.

"I did get some sleep," he proceeded to say to U Po Thein. "This," presenting the young man with gold teeth, "is my secretary. We've already found a building near the bazaar for our office."

Although U Po Thein had risen from his seat and pulled out a chair for him to sit on, U Saw Han continued standing with his pith helmet in his hands as he spoke. U Po Thein's face smiled pleasantly and nodded at U Saw Han's secretary.

Then U Po Thein said, "This is U Kya Ngan, a paddy broker," introducing the Chinese broker, who had been leaning on the handle of his curved walking stick and staring at the newcomer.

He was so happy to be introduced that he stood up and said in Burmese (with a Chinese accent), "Pleased to meet you, sir.[14] Please let us know if we can help you in any way."

U Saw Han looked at the smiling, eager face of the Chinese man and said sedately, "Thank you very much." Way Way saw Gaw Naw and U Than Kyu, the two tenant farmers, gaping at U Saw Han and began to criticize them in her mind, thinking them very uncouth. She was ashamed and embarrassed at what U Saw Han would think of their sitting room. Glancing at the table, she saw the white enamel tray holding a teapot with a broken spout and cups set out for the plain green tea traditionally offered to visitors to a Burmese household. Her heart turned over for fear he might notice.

U Po Thein was saying, "There's no need to feel embarrassed about anything. The house we arranged for you isn't very nice, and we feel badly about it. We'll call a carpenter to mend the gate. If you need anything, please let me know."

U Saw Han appeared rather forbidding, but he spoke politely. "Thank you. I apologize for bothering you with finding me a house. If there is anything you want to see me about, please feel free to come to my office. The hours are from 8:00 a.m. to 12:00 noon and 3:00 to 5:00 A.M."

---

14. The speaker uses *bogyi*, a term of address referring to Englishmen.

Way Way could hardly believe her ears, listening to him say this in abrupt and halting Burmese. She thought, Here we are living next door to each other, and the man says to come and see him in his office! What incredible formality!

U Po Thein had realized from the start, when U Saw Han refused to sit in the chair he was offered, that he was not reacting as a Burmese would in a situation set up for natural conviviality. He was deliberately keeping aloof, not wanting to mix.

"Well then, . . . I will take my leave now," said U Saw Han. Way Way did not look up. She could not raise her head. Her heart fluttered madly until the sound of his footsteps died away. In her mind she could still see U Saw Han's reserved face, in contrast to the circle of smiling friendly faces. He was quite good-looking, with a wide forehead, shapely nose, and an air of distinction about him.

"The man seems quiet and poised and very dignified in his ways, U Kya Ngan," remarked U Po Thein, "but very English. Seems he went to work with the company after finishing his degree not too long ago."

U Kya Ngan, pouring himself some tea, gave his opinion, "Not bad. Seems nice enough. Quite good-natured."

Daw Thet entered from the back room. "What in the world? Has he gone already? I just saw him a minute ago and went back to order some coffee. Oh dear, you didn't urge him to stay." Scolding and talking in this fashion, she turned to Meh Aye, the servant girl, and said, "Well then, girl, give the coffee to the Chinese gentleman."

Seeing the black lacquer tray on which sat coffee cups with coffee spilled into the saucers, Way Way thought, It's just as well they were brought in only after he left.

❖ 3 ❖

The 8th day of the waning moon in December.

Dear daughter,

I am replying to your letter. I am glad to hear that you will try to abide by the advice and precepts I wrote to you about in my last letter.

I would like to further explain the Four Noble Truths of the Most Excellent Law, to help your understanding as you meditate upon them.

The Law of Truth has four principles; they are the principle of pain and suffering, the principle of the origin of pain and suffering, the principle of the cessation of pain and suffering, and the principle of the Way. Of these, the principle of pain and suffering and the principle of their origin are of this world; the principle of their cessation and the principle of the Way go beyond this world.

The pain of being born, the pain of growing old, the pain of sickness, the pain of living with those we do not love, the pain of separation from those we do love, either in life or by death . . . such instances of the principle of pain afflict all living beings. Those who are afflicted by such suffering cannot be happy. Those who have themselves experienced it know the principle of pain to be a fact. Until suffering and unendurable pain comes one may, perhaps, live in contentment, but grief and mourning can consume the sufferer like a fire ablaze. If you examine the origin of the principle of

17

pain and suffering, you will find that it lies in the tug of desire and the deceit of ignorance.

My daughter, the desire represented by sexual love leads to new life and the renewal of existence. If one is too attached to life in this plane of existence, this in itself is the principle of origination that brings pain into being, through desire and wanting.

This unworthy Law of Desire inevitably gives rise to suffering and misery. Each living person, each living creature, wishes to experience sensual pleasure but does not know or think that this will lead to pain and suffering.

The extinguishing of all suffering is Nirvana, which is freedom from greed and freedom from all defilements. The state of Nirvana is perfect calm and serenity, with no more death, change, or rebirth for mankind or celestial beings. The noble Law of Nirvana is the concern of the contemplative monk who is capable of winning the knowledge or wisdom of Nirvana . . . The capacity to see everything in a state of flux can be attained by ascetics through practicing for eons . . . a hundred thousand or hundreds of thousands of years.

To achieve this ultimate goal of Nirvana, there is the Eightfold Noble Path, which consists of the eight rules of right conduct. These eight rules can carry you clear of the suffering of wrong living. They can reduce greed, anger, delusion, and other such defilements to nothing.

The Eightfold Noble Path consists of:
Right Understanding (Comprehension)
Right Resolution (Aims, Intention)
Right Speech
Right Action
Right Livelihood
Right Energy (Effort)
Right Mindfulness (Minding what is right)
Right Concentration (Meditation)

These eight rules of the Way are related to this world and the other world, whether you are concerned with the way you are living in this world or whether you are trying to attain Nirvana.

In short, daughter, of these eight the most important is Right Understanding. It is important, daughter, to be able to see things as they truly are, since it is only in this way that we become virtuous.

My daughter, once you have the right understanding, you will then have right intentions, you will say the right words, you will perform the right actions, you will live rightly. You will put forth the effort to be diligent in the right, you will be heedful of the right, and your mind will be fixed on what is true.

If you do not understand things rightly, your viewpoint will be wrong, your views will be falsified and will lead you to wrong action. You will live wrongly, your efforts will be for the wrong, and you will constantly be fixed in falsehood.

Not everyone can at all times hold to the right understanding of the Way. At times they will see rightly and at times wrongly, but the right views are always of the highest importance. In the other world, however, the right view or Truth will always prevail. It is steadfast and indestructible.

Dear daughter, your mother feels bound to write this exhortation to you. It comes with a special love so that you may be able to keep in your heart the Eightfold Path, which contains precepts for our lives in this world. As I wrote in my October letter, keep in mind and practice charity, duty, knowledge (knowing right things from wrong), almsgiving, wisdom, and purity of conscience.

Those who are alert and mindful are able to do more meritorious deeds than those who are negligent and unmindful. Only those who have a sense of shame and fear can be virtuous, while those who are brazen and shameless cannot have good morals. Therefore, I urge you to cultivate the seven rules of virtue.

Do not worry about me. I am meditating and practicing the Law so as to be free from the bonds of rebirth in the 37 planes of existence.

Thila Sari
Red Cave Stream
Sagaing Hills

Way Way's voice trembled towards the end of the letter, as she read it aloud. U Po Thein, reclining on the armchair, was listening intently, his legs extended on the wooden arms.

As soon as Way Way finished reading, Daw Thet sputtered sarcastically, "Oh sure, now she's a holy person devoted to the service of religion, without the cares and entanglements of existence, at ease and at peace . . . ." Then, as though deep in thought, she pressed down with her thumb on the ashes of her unlighted, partially smoked cheroot and gazed into space.

Way Way controlled her welling tears from flowing onto the letter she held in her hand. U Po Thein coughed, cleared his throat, and sat up to spit. From where she sat, Way Way could see clearly the blood that streaked his spittle in the cuspidor. Her face filled with alarm as she bent her head to avoid looking at it. Her tears flowed down and blurred the words of the letter.

U Po Thein said, "When you reply, daughter, don't say anything about my not being well. Let your mother meditate with a calm and peaceful mind."

Way Way remained quiet, her head bowed. Her mother's face as it had looked before she became a nun entered Way Way's mind. Her mother had been a beautiful woman, as beautiful and gentle in person as she was in thought and disposition. Since Way Way had lived close to her mother till the age of twelve, she was able to recall in detail her every mannerism—the way she combed her hair, the way she dressed, the way she spoke, the way she walked. She remembered how her mother would go to the Sagaing hills during the Buddhist Lenten season each year.[15] She

---

15. For three months during the Burmese rainy season (approximately May to July), Buddhist monks practice special ascetic exercises, live austerely, and do not perform ceremonies such as those of marriage. Unlike Christian Lent, this tradition does not commemorate events of

remembered how her mother had hated to travel alone, so her father had to take her there and leave her for a month or so. Before her meditation period was over she would write her husband to come and escort her back home to the Irrawaddy delta.

Way Way remembered that some years when the trip did not work out, her mother was unhappy and restless, lamenting the fact with murmurings and complaints. She changed so much that, two years before she donned the habit, it was apparent to everyone in the household that she would eventually do so. She talked less. She spent time each day on a multiplicity of religious observances. She constantly worked the beads of her rosary, which never left her hands. When she sat at prayer, she sat so long that she was unconscious of time and seemed to be in a trance. She read the scriptures until midnight. She always spoke in terms of religious parallels, so that Way Way was exposed to the Buddhist view of existence when she was but a child. Her mother did not seem to enjoy her food or take any pleasure in her apparel. She removed all her jewelry. She even took off her earrings, which every Buddhist Burmese woman wears from young girlhood, and gave them to Daw Thet saying, "Sister, you wear these from now on." She lost interest in the family business and was not aware that she had stopped participating in it. Indeed, she was not aware at all that she had cut herself off from her family.

When U Po Thein had said teasingly, "You may as well leave the society of man and become a nun in Sagaing," she replied gently, "Just give me leave to do so. I am ready."

When U Po Thein had mumbled and grumbled about this withdrawal from the world, Daw Thet's refractory answer was, "Then it might just as well be withdrawal to the hills of Sagaing." She too had meant it as a joke.

Then one year, when Way Way was in the seventh standard, her mother went to Sagaing to meditate and never returned. She wrote telling U Po Thein that she had become a nun, asked for his acceptance of the fact, and gave her permission for him to be free to marry again if he so desired. Way Way cried her heart out when

---

the Buddha's life, but is said to be the result of instructions given by the Buddha to his followers. In the latter half of the twentieth century increasing numbers of laypersons have shown an interest in observing this "Lenten" season in ways similar to those of monks.

she was told that her mother had become a nun. U Po Thein had loved his wife so much that he had always acquiesced to her wishes and therefore Daw Thet censured him, saying, "It's really you who is responsible for this, you know. You have always given in to her, and you have only yourself to blame."

U Po Thein was heartsick and could not understand or accept what happened. It took him a long time to get over it, but he tried to explain his wife to Way Way and the others saying, "For the kind of person she was, the religious life is really best." When he was alone, however, he would grieve and sink into depression.

Daw Thet's heart went out in pity for her brother and her small niece, and she felt bitter towards her sister-in-law and thought, How could she be so cruel!

When Way Way finished her seventh standard exams and school closed for the hot weather, she cried and fretted about, wanting to see her mother. U Po Thein sent her off with Daw Thet as he himself could not bear to see his wife. After this, Way Way went once a year to see her mother. It had now been five years. Way Way's brother, Ko Nay U, and her sister Hta Hta, who lived far away, were at first quite upset about their mother; then they rationalized what she had done by saying, "Well, it really is a meritorious action . . . ."

U Po Thein chose not to see his wife after she left, and never wrote to her. He still sent her support regularly, however, and tried to get on with his life as best he could. Way Way was aware that her mother had severed all feelings for her father but that her father still cared deeply. It made her unhappy every time she thought of it. Although her father did not read the letters that came from her mother, he would ask Way Way to read them aloud while he listened. All through those five years, Way Way's mother never mentioned her father, and Way Way could not understand how her mother could do that. In the beginning, just after her mother had left home, Way Way, aware that her father was filled with longing and sadness, would write and tell her mother, but her mother never mentioned him in her letters. Remembering now in flashbacks her mother's going from the world into the nunnery brought it all back afresh.

"She brought her karma into this life from her previous existence. That is the reason she could break off her ties so completely. I think she wanted to leave after Maung Ne U and Hta

22

Hta married and left home, but she waited because Way Way was too small at the time," Daw Thet said slowly, not looking at either Way Way or her father, as though her thoughts were way off somewhere in the past. Having started on this theme, she wanted to continue but was prevented from doing so by a spasm of coughing from U Po Thein. When he stopped, Way Way looked up and saw her father's peaked and wan face. She was aghast.

"Have you taken your medicine yet?" asked Daw Thet. "Personally I don't go along with those injections and things. I think Burmese medicine is better, myself." She was truly upset about her brother's condition.

Early that morning, on returning from the godown where the paddy was stored, U Po Thein had started coughing and there had been blood. The whole household was startled out of their wits. U Po Thein had never experienced such a thing before and was himself even more terrified. His face turned as white as a sheet and his feet and hands went cold. They ran at once for the doctor.

The doctor told them it was not tuberculosis, only an excess of blood, but they all thought he said that to reduce their fears and believed it was indeed tuberculosis. Way Way was extremely worried about her father and longed for her mother to be with them at this time.

"Is it time for my medicine?" asked U Po Thein.

Way Way looked down at her watch. "It's one o'clock. You'd better take it," she said as she went to fetch it for him. After taking the medicine, U Po Thein climbed slowly up the stairs to lie down for a nap.

"I worry about your father so," groaned Daw Thet as she got up to leave.

Way Way walked across the room and sat at the desk in order to reply to her mother. She read her mother's letter once more. She was tired of reading her religious exhortations. Sometimes she discerned their meaning, but most times she did not. She really never sat down to study their meaning deeply and had never really caught that feeling which led to religious ardor and understanding. She remembered some of the religious tenets like the Three Truths, the Eight-Fold Path, the Seven Rules of Living for an upright person, and so on, and she could recite them, but that was about it.

Dear Mother,

I am writing this in reply to your letter, which we were happy to receive. Since Ko Nay U's eyes were troubling him, he went to have them checked at the Billimoria Clinic in Rangoon; he will be away for about ten days. Father sent along the bag of rice and tin of oil for you. We were very happy to hear from Hta Hta that they were being transferred to Maubin. It is so much closer to us. Daw Thet is in good health. She received that herbal medicine from Uncle Thaike, and she has made up the mixture and is using it.

The Abbot of Ywagalay sent us two religious relics for veneration as an aid to our meditation. I stitched up your velvet blanket and sent it to the abbot as an offering.

As for Daddy, just this morning . . . .

Way Way did not write any further and stopped to consider whether she should go on, especially after her father had requested her not to. But she wanted very much to write and tell her mother, and wanted her mother to be concerned for her father. She thought, No matter how apart much of their lives have been, it's just not right to be indifferent in these circumstances. When she writes and Daddy hears me reading of her concern for him, she imagined, it'll surely help him to get better. So she continued:

As for Daddy, just this morning he coughed blood, so all of us are extremely worried. We called the doctor and he gave him some injections. He seemed a bit better this evening. Daddy says not to tell you and to allow you to meditate with a peaceful mind, but I want you to know what has happened.

I will respectfully try to persevere in following out the precepts and instructions you sent me, Mother.

Way Way sat reading over what she had written when she heard a noise in front of the house and looked up. She saw U Saw Han striding toward the house, a cigarette tin in one hand and his

24

hat clasped in the other. She was taken unawares and stared at him for a second.

"Is your father in?" U Saw Han asked, halting at the entrance. Her eyes looked at him but they hardly dared register what was in front of them. Way Way stood up and said, "Yes, he is. Please come in."

Walking softly, U Saw Han approached the desk and said, "Is he sleeping? If he is, please, there is no need to wake him up."

At a loss as to how to answer, Way Way said, "Daddy went upstairs earlier. I don't know whether he is asleep. He wasn't feeling well."

U Saw Han was looking straight at Way Way. According to Burmese custom it was too direct a look. "Oh, is he not well? What happened? Then, certainly, don't wake him." While U Saw Han awaited her reply, it seemed that his features softened into a smile.

"He went to the godown this morning, and on his return he coughed up blood."

Before Way Way finished telling him the rest, his face took on an expression of alarm and he asked, "Didn't you call the doctor?"

"Yes, we did," said Way Way quietly. "He was given some injections."

He had a natural scowling expression and Way Way thought, When one first meets him one gets the impression that he is haughty and aloof, but when one actually talks to him he is quite warm and friendly. She was beginning to change her mind about him already.

"What did the doctor say?" he asked.

She found it easy to respond to him directly as his questions showed interest and caring, and this encouraged her to tell him more. "The doctor said it was not tuberculosis, that it was just the body's mechanism being overheated, like a nose bleed, and that we were not to worry."

U Saw Han's face looked thoughtful as he asked, "Has he ever had this happen to him before?" Although he was pleasant and asked questions in a gentle persuasive manner, he seemed upset and regarded Way Way in a serious manner.

Way Way looked up at him through her eyelashes and smiled, "No, never," she said quietly, shaking her head for emphasis.

25

"Well, . . . don't worry too much, but on the other hand don't be too negligent either. As to the business I came for . . ."

They had been standing all this time, and before going on he looked at a chair in front of the desk and said, "May I sit down?"

"Oh yes, please do," said Way Way. She sat down at the same time as he did and found herself face to face with him.[16] She quietly asserted her dignity by sitting in a businesslike manner and showing deference by waiting for him to speak.

"Please tell your father, when he awakes," U Saw Han went on, "that a telegram came from the firm accepting the price he asks. But it cannot be done immediately as the barges will take a week to get here."

"If that is so, I don't think the deal will be feasible. It has to be transacted immediately," said Way Way. "The next lot of paddy we will be receiving got wet, and it would not do to mix the two lots in the godown. Only when the present paddy has been removed can we put in the new stock."

Quite taken aback at this, U Saw Han listened with a smile. "Do you have a lot of paddy? When is it coming?" he asked, regarding her steadily.

Way Way took a large account book out of her desk drawer and, opening it, looked at the figures and said, "A large amount. We have 3,000 baskets out of our own fields. And there will be more from all the other fields."

U Saw Han looked admiringly at her and at the large book and then back again at her. "Your name is Way Way, is it not?" he asked, and Way Way smiled at him and nodded. U Saw Han looked at Way Way's smiling face and child-like manner of nodding instead of answering, and thought it very charming.

"Way Way, don't you attend school?" asked U Saw Han, who took a handkerchief out of his pants pocket and wiped his face.

"Since Daddy was alone, I left school when I finished the seventh standard."

"Oh, then the lady I saw was not your mother . . ."

"No, she is my aunt."

---

16. In polite Burmese society it is frequently considered embarrassing for a young, unmarried girl to sit tête-à-tête with a bachelor.

U Saw Han put his handkerchief back into his pocket and said, "Oh, I thought she was your mother. Please don't think me nosy." He got out some matches, lit a cigarette, and drew on it.

"No, I don't think that," she said.

He took a long draw of his cigarette, his eyelashes fluttering slightly, and asked in a serious tone, "Has your mother passed away?"

Eyes downcast, Way Way hesitated to answer. She glanced up suddenly and saw U Saw Han's face regarding her with a tender expression.

"My mother is alive. She is a nun in Sagaing. It has been five years since she left. That's the reason I'm not in school. I help my father with his work."

Way Way turned her face away after speaking, and U Saw Han looked at her gently and was quiet. Although outwardly quiet, inside he was in a state of upheaval. As he looked at Way Way his heart seemed suddenly to pour out its love for her in her poignant, sad existence. He sensed a dim stirring inside Way Way's heart, a hint of a capacity for happiness.

"Oh . . . when did you come in, sir?" Daw Thet's voice asked as she emerged from the back of the house into the room. She did not come any closer to U Saw Han but talked to him from a distance.

U Saw Han stood up and answered, "I just arrived. I am sorry to hear of U Po Thein's ill health." He sat down after he spoke.

"Seems like he caught something. It just happened this morning. The doctor says not to worry."

"Yes, ma'am."

Daw Thet wanted to go on talking but U Saw Han had turned towards Way Way. Yet Daw Thet did say, "Don't go yet. Have some coffee."

"Oh, no thank you," said U Saw Han, "I only drink coffee in the evening. Please don't bother."

Way Way had been feeling as if she ought to offer refreshment to U Saw Han. In their house it was customary to offer coffee to anyone who came to visit, regardless of the time. She now made a mental note of the one guest to whom they need not offer coffee.

"I'll make certain that arrangements are made for the paddy barges to be sent as soon as possible. I'm sorry to intrude on your work time, Way Way. You are very young and it is really commendable that you are such a help to your elders. I will take my leave now." Then U Saw Han also said goodbye to Daw Thet, and left.

Smiling a little uneasily, Way Way muffled a laugh and said to Daw Thet, who had in fact barged into the room after she could no longer restrain her desire to hear what was being said between the two, "I knew you were standing behind the screen all the time."

❖ 4 ❖

The morning light was shining bright and clear, and Way Way looked outside as she opened the windows. Growing in the fork of the mango tree at the front of the house, a wax orchid plant fell in a trail of flowers, its blossoms swaying like a line of dancers. It was a beautiful morning. There were pigeons in the mango tree, too, jostling and pecking each other. The mangoes, already close to full size, grew profusely in clusters. Way Way turned back to the room and saw the sunlight streaming in from the windows onto the polished wood of the new furniture and her heart filled with pleasure at the sight.

Before leaving for Rangoon, her brother had asked what he could bring. She had said she wanted some new furniture like the set of low tables and chairs she had seen at the township officer's house. Way Way and the servant girl Meh Aye had stayed up until midnight the night before, polishing the floors so the place would be ready when her brother arrived early the next morning. Using a mixture of kerosene and paraffin, they had polished and polished until their arms nearly dropped off.

The marble-topped table and accompanying chairs, to be used now as a dining set, were taken into the middle room behind the screen. Way Way had decided to have their meals at a table sitting on chairs because they could be seen from the upstairs of the house next door when they sat eating around the low table on mats on the kitchen floor. She had been very uneasy at mealtimes ever since U Saw Han had moved in. Only now did she feel that she could relax and eat without fear of being observed.

For two full days Daw Thet had sat at the sewing machine to finish the set of poplin curtains exactly like those hanging in the windows of U Saw Han's house. When Way Way finished polishing the floor, she hung the curtains. She set her alarm clock before

29

turning in for the night, but rose before it went off. Both she and Meh Aye came downstairs. She switched on the light, anxious to see if the floor had been done well enough, and then the two of them lifted the large cane armchair that U Po Thein usually sat in and moved it to the front end of the room. Since it did not look right there, they moved it to a corner. Not satisfied with that either, they moved it back to its original place in front of the screen that separated the middle room from the sitting room. Then, after being moved here and there, the desk and its chair were settled in a corner at the rear of the room. She decided to get rid of the old wooden settle, which she could no longer stand the sight of, and put it outside as soon as it was light enough to open the doors. Way Way then went into the middle room and took a new white table cloth and spread it on the marble-topped table. From now on this is where they would have breakfast. She placed cups and saucers around the table and stood back to look at the effect.

Then suddenly she heard the boat whistle and ran off to finish making herself presentable. She kept busy with things upstairs and downstairs while the boat docked. When she finally saw the furniture appearing, the tight feeling in her chest disappeared. Her brother had sent the furniture on ahead with coolies and had gone to his own house first. Way Way quickly unwrapped the packing and arranged the furniture around the room exactly as she had planned the night before. In the clear morning light the room appeared quite elegant. She thought, Now it looks sophisticated and Westernized. If only there were a carpet to put under the furniture, it would really have class.

She then asked Meh Aye to go outside and pick the wax orchids from the mango tree, as she wished to place them in a bowl on the coffee table. Way Way looked at the transformed sitting room and thought of U Saw Han. She was satisfied and pleased to think that the next time he came, they could receive him properly with up-to-date furnishings.

U Po Thein came downstairs. Seeing the sitting room changed around, he thought, Young people nowadays want to be so modern and fashionable. After looking around at the freshly cleaned and orderly sitting room, he added to himself, I rather like it this way; I like it very much indeed.

30

"Daddy, Ko Nay U says he'll come over later. I've made some coffee for you. We've turned the marble table into the dining table." Way Way appeared cheerful and bright. She saw that her father looked rested, and this observation of a change for the better made her happy.

U Po Thein sat at the marble-topped table and was surprised to see there the china that was usually stored away in the cupboard, and a new table cloth, starched and gleaming white. The table was laid with the new tea set as though company were expected. He observed bread, butter, ripe papaya, and bananas, and was a little taken aback at the kinds of food selected. U Po Thein was used to having his breakfast in his armchair, his legs tucked under him and his coffee-cup and plate of food perched on the long wooden arms. He was unaccustomed to sitting formally at a table and felt rather intimidated by the white table cloth and new cups. He never ate papayas or bananas so early in the day, only after a meal of rice and curry. All this was new to him. My daughter is acting strangely, he thought. "Daughter, if we use the new plates every day, won't they get old-looking soon?"

"If people saw us use the old plates and cups from the kitchen on this table, it would never do," she replied as she fixed his coffee. U Po Thein mused over the words "if people saw us" and "it would never do" as he ate his meal.

Way Way sat down at the table facing her father. Turning her cup right side up, she poured herself some coffee and looking up at him said, "How did you sleep last night, Daddy?" Her father regarded her steadily, and she began to feel a little uncomfortable about putting on these airs about sitting at a table.

"I slept quite well, didn't cough once all night. I coughed once or twice when I woke up in the morning, but there wasn't any blood."

"Then you are going to be all right!" she cried with relief. "I asked Aunt Thet to buy some cucumber melons from the bazaar. They say that eating cucumber melon with sugar cures you, so you'll be sure to have some, won't you, Dad?"

U Po Thein nodded in agreement. "I really don't think it is tuberculosis," he said as he smiled and shook his head.

"It's just something caused by fear. If you worry about having a certain disease, you get the symptoms. What you had is just a little excess blood, like a nose bleed. They say that some-

31

thing like this happened to Uncle Po Myaing and he's all right now. Never had it again. Don't think about it or dwell on it, Daddy." Way Way talked a lot to cover up her uneasiness. She felt awkward in front of her father because of all the changes she had made, and could not relax and eat normally.

Her face fell as she heard her name called out—"Way Way!"—from the front of the house. There was a sound of footsteps striding in and then her brother appeared, exclaiming loudly, "My, my, aren't we stylish!" Wide-eyed, he took in the dining table and continued, "It's a white man's house!" and began laughing. His laughter sounded strained, as if he did not really find it funny but was ridiculing her.

Way Way was hurt and her face looked pained. Glancing sideways at him, she said with a pout, "Oh you *would* say something like that!"

In appearance Ko Nay U was light-skinned and built quite short and stout. He had large, prominent eyes which were always ready to smile or laugh, giving him a pleasant-looking face. Because he loved to chew betel, his teeth were stained red and one of his cheeks was always puffed out with a wad of it. His hair was cropped very short, European style. He wore a short-sleeved shirt, a cotton longyi with large checks, and a big belt around his waist.

"You said ten days, but you were gone much longer," U Po Thein said. He had to turn his body sideways towards his son because he was sitting up so close against the table.

"Have some coffee," said Way Way to Ko Nay U as she poured him the cup meant for Daw Thet when she returned from her morning trip to the market.

"I had to have injections for my eyes. Seems I'm supposed to wear glasses, but I don't want to, so I just brought medicine for them. What's this I hear about your not feeling well, Dad?"

"Who told you that?" Way Way asked across the table.

"Aunt Thet, of course. She stepped in at our place on her way to the market this morning and told us." Then to his father he said, "How are you now? It's really got me worried," said Ko Nay U as he slid into a chair and sat at the table.

U Po Thein straightened himself around and replied, "We were just talking about it. I'm much better. My pulse is normal. The blood was just something like a nose bleed."

"If that's the case, it is really good news. Tuberculosis is a serious illness and even got my in-laws worried. My father-in-law asked me to persuade you to go to Rangoon for treatment."

"Drink your coffee." Way Way poured coffee into a cup and pushed it towards him.

Ko Nay U looked under the table and said, "Where's the spittoon?" Wanting to spit out the betel juice in his mouth, he looked all around but Way Way had banished the unsightly spittoons to the back room and had to run out to get one for her brother.

"Did you write your mother a letter when you sent her the bag of rice?" U Po Thein asked Ko Nay U.

"I sent it registered freight on the train, with a letter attached. She should have received it by now."

U Po Thein had never ceased to care deeply for his wife but did not want his children to have an inkling of the strong feelings he still held for her. He had developed the habit of talking about her with a guarded self-composure and dignity.

"What else did you buy in Rangoon?" asked Way Way. "The furniture is great."

Her brother poured his coffee into a saucer to drink, and to prevent the tablecloth from getting stained Way Way quickly placed another saucer in front of him on which to set down his cup. "I like my coffee cooled before I drink it," he said as he slurped it in one gulp. "I bought the furniture at the Bombay Burma Company because U Haji Ahmed's furniture was priced too high. Do you like the colors? I don't care for light-colored wood, so I chose the dark reddish brown, like ripe thabyei. I didn't buy anything else because I was on the lookout for second-hand books for the library I'm opening. That takes a lot of time."

Ko Nay U was planning to open a library in the town. Ever since his school days he had been unable to live without reading, and always had his nose in a book. He bought and read every newspaper, magazine, and new novel that came off the press. Since his marriage he had had to give the rice business priority, but his heart was not in it. He had always wanted to go to Rangoon and set up a bookshop for magazines and works of fiction.

Suddenly Way Way heard the sound of U Saw Han's footsteps and her heart turned over. The newly acquired sitting room furniture was out there to greet him first. Way Way was trying to show him that although they lived in a country town they were not bumpkins and had some taste. Of course, we do not come up to the standards of his house, with its stuffed sofas and wool carpet, but this much in a country place isn't so bad, she reassured herself. "I think that's U Saw Han," she said.

U Po Thein got up from his seat and, taking off the scarf that was wrapped around his neck and leaving it on his chair, went out to the front.

Ko Nay U leaned forward in his seat and said laughingly in a low voice just loud enough for Way Way's ears, "Master Chicken Shit."[17] Way Way was worried that her brother might be heard out in front and punched him on the shoulder, telling him silently not to clown. Ko Nay U grinned widely, showing all his teeth, and was soon convulsed in soundless laughter.

"I heard you were not well, Uncle.[18] How are you now?" U Saw Han's voice was heard to say.

"Oh, I'm much better. I was frightened because of the blood, but was only something like a nose bleed the doctor says, so that must be it." He then called out to his son, "Maung Ne U . . ."

Way Way tapped her brother on the shoulder and said, "Go on. Father's calling you." Ko Nay U straightened his face and went out front. Way Way followed.

"This is my son. He's the manager of the Thukadama Rice Mill."

U Saw Han, dressed in a long-sleeved white shirt and long white pants, put his white pith helmet under the arm of the hand that held a tin of cigarettes, and extended his free hand to shake Ko Nay U's.

Ko Nay U shook hands pleasantly and said, "Good to meet you," and pointing to a chair said, "Please sit down." With a smile, U Saw Han nodded and sat down on one of the brand-new chairs that no one had sat on until then. Ko Nay U then introduced Way Way to him saying, "This is my younger sister."

---

17. A rough approximation of a slang term used to ridicule Burmese with English pretensions.
18. It is considered rude to address a person by his given name after a certain point in familiarity is reached. Here "U," which we might in this instance translate "Uncle," is used alone as the term of address.

U Saw Han stood up from his chair and said, "Yes. I had the pleasure of meeting your sister yesterday. Come, Way Way, do sit down." Smiling, he sat down again. "Way Way is a real asset to you in your work, isn't she?" U Saw Han said to U Po Thein. "Yesterday, she let me know that the cargo boats were going to be too slow in arriving, so I telegraphed Rangoon a second time."

U Po Thein smiled and said, "I'm fortunate indeed to have her. I can take it easy and leave everything to her." Way Way was a little embarrassed to have them talk about her right in front of her like that, and stared uncomfortably at the vase of flowers.

"What year were you in college?" U Saw Han asked Ko Nay U, who sat slouched in the chair with his legs crossed.

"1935," he replied.

"I left after my B.A. in '33. Which hostel did you live in?" U Saw Han asked again, his face quite relaxed and at ease.

"Tagaung Hall," answered Ko Nay U.

"You weren't there for the student strikes, then."

"I didn't go back to college when the strikes were over. I got married and left school."

U Saw Han looked across at Way Way and said, "Don't you want to go to college, Way Way?"

Since U Saw Han's manner when he talked to Way Way was as to a child, she shook her head like a child and said, "No, I don't want to anymore," and smiled.

U Saw Han looked down at his wrist watch and said, "I must be getting along to the office. I have an eight o'clock meeting with some brokers who must now be waiting for me." As he stood up he began to speak. "Well . . ." U Saw Han seemed to be considering something, then said to Ko Nay U, "Why don't you come to my place for dinner this evening. You too, Uncle, and Way Way. I invite you all. Please come."

Ko Nay U smilingly replied, "Oh no, let it not be said that we have eaten a meal offered by the guest before we have invited him."

"'Guest,' 'host'—let us not think in such terms. I invited you first. You don't have any previous engagements, do you?"

U Po Thein was reluctant to accept, but found it even more indelicate to argue about an invitation. Way Way, looking bashful with downcast eyes murmured, "Oh, please don't trouble . . ."

35

"No need to feel shy. Please come. I'll have everything arranged." U Saw Han looked into each of their faces in turn while he spoke and then said to U Po Thein, "Well, I'll be on my way." Turning toward Ko Nay U and Way Way, he tossed out a "Cheerio!" in English and left.

Way Way spent the rest of the day feeling very uneasy about the fact that it would not appear proper for a young girl to eat a meal in an unmarried man's house. She was afraid of what people would say.

"Oh for crying out loud, girl, your father and brother will be with you, and you cannot refuse an invitation to a meal by a respected person like that! It would be very rude," said Daw Thet.

Even though Daw Thet was persuasive, Way Way was fearful and undecided all day long. As evening approached she became quite agitated. She could see the large dining table next door from her upstairs window, and became worried all over again as to how to use the knives and forks set near each plate. She was thoroughly intimidated by the sight of things she had never seen before. She had occasionally eaten a chicken pilaf with a spoon and fork at a *danbauk* shop in Rangoon, but never had she seen such an array of cutlery as on U Saw Han's table. She was so frightened that she could hardly look it. She wondered what the two spoons lying alongside each other at the head of each plate were used for. She also noticed freshly-cut tiger lilies arranged at the center of the table.

Since she began her bath only at sundown, she had to finish getting ready by lamplight. She wore a thin muslin blouse and yellow Mandalay silk *tamein*[19] in a traditional royal pattern. At Daw Thet's insistence she took off the plain gold chain and put on a diamond necklace, but she adamantly refused to wear the diamond solitaire earrings because she thought they made her look too old. She moved the diamond bracelet from her left hand to her right and wore a wristwatch in its place. When she was completely dressed, Way Way looked at herself in the full-length mirror on the wardrobe door and began to wind a string of fresh jasmine around the chignon at the back of her head. Daw Thet hovered about, lovingly and proudly commenting, "Rub off the

---

19. A type of longyi worn by a woman.

36

sandalwood paste above your ears," and "There's no powder on the nape of your neck." It took a long time for Way Way to finish dressing, due to the fussy ministrations of her aunt.

U Po Thein wore a pink gaung-baung, the end of which hung down to touch his shoulder. He wore a Mandalay silk jacket that buttoned across his chest, and a brand new reddish copper-colored Bangkok silk longyi. While waiting downstairs for Ko Nay U to arrive, he called up, "Way Way, aren't you ready yet?"

Way Way put some cologne in her handkerchief, clenched it in her hand, looked one last time in the mirror, and said, "Coming, Daddy," and then came running down the stairs.

Although she had told her brother that morning to come suitably dressed, she worried that he would not. He turned up only at seven o'clock. He was dressed in a jacket made of *pinni*, a kind of homespun, a black Bangkok-style silk longyi, and leather thonged sandals.[20] Way Way wondered critically why he had not worn Western shoes.

"Well, let's go," U Po Thein said as he led the way. Way Way and Ko Nay U followed him side by side. When they got to the front of the house next door, Way Way saw a heavy curtain hanging over the doorway to assure privacy from the main street. In front of it stood an Indian watchman, resplendent in a white turban and a long white knee-length coat with brass buttons all the way down. He looked very impressive. When U Po Thein's party entered the compound, the doorman stood up straight, his feet together, gave them a salaam, and drew the curtain aside.

The room inside was lit with a diffused greenish blue glow. U Saw Han, dressed in a long-sleeved white shirt and long black serge pants, arose from the sofa and came forward to greet them. "Please," he said, turning first to U Po Thein, "Don't take off your shoes, keep them on. Don't take yours off, Way Way."[21] U Po

---

20. The costume is deliberately nationalist. Inspired by a similar movement in British India, in the 1930s Burmese men with nationalist sentiments often made a point of wearing *pinni* homespun to protest the importation of cloth from England. The black (rather than brightly colored) longyi, and the sandals (rather than Western shoes) were also part of the pointedly simple and indigenous costume.

21. According to Burmese custom a person automatically removes footwear upon entering a house, just as a Western gentleman might

37

Thein had taken off his velvet sandals, but out of deference to U Saw Han's requests he put them on again even though he felt uncomfortable doing so. U Saw Han wouldn't let the others take off their sandals either.

Way Way and Ko Nay U sat down on the sofa. Since the sofa and the two matching stuffed chairs were placed around the edges of the large carpet, the people sat quite apart from each other. Way Way was gazing at the porcelain vase that held an arrangement of New Zealand Creeper. Ko Nay U started the conversation by asking U Saw Han, "Well, what do you think of my house?"

"Oh I like it, but since the roof is made of zinc it gets very hot upstairs in the afternoons, so I usually have to rest downstairs at that time."

Way Way looked at the chaise lounge covered with the dark blue Mandalay silk and thought, That must be where he rests in the afternoon. She decided it was certainly much better to see things in detail from the inside than trying to look at the room from upstairs next door. She studied a wooden figure on a shelf. It was a carving of a young man wearing a gaung-baung, no shirt, and a longyi tucked up between his legs; he was playing *chinlone*, a kind of Burmese kick-ball. Underneath was neatly engraved *Playing Chinlone*.

Way Way noticed that Ko Nay U's attention had been directed to the carving from the moment he sat down. As he looked at it, his mood changed and he began thinking of the state of art and culture in Burma. He felt that Burmese art and culture could compare favorably with any other country in the world. But since the country had fallen under colonial rule, its culture had been kept in the shadows and neither recognized nor encouraged. A powerful desire to overthrow the colonial power came over him as he sat musing. U Po Thein settled himself back in his sofa and began casually observing the room.

U Saw Han asked each guest in turn, "Well, then, what would you like to drink?" Turning to U Po Thein he said, "I imagine you don't drink whiskey; would you like some orange squash?" Then, "Ko Nay U, what will it be, whiskey or brandy?" He used the English words for these drinks. "And you, Way Way?"

---

instinctively remove his hat.

38

U Po Thein looked at Ko Nay U before he replied. He was thinking, So he entertains his guests with liquor. He felt uncomfortable about this, but thought it rude to show surprise. When Ko Nay U said, "I don't drink either," U Po Thein said, "Why don't we all just have orange squash?" Way Way was relieved. The mention of strong drink made her nervous.[22]

"Maung Mya!" U Saw Han called out. Maung Mya appeared from behind the screen, dressed in a white cotton jacket fastened with buttons, a maroon Mandalay silk longyi, and a red gaung-baung. He bowed respectfully, hands behind him. "Orange squash, and a whiskey." Ko Nay U gave Maung Mya a cold, censuring look the whole time he was in the room.

U Saw Han opened his silver cigarette case and went over to U Po Thein, who leaned forward and looked up at him and said, "Thank you, I don't smoke." U Saw Han then offered a cigarette to Ko Nay U. Only after Ko Nay U had taken one did U Saw Han extract one for himself and put it in his mouth. He then placed the cigarette case on a low table nearby. Taking a lighter from his pants pocket, he lit it and then offered the flame to Ko Nay U, who bent forward and lit his cigarette. When Ko Nay U had finished, U Saw Han lit his own cigarette and returned to his seat. The way he accomplished all this, the way he shook the lighter to extinguish it, even his gait as he returned to his seat, everything struck Ko Nay U as being exactly the mannerisms of an Englishman. Gosh, Ko Nay U thought, he has become one!

"I was not really supposed to have come here," U Saw Han began. "Mr. Pugh was to have come, and I was to have gone to Upper Burma, which is very hot, but I persuaded him to go there instead. I wonder how the old boy is doing in the heat, ha ha."

Everyone was silent listening to U Saw Han's words. He certainly has taken on the sly and clever ways of the foreigners he mixes with, thought Ko Nay U.

Maung Mya brought the glasses of orange squash on a lacquer tray lined with a white lace doily. Each glass had a little cover of mesh weighted with beads sewn along the edges. Because

---

22. In proper traditional Burmese families drinking liquor at home is taboo. Men do drink, but only in the company of other men outside the home in pub-like establishments, never in front of elders or womenfolk.

Way Way was served first, she took the glass nearest her on the tray. When the glasses of orange squash had been taken, Maung Mya went to the back and returned almost immediately with a bottle of whiskey, a glass, and a soda bottle on the tray. As U Saw Han poured about a finger of whiskey into the glass, Maung Mya opened the soda bottle and poured some into it. Way Way looked at the amber-colored liquid in U Saw Han's glass and her heart began to beat fast like the waves in the ocean.[23]

U Po Thein sat drinking his orange squash with dignified composure, keeping his thoughts to himself but thinking, He drinks like an Englishman.[24] As U Saw Han got a little liquor into himself he seemed to become slightly more talkative. He started chatting about exporting rice and how, thanks to the English companies, the price was the highest yet on the world market, and so on. Ko Nay U got more and more depressed as he listened to him. Ko Nay U had learned much about the rice market since going into the business after leaving college, and he had become aware of the manipulations of the English companies in diversifying the market. He seethed at the injustice of it all. Now, however, he controlled his temper and listened to U Saw Han without any outward sign of his feelings.

A conversation then started up between U Saw Han and U Po Thein on the same subject of rice. Way Way kept eyeing the whiskey glass, and her thoughts jumped about uneasily. Then the pleasant tones of a gong broke in on her thoughts. All conversation stopped at the sound.

U Saw Han stood up from the sofa and with extreme politeness and hospitality said, "The meal is ready. U Po Thein, please come in. Come Ko Nay U, come Way Way."

Looking up from her chair, Way Way caught U Saw Han's eyes as they were signalling them to rise. As though compelled to obey and unable to resist, she stood up first. Each person was

---

23. A traditionally brought-up young Burmese girl would feel very uneasy but also excited in an ambivalent way to be in the presence of men dringing alcoholic beverages.
24. That is, U Po Thein was thinking that U Saw Han was able to drink socially and merely get more relaxed and expansive, as Englishmen reputedly did, rather than drink to get drunk like the stereotypical Burmese.

placed in the dining room according to U Saw Han's direction.[25] There was a candle in the center of the table. Way Way and U Po Thein sat side by side. U Saw Han sat directly opposite Way Way. U Po Thein had never before eaten English food, and as he looked down at the table setting to which he was unaccustomed, he was distressed at his inability to solve the difficulty. Way Way, looking down at the gleaming cutlery, was wondering which fork or knife to pick up and in what order. Anxious about doing the wrong thing but not wanting U Saw Han to notice, she did her best to maintain a pretense of composure. Ko Nay U looked quite natural. Looking at a large painting on the dining room wall entitled *Up-country Boat*, he asked, "Whose painting is that?"

Placing his napkin on his lap, U Saw Han answered, "U Ba Nyan painted it." Neither her father nor her brother touched their napkins, so Way Way, who had waited for them to do so, went ahead and followed U Saw Han's example by taking her napkin and placing it on her lap. Maung Mya, the butler, appraised the situation and placed the others' napkins on their laps for them.

Way Way observed the table setting with an eye to copying it and tried to remember the details. Maung Mya placed soup plates in front of each person. He ladled some clear chicken broth into Way Way's plate and then served the others. While Way Way and U Po Thein watched U Saw Han to see which spoon he would pick up, Ko Nay U grabbed the wrong one and started on his soup. Way Way picked up the round spoon as she saw U Saw Han doing and thought, Uh-oh, my brother has done the wrong thing. She looked across at him, wondering what to do. He went on spooning his soup with an air of nonchalance, not in the least embarrassed.

U Po Thein was the last to pick up his spoon and said very simply, "I've never eaten English food, only Burmese food, so I don't understand these English customs at all," at which everybody laughed.

"Don't worry, please. Don't be hesitant," said U Saw Han. He also showed concern for Way Way. "Do you want your bread buttered, Way Way?" he asked. There was toast in a silver rack

---

25. Seating guests in this way is not a Burmese custom, except for giving the best seats to one's elders and monks.

near the centerpiece of flowers. He took a slice of toast, buttered it, and placed it on the small plate at the side of her dinner plate and said, "Please eat, please eat, Way Way."

Way Way was shocked and extremely nervous about the way he showered his attentions on her from the time she sat down at the table. And right in front of my father and brother too, she thought.

Because Ko Nay U understood the English custom of men deferring to women and putting "ladies first," U Saw Han's behavior had not bothered him, yet all the while he was thinking, Gosh, and the man has not even set foot in England. Can you imagine when he gets there! But he controlled his feelings and was quiet.

Maung Mya cleared away the soup plates and then brought out more dinnerware. Way Way took note of the fact that all the plates matched and had a dark green and gold border. Fried fish cut in squares and potato chips were then served on a large platter shaped like a duck egg and offered first to Way Way. She picked up the large serving spoon and fork and tried to help herself but found it difficult to handle; therefore U Saw Han stood up and served her with ease and dexterity. Way Way watched the way he handled the serving pieces, and when the next course of roast chicken and potatoes and green beans was served, she did quite well on her own. She sat admiring the composition of the chicken, potatoes, green beans, and red beets on her plate. The aroma that arose from the food was different from Burmese food. As she ate, she thought it tasted pleasant and different.

U Saw Han and Ko Nay U fell into a bantering dinner conversation. Ko Nay U said jokingly how much better food tasted eaten Burmese-style, with the fingers, than with silverware, and how ngapi was essential to a meal. He was pleasantly open about it and everybody laughed a lot.

"Did you wear clothes made of homespun in your college days?" asked U Saw Han as he broke off a piece of bread in a deliberate, almost ostentatious way and ate it.

"Oh no. I began to wear it just before the strikes broke out at the university. In the beginning, I wore silk longyis and patent leather shoes, and my hair was styled in the Western way, combed back slick and shiny. It was only later that I cropped my hair and wore homespun and wooden clogs."

42

Although U Saw Han laughed lightly and joked, he summed up Way Way and her father as quite simple folk and Ko Nay U as a contrary-minded country bumpkin. Maung Mya went around the dinner table several times in the course of serving the meal. As long as there was silverware remaining on the table, the courses came one after the other. Way Way relaxed as the meal progressed, and she became quite adept at using silverware. At the end of each course she would gather up her fork and knife and lay them along side each other on the plate. U Saw Han was aware of her every move; nothing escaped his attention. He noted her likes and dislikes and how much or how little she ate, and was very solicitous of her needs. He realized that this was her first English meal and was pleased that she learned so quickly. U Po Thein did the best he could and ate slowly. As he ate, he reflected that English food was rather bland and on the sweet side; it seemed to him that it was somewhat like eating snacks instead of a real meal.

After his conversation with Ko Nay U, U Saw Han turned to Way Way. Although he was a little lightheaded because of the drink, unlike some he never lost control of himself. He maintained his dignity and this amazed Way Way.

"Way Way, you are not eating very much at all. Why is this? I know. It is because you keep seeing all those figures from your account book. Don't worry, the paddy barges will arrive. Relax and eat more, please," U Saw Han said smiling at her teasingly. He looked eagerly across at her face, bathed in the pink glow of the light, and it seemed to him that she looked like a rosy-faced English girl, the heroine of many a novel written in the English language.

When Maung Mya brought in the pudding topped with blobs of cream, fluffy and fragrant, Way Way looked closely at the serving bowl before helping herself. She recognized the same kind of bowl that they had at home, used on very special occasions as finger bowls in a Burmese-style meal. So it is not meant to be a finger bowl after all, she reflected.

Coffee was served at the end of the meal. Way Way looked curiously at the tiny coffee cups that held about a mouthful each and thought, as she stirred the sugar and cream, They look as if they belong to a child's tea set.

After they had eaten, they went back into the sitting room, talked a while, and then got ready to leave. U Saw Han's teasing voice was saying at the doorway, "The paddy barges will arrive, Way Way, so don't worry at all," and "Be sure to sleep well." His "Good night," in English, reverberated in her ears as she walked home in a trance, hardly aware that her feet were touching the ground.

❖ 5 ❖

It was beginning to drizzle. Only when she felt the tiny drops blown in by the wind did she get up to close the window. Looking out, she saw an overcast sky and heard the sound of rain in the distance, and groaned. It's going to rain again, she muttered to herself. Way Way had now to be concerned about the rain. On very wet days U Po Thein just stayed in bed. In the summer, when the days were warm and dry, he seemed to improve, but when the rains started his symptoms returned. Every time he coughed there was a little blood. There seemed to be no easing of his condition all through the long rainy season. On especially rainy days he coughed even more, and the spasms brought on a sweat that left him limp and exhausted. U Po Thein would remain resting all day except in sunny weather, when he would venture out of his room and come downstairs in the mornings.

There seemed to be more happening in the fields during the rains, and the farmers would appear often on this matter and that. Way Way would take care of most of the problems, and only when she could not did she let them go upstairs to bother her father. "You just rest, Daddy, and don't worry about the business," she would tell him. "Let me take the responsibility for the time being." She continually coaxed and encouraged him in this manner. He in turn would put up a front of trying his best to get well, for his daughter's sake, and of not worrying about the business, but inwardly he had already accepted that he had a terminal disease and no chance of recovery.

Way Way clung to the bars on the window[26] and gazed out at the rain. She seemed to see her mother's face among the

---

26. It is common for Burmese houses to have metal grilles on the windows to guard against thieves.

45

raindrops. She yearned for her mother and her heart ached for her ailing father, who needed his wife's care in his condition. How could she have the heart to leave him and all of us? she thought sorrowfully. She thought about her family, all split up and living apart—her sister, her brother, her mother—and realized again that her father would be terribly alone if she were not there. There would indeed be no one else.

Her thoughts turned to her sister, Hta Hta, who lived far away from them and could not share the worries and problems of home. Way Way thought, She's lucky, Hta Hta is. As far as she could recall Hta Hta had never experienced any problems connected with the family. When she lived at home their mother had always been there to keep things in order, so she had had a settled atmosphere in which to study during her school days, and as soon as she finished high school she got married. Now that her father was ill and needed care, she could not help out because she had responsibilities to her own family. She had written them regretfully many times explaining how it was with her, and had written again only recently. On thinking over her sister's circumstances, Way Way began to realize the lack of freedom in the life of a married woman and to worry about her own possible marriage. If she ever married, she thought, it would have to be someone who could live with them so she would not have to leave her father alone. She thought that even though her mother, her brother, and her sister had left her father, she could never do so. Her own position became clear to her as she pondered these matters.

Her mother had replied to her letters, instructing them in methods of care for her father and advising them in regard to the medicines he should take, but there seemed to be no underlying anxiety for him. Way Way thought to herself, How cold and unfeeling she seems; how can she be so detached? So it was that Way Way alone bore the weight of her father's illness and all that it involved. The business affairs also fell on her shoulders. Ko Nay U was kept so busy with the business of his in-laws that all he could manage was to come once a day to see his father and inquire after his health. Even then he would be called away to attend to something or other in his work. Aunt Thet was the only one who remained with Way Way and her father. Although she and Way Way's father were not brother and sister with the same parents, she was even closer than if they had been.[27] She was deeply attached to both father and daughter, and cared very much about what was happening to them.

Way Way's face was wet with rain as these gloomy thoughts surged through her mind as if driven by a fevered pulse. A roaring noise filled the whole countryside from the direction of the river. It was U Saw Han's motorboat. Way Way's train of thought snapped as her ears were deafened by the roar of the machine. Closing the window, she returned to her desk. She had been working on an account of a sale of paddy from Kyait-pi to U Saw Han's firm. She heard the sound of a motorcycle, then went back to the books. The rain came down suddenly, hard and in torrents. In the midst of her accounts she made a mental note that the rain started after the boat docked, and the motorcycle had started up after that. Relieved, she said to herself, It's just as well.

Way Way looked out through the door and saw U Saw Han coming in the direction of the house. His head was down, his raincoat was flapping about him, and his Indian watchman held an umbrella over him while trying to keep up with his strides. As he neared the house, she looked down at her account book. He stood by the front door before entering, while the Indian divested him of his wet raincoat. He smiled at Way Way in greeting. She smiled back at him, the tip of her fountain pen brushing her lips.

"Hey, young lady, how's your father today?" Placing his leather attaché case on the bench and dragging the chair in front of it towards the desk, he let out a long sigh before he sat down, exhausted.

"Dad's much better today compared with yesterday. He spent the morning downstairs and went up only when it began to threaten rain," said Way Way.

"Did the doctor come this morning?" asked U Saw Han.

"Yes, he did. He gave Dad an injection," replied Way Way.

Although U Saw Han regarded Way Way as a youngster twenty years or so younger than himself, she could not do business with him relating to him on a youngster's level. She could only be effective as an equal and an adult. At the beginning of their

---

27. In Burma, first cousins—as Daw Thet and U Po Thein appear to be—are usually called brother and sister, and grow up in the same extended family.

acquaintance, Way Way thought of addressing him in the customary way as "Ko," or "older brother," but since she already addressed her brother in that fashion, she could not bring herself to use the term for someone else. She could not call him "Uncle," as he was much younger than her father's brother, U Po Myaing, whom she called "Uncle," so it was quite awkward at first determining how to address him. She decided to call him "U Saw Han" in a strictly professional manner, which was acceptable in their business context. So, calling him "U Saw Han" at work, Way Way assumed a certain maturity and poise as his equal and contemporary. U Saw Han, on the other hand, seemed to become younger in her presence, with his bantering, teasing style and his habit of calling her "young lady."

He took a puff of his cigarette and thoughtfully studied her face as he exhaled. Then he said slowly, "I have something on my mind that I have wanted to talk to you about but have hesitated to do so till now. I hope you will listen to me and not be offended. Please do not use the cups and plates your father uses. Please keep them separate from yours. I implore you not to use his. Prevention is the best way. It is better to stop things before they happen, as the saying goes. Right?"

Way Way's face fell. She was stunned and just stared in front of her. She looked pathetic as U Saw Han watched her. To Way Way the thought that this was a communicable disease had never crossed her mind as she tended her father and nursed him at close quarters. U Saw Han's warning came as a shock and she could not accept what he was saying. It was very upsetting to think of keeping all the utensils he used apart from the others, though they lived in the same house. True, it was for her own good, but hearing about it directly in this was made her pity her father more deeply than ever and left her utterly dejected.

"Please keep in mind, Way Way, that I had to say this for your sake."

Way Way nodded sadly, heavy and numb, remembering that it was done out of concern for her, although she did not want to admit it in the least. She noticed that U Saw Han seemed perceptibly relieved, and although she did not like what he said, she accepted his apparent solicitude.

Changing the subject, he went on, "It was raining heavily when I got to Kyaitpi. Some of the paddy on the barge got wet

48

and I had to wait till the rain stopped. It was a mess. Have you ever been to Kyaitpi, Way Way?" She answered in the negative, quietly and slowly. U Saw Han looked steadily at Way Way as she spoke, and saw before him an upright little person with an unusually strong sense of duty. It did not detract from her youthfulness, and indeed seemed to enhance the natural grace already there. Coming to Moulmeingyun, he had been struck by her the first time he set eyes on her and had looked long and hard. From that time on he had met her many times and had always found himself looking intently at her. It was extraordinary to him that somehow it seemed as though he had never seen another girl before, and that finally he had found everything in this one girl.

Way Way dropped her eyes, uncomfortable at the long silence and his looking so directly at her. She turned the pages of her account book and began to study it.

"Poor kid," U Saw Han said, using English for the first word, "trapped at home, mother far away, sister someplace else, . . . poor little spinster . . . tough isn't it?" He laughed loudly, and his eyes were bright with compassion for her. Way Way put her head down to hide her smile. The rain subsided and the Indian watchman could be seen nodding as he sat leaning against the brick wall of the house.

Way Way continued adding up her paddy prices. She looked down at her watch and at U Saw Han, who then blurted out, "I've stayed too long." Again resorting to an English expression, he added, "Sorry, Way Way."

Startled, Way Way was unable to speak at once, but then exclaimed, "Oh no, it's not that. I wanted to say something to you and looked down at my watch to see what time it was."

"Oh?" said U Saw Han, "What is it, Way Way? Tell me, tell me what it is!" U Saw Han saw an expression of diffidence on her face that was so singular it moved him inexplicably.

Then she said, "I hesitated to say this when you came in because it wasn't the right time, and I thought you'd refuse." U Saw Han sat up in his chair and without moving a muscle, fixed his attention on her, trying to get the import of what she was saying. "It is now four o'clock and I'd like to offer you a cup of coffee, since the weather is so bad and all."

49

U Saw Han drew a deep breath, smiled, and mopped his brow with his handkerchief. "Of course I'll have some coffee. I was awfully worried as to what it was!"

Way Way's face brightened up at his words like the moon coming out of an eclipse. Giving him a glowing smile, she started up and said, "I'll get it for you. I won't be long."

Daw Thet was in the kitchen starting supper. She had not known there was company, and got all flustered when Way Way told her what she had come in to do. "Dear me, did he say he would have some?" she queried.

It was almost ten months since U Saw Han had first arrived. He never ate anything they offered him, so they just treated him like an Englishman, a foreigner, and left it at that. U Saw Han had fixed times for meals and he never came over to join the family for an informal, potluck meal.[28] That U Saw Han had said he would have coffee at their house was to Daw Thet as astonishing as an Indian saying he would eat ngapi.[29]

For Way Way the preparation of one cup of coffee became terribly complicated. First, a pretty cloth had to be picked out and placed on the tray. Then the cup she had was not satisfactory and had to be changed, so there were trips back and forth between the dining room and kitchen. The coffee was then made and put into the cup. The tray was ready and about to be taken in, when it was put down again. "Oh no . . . Aunt . . . It won't do!" cried Way Way.

Daw Thet, watching Way Way's retreat to the kitchen, asked, "What won't do?"

Way Way was hurriedly taking more tea things out of the cupboard, for she had just remembered that they had recently bought a brand-new tea set complete with sugar bowl and milk pitcher. U Saw Han might not like his coffee mixed by somebody else, she thought, and it would not do to serve him coffee Burmese-style, milk and sugar all mixed in. He would like to fix it himself according to his own taste. So she reset the tray again.

---

28. This kind of casual meal is widely accepted as a mark of friendship in Burma.

29. According to popular stereotype, Indians in Burma never learn to enjoy the strong-smelling fish paste no matter how "Burmese" they become.

Way Way carried out the tray herself. U Saw Han looked up and saw it. A pleased expression crept over his face. "Way Way, you have some too . . ." he said.

"We have ours around noon. It's almost time for our evening meal. I won't have any if you don't mind," she replied.

U Saw Han knew that this was not the customary way of serving tea in country places and that all had been done especially for him, and it pleased him immensely. He liked her even more for it and started fixing himself a cup.

On his way home from the library, Ko Nay U could see U Saw Han from the main road and thought it unusual that he was drinking coffee. "My brother's here," said Way Way, and U Saw Han turned around and stood up to greet him.

"I've come to see Dad. Please, continue with your coffee. I'm going upstairs." Ko Nay U went to the stairway but stopped on the first or second step as though remembering something, and said to Way Way, "Ko Saw came from Maubin and brought a letter from Hta Hta. She's coming here at the end of the month."

Way Way went over and took the letter her brother handed to her. U Saw Han made himself a second cup of coffee while she read the letter and, as she was putting it back in the envelope, said without looking at her, "Now that your sister will be here, Way Way, you'll have time to rest and take it easy. So take care of your health, please."

Filled with happiness at the thought of seeing her sister, Way Way listened absent-mindedly to his words without thinking of what he meant.

❖ 6 ❖

Way Way and Hta Hta stood at the door and looked in. The room was furnished with chairs and tables and two second-hand bookcases. There were about fifty school-room chairs. Banners in large Burmese letters proclaimed mottoes such as "Respect the Present," "Clean Living, High Thinking," and "Burmese is *Our* Language." There were about thirty guests already seated. There were elders of the town and younger men, but no women.

Ko Nay U, who was standing in front of the bookshelves, saw his two sisters at the entrance and came towards them saying, "Come in, come on in . . . the ladies haven't arrived yet."

Way Way smiled and nodded at Saya Chit, who was sitting quite close to the door.[30] Saya Chit stood up and came towards them smiling. He looked hard at Hta Hta standing by Way Way's side, and came closer wondering who she was. "Oh, Hta Hta it's you! I didn't recognize you! When did you arrive?"

Hta Hta smiled at him, thinking, My, but he's lost weight! Smilingly she answered, "You and the family are all well, Saya?"

Saya Chit was about fifty years of age, slightly built, light-complexioned, with a faint mustache. He had taught Burmese language and literature to the seventh standard level for many years. Because he knew his subject and taught it well, and was cheerful and considerate, he was well liked by all his students.

When she was in school Hta Hta always knew more people than Way Way, and she was soon surrounded by her old school-mates each welcoming her back in turn. "I came to see my father, who is not well," she said. "Got here only yesterday. Luckily I'm just in time for the opening of the library."

---

30. The honorific "Saya" indicates that the individual bearing it is a teacher.

52

If it had not been for Hta Hta, Way Way would not have attended the ceremony. Since leaving school, she seldom went out of the house, and since she was not used to going out alone, it seemed as if she could only do so when escorted by Aunt Thet.[31] Hta Hta on the other hand was used to going wherever she liked on her own, even before she was married. She was quicker than Way Way in speaking, in thinking, and moving. She had wanted to hear her brother speak at the library and had dragged Way Way along with her.

Ko Nay U and Hta Hta were very much alike in temperament. They were both very active in civic and community affairs, were avid readers, and had many friends. Hta Hta was even more high spirited than Ko Nay U, quite the opposite of Way Way. Hta Hta was as strong and vibrant as Way Way was soft and quiet.

Way Way left Hta Hta with her circle of friends and went quietly to the front row, bending over in a respectful posture as she went down the aisle, as if shrinking from the audience. Having greeted everyone, Hta Hta went to join her sister. Her old teacher, Saya Chit, sat on the other side of her.

It was about four o'clock in the afternoon. Not everyone had arrived. Way Way reached up to the back of her head and tightened her hair knot. She was worried about things at home and fretted that the event had not even started. "It would be terrible if Aunt Thet forgot to give Dad his medicine," she whispered to Hta Hta, who replied, "Come on, you know that you gave her specific instructions. Of course she's not going to forget. Don't worry so." Hta Hta then turned around to look at the hall and said, "The place is full now, so stop worrying, they'll be starting soon."

Ko Nay U went over and stood in front of the table, and people stopped talking. There was a hush. He leaned against the table, rubbed his hands together, looked at the audience for a second and said, "Today we are able to open a library in our town because of the hard work of a group of young people. Today is a happy day for everyone who loves literature and books. We hold in remembrance and honor those many writers and artists who

31. In the prewar era it was still thought quite improper for a young unmarried girl raised in the traditional manner to walk about on her own, especially in a small, conservative town.

have kept the historical heritage of our country alive for us." Ko Nay U stopped speaking for a moment, bowed his head with his arms behind him, and then went on, his audience listening intently. "It is the duty of all of us today to keep our literature and knowledge alive and shining brightly. At this time in our country's history, we are not able to plan for ourselves or our country, and our foundations are weak and shaky. Burmans who call themselves Burmans study a literature which keeps them slaves, turns them into cultural hangers-on, appendages like tails, causing them to lose pride in their own literature and diminishing their knowledge of the most basic elements of their own language. The aim of opening this reading center is to increase the knowledge and awareness of our young people and to start them on the right path. A library is a repository of all that is valuable in a culture, a place where people can learn about their culture, increase their knowledge, and share it with others. So then . . . I invite everyone to come . . . come and use your library. Come in your spare time to study and learn."

Everyone listened raptly to Ko Nay U, and not the least among his listeners was his sister Hta Hta, who, quite taken with her brother's speech, thought to herself, Hmm, he's certainly a good speaker; he'd do well in politics.

Ko Nay U then spoke briefly about the objectives of the library project and frankly told them of some of the difficulties they had encountered at the beginning and along the way. He did this to unite them all, in an intimate way, behind a common cause. He urged them all to be constantly vigilant, and on that note ended his speech. The enraptured audience backed him completely, and were so moved by this speech that they stood up one by one to express their approval.

Saya Chit whispered to Hta Hta, "Maung Ne U has been disillusioned by the colonial educational system ever since he went to college."

Way Way sat sedately listening to it all. People started leaving the library at about six o'clock. Way Way and Hta Hta were about the last to come out of the building and join the crowd in front. Ko Nay U came up to Hta Hta and said, "I was going to open the library when I returned from Rangoon, but what with one thing or another it just couldn't be done. There are really very few people who will do voluntary work, when you come right

54

down to it. I also insisted on a well-planned, systematic procedure from the beginning, so it got delayed further."

Hta Hta teased, "You really should be in politics," to which Way Way replied, "Now don't go encouraging him. Soon he'll be becoming a thakin, and get thrown into 'His Majesty's royal lodgings.'"[32] At this, Ko Nay U raised his clenched right hand in the Thakin salute and chanted, "We Thakins, We Burmans!" Some of the bystanders smiled quietly at his clowning as they left.

Since it was almost dark the sisters hurried home. Greatly concerned, Way Way said, "Ko Nay U became a member of the Dobama Asiayone Party[33] when he went to Rangoon. Ma Ma Than told me that. I had to tell her, 'You better control your husband's actions or he'll end up with a bloody nose.'"[34] Way Way's voice sounded faint and tired and out of breath as she hurried along.

"So what if he did join?" said Hta Hta abruptly.

Unable to stop suddenly in her tracks, Way Way slowed herself to a halt. Standing aghast she cried out, "Why, it's against the law!"

Hta Hta laughed aloud and said with a touch of arrogance, "Dear 'Fraidy Cat, you're scared."

Then, just before they reached home, U Saw Han emerged from his house and met them on the road. "Hey, young lady, where have you been?" he greeted Way Way. He smiled at Hta Hta, whom he appraised with interest.

Way Way could not answer at first. She was embarrassed and tried to appear natural and said, "We've just returned from the library. This is my sister Hta Hta. She arrived yesterday morning."

U Saw Han smiled courteously and said, "Ever since she got the letter about your coming, she's been beside herself with joy,

---

32. That is, prison. "His Majesty" is here, of course, King George VI of Great Britain, Burma's colonial ruler.
33. The Dobama Asiayone ("We Burmans Association"), popularly known as the Thakin Party, was founded on 30 May 1930 by Thakin Ba Thoung. It was the principal prewar nationalist political organization.
34. That is, he would be hurt in confrontations with the police, who in the 1930s frequently broke up political gatherings and demonstrations with baton charges.

oblivious of everything around her, just talking about you all the time. I am happy to meet you. Won't you come in?"

Hta Hta observed U Saw Han's behavior with a faint smile. Way Way said, "Please . . . forgive us this time for not coming in, but father should be given his medicine."

Smiling gently until she finished, he said, "I went to see your father earlier. He seemed much better and was sitting downstairs. I also saw him take his medicine, with my own eyes, so now please, come in for just a minute." U Saw Han was quietly adamant, and Way Way threw Hta Hta an imploring look. She seemed unable to resist any further. U Saw Han began again, "Oh Hta Hta, do come in for just a little while, please, since you are here right in front of the house. Come in for just a moment."

Hta Hta's observant eyes glanced from U Saw Han's face to Way Way's and felt that it was up to her to settle it. "Well, let's just go in for a moment," she said to Way Way. Since her arrival Hta Hta had heard from Daw Thet and Way Way, as much as she needed to know about U Saw Han, and had been able to guess the rest. She looked around the sitting room before she sat down and thought at once how Westernized it was.

U Saw Han was busy calling Maung Mya to bring some orange squash. He went into the dining room, brought out a large parcel, set it down next to Way Way, and said with a smile, "I have a surprise for you Way Way. I ordered these things for you from Rangoon. They arrived this morning. Open up. Take a look."

Way Way looked in astonishment at the parcel and tried to open it, but she was too slow for U Saw Han, who began to open it himself. In the parcel were all kinds of treats from Barnett's Store in Rangoon: biscuit tins, chocolate, candy, and pretty little sample-sized boxes of sweets.

"I ordered 'little' things on purpose for the 'little lady,'" he said. He could not take his eyes off Way Way's blushing face. It seemed he could not help himself, in spite of the older sister's presence. Only after giving Way Way the gifts did he talk to Hta Hta. Hta Hta began telling him that there had been another sibling in their family born between her and Way Way, but the child had died. He was very interested in what she was saying, and turning to Way Way said, "No wonder the young lady is so young."

56

Hta Hta looked at Way Way, who was in an agony of embarrassment, her face wet with perspiration and looking as if she did not know where to hide. Hta Hta wondered, Why is she so embarrassed? They continued to talk for a while and then the sisters stood up to leave. U Saw Han looked at them together. Hta Hta was taller and quite slender. Her forehead was wide and she had fine eyes. She was a little darker in complexion than Way Way, and had clean-cut features which, though not as pretty as Way Way's, were remarkable and attractive in their own way.

Hta Hta led the way out with Way Way close on her heels, but U Saw Han detained Way Way showing her the telegram about the paddy prices. Holding the curtain that hung over the door, she had to listen to him. Only when he finished was she able to catch up with Hta Hta. They hurried along together without speaking.

U Po Thein was still sitting downstairs on the cane armchair waiting for his daughters and talking to Daw Thet. He greeted his daughters with a cheerful face when they came in. The kind of love he had for each of his daughters was different. He loved his older daughter more, but he felt an indescribably infinite tenderness and compassion for his younger daughter.

"Daddy, have you taken your medicine? Have you had your soup? Did you enjoy it? Oh look, he's even chewing betel nut!" said Way Way all in one breath while Hta Hta stood quietly looking on. It had been about a month since he had come downstairs, and the empty armchair had been very conspicuous and upsetting. Seeing her father out of bed and sitting downstairs in the chair made Way Way deliriously happy.

U Po Thein did not go upstairs for some time. He sat and waited for his daughters to finish their supper. He had cheered up considerably since Hta Hta's arrival, and Daw Thet said that her visit had brought his old lively spirit back. The quiet house had become alive and joyful. Wherever you looked everyone had a happy face. The girl in the kitchen, Meh Aye, did not mind the extra work caused by a guest in the house; she kept busy and happy as though she were helping to prepare food for a neighborhood feast. All the unhappiness of living apart had gone and they were happy to be together again.

That night the two sisters, lying side by side on the bed, could hardly sleep because they had so much to talk about. They laughed and chatted endlessly about all kinds of things. They also talked about their mother. There, their ideas differed. Way Way lay back quietly, her fingers clasped on her forehead. "Cold and unfeeling, that's what she is. Mother is just cold and unfeeling and alienated. She's just cut herself off from us," said Way Way bitterly.

"Yes, but don't you see, it isn't just you and me she is cut off from, but Dad, Ko Nay U, and Daw Thet, all of us, and that's just it. She is practicing the Buddhist rule of *uppeka*."[35]

Way Way thought about this and tried hard to put her whole mind into trying to understand the meaning of the concept, but try as she might it was impossible to comprehend it in so short a time. She could only try to grasp what it meant at her own level, and even then it eluded her. Finally she lost the thread of her thinking, including thoughts of her mother, and she did what she always did when she could not understand something, which was to change the subject.

"Is it true," she said to Hta Hta, "that marriage is nothing but trouble, and that when you get married all you are doing is getting yourself into a whole bunch of problems?"

Hta Hta was amazed and looked curiously out of the corner of her eye at Way Way. Strange how she got to this subject so suddenly, she thought. "I don't know how to explain this to you so that you will understand," she answered. "It is true that you are asking for trouble because you have a new set of problems when you get married, but if you know that there will be these particular problems and go ahead and solve them as they come along, then there is nothing more to be said. But if you see beforehand that these problems cannot be solved no matter what, then that's serious and you shouldn't get married. One has a responsibility to work things out and to be in control of one's life. . . ."

Way Way was silent, thinking about what she had just heard. Hta Hta guessed that she was thinking about marriage. When one reaches a certain age, one invariably has thoughts about it and desires it, Hta Hta mused to herself. She thought, Love and

---

35. Freedom from all kinds of desire and attachment, a neutral state of mind, equanimity and indifference to one's own enjoyment or suffering.

marriage go together as one whole, complementing each other. Love is essential for the stability of a marriage, but for dealing with life itself it is essential for each individual person to have an inner confidence and self-sufficiency. As far as she was able to tell from her own experience, marriage was not right for Way Way at this time, and she should not in any way be encouraged into taking such a step.

❖ 7 ❖

Hta Hta awoke in the night and looked around drowsily. She did not know when they had dropped off to sleep, what time it was now, or when Way Way had gotten up and left. The mosquito net was not down, the window not closed, and the light still on. She could see the dim moonlight outside. Apart from Daw Thet's snoring, which sounded as though she had fallen into an exhausted sleep, the house was silent. She heard the barking of dogs far off in the distance. She could not tell whether it was just one dog barking or different dogs barking one after another. She shut her eyes in a kind of stupor but would not let herself sleep; she had to tell Way Way to close the window at the foot of the bed so it would not rain in on the covers. Hta Hta waited for Way Way to return from the bathroom and wondered what was taking her so long. With a groan, she got up to close it herself. She staggered sleepily to the window. When she got there, her eyes suddenly widened at what she saw, and she stood shocked. Her whole body froze except for her hands, which trembled violently as she held on to the window.

Hidden from the main road by the big mango tree, but revealed in the faint dappled moonlight shining through its branches, U Saw Han and Way Way stood facing each other, his arms around her neck embracing her. At first, seeing them suddenly in the dark, you could not tell who they were, but when you saw their silhouettes you knew it could be no one else but Way Way and U Saw Han. U Saw Han had on a dark coat and pants, and Way Way was dressed as she had been earlier. They could not see Hta Hta from where they stood, but she could see them well. As soon as she realized who they were, she did not want to see any more. She rushed back to her bed and threw herself down on it.

Her heart pounded fearfully. Never in all her life had she experienced such palpitations. She became extremely exhausted, and had to force herself to take slow breaths to calm down. She heard the stroke of one beaten on a piece of iron by some night watchman to announce the hour. It sounded very close. She was confused and did not even know how to begin thinking about this problem, but was unable to drive from her mind the picture of U Saw Han's embracing form and Way Way's upturned face. Those two are already involved with each other, she said to herself, coming to a starting point. She began thinking about U Saw Han and how much he admired the British, how un-Burmese he was in behavior, and how different his life style was from their own and that of everyone they knew. Then she thought of Way Way and her innocence, her lack of sophistication, her youth and child-like ignorance of life. To think of them as a couple alarmed her even more.

She heard Way Way's footsteps coming softly and slowly. Hta Hta, calmer by this time and more in control of herself, listened to the footsteps. When they neared the bed, she opened her eyes and looked at her sister severely. This completely startled Way Way, who acted as if she had seen a ghost. Unable to bear Hta Hta's stern eyes upon her, she began to retreat into herself and to blot out the fact that she was there. She did this almost to the point of denying her very consciousness. Hta Hta sat up and swung her legs over the side of the bed. "Way Way," she called in a low voice.

Hta Hta's voice shook Way Way from her trance-like state. Thoroughly ashamed, she hung her head down and was on the verge of tears. Hta Hta did not have to say more. Way Way knew that she had seen them. Looking at her sister so cowed and frightened, Hta Hta's heart dissolved in pity. She did not say a word, much as she was against what Way Way had done. Instead she thought to herself, The poor girl, now grown to adolescence, has had to take care of herself without a mother, is lonely without the company of her sister or brother, and is obliged to take on the burden of the whole house and the family business, and a sick father, with no time for herself. She's lonely and only human. She cannot really be blamed for going out in the dark to meet a lover. So, gradually understanding things, the older sister forgave the younger instead of berating her.

61

With an anguished face, Hta Hta stretched out her hand and said, "Dear little sister, don't be distressed. Come and sit beside me and talk."

Hearing the gentle tones of her sister's voice, Way Way sat beside her with her head still hung down from embarrassment. "Have you and U Saw Han been in love for a long time?" asked Hta Hta. Way Way shook her head in the negative. "Then it's not been long," said Hta Hta. Way Way nodded and looked timidly up at Hta Hta with her eyes brimming with tears and full of love for her. Seeing her face, Hta Hta choked up and could not ask any more questions.

Then Way Way said, "It was really nothing at first . . . just ordinary . . . It was the day before you came . . . he . . ." and did not continue. Hta Hta regarded Way Way quietly. Although she did not say more, Way Way was recalling to herself the course of events and tracing how one thing had led to another. Knowing that the paddy in the godown was wet and beginning to smell of mold, she knew she had to stop the new paddy, which was soon to arrive by boat, from being mixed with the wet grain. She had planned to ask Daw Thet to go to the godown and prevent that, but her aunt had not returned from the monastery. So, leaving Meh Aye with her father, she had hurried off to the godown. It was about three o'clock in the afternoon and as she hurried along the road, who should she come face to face with as she turned the bend but U Saw Han returning from the office. U Saw Han had been taken aback at seeing her so unexpectedly, and anxiously asked, "Way Way, what's happened? Is it your father? Are you going for the doctor?" Way Way explained what she was doing. U Saw Han said, "If that's the case then, I'll come with you to the godown." Way Way was aware of the impropriety of a young girl like her walking down the road with a man, and was afraid of being seen by neighbors. She hastily replied, "It's all right, I can go by myself. I can go by myself." U Saw Han did not realize why she did not want him to accompany her, and went along anyway. He talked the whole way, while Way Way concentrated on getting where she was going as soon as possible without being seen. "In my eyes, Way Way, you are still a child, but the work you do is that of an adult. I am sorry you have to do it. I have great regard for you, and I want to help you in any way I possibly can," he went on.

62

Way Way had been unable to say a single word, so fearful was she that people would see them together. Only when there were a few other people on the road as they neared the godown, did she relax a little. She went to the hut near the godown where the caretaker, Ko Nyo, and his wife lived, while U Saw Han walked around the godown. Way Way found only the wife, for Ko Nyo was still at the bazaar purchasing some kerosene oil. He had run out, and needed it for his lamp during the night watch. He had come to the house about it earlier and Way Way had given him some money. She gave the message to the wife and then looked around for U Saw Han, wondering where he was. She saw him looking at the river from under the acacia tree on the north side of the godown.

Way Way had walked toward where he was standing. "Oh, what a breeze!" she had said, when a sudden gust of wind blew against her, and she had to struggle to keep her tamein from sticking to her body. U Saw Han turned towards her and noticed the bangs on her forehead being blown about and he was fascinated by them. He said, "This is what I call fresh air. It's so fresh and clean. Let's stay out here a little longer and enjoy it."

He looked at Way Way with hazy eyes. She pretended not to notice and gazed at the river. Neither of them spoke. As U Saw Han looked at her he had to control the strong wave of emotion that rose up in his heart for her.

"Let's go," Way Way had said, and U Saw Han nodded and swallowed hard. He was in a daze as they walked back together. They did not follow the same route as when they came and took a short cut instead. They could get to the main road much more quickly by crossing a small ditch. U Saw Han jumped across it and stretched out his hand for Way Way. She was embarrassed to hold his hand. Seeing her so shy and not even daring to look at him, U Saw Han was so entranced that he could hardly contain himself. Way Way jumped over the water on her own, but he caught her hand to steady her and then would not release it. It seemed to her that he not only held her hand in his, but that he had her whole self trapped in his grasp. Just the thought of the two of them walking hand in hand like this almost made her heart stop. "Way Way, do you love me?" he said. At that instant, it seemed as if a motor had started up inside her and left her weak. Even remembering it now made her feel weak all over.

Hta Hta, who had been determined not to ask any more questions, could not hold back and said, "Do you and U Saw Han meet like this every night?"

"No not every night," replied Way Way, "Tonight was the only time. When he detained me at the front door of his house this evening, he begged me to meet him down there. He said he would be waiting for me."

Hta Hta did not want to ask or hear any more. She got up and moved away. Way Way asked anxiously, "Don't you approve of him and me?"

Hta Hta turned around to face her and said, "As long as you love him, that's all that matters. Don't let anything disturb you, Way Way, it will be all right." Then she got up to close the window.

U Saw Han was at least twenty years senior to seventeen year-old Way Way, far too wide a gap for anyone to agree to the match. But if they loved each other and asked for approval, it would have to be given. Certainly if the elders had made the match, U Saw Han would have been rejected. Hta Hta lay in bed thinking seriously about Way Way's future. She knew that she herself was indulging her younger sister, and wondered how her father and her brother would react. She was quite certain that her brother, with his predisposition against the English and his nationalistic feelings, would not give his consent. With regard to social status, and as a provider, U Saw Han would exceed what any woman would expect. There might be a few township officers and commissioners who were called "your honor" by other Burmese, but to find someone whom they called "Thakin" was quite rare. Hta Hta tried to put herself in Way Way's place. She considered U Saw Han's rank and impressive personage, but when she came down to it, she absolutely abhorred a Burmese who tried to ape the British. Hta Hta examined it from every angle and thought with a sigh, Will it work? She shuddered as she thought of Way Way's reaction to the sight of amber-colored liquid in a glass.

Way Way was crying quietly, the tears streaming down her face, her back to Hta Hta as she lay beside her on the bed. She was thinking about her life. She knew that she was responsible for the house and for her father, and felt that she should not have any other concerns. She should not in these circumstances have a suitor. It would be like breaking faith. Her thoughts were in turmoil, thinking about her love for her father and the attraction she felt toward her suitor. She who should be at her father's side, at home, had stepped out the home and found herself at the side of another love. Way Way tried to decide between the two, hoping that her feelings for one would give in to those for the other. But as soon as she decided in favor of her father, she found she had not lost her feelings for her lover. And when she decided in his favor, all her feelings for her father pulled her back. She had never experienced such feelings before.

Hta Hta got up and switched on the light. Way Way quietly wiped her eyes and closed them. Hta Hta's reddened face could be seen in the light. Heavy with sleep, she went to get a drink from the table where a pitcher of water and glasses had been placed. She stood there for a long time. Way Way said, "Aren't you asleep yet?"

Hta Hta felt a shiver go down her spine. "I got up to get a drink of water. Aren't *you* asleep yet?"

Way Way got up and scrutinized Hta Hta's red face. "What's the matter?"

Hta Hta looked at Way Way's tear-stained face and said, "Nothing. I couldn't sleep, so I started planning for when you two get married."

"Get married?" Way Way's eyes widened and her mouth gaped. "Way Way, when did U Saw Han say he was going to marry you?"

Way Way, greatly distressed at the thought of marriage, shook her head and said, "He never said." After seeing U Saw Han in the godown, all they had spoken about when they met was about love. She had not heard the word "marriage" until Hta Hta mentioned it. Way Way had not related love to marriage. It was too speedy for her.

"What about you . . . when do you think you want to be married?" asked Hta Hta.

"I don't know . . . I haven't thought about it yet . . . I don't want to get married."

"Goodness, girl, how can you not get married? What are you saying?" Hta Hta said with a frown. "Well," she continued, "I guess things have not got to the stage of discussing marriage plans as yet, but I wouldn't drag it out too long, if you ask me. When you feel you can discuss it, I want to make a clean breast of it to

Father, and arrange things to suit both sides before I leave. I think it's best that way."

Way Way's thoughts were muddled. She winced to hear the word "marriage." "I will not marry for a long while . . . it won't do to get married yet," she insisted.

"What do you mean, 'won't do'? How can you carry on, the two of you, without being married?"

"But what about Daddy?" Way Way's voice rose in an inadvertent shout.

"What *about* Dad?" said Hta Hta, "Are you worried that if you got married Dad would be left alone? It would have had to happen sometime. We can't stop you from getting married just because Dad will be left alone. You can't be a spinster because of Dad. When you two get married, Dad will adjust to new arrangements. We'll just have to think about it and make arrangements, that's all."

It became more and more difficult for Way Way to think. If she did marry U Saw Han, she thought, she would have to be apart from her father, and that was a fact. It would not do to be away from him at this time, with him sick and the business likely to get out of control. She became more and more confused about it all, so before she slept she made a vow to put off getting married as long as she could.

❖ 8 ❖

It was a sunny afternoon. A sampan could be seen drifting along
in a current made by a breeze blowing across the expanse of water.
Ko Nay U looked down at his watch, then, craning his neck
towards the river, studied it intently. He turned to Ko Khant, a
lawyer and secretary of the library, and said, "It's four o'clock now.
Do you think they'll make it?"

As he sat down wearily on his haunches, Burmese style, Ko
Khant said, "Oh, I'm sure they'll come."

There were crowds of people on the bank of the river. Sitting on a stool in front of the Chinese tea shop was Ko Aung Sein,
perspiration mottling his powdered face. Taking the end of his
long sarong of the traditional royal style, he tucked it behind him
with an affected air and went into the water on the tips of his toes
to look across the river. The throng of happy children near him
cried, "Dance, Uncle, dance! Now! Please!" egging him on to do
a show.

Ko Aung Sein had rented the male dancer's outfit he wore.
The starched cotton jacket was quite crumpled from his constant
sitting and standing. Retying his costume turban, which was more
resplendent than the real thing, he shouted to the children, "Wait,
will you? You'll just have to wait!"

Hearing the outcry, Ko Khant smiled and said, "Aung Sein is
turning into a real monkey sideshow."

A voice near Ko Khant said, "I hear that the Nagani book
shop has sent you some books."[36] The voice belonged to Saya
Chit, the school teacher.

---

36. "Nagani" means "Red Dragon," indicating that the firm is a leftist
publishing company.

Ko Khant replied, "Yes, Saya. Three books. One by Thakin Nu called *The Way Out for the Poor, Socialism* by Thakin Soe, and *Capitalism* by Thakin Ba Hein. The book on socialism is really about communism: no landed property, no landowners, no private ownership. That's what it says."

Ko Nay U, whose attention centered on the river all this while, said with a groan, "If they left Wakema at noon, they should be here soon."

"There they are! There they are! Over there! Over there!" came a shout from the group at the river bank. But Ko Aung Sein said, "It's just lotus plants, man!" causing a guffaw from the crowd, which was all tuned up to a festival mood. The news had spread all around town that some thakins were coming from the Dobama Asiyone. The town crier had gone around saying there would be a meeting in the movie theater that evening. Ko Nay U had met and discussed the setting up of a chapter of the Thakin Party with many of the town's young people. In anticipation of this, an invitation had been sent to the Dobama Asiayone in Rangoon, asking for some prominent thakins to speak to the public.

On his recent trip to Rangoon Ko Nay U he had met an old friend, Ko Thein Maung, who had become a thakin. This friend had taken him to the party headquarters to meet the other members. Thakin Ba Sein, Thakin Htun Ok, and Thakin Nyi happened to be there. "We have a new vote from the jungle.[37] This guy's a rich man's kid. We won't starve while he's in town. He'll feed us." said Thakin Thein Maung, introducing him in a gravelly voice. They all became friends almost immediately, and were soon on easy, familiar terms. Ko Nay U had been tremendously excited to meet people who shared his views on national independence as well as his anti-imperialist feelings. Greatly stimulated by all the talk, his nationalistic spirit was roused to battle pitch and he joined the Thakin Party that same day.

The news that Thakin Hteit Tin Kodaw Gyi, Thakin Ba Sein, Thakin Nyi, Thakin Htun Ok, and Prome Thakinma Ma Thein Tin would come to speak had spread all over the town of Moulmein-

---

37. The speaker jokingly alludes to the provinces outside the capital city as "the jungle," and treats Ko Nay U as something of a "country boy."

gyun, and a large crowd had assembled on the river bank to greet them. Included in the large crowd were many people from remote jungle places, who had come expressly to see Thakin Hteit Tin Kodaw Gyi, a scion of the Burmese royal family.[38] The crowd on the river bank slowly grew larger. Ko Nay U was happy to see the joyful but orderly throng, adorned in their best festival clothes.

A small motorboat with a fluttering flag came into view round the bend of the river. The flag had a hammer, sickle, and three colored stars. The welcoming drums began to beat loudly, "Gyein . . . gyein . . . gyein . . . gyein . . . ," before the craft neared the bank. Standing at the helm a good looking, light complexioned, bright-eyed man, wearing a homespun jacket and a pink gaung-baung, could be seen as the motorboat moved towards the causeway. He was Thakin Htun Ok. He stretched out his arm and shouted, "Thakin myo hay! (We thakins!)" Ko Nay U and the others standing on the causeway shouted in reply, "Dobama! (We Burmans!)" The crowd joined in.

"We thakins!" the shout came from the boat.

"We Burmans!" came the reply from the crowd.

"Our Noble Cause!" came from the boat.

"May it succeed!" the crowd replied.

These words reverberated all over the area in a tremendous roar. Thakin Hteit Tin Kodaw Gyi, the royal descendant, did not come, much to the disappointment of the people from the remote areas. Before going to the meeting hall, the crowd first circled the town in a long procession, with the big drum in front. The dancer, Ko Aung Sein, was in his element. He leaped about, dancing his heart out as they moved along. The townspeople stared in wonder at the line, especially at the lady member of the Thakin Party, who was also wearing clothes made of homespun.[39] The procession wound around the town and passed in front of Way Way's house. Way Way and Hta Hta were waiting at the gate to see it.

U Saw Han met up with the procession on his way back from work, and stepped to the side of the road to let it pass by. Hta Hta

---

38. This individual's name denotes royalty of some degree because it begins with "Hteit Tin," which means "the uppermost."
39. She is indicated by the appellation "Thakinma," "ma" being a suffix meaning "female."

saw this and nudged Way Way and said, "Look over there." Way Way saw U Saw Han, his European-style white shirt and pants contrasting with the thakins in their homespun, and she could hardly bear to watch. It made her very uneasy.

Just then her brother, Ko Nay U, dressed in pinni homespun and wearing a bamboo coolie hat,[40] came walking along the road with some of the thakins. When he saw U Saw Han he saluted him thakin-style, with outstretched arm, and grinned at him. U Saw Han gave him a weak forced smile in return. Dodging the crowd, he came to Way Way's house in a roundabout way. Way Way and Hta Hta smiled at him in greeting. Hta Hta remained at the gate while Way Way followed U Saw Han into the house. When he got inside, he looked around and asked Way Way if Daw Thet was about. Way Way shook her head in the negative, and U Saw Han pointed upstairs indicating that he surmised that she was upstairs. He came close to her and whispered, "Let's meet tonight."

Way Way's face clouded and she turned to the front of the house in the direction of Hta Hta, who had her back to them and was still watching the procession. "No, no. I don't think so. My sister saw us the other night from upstairs."

U Saw Han gasped. His face went ashen, his lips drew together tensely. After a moment, he asked softly, "What did she say?" He looked down at her unhappy little countenance, waiting in suspense for her answer.

Way Way, upset and breathing fast, was at a loss as to how to answer, and hung her head dejectedly. Just at that point Hta Hta came back into the house and they had to constrain themselves and sit down with her. She guessed that something was wrong from their strained faces, so she put on an air of ease and said to U Saw Han, "Well, it seems that Ko Nay U has become a thorough-going thakin." She smiled as she said it.

U Saw Han forced a smile and replied, "What does your father say about it?" Then turning to Way Way, he said teasingly, "And what about you, Way Way, don't you want to join the thakins too?"

---

40. The conical coolie's hat, like homespun, emphasized the use of indigenous products. It also symbolized solidarity with the lower classes.

Way Way smiled, not really wanting to, and replied, not looking at him but at Hta Hta, "Daddy doesn't tell his son to stop doing anything. Ko Nay U's opinions have changed, somehow, since he left high school. He is now interested in politics."

"What about you, Hta Hta, aren't you interested in politics?"

At first she was going to answer seriously, but changed her mind and said lightly, to match his half-joking question, "Well, let's say that I am just keeping my interest on hold until my better half, the good doctor, retires from government service."

U Saw Han liked her answer and guffawed. It seemed absurdly funny to him that Hta Hta's husband could lose his government job because of his wife's proclivity for politics. "I know your husband, Ko Thet Htun. Although we weren't friends, he lived in a room close to mine when we attended the university. He was a good sort. People used to call him Phongyi,"[41] said U Saw Han.

"Yes," said Hta Hta, "When we heard from Way Way's letters that a certain U Saw Han had arrived next door, he told me that he knew you, too." Then turning to Way Way, she said, "Why don't you get him an orange drink?"

As Way Way left the room, U Saw Han looked at Hta Hta's composed face and asked uncomfortably, "How long will you be staying here, Hta Hta?"

"I was going to stay only ten days because I was anxious about the children, but both my father and my sister are pressing me to stay longer, so I decided to stay on for a month. I've written to my husband about it already."

"Before you leave, you must come to my house. I don't have anywhere to go in this town. I sometimes go on inspection tours, but that's about it. I just go back and forth, from office to home and home to office. I come here now and then, of course."

Hta Hta listened quietly and, when he had finished, asked, "How long will you be stationed here?"

"I can't say. Whether they'll just keep me here or send one of their own men,[42] I don't know."

---

41. The nickname comes from *phongyi,* meaning a Buddhist monk.
42. That is, an Englishman.

They were both silent for a while. Hta Hta was thinking quietly. U Saw Han lit his cigarette and wondered what was going on in her mind. He could see that she was troubled. Hta Hta was worried about Way Way, who was very young and could be taken advantage of easily. She wondered why U Saw Han had not married. She worried that after going too far with Way Way he might not be able to marry her. Hta Hta gave out a little sigh and said, "When Dad is better, I am thinking of taking Way Way with me for a visit. She never gets to go anywhere. She only just manages to see mother about once a year, and that's it. As the family business seems to depend on her, even to invite her seems difficult."

"Are you taking her to Maubin?" U Saw Han blurted out in great consternation and then quickly regained his composure. To add to his being disconcerted that Hta Hta knew about them, this sudden information that she might take Way Way away quite knocked him off balance. He wondered if they disapproved of him because he was so much older than Way Way, and were trying to break them up. He started to feel depressed.

Way Way came back from the kitchen. Behind her was Meh Aye with a tray with two glasses of orange squash. The girl held the tray with both hands and walked respectfully in a bent position. Way Way placed a glass in front of U Saw Han and then one in front of Hta Hta and said, "Please have a drink."

U Saw Han picked up his glass and was about to drink when he set it down and picked up Hta Hta's glass and handed it to her, saying, "Here, Hta Hta, here's your drink. Please drink."

Hta Hta took the glass and started to drink. Way Way was sitting silent, her eyes cast down. Putting down his glass with half of his drink still remaining, U Saw Han turned to Way Way and said, "I hear you are going to Maubin." Way Way was dumbfounded. Hta Hta had never mentioned anything of the kind to her and she turned her astonished eyes toward her sister, wondering what she had told him. U Saw Han took in the surprised expression on Way Way's face and the look she gave Hta Hta. He had thought it had all been arranged. How could he stop Way Way from going, he thought frantically; he must see her alone. Hta Hta, in turn, was trying to figure U Saw Han out, as always. Seeing him visibly upset over Way Way's impending departure, she wondered what that meant. Way Way will not want to leave home.

72

I'll have to persuade her against her will, Hta Hta noted mentally. Way Way was sitting silently, not saying whether she was going or not. With her eyes downcast, she seemed wrapped in a brown haze. It drove U Saw Han to distraction.

"I believe Maubin is famous for it's mosquitoes. I've never been there myself," he said as he picked up his glass, gave it a swirl, and drank up.

Way Way listened to U Saw Han patching up the gaps in the conversation and sat with her head bowed, rubbing the nail of one of her fingers with her thumb.

"Ah, don't mention mosquitoes!" said Hta Hta. "As soon as it gets toward evening, we have to put the house under mosquito-netting. We have to put netting over all the doors and windows."

Just then Maung Mya appeared without his gaung-baung.[43] In his hand he held a telegram, which he presented humbly to his master. Way Way watched as he opened the telegram, read it, and then said to Maung Mya, "Fine. You may go." After Maung Mya had left, U Saw Han placed the telegram in it's envelope and, putting it in his pocket, said, "I'll have to return to the office. Something has cropped up at work," and stood up. He took his leave of Hta Hta and looked at Way Way with a special, concerned expression. He left the house and went out on to the road deep in thought. His head was lowered and foremost on his mind was Way Way's dejected little face. Wondering again if Hta Hta was trying to break them up, he became uneasy.

As he neared the movie theater, which was on his way, he heard voices singing so loudly that his ears could hardly stand the noise. "We citizens of Burma, one and all, believe that this land, this country belongs to us. We BURMESE, We THAKINS!" the song went on.

---

43. This nuance emphasizes that even a person like Maung Mya, a servant, knew that, in contrast to the English-style house of U Saw Han where he worked, it would be too much for a servant to wear a gaung-baung in a Burmese house in a casual everyday situation. It would look more than ridiculous.

❖ 9 ❖

When Hta Hta appeared in the upstairs front room, U Po Thein was lying back in his arm chair. Putting his book down on the table, he looked at her from behind his crystal eyeglasses. "Have you heard whether Maung Nay U's house guests have left?" he asked.

"Yes, they've gone. They talked at the movie theater last evening, and left this morning," she replied. Hta Hta studied her father's face. Despite his being house-bound for a month, his complexion looked fresh. The short hairs on his close-cropped head were white and matched his moustache. Although his face appeared thinner and his temples and cheeks a bit shrunken, he did not look emaciated. As always, his face had about it a look of calm and an inner peace. "I've just written Mother a letter," Hta Hta went on, "I hope it won't upset her."

"Oh . . . what sort of letter, daughter?" asked her father. U Po Thein's face became slightly more dignified, as it always did when his wife's name was mentioned.

"Oh I haven't mailed it yet. I was going to consult you first, of course. It's about Way Way." Hta Hta lowered her eyes and stopped talking. U Po Thein waited in silence for her to continue. He was thinking over what she had just said.

"I think it would be good to get Way Way married," said Hta Hta. "U Saw Han from the other house desires very much to marry her. They care for each other and are in love. Way Way does not want to get married and resists. She says she cannot part from you yet. What do *you* think, Dad?"

They were both quiet for a while. Then he suddenly bent over to expectorate in the spittoon and said calmly and pleasantly, "Daughter, when a young girl reaches a certain age it is the same as when a fruit is ready to ripen or flowers to bloom. I have been

74

observing the young man in question since he arrived, and I wonder if marriage would be suitable. Does Way Way love him?"

"Yes, she loves him. I bumped into U Saw Han on his way to work when I was going to Ko Nay U's place this morning. He wanted to talk to me, so I stopped by his house on my return."

Hta Hta had been quite taken aback when she talked to U Saw Han; he had turned out to be a rather different person than she expected. She had worried that he had been trifling with Way Way's affections and taking advantage of her tender age. Instead, it appeared that was not only utterly serious, but had concerns about the family's acceptance of him. She also had not anticipated the speed at which their conversation would move.

"Since you now know about Way Way and me, let me at last speak out openly. The feeling I have for Way Way is not just a passing fancy. I love her deeply. I loved her the moment I set eyes on her. Later, as I got to know her, I was filled with even more love and compassion for this little person carrying such burdens. I could hardly bear to watch her with all those adult responsibilities. She is but a child in my eyes. If you and the family approve and give your consent, I am ready to marry her at any time."

When Hta Hta had heard these words, she felt as if a huge load had slipped off her back. She told him she would consult their father first and took her leave. She filled her father in on the details and background so that he would understand the situation better, and then waited to hear what he had to say.

"Well," he said, "If they love each other, I have no cause to oppose it. I want my little daughter to be happy, though as I just mentioned, their life styles are very different. But it's up to her to decide .... What about Daw Thet? What does *she* think?"

"Aunt says if Way Way loves him, get her married off, the sooner the better. I haven't told Ko Nay U. I'm sure he won't approve."

U Po Thein's eyes were staring off into space. He was back in a past time, oblivious of his surroundings, his heart beating rapidly as he pictured his wife, Daw Mya Thet, sitting demurely near him, hair combed back neatly and wound into a knot around a comb, her blouse crisp and laundered by the Indian laundryman, and wearing a longyi of a silver weave with black specks. She is sitting near him but not looking at him. Modestly averting her eyes, she is saying politely, "Since the children are in love with each other, please allow them to be married." He was remembering the time his wife came to intercede for Hta Hta before she was married to Ko Thet Hnan. U Po Thein turned and smiled at Hta Hta.

Seeing her father smile, Hta Hta assumed he was smiling at what she had just said and laughed, "Yes, Daddy, it is true. Your son has joined the thakins and his national spirit is high. He can't stand the sight of U Saw Han because he is so English in his thinking."

Way Way came into the room with a glass of milk. She had just bathed and put on fresh clothes. Her long, black hair, which had just been washed, was hanging down loose to dry. U Po Thein looked at his dear little daughter, took the glass of milk from her, and said, "Way Way, don't let your hair hang loose. Make a knot at the ends, as the tips are already dry."[44] Daw Mya Thet, Way Way's mother, used to knot the ends of her hair whenever she washed her hair and let it hang loose to dry. There was hidden pain in her father's voice as he spoke.

Way Way smiled, gathered her hair from the back of her shoulders to the front and began to knot it at the ends. U Po Thein watched Way Way intently, and Hta Hta left her place and moved unconsciously toward Way Way. Having knotted her hair, Way Way let it fall back over her shoulders. With a cheerful face, she picked up her father's empty milk glass and left the room.

Everyone said that Way Way had never looked as pretty as she did that evening. The whole family seemed especially aware of her, and noted the way she talked and behaved. Her smiling and laughing ways tugged at their heartstrings. Just calling her name—"Way Way!"—seemed to give them pleasure. The two sisters went for a walk along the river bank that evening. Daw Thet watched them from the doorway until they were out of sight.

---

44. Burmese women traditionally wear their hair uncut, and long, well-kempt hair is much admired. At the same time, according to old-fashioned or merely conservative sensibilities, there is something faintly immodest about hair that is allowed to hang loose rather than gathered or tied in a coiffure.

Hta Hta proceeded to tell her sister about her conversation with U Saw Han that morning, which surprised Way Way. She seemed pleased and cheerful as they walked along.

"I was afraid he was toying with your feelings, but he is dead serious and loves you very much and says that he is ready and willing anytime." Hta Hta then stopped talking and walked on in silence, wrapped in her own thoughts.

She was thinking of when she and Ko Thet Hnan fell in love. Recalling the first time she met her husband, her mind went back to a river scene and a little boat. Because of the low water level, the boat could not land at the usual place and was being shoved through the mud to the bank. There were two men on the boat, one a cleanly dressed and dark-complexioned man with sunglasses, the other a boatman without a shirt, a faded old longyi wrapped around his head. Hta Hta watched the little boat from the house on stilts in the rice mill compound, which belonged to the parents of Than Than, Ko Nay U's wife. As she watched, the man in the sunglasses stood in the prow of the boat and looked at the oozing mud. Then, hitching his longyi up to his knees and carrying his small leather bag, he stepped into the mud. Behind him came the boatman, maneuvering skillfully through the mud and taking the leather case from him. As she watched the person plodding with difficulty through the mud, she heard Than Than's voice near her say, "That's the new doctor. He's come to see old man San." Hta Hta watched him wade through the mud, hoist himself onto the pier, walk to a hut inside the mill compound some distance away, and, bending over, enter a small adjoining cattle shed. She watched until he was out of sight.

The memory of that first time never left her. "Old man San caught his leg on a sharp snag and it became infected. He went to the hospital on the other bank for treatment for four or five days, but then it got so swollen that he couldn't stand up. The doctor missed him and was worried; he enquired about the old man and came to see him. He comes over every evening and treats him free. He really cares about that old man. He's a very good person, the doctor." Than Than's words found their way into Hta Hta's heart, and great regard and admiration for him turned into love as time went on.

The circumstances in which the two sisters had met their true loves, one walking with shoes on a wool carpet, and the other

77

barefoot in oozing mud, were as dissimilar as the feelings they engendered.

Turning to Way Way, Hta Hta said in a straightforward manner, "It certainly looks as if he loves you sincerely; but what about you, do you love him?"

Way Way was taken aback at the directness of the question and could not answer. Then she said, "How do you want me to answer you?"

Hta Hta said, "Just tell me why you like him, why you love him." Hta Hta smiled encouragingly at her and Way Way started thinking slowly, looking at the ground.

Hta Hta waited as they walked along and then Way Way said softly, "He loves me so much that I love him back, that's all."

Hta Hta could not believe her ears and looked at her stunned. Then an expression of great pity and tenderness came into her eyes. Way Way was thinking over her answer and feeling a little shy, then she asked Hta Hta "What did Daddy say?"

Hta Hta would have liked to have asked more questions but did not want to make it difficult for her sister. She said, "Father says if you love him, if you are happy, he has no objections. He agrees, and says that your lifestyles are very different but that it is up to you to decide what you want to do with your life and how you are going to handle it."

Way Way, who had not looked critically at U Saw Han's pro-English attitude, and indeed did not think the difference in their ways might be a drawback, took her father's remark lightly.

"I don't know how Ko Nay U will react," said Way Way. Hta Hta, interrupted in her train of thought by this introduction of a new person, said, "Oh I don't think he will say anything against it, but knowing him you can never tell," and laughed.

"Oh yes, he's is something else," said Way Way.

Just then one of the neighbors called to Hta Hta from her front yard, and she stopped to talk; feeling shy, Way Way went on by herself. Hta Hta caught up with her and went on with the conversation. "I told U Saw Han that he could come to see you this evening if he wants to. You should have seen his face light up. He looked as sweet as honey by the time I left him."

When Way Way heard that he was coming that evening her reaction was mixed. She worryied about it, and felt both nervous and somewhat afraid. They walked along the river road and followed the bend to Ko Nay U's house. Than Than came hurrying to open the gates, blouseless and with her longyi tucked up under her armpits, a towel over her shoulders. Ko Nay U was in the house, wearing a tee shirt and perspiring freely, bent over a meal.

"We Thakins! We Burmans! Our Cause! May it prosper!" he teased them in greeting, extending his arm in the thakin salute. "Come in! Come on in, girls, come and join me," he said, inviting them to eat.

Than Than spread a mat near the low round table on which the food was arranged, and Hta Hta and Way Way sat down. Hta Hta looked at her brother. He was eating his meal with great relish as he talked to them animatedly about his success at founding the Thakin Party in town. As he talked to Hta Hta, he turned to his wife and said, "Don't keep asking Way Way to eat, Than Than. She only eats at a table sitting on a chair, not on a low table sitting on the floor." He was teasing, but was right on target. Way Way, bashful, punched him on the shoulder. Hta Hta's face changed imperceptibly as she looked at them together and realized in a flash that Way Way was going to be an outsider to their warm and loving family, which had always been noisy and close. Her heart was heavy. She chattered on but without real enjoyment, and she had to be careful of what she said.

They finally left just as the sun was setting. The last rays had been gathered in and it was dark except for the dim street lights. It was that time of day when dark and light intermingled, and soon they were home.

Hta Hta and Daw Thet went upstairs, and Way Way sat at the desk looking towards the road waiting for U Saw Han to come. Meh Aye was waiting near the door with the keys to the gate. U Saw Han appeared and Meh Aye let him in. She then locked the gate and went to the back of the house.

U Saw Han saw Way Way with her head down on the desk. He crept up softly until he was facing her, put his hands on his hips, and said in a loud whisper, his head almost touching hers, "Young lady!" Way Way lifted her head slowly until she could see his face, and smiled. He came very close to her face, which was streaked with tears; he could not bear to see them. He sat down on the desk and there was a sudden fragrance of hair lotion and soap as he took her hands into his. "Hta Hta told me that she would talk to your father. What did he say? Let's get married as soon as possible," he said huskily.

Way Way did not move. She would not answer and just sat silently, which made U Saw Han uneasy. It was difficult to know what she felt or thought. He wondered whether being so young made her apprehensive about taking such an enormous step as marriage. If she did not want to marry him, did she really love him enough? He was confused as he tried to fathom her silence; he had some real misgivings.

What was actually going through Way Way's mind at the moment was anxiety over her father's nosebleeds. She was unable to think straight or answer him. Then she tried to focus on marriage and whether she wanted to marry just yet. She thought that if she was happy thinking about marriage, then maybe it was a sign that it was all right. But try as she might she could not get her mind and her feelings together. She had a hard time trying to imagine herself married to U Saw Han, and a harder time still picturing herself leaving home. Way Way sat silent. She looked down and saw U Saw Han's hand holding hers. In her mind's eye she could see her father and her aunt left behind in the old house, her father lying back in the old cane arm chair and her aunt sitting beside him, both looking forlorn and not talking to each other. She could see the sad expression that sometimes came over her father's face since his wife left, and it haunted her.

She tried to reassure herself that the two houses were actually very close to each other and that she would be able to visit her father frequently, but also nagging at the back of her mind was the fact that U Saw Han could be transferred from Moulmeingyun at any time and that she would then have to leave with him. She started trembling just imagining it, and could think no longer. Way Way tried with great difficulty to smile at U Saw Han and said, "Later . . . , we can think about it later."

"What do you mean 'later'? Way Way, don't you want to marry me? What do you mean?" he said with his face contorted and his voice strangely hoarse. His face showed signs of suppressed emotion.

Way Way felt drawn to his ardor, but not completely, as one who had not yet abandoned the props she had hitherto depended upon. She felt she could marry him immediately if it were not for her father, and wanted to tell him that but the words would not come out. She realized that such an argument would not hold, as it implied they would have to wait indefinitely, as long as her father was alive. And she sadly had to admit there was certainly no hope of her mother ever returning, either.

"Say something, girl, don't you want to marry me?"

"It's not that . . . ," she said.

He looked at her, wondering why she was so downcast and sad, when the reason slowly began to dawn on him. "Is it because of your father being left alone? Is it?" he said, quite upset. She nodded her head without answering. "Listen, Way Way. It will be even tougher if you take things so hard. It isn't that I don't have compassion for your father, but you have been saddled with the entire problem. Your mother did what she wanted, and your brother and sister both left to get married, and now you are left alone with the consequences. It is in the established order of things that one leaves one's parents in due course. What does your father say?" He turned her face to look into her eyes and immediately enveloped her in his arms. Her sad little face smiled up at him; she felt comforted.

"Hta Hta says that Father told her it was all right with him and that I could decide what I wanted to do. But if I marry you, what will become of my poor Daddy? What should I do?" The tears began to well up in her eyes as she struggled to smile. U Saw Han could hardly control his feelings as he saw her smile through her tears. Bending down so that their foreheads touched, he said passionately, "Way Way . . . , I could just sweep you up in my arms and carry you home right here and now."

Way Way closed her eyes, completely overwhelmed by his emotion. She felt as if she were tossed about on waves and made seasick, while his voice, close and urgent, found its way into her ears and heart. The tears came streaming down her face.

U Saw Han took a handkerchief from his pocket, wiped her face gently and said in a murmur, "When Lent is over, we'll get married. I am going to talk to your father."

Way Way reached out and took his hands and held them tight and looked at him full in the face as if about to say, Please, please, let's wait a while; not yet. But the words stuck in her throat each time she tried.

81

❖ 10 ❖

Half awake, Way Way squinted in the darkness. A cold draft from the window had awakened her. She reached for the velvet blanket at her feet. Her eyes opened wide in astonishment as she heard a faint but steady breathing beside her. Puzzled, she focused on the sound, clutching the blanket. Only when she felt the breath on her skin did she become completely conscious of where she was. She pulled the blanket over her head, clasped her hands over her chest, and shut her eyes tight.

Closing her eyes she sees a pretty dancer, slender and supple, dancing in the lamplight as pleasant sounds from musical instruments wafted through air. The dancer's gossamer green scarf loosens from her shoulders, falling gradually to the floor. As she twirls around, the scarf drags behind. A tall, thin, dark-complexioned man dressed in a green royal sarong, a short-sleeved tee shirt, and a pink gaung-baung appears on the scene. He picks up the scarf, winds it around her shoulders, and pulls her down with him in time to the music, which ends with a clash of cymbals as they both fall to the ground. She hears a great roar of laughter from the spectators. Before it subsides, she pushes away the blanket, and with heart pounding, opens her eyes. She turns her head on the pillow to look next to her. She sees U Saw Han facing her, sleeping on his side.

Her heart beat hard as she remembered. She was married to U Saw Han that day. It seemed like a dream. Thoroughly awake by now, she began to recall the wedding. It brought back to her mind the scene of U Saw Han participating in the dressing of the bride. She could see him rearranging the sprig of gold *mahur* flowers that Hta Hta had fastened to the side of her headdress. He had chosen the color and style of the bridal outfit and had gone along to Rangoon when the bride's trousseau had been purchased.

82

He had insisted that her outfit be according to English tastes. Instead of covering the bride with jewels, the customary Burmese way, he had her dress with restraint.

There he was, among the group of women dressing the bride, standing with folded hands watching Hta Hta fix the bride's hair, and giving his opinion about the *samei*, the tassel of hair that hangs down fetchingly to one side. He did not just look on quietly, but joined in to help. He watched Way Way as she was being made up as though he could not get enough of the sight of her, and he watched her reflection in the mirror as well. When the time came to get into her outfit, she threw him an imploring look but he said, "Put it on, Way Way. I won't watch. I'll turn my back," and he went to the window and looked out.

"Gosh, he's sure a persistent one," whispered Hta Hta into Way Way's ear. Smiling, Daw Thet mockingly thrust out her chin at him. The bridegroom did not change his clothes until the bride was almost ready. His outfit, the gaung-baung, the elaborate longyi, and silk jacket were laid out on the bed of the bridal chamber.

"Hey, young lady! Take a look at me," he said after putting them on. Way Way did not know how to take this in front of everybody. She blushed furiously and looked up at him timidly. "Hta Hta, isn't the diamond comb a little lopsided?" he asked, looking at Way Way's coiffure.

"Oh, no, it isn't," Hta Hta replied.

"Isn't it too heavy on your head, Way Way?" he asked. "Are you cramped from sitting too long? Aren't you going to eat anything?" One could hear him constantly saying something or other as he kneeled by her stool in front of the dressing table mirror.

She was ready. The ceremony began. They descended the stairs together. She did not want to hold the large bunch of flowers in the English style. The wedding bouquet was of expensive imitation English flowers tied with a white satin ribbon, specially ordered from Rangoon. She felt ill at ease carrying it in front of all the people, but she did it to please him. She had her eyes down and did not look at anyone in the assembled audience, but glanced up at her father. She saw him dressed in fine clothes, his face thoughtful and reflective. She was so moved at the sight of him that she missed a step.

She and U Saw Han sat together as bride and groom on ceremonial cushions, heads bowed in the traditional manner. Her controlled outward demeanor belied her inner thoughts, which were coming and going as they pleased. She seemed to have little control over them. Irrelevant thoughts darted about, quite unconnected with what was happening. As the welcome address was being read, Way Way looked across to the paddy fields, where she saw swarms of tiny crabs coming up from holes in the ground. Her neck ached as she sat with her head down. She felt dizzy and her head felt heavy with the hairdo and the ornaments in it.

Hta Hta sat behind, fanning her. Way Way's eyes fell on the pattern on U Saw Han's sarong. She noticed the interlinking of pink threads with blue and brown in the traditional *cheik* pattern. Having nothing else to look at, she stared at the design. As she sat she recalled, above the sounds of the speeches and the music, Ko Nay U's voice three months ago. They had just seen Hta Hta off at the wharf. "I don't want to come between you two, Way Way, but I must let you know how I feel," he had blurted out when they were alone. "I don't approve of the match at all. Do you really think you will be happy married to him?" This conversation could hardly bear recalling, and she quickly turned her mind to other things. She thought of the huge wedding cake that U Saw Han had ordered from Rangoon; it would have to be cut. Then she thought of Hta Hta's wedding and compared it with this one. It seemed to her that she did not mind her own wedding, half-English and half-Burmese as it was. She then thought of U Saw Han's agreeing to stay in the bride's house for seven days after the ceremony, as was the traditional Burmese custom. She did not want to think about her moving into the groom's house after that, so she forced herself to listen to the gift list, which was being read aloud.

Her mind had been in a flurry all day, and now as she lay awake in bed she still could not quiet her thoughts. The fact that she was really and truly married could not escape her. She thought with sadness and remorse of her lost virginity. She felt trapped under the the velvet blanket. She had married because of U Saw Han's importunity. In surrendering to U Saw Han's burning ardor, she had not considered her own feelings, nor had she let him be know how she felt. In the period after the betrothal had been settled upon, she had stayed close to her father and spent as much time with him as possible. U Po Thein had been more cheerful than ever and planned a big wedding for his little daughter. He sat daily with Daw Thet discussing details. It had taken a month to construct a wedding pavilion in front of the house to accommodate all the guests. It had been decorated with flowers and looked like a veritable bower. Her father had said that expenses were not to get in the way, and had gone on expanding his plans till Way Way had to step in and curb him.

She also kept a strict watch to see if he had shown any signs of brooding over her imminent departure, but she could find none. It seemed as if he had forgotten his illness and did not act like an invalid. He was hiding his real feelings and so was she. Neither of them had talked about the future and what would happen to the family business after her marriage. Her impending departure seemed to make her more and more attached to the old house and its pots and pans as she realized that she was not going to be living there anymore. In this mood she reflected to herself that, after all the pain and hurt of parting with her mother, she was now going to part with her father. She knew that the pain she felt at this moment would only get worse.

For them all to live under one roof was what she wanted most, but she knew that it was not possible because of U Saw Han. She realized that it would be an ordeal for him to put up with them even for the seven days. Way Way wiped away the welling tears with the palm of her hand and looked out of the window and saw only darkness. Her thoughts, over which she had no control, drifted away into the dark.

U Saw Han had been quite intoxicated as he watched the dance performance in the wedding pavilion that evening. When the star lady dancer of the performing troupe had wished the bridal pair "a hundred years of married life," U Saw Han had stood up unsteadily, taken a wad of banknotes from his pocket, and given it to the dancer. Way Way had known that he was too drunk to realize how much he gave, and she did not know how to hide her shame in front of all the people. She had always told herself that he held his liquor well and was not like others who lost control, but she had never seen him like this, all bleary-eyed and unsteady.

He had gone over to his house after the ceremony to entertain a group of Englishmen from his company who had come

85

up for the day from Rangoon. She did not know how much he had had to drink, but when he returned after his friends left he smelled of liquor, and it frightened her. She watched the dancing without enthusiasm, her eyes glistening with unshed tears. The smell of intoxicants made her dizzy, but she had to bear it. It seemed that she could not escape from it that night.

Way Way closed her eyes, which had been staring out into the dark all this time. She shut them tight and knit her eyebrows in an effort to blot out her thoughts. Then she quietly put the blanket aside and got out of the bed. She made her way down the stairs, feeling her way quietly in the dark. She switched on the light in the sitting room and looked at the time. It was four o'clock.

Later, upstairs, Daw Thet rose hurriedly from her bed. The dawn was lighting the sky with many hues of red. A new day had begun. She heard the sound of the monastery bell in the early morning. Last night she had stayed up past midnight watching the dance performance to the very end. She was late getting up. She had not cooked the food for the monks. She hurried down the stairs and stopped halfway. Goodness me! It isn't light yet and breakfast is ready! she exclaimed to herself. The round marble table was laid. A fine display of china and silverware gleamed under the light above it. Way Way had set a splendid table. She had tried her best to set a table just as good as they did at U Saw Han's. She was worried that in the seven days he was here, things would not be as nice as they were in his own house.

Daw Thet was taken aback, but she soon began to admire Way Way for her diligence and industry. She smiled as she continued down the stairs. Daw Thet came into the kitchen as Way Way was slicing the bread into very thin slices. Way Way spoke first. "Auntie, your rice for the monks is already cooked—there on the stove."

"My goodness, young lady, you needn't have cooked the monks' food as well as our breakfast!"

Way Way was embarrassed. She said shyly, "Oh it was nothing. Just the rice. And I only set the table."

"Tsk, tsk . . . , this early in the morning!" Daw Thet declared wonderingly in a mildly disapproving voice as Way Way set off to wash her face.

"Just getting things started early. I had qualms about leaving it to Meh Aye," Way Way replied as she left.

Outside, the sun was coming up and the world was awakening. The birds were singing little pleasant morning tunes, enjoying themselves in the early sunlight. The cool morning breeze revived the flowers. The air was redolent with the fragrance of flowers. To see these sights made one's heart overflow with a feeling of well-being. To hear the sounds brought peace and harmony to the senses. Way Way went to U Saw Han upstairs.

"Time to get up. Time to wash your face!" She pulled him up by his hands and took him to the table on which stood a white enamel water pitcher and basin. She poured some water for him and waited nearby.

Not getting on with his ablutions, he held Way Way by both shoulders and, speaking in the same wheedling tones one might use with a child, he hugged her and said, "Young lady, what time did you get up and leave me all to myself? It was odd getting up with you not there. From now on, we get up at the same time. Do you hear? Promise?"

She winced inwardly when she heard his words, but nodded in agreement, trying to be pleasant. She poured more water so that he would begin, and only then did he start.

Aware that U Saw Han was awakening, Hta Hta had come downstairs to prepare an English breakfast. Soon the aroma of coffee permeated the house. The thin slices of toast were ready, brown and crisp, and a very special bunch of Nathapyu bananas, wonderfully fragrant from ripening to perfection in an earthenware crock, sat on the table. The smell of crisp bacon filled the air. The Variety Biscuit tin, the jam, and the butter were on the table. Seeing that the salt and pepper were missing, Hta Hta opened the sideboard to look for them. As she did so, she heard a voice behind her.

"Miss, may I go upstairs?" Hta Hta recognized the voice of Maung Mya, the servant, and turned around. She saw him, dressed in a spotless jacket and pink gaung-baung, a clean starched napkin on his left shoulder, and a large tray held over his right shoulder. A teapot, creamer, sugar bowl, two cups and saucers, bread, butter, eggs, grapes, cake, and toffee and boiled sweets were on the tray.

Oh my God! she thought in stunned silence, her heart beating fast. To her it was the proverbial situation of the black elephant not daring to look at the magnificence of the white elephant. The grand dining table was not worthy of comparison with the tray on Maung Mya's shoulder; it seemed to withdraw into itself as though not wanting to confront the magnificent tray. Everything on the table seemed to fade and diminish, everything except for the delightful and pleasing bunch of bananas which were prominently displayed. Hta Hta's eyes flashed with fire. She had to try to control herself as she glowered at Maung Mya. She calmed herself and gradually let out a long breath and said, "Yes. You may go up."

Maung Mya, very circumspect, with a deportment befitting a butler in an English household, went soundlessly up the steps.

"Oh, it's all been prepared downstairs!" Way Way let out a loud startled voice. Very upset, her lips quivering, not looking directly at him, her eyes brimmed over.

At this, U Saw Han took her face in his hands, pulled her to him and blew on her face till her bangs were wafted about. He then laughed aloud and said, "I ordered it because I wanted to have breakfast alone with you, just the two of us." He sat Way Way on the edge of the bed, put the table in front of her, and drawing up a chair, sat down facing her. Maung Mya set the tray on the table, retreated a few paces, and stood.

Way Way sat all bunched up with her head bowed. U Saw Han had no inkling of the upheaval going on inside her. He was so delighted to be having a meal with her, all to himself, that he was dizzy with happiness. He went on talking non-stop; she did not utter a word.

"First, you are to have two eggs. You will have to have two eggs every morning from now on. Only when you have two eggs will I let you have coffee and toast . . . now remember that . . . do you hear?"

She gazed at him as he cracked the egg with a teaspoon while continuing to talk. Her thoughts were downstairs with Hta Hta and her father having breakfast without them. She could picture them in her mind and wanted to cry her heart out.

"There you are, young lady!" he said as he handed her an egg. He fixed her coffee for her, buttered her toast, and peeled grapes and put them into her mouth, one at a time. U Saw Han was solicitous and very busy, as though looking after a doll he had come to own, a doll which, in his mind, required his care. As to how the doll was feeling inside . . . .

When they were done eating, and before Maung Mya left, she heard him order lunch for twelve noon, so she came to understand that he was not eating at their house. He did not seem to have the least compunction about what he was doing. That he was a guest in their home yet was having his meals next door did not seem outrageous to him at all, neither did he seem to feel the need to inform the family of his plans.

Maung Mya left with the tray. Way Way went cold as she thought, Now they are seeing him downstairs. She was so tense and upset that she could hardly breathe or let out her sobs. She waited a long time, unable to go downstairs after U Saw Han had left for the office. She could not face her family. It upset and embarrassed her that she could not eat with the rest of her family, that she was kept separate from them. It felt as if someone had thrown sand in her eyes. She fell on the bed and sobbed with her face flat on the pillow. The whole pillow was wet with her weeping.

While Way Way lay sobbing, Hta Hta came into the room softly and tenderly patted her on her shoulder and said soothingly, "Don't cry, little sister, don't cry." Hearing that, Way Way cried even harder.

❖ 11 ❖

U Saw Han quietly studied Way Way's face as he poured himself a drink. He could see by the expression on her face and the way her chest rose and fell as she breathed that something was wrong. Her eyes were listless and dull. He took a gulp from his glass, put it down, and said, "Hta Hta leaves tomorrow, doesn't she?"

Way Way did not answer at once. Then she said in a flat voice, "Yes, she does." She stared in front of her with her lips compressed.

Hta Hta had not returned home immediately, remaining behind after the wedding to settle her father in his new routine. While tending to her father she also took care of Way Way and had been specially considerate and gentle with her. Way Way would have found it very difficult had Hta Hta not been there. During the seven day period, Hta Hta had helped to get her downstairs to do a few chores and make things normal for her. She even helped tie her hair at the back of her neck and other sisterly things that no one else could have done in quite the same way.

No one in the house had any idea what Way Way was going through or guessed that she was excruciatingly embarrassed about her husband's behavior. She did not want to remain in the house for the seven days. She had found it unbearable from the very first day or two; the family home had become just a place to sleep at night. According to U Saw Han's wishes, she had to go over to the other house for meals. She could have died every time they left to eat; she felt terrible and could not look her family members in the face. And then Ko Nay U would say something like, "Well, he's an Englishman. He's not used to our food."

Hta Hta knew that Way Way was constantly embarrassed about all this. She tried her best to tell her not to mind and that they understood U Saw Han's not wanting to eat their food. She told Way Way to just accept the situation; it did not really matter. Daw Thet, though she never mentioned it aloud, could not get over the fact that the two had not eaten a single meal in the house since the wedding. Whenever they left to eat, she smiled a small, hurt, derisive smile. U Po Thein never said a thing about this strange son-in-law who had not grown any closer to the family. U Po Thein was a quiet man by nature who kept his own counsel on everything.

Way Way had wanted U Saw Han to fit into the family circle during the days they spent under the family roof, but she found it very hard to persuade him to do so. He was so Westernized in his way of doing things that it was difficult for her to guess just how to approach him. For his part, U Saw Han was thoroughly captivated by Way Way. He valued her as he valued his very life. He wanted to cherish and adore her. He wanted to put her in the palm of his hand as he would a tiny weak creature and blow gently on it. He was so enchanted with her that he wanted to feast his eyes on her, and could not let her out of his sight. He wanted to savor her as he would a sweet-and-sour plum. His happiness overflowed and he lacked for nothing.

He knew that she was upset at her sister's impending departure. He also knew that she was anxious and afraid for her father. He regarded anxiety and worry and all the things that upset her as enemies of her existence. Now that she is in my care, I will protect her from them, he vowed. These worries and responsibilities have come along with her, but I plan to get rid of them. The little flower called Way Way will never droop or lose her color, she will always be fresh and fragrant. It has been pitiful to watch her carrying burdens too great for her years. I am the only one who can free her and make her happy.

"What else did Hta Hta say, Way Way?" he asked.

Way Way forced herself to sound cheerful and said, "She told me to check on Dad very often."

U Saw Han's face darkened. It was not that he did not want her to see her father, but he was afraid that she would catch his disease. Because he loved Way Way so much, he had stayed the seven days in the house despite of his misgivings about tuberculosis germs. He wanted Way Way to be examined by a doctor, but he knew that he should not force the issue right away.

91

"Go and see him about once a day, of course, but while you are there don't get too close to him. I don't want you exposed to the germs and catching something. I worry about you so much, Way Way."

When she heard this, Way Way wanted to burst out crying. She had thought that she would be able to come and go as she pleased when she came here to live, as the houses were next to each other; in fact she had counted on it before they had married. It had made leaving home bearable. But now she found it hard to breathe. She felt as though someone were squeezing the life out of her. It was true that he loved her very much and was extremely worried about her, but she did not want to visit her father just once a day, like a visitor, asking for news and keeping her distance from him. She could not bear to hear U Saw Han go on about it. Although she was here in this house, her thoughts were there, in the other one. With tears filling her eyes, she longed for the old house as she thought of her father somewhere in it. She thought that it would be time for him to drink his broth about now. Was he having it on his armchair downstairs, or was he upstairs? Oh Daddy, she cried to herself, I'm only supposed to come to see you once a day!

She was unwilling to accept this. Recently, she had gone through so many things unwillingly, beginning with her wedding. Now she was being forced to stay away from her father, seeing him only once a day. Now that she was married, she would be forced to do whatever another person expected of her. She would just have to steel herself and follow her husband's wishes.

Glass in hand, U Saw Han came towards Way Way, sat on the arm of her chair, and put his arm around her shoulders. He bent his head close to hers and said, "Don't look so sad. Smile, smile, smile," over and over. Way Way gave him a little smile, the smile that had captivated him from the very first time they met. U Saw Han was reassured on seeing that smile, which started with the dimple on her cheek before it reached her lips. He finished his drink quite happily. Relieved, U Saw Han said lightly, "Did you nap this afternoon? Did you? Huh? Huh?"

"I dozed off for a while. When I woke up, I came down because it was hot upstairs."

"Then?"

"Then I was bored, so I read a little. As I was reading I got hungry, so I ate an orange."

"How many did you eat?"

"One."

U Saw Han put his glass down on the carpet near him and caught the little finger that she had used to show "one." He looked at the little face turned up to him as she spoke. It was the delicate, pure face of a child. His expression softened, and moving even closer to her, he said, "Next time, eat lots and lots of oranges. Do you hear?" He went on, asking "Then what did you do?"

Way Way's life already followed a schedule devised by U Saw Han in the two weeks she had lived under his roof. In the morning they got out of bed together, washed their faces together, and combed their hair in front of the mirror, she sitting on the dressing table stool and he standing behind her. She was not allowed to leave the bedroom until the breakfast gong sounded. He chose what she should wear. He liked her wearing white in the mornings, and chose her blouse, her camisole, and longyi with a lot of white in the design. She had to wear slippers in the house. She descended the steps in them, U Saw Han clasping her about the waist.

She had to sit up straight at the table. After eating a whole plateful of porridge, she was given toast and eggs and coffee with lots of milk in it. When she first went to live there she had addressed Maung Mya as "Ko Mya," just as any well brought-up Burmese girl would call a male who was older than herself. U Saw Han came down on that like a ton of bricks, and absolutely forbade it. Maung Mya was a servant, not a friend or family member.[45]

After they were married and she first came to the house as its mistress, both the cook and watchman, dressed in their best clothes, had come and kneeled before her and salaamed her as the mistress of the house, just as servants might do in an English household. It was no use asking the cook what his name was; she

---

45. "Ko" here is both honorific ("older brother") and informal or family-oriented. A servant in a Burmese family would likely be addressed in this way and treated as a member of the extended household; in a British household such familiarity, never mind respect, would be considered intolerable if extended to a servant.

was obliged to call him "cook"—in English—just as U Saw Han and the English sahibs did. The watchman had to stay outside day and night, and did not enter the house unless invited. The cook, likewise, stayed within the confines of the kitchen, usually separate from the house, unless asked to do something inside.

When not serving meals, Maung Mya was always busy. His work in the house was arranged according to a schedule. His duties were to make beds, tidy rooms, straighten the living room, wait on table, clean the silver, wash the glassware . . . . Whenever one saw him, he would be busy, cleaning and polishing and making the house neat and tidy. He kept the house as well as or better than a woman.

After breakfast, Way Way had to go to the front room to fill U Saw Han's fountain pen with ink and fasten it to his shirt pocket, fill his cigarette case, which he then put in his pants pocket, and strap his watch onto his wrist after checking it for accuracy. Those were her morning chores before he left for the office. He returned for a meal at noon. When they sat at the table she had to put aside any desire to mix the food and eat with her fingers as she was used to. She had to use cutlery according to the acceptable standards of another culture. As a result, she never enjoyed anything she ate and always felt vaguely unsatisfied. Whenever she went next door, she would run to the kitchen and take leftover rice from the pot, fried onions, fried garlic in oil, fish sauce, and red chili peppers, mix them all up in an appetizing way with her fingers, and really enjoy eating. It greatly satisfied her inner hunger. All this was usually done in a furtive manner. Daw Thet would sigh and say, "Way Way, it worries me to see you this way."

Way Way had to dress up formally every day as though she were a guest in her own house. She ate her meals with elaborate pretensions, was waited on during the many courses, and wore closed-toe "lady shoes." As soon as U Saw Han left for work she ran upstairs, kicked off her shoes, and walked about the house barefooted, Burmese style, free and unhampered. She had to take a nap after her noon meal regardless of whether she felt like one or not. After the nap she had to get dressed for the evening. She lived a very routine, restricted life. When she went to bed at the same time every night, she would think, "Another day of duties and obligations over with."

94

U Saw Han always wanted to know what she had done and how she had fared while he was away at the office. He questioned her as he would a little child. She had to tell him every little thing when he came home.

"After eating . . . I knitted for a while and then went to see my sister."

"Wasn't the sun hot? Did Maung Mya take you over there with a parasol?"

She would have been mortified if Maung Mya had followed her like a royal umbrella-bearer. She would have been so embarrassed that she would have missed her footing and tripped. She would have been conscious of people seeing her and thinking she was putting on airs. She would have been soaked with perspiration trying to make herself as small as possible under the parasol.

"I went across on my own. I didn't ask Maung Mya."

Displeased, he shook his head and said, "Next time you are not to go out in the blazing sun if Maung Mya is not along."

The smell of whiskey was strong. She was getting used to it by now. Although there were all kinds of drinks in the house—whiskey, brandy, wine, and champagne, bottles and bottles of it—U Saw Han was not one of those who drank from sunup to sundown. He drank with control and only at certain times of the day. She did not have to worry about him on that score. When he returned from work, he took a drink and the glass never left his hand until it was time for dinner. Only then would he set it down.

The setting sun filled the sky with a twilight glow. U Saw Han sat in a chair opposite Way Way. The cool evening breeze blowing in from the window made him slightly light-headed. Way Way left her chair and went to the window and looked out at the sunset, taking consolation from the sight. The sky was a rosy pink and spread across with clouds. U Saw Han mixed himself another drink and looked steadily at Way Way standing framed in the colors of the evening. He was looking at the lovely Way Way, enjoying his drink, and feeling at the height of well-being, when the curtain parted and in walked Hta Hta. U Saw Han put his glass down and rose to greet her.

"Hta Hta, I hear you are going to leave tomorrow."

She handed Way Way a letter and sat down. "Yes, I'm afraid I have to leave."

U Saw Han picked up his glass and went to sit by Hta Hta on the sofa. He asked Way Way, "What's in that letter, Way?" He turned to Hta Hta and said "Is your father all right?"

Way Way was just opening the letter and Hta Hta answered for her, "Oh, it's a letter from Mother. Dad is fine. He tires easily but otherwise there are no symptoms."

"Well, he's getting on in years and can't do things as he used to. He'll just have to take things easy," said U Saw Han.
He kept looking at Way Way as he talked to Hta Hta. He thought he saw a shadow cross Way Way's face as she read the letter. He thought to himself, I wonder what the nun is bothering her about.

U Saw Han had never spoken to Way Way about her mother. He had no patience or respect for a woman who would leave her family and home to become a nun. He could not understand and had no sympathy for the whole business.

Way Way, engrossed in the letter, heard only bits of the conversation. Her mother's letter was different from the usual ones because it did not have the customary sermon but was full of advice about marriage.

Dear Daughter,

According to the wisdom of the elders of long ago, there are three things that cannot be undone. They are (1) getting married, (2) building a pagoda, and (3) getting tattooed.

Regarding the first, keeping one's husband's material resources and his future welfare uppermost in one's mind is vital to a marriage. Considerable reflection and discretion are needed to make a marriage successful. Now that you have attained the honorable state of matrimony, you need to develop the right qualifications and disposition according to the world of nature and humankind.

As to my past marriage, it was a matter of obeying my parents, who arranged it. I wanted to make them happy. For myself, I did not have any desire whatever to have a home and family. During my life with your father I was allowed to attend retreats every year during Lent, for he never failed to grant my wishes and desires. He is a truly good person, and has always been utterly considerate and kind to me. I first made an effort to break away from the world when my son Maung Nay U was born, but out of consideration for your father's goodness I gritted my teeth and stayed with the situation. I decided to wait until all my children were grown, and meditated continually as I waited for the day to come when I could leave.

Finally, I was able to leave all earth-bound cares due to the goodness and generosity of this husband. He not only allowed me to leave, but contributed to my upkeep, hence enabling me to practice the Law without hindrances. To him, I owe an immense debt of gratitude.

You can say that because of my good karma, I have had the good fortune to have had such a man for a husband. It is the subject of my fervent prayers that you also now have such a man as husband.

Way Way held the letter in her hand and stared straight ahead, deep in thought. She had always felt closer to her father than to her mother. She realized at this moment what a completely unselfish disposition he had, causing him to push his own needs into the background to allow for her mother's needs for growth according to her nature. She admired and loved her father more than ever, and wanted to emulate him in his unselfishness. Normally she would have run to her father and read him the letter; it would have made him so happy to hear what her mother had written.

"Young lady, what's the matter? Why so thoughtful?"

"Oh, nothing unusual, just the customary exhortations and such," she replied nonchalantly as she handed the letter to Hta Hta. "Don't forget to read it to Dad," she reminded her.

"Hta Hta, if these letters keep coming, I'm afraid our little lady will become a nun. You won't catch me sending rice and oil, I'm telling you right now," joked U Saw Han.

Hta Hta smiled and waited for U Saw Han's laughter to subside before she said, "Worried about her? There's no one who is more conscientious about her duties and frets about them the way she does. No way. She'd never leave them and go off to be a nun."

"If there's anyone who is likely to do it, it is Ma Ma Hta," said Way Way.

The light suddenly came on. Maung Mya entered with lemonade for Hta Hta. U Saw Han said, "Hta Hta, would you prefer champagne?"

She replied laughingly, "I don't drink stuff like that. I'm off to Sagaing." U Saw Han drained his glass, set it down, stood up, and took a handkerchief from his pocket and wiped his face. He then cleared his throat in an attention-getting manner and, turning to Hta Hta, said smilingly, "Now that you are here, Hta Hta, I wish to make a formal complaint about a certain young lady who is very naughty indeed. She makes a big fuss about taking her medicines. Also, she does not like eggs and milk and won't eat them much. She says that the eggs and milk have a fishy smell. She only wants to eat things that are sour and spicy hot. She also says that she does not like the taste of boiled drinking water; she says it does not quench her thirst and keeps on drinking unboiled water."

U Saw Han was quite satisfied with his speech. Way Way sat smiling, with her lips slightly parted and her eyes down, rubbing one palm with the other. Hta Hta looked at Way Way. As she tried to fathom her sister's mind and heart, she was not deceived by Way Way's outwardly calm appearance.

❖ 12 ❖

Way Way ran hurriedly over to her father's house when the servant girl had come and said, "Your father has fainted." U Saw Han had gone to Wakema in the early morning and was not expected back until late afternoon.

"Daddy," Way Way called softly as she bent over the side of his bed. Daw Thet was sitting by the bed attending to U Po Thein. Ko Nay U was dozing in the armchair with his hand on his forehead; he sat up and looked toward the bed when he heard Way Way come into the room.

Her father did not answer her so she called again softly, "Daddy." U Po Thein mopped the perspiration from his brow before opening his eyes. Apart from a trace of fatigue on his face, he looked quite good. "How are you now, Daddy?" Forgetting her husband's instructions not to get too close, she took a fan from the top of the pillow, drew nearer to her father, and fanned him gently.

"I had a bit of a coughing spell earlier, but it's stopped and I'm much more comfortable now."

Way Way put on a cheerful face, though in fact she was still upset. "He was fine this morning. He was even going downstairs, but I suggested it wasn't such a good idea," Daw Thet informed her. "It was after he had the rice porridge and milk that he started coughing and choked . . . . My, what a turn it gave us all! Luckily, Ko Nay U was here and ran for the doctor. The doctor gave him a shot."

Way Way turned to Ko Nay U and asked, "When did you get back?" Under orders from his political headquarters, Ko Nay U was often away, out in the countryside organizing and speaking.

99

"I got back late last night, so I slept at the mill and came over early this morning. I even saw U Saw Han's little motorboat. He waved at me," Ko Nay U answered.

Daw Thet turned to speak to Ko Nay U. "We read in the newspapers that the big Yenangyaung strike has begun and that the strikers have started marching towards Rangoon. Where are they now?"

"They've reached Magwe, and the leaders have already been arrested," Ko Nay U replied.

Way Way thought that discussing political news would be confusing for a sick person, and changed the subject. Turning to her father she said, "Daddy, did you get any sleep last night?"

"Yes, dear, I did get to sleep. I've lost my appetite somewhat, though. Have you replied to Hta Hta's letter?" The patient's face looked good, but his voice was not his normal one. He had been ill for some time. The wedding had taken its toll and he was mentally and physically exhausted. He tried to improve his health through mind control and sheer will power. Sometimes he would get better and the illness would abate, but then, in the middle of a good spell, he would fall ill again. After this had happened many times he gave up on getting better. The idea that the end was not too far off became fixed in his thinking.

Ko Nay U said, "I like Hta Hta's idea for you, Dad. Since I am taking over the business now, it would be a good idea for you to go to Hta Hta's, where her husband the doctor could keep an eye on you."

Hta Hta had written that her husband had been transferred to Rangoon, and suggested that her father come live with them and get the best medical treatment. Ever since his illness started, Ko Nay U had wanted to take his father to Rangoon for treatment. For Hta Hta and the doctor to keep him at their home and take him to see specialists, was in his view an excellent idea.

"Should I go, daughter?"

When Ko Nay U heard these words he looked at Way Way and told her silently with his eyes to persuade him to go. Way Way felt that this move would mean further separation from her beloved father. Her heart sank, but she did not show her feelings. She was sad that he would perhaps be a long time in Rangoon.

"Daddy, it would be a good idea, if you want to. Ma Ma Hta is worried for you here. You will have the very best doctors over there. Shall I tell her you are coming when I write?"

Daw Thet chimed in, "Yes, indeed, I think that would be the best thing for him, myself."

"Well if that's the general feeling, go ahead and write to her and say that I'm coming with Maung Nay U and Daw Thet. Maung Nay U can move into this house and Way Way can keep the girl, Meh Aye, for running errands and helping out . . . ."

U Po Thein then turned drowsily to his side. One by one they tiptoed out of the room, leaving only Way Way sitting near him. He had his back to her and she cried silently, wiping away the tears from her eyes as she fanned him. Those words of his, asking her permission, "Shall I go, daughter?" just broke her heart. He was aware of Way Way's feelings without her having to say a word. He knew that she wanted with all her heart to come over to the house and be at his side to nurse him constantly, but was restrained by her husband. He knew that she fretted and pined for him in secret, and longed with all her heart to be near him. The wonder of it was that he sensed and understood it all, and asked her permission. It was exquisite.

All was quiet in the room. She looked around the bedroom lovingly. As she did so, nostalgia for her childhood welled up in her. He had left it exactly as it had been when her mother was there. The double bed, although ancient, was durable. The balustrade at the foot of the bed was firm and strong. The carved headboard was high and had a hint of cobwebs in the crevices. The round bedside table bed held religious books on one half of it and the on other half were medicine bottles, glasses, a box of toothpicks, eyeglasses, and a pair of tweezers. The dark wooden wardrobe with the full length mirror on the door was still in the same place against the wall. This was where her mother had kept her clothes. The bookcase with glass doors, still full of her mother's religious books, stood beside the reclining chair.

Way Way looked at the windows, which let in lots of light but in hot weather also benefitted from the shade of the large *padauk* tree outside. Her attention was drawn to the framed picture on the wall hanging above the clothes pegs. It was a group picture of the whole family, taken at Ko Nay U's shinpyu ceremony. Her mother's hair was decorated with jasmine buds.

Near her mother was Hta Hta, her hair worn in the adolescent *sadauk* style, and Way Way, leaning against her father, her hair in a topknot and bangs in a little-girl style.

A pang struck Way Way's heart as she looked at her father's prone figure on the bed in the room where everything had been kept exactly as it had been when her mother lived in it. Meh Aye came in quietly and whispered in her ear, "Daw Thet says to tell you to come downstairs and eat a meal with Ko Nay U, who is waiting for you. She says that I should stay here."

Looking over at her father's face and giving the fan to Meh Aye, Way Way wiped her eyes with her handkerchief and left the room quietly. She glanced at her old room as she passed. Her bed and dressing table were bare. Her empty bed, indeed the whole room, looked at her as if they regarded her as a stranger.

"Come on and eat," Ko Nay U said. "Since it's ready and you're here, have some. The Englishman won't be back for a while yet," he said grinning and handing her a plate of rice. As best she could remember, this was the first time she had eaten a real meal in her father's home since her marriage four or five months ago. In her own house she always had English food, which did not satisfy her. Whenever she could, she would come into the family kitchen, grab a plate, mix whatever food there was with her fingers, and eat it enthusiastically. She preferred to eat in the kitchen.

Today she had eaten a large breakfast and was not hungry, but it would have hurt her brother's feelings if she had not eaten with him, so she joined him.

Her brother said, "When I saw that we had some of your favorite *ponyegyi*,[46] I told Meh Aye to bring you down here. I'm sure you don't get this at your house, so grab your chance and have some," said Ko Nay U as he spooned the sauce onto her plate and began to eat heartily.

No one talked to Way Way about her married life. There were many things they did not understand about it. Mentioning it would only have made her unhappy, so they left her alone to live her own life.

---

46. A special kind of spicy bean sauce from the Shan hills.

Although she was not hungry, when she smelled the generous portion of ponyegyi, she knew she would be able to eat. She mixed the ponyegyi with all the rice in her plate, added nganpyaye,[47] sprinkled crushed hot chili peppers over everything, and mixed it with her fingers. Daw Thet passed her some raw garlic cloves and powdered dry shrimp, and said, "Here, mix these in too."

"Aren't you eating yet, Aunt?" asked Way Way.

"I'll eat later. You two go ahead. I'm going to bathe first," she replied, and went to the back of the house to the kitchen.

Way Way did not dare eat the garlic. If her breath smelled of it that would be enough to cause a court case, she thought, so she just helped herself to the powdered dry prawns.

"I think it would be best for Dad's sake if he lived with Hta Hta, as there will be doctors available and it would be easier on him," said Ko Nay U.

"And what about you, when will you move in here?" asked Way Way.

"Oh, we'll have to get organized quickly."

The ponyegyi tasted particularly wonderful today. It was all nice and sour and hot and tasty. The accompanying soup of transparent noodles with black pepper was delicious sipped along with each mouthful of rice, and helped the food slip down easily.

"What do the strikers do for food out on the road?" asked Way Way.

Ko Nay U could not eat the next mouthful. The one thing he enjoyed more than food had cropped up. "Oh, there are lots of people to feed them; they march fifteen miles a day. There are kitchen units, medical units, and all kinds of units. They will have provisions and all manner of help."

"The Company[48] won't give in a bit to their demands, will they?" asked Way Way.

"Well, what can you expect from capitalists? Not only have they not budged for eleven months, but they kicked the workers out of their row houses. We'll have to demolish these 'white-

---

47. Another sort of pungent fish sauce.
48. That is, the British-owned Burmah Oil Company, or BOC.

faced' companies. Only when they go will we have enough room to breathe."

"Ba Maw's government will have to go.[49] Not only are there the oil strikers from Yenangyaung, but a whole army of farmers from Pyu and Thanutpin. Two thousand strong, marching toward Rangoon. They've arrested all the leaders, but a search is already on for new leaders to take their place. All our committees from the countryside have been asked to submit names of leaders."

"Oh, please don't go and be a leader," said Way Way, frightened.

Ko Nay U laughed. "When I heard about the 'white faces' using horses to charge into the crowds and beating people with *lathis*,[50] I was so angry and my nationalist pride was so wounded that I could have taken on the English myself! Only my concern for Dad kept me from rushing off to Magwe. I wrote to Thakin Thein Maung asking if I could help in any way. I also sent them some money. My father-in-law got quite upset with me."

Way Way studied him out of the corner of her eyes.

"Have some rice," he said to Way Way, "and I'll polish off the rest."

Way Way took two spoonfuls of rice from the dish, put ponyegyi generously over it, and started mixing it with her fingers. The rich brown sauce was smeared all over her white fingers, all sticky and gooey and delicious. Ko Nay U, eating with his head down, was thinking about his sister and noticing her evident enjoyment. He suspected that she ate all her meals with a spoon and fork, and took little helpings that she never really enjoyed, just to make a pretense of eating. They both were bent over their food and happened to simultaneously raise their heads, when both their eyes widened at the same moment. For U Saw Han suddenly appeared in the doorway.

Way Way's face fell as a cold chill went through her, her fingers suspended in midair. Ko Nay U turned his head and said,

---

49. Dr. Ba Maw (1892-1962?), a lawyer and separationist activist, was education minister during the 1936 university strike and in 1937 formed a coalition of parties and individuals which became Burma's first government after separation from India. This goverment continued, somewhat reorganized, under Japanese rule.
50. Police batons.

"Come on in, come and join us in the meal. We didn't know you were back. Didn't even hear your motorboat."

U Saw Han came towards the table, obviously upset. Ko Nay U saw Way Way's ashen face and felt his chest constrict. Caught off balance, Way Way looked like a crow captured by boys. She said sheepishly, "Father took ill, so I came over. How did you come across the river, dear? We didn't hear your motor-boat." She was trying hard to keep her voice from cracking.

U Saw Han's eyes swept around the table, taking in all the details of Way Way's plate and food-stained hands, and said to Ko Nay U, "The engine broke down and I had to come back in the Indian's boat." As he spoke to Ko Nay U, his eyes went over to Way Way's face and plate several times and then he said to Way Way, "Maung Mya told me you were here, so I came over."

"Way Way is extremely fond of ponyegyi so we begged her to stay. We really had quite a time getting her to eat," said Ko Nay U, trying to make things easier.

U Saw Han pulled himself together and with a controlled smile said to Ko Nay U, "How is your father now?" Feeling wounded by Way Way, he did not look in her direction.

"Dad was very tired, but he's better now and is dozing," Ko Nay U replied.

U Saw Han looked with some disdain at the dishes and the bare table and said, "Please continue eating. I'll be getting back to the office."

In contrast to the soft tread when he entered, his foot steps now sounded angry and overbearing as he left. Only when she saw his back did Way Way remember to adjust her facial expression in front of her brother. She forced herself to smile and said lightly, "He absolutely hates it when I eat hot peppery food." The abrupt change in mood from one of a brother and sister's light-hearted enjoyment of each other's company at the family table, to one of sudden uneasiness and gloom was almost ominous. It could hardly bear thinking about. Thoughts went spinning through Way Way's head, confusing her. She had lost the desire to eat, but absent-mindedly mixed what remained and forced herself to swallow, continuing to pretend that it did not matter. The food was tasteless. Her brother wanted to tell her that she did not have to eat it if she did not want to, but hesitated and pretended he had not noticed she was upset. Nor did he joke about the situation, as that would reveal he had noticed her sudden loss of appetite and understood how upset she was.

"The soup is nice and peppery," he said as he took a little more rice to appear natural. He then stood up as though he were finished, so that Way Way would not have to pretend anymore, and she finished too. Way Way washed her hands but could not look at Ko Nay U straight in the face; she went to the back of the house towards the kitchen and bathroom and called out to Daw Thet, in a voice loud enough for Ko Nay U to hear, "I'll be going along now."

Her aunt answered from her bath, "Don't go yet. Maung Saw Han hasn't even returned."

Way Way didn't reply but went back to the table. Aware of her feelings, Ko Nay U had wanted to give her the freedom to leave if she wanted, and had gone upstairs to see to his father to make it easier for her. Way Way glanced up once towards the stairs and then hurried out.

Outside, the sun was burning and bright. She returned to the house next door in all this bright light, which was not as hot on her as she feared the disgruntled U Saw Han would be when she met him.

She found U Saw Han, who had said he was going back to the office, sitting back on the sofa with his glass of beer nearby, smoking dejectedly. When he saw Way Way come in, he changed his expression somewhat and looked straight at her, still dejected. His eyes were blurred. Way Way could not avoid facing him, so she walked up slowly and said, "Dear, don't be angry . . . ."

U Saw Han frowned, picked up his glass, and drank from it without looking at her. Only after he finished did he put down his glass, leaned back, and smiled. "Do you know that I'll never be able to tell you just how much I love you, and that you don't love me as much as I love you? Isn't that true?"

With downcast eyes, Way Way stood in front of him like a naughty school girl who had done something wrong.

"You are so fragile that I worry that even a gentle breeze might hurt your tender skin when it blows on it. I always want the very best for you, the finest and the most beautiful. I spend a lot of time thinking about the best for you, but as soon as my back is turned, it seems you go out and play in the mud and get yourself dirty."

Her face fell, her voice seemed to swell, and tears streamed down her face, not because U Saw Han was finding fault with her for doing something he didn't like, but because she was curiously upset about her own predicament. She was one person in one house and a different person the other, and she could not separate the two.

She could not stand up any longer, so she went to sit at the desk. Her handkerchief was wet from crying. U Saw Han finished his beer and came to Way Way. She sat quietly, the tears welling up in her eyes. He sat on the desk and, though at heart still uneasy and almost afraid to touch her, tenderly caressed the wisps of hair on her forehead and said, by way of apology, "This happened because I love you so, my darling Way."

❖ 13 ❖

The wind was strong and gusty; the hot sun shone down, burning the skin. Trees flashed past on the riverbanks and the prow of the little motorboat stuck up out of the water, making one wonder whether the boat even touched the surface of the river. The noise made one's ears ring.

U Saw Han placed his pith helmet on Way Way's head. To keep it from flying off, she had to hold on to the strap. U Saw Han had his arm around Way Way, and every so often he would smooth down the wisps of hair that flew loose on her forehead. They were forced to gaze silently at the scenery, for it was impossible to speak above the noise of the engine. The sunlight looked green through their sunglasses and even the sky took on a greenish cast.

Groves of trees, open fields, and rows of small thatched huts came into view as the engines droned on. Every now and then they passed people standing and gaping at them. The water at the side of the boat formed whirling spirals and sprayed out in an arc. Way Way was enchanted by the sight of the sunlight glittering on the spray through her blue-green sunglasses. U Saw Han worried that Way Way's little finger would tire from hanging onto her pith helmet's strap, so he held it for her with the same hand he placed around her shoulders.

Now that her father was in Rangoon, Way Way did not know what to do with herself. She felt a great emptiness inside her and accompanied U Saw Han on his trips out of town. At the beginning she was in quite a state and cried every time she looked at her father's house. Since he[51] had stipulated that she visit her

------

51. Here Wei Wei uses the familiar honorific "Ko," literally meaning "elder brother." (See footnote 45, page 93.) This is the form

father only once a day, she had gone over to be near him the moment U Saw Han left for the office, and remained all day until just before he returned. Before her father left for Rangoon, he would wait for Way Way every day in his chair. At times he would gaze at his daughter, his eyes full of unspoken words. They could not bear to look at each other directly and avoided eye contact. He gave her her mother's jewelry, which she received with feigned cheerfulness.

It seemed impossible that four or five months had passed since her father had left, and all that remained for her now was to wait for letters about him from Hta Hta. It was said that he appeared fuller in the face and looked good, but that he tired easily and had to stay in bed on doctor's orders. She longed to go to see him.

Since her father had gone, she had been over to the house about once a month or so. Her brother, who was now living there, was so busy going to Rangoon and travelling all over the countryside for his political work that he was hardly ever home. She was the one who went to see him, as he never came to her house. If he had any urgent news, he sent his wife, Than Than.

U Saw Han took a piece of chocolate from a tin on his lap, unwrapped it, and put it in Way Way's mouth. Way Way got heartburn from eating chocolate, so he also gave her ice water from a thermos they had brought on board. U Saw Han's complexion was much darker than when he had first came to Moulmeingyun, for he often made trips in his motorboat and his skin was sunburned.

It was only because Way Way implored him to take her with him that he had consented. Concerned as he was about her health, he would worry that she was getting too much sun or too much wind. Not long ago he had become very alarmed when she coughed one night, and had turned absolutely ashen when he discovered that she was running a low temperature. She made light of it and said it was nothing, that she coughed because her throat tickled. To make certain, he had called the doctor right then and there, even though it was late at night. The doctor had come and examined her, and laughing a little said it was just a

---

commonly used by married women to address their husbands; it would be impolite to refer to him directly by his given name, and "Ko" in this case has the emotional equivalent of the English "dear."

109

common cold; the cough was quite ordinary and nothing to worry about. However, seeing how tense U Saw Han was, the doctor had said, "But do be careful."

After observing how upset U Saw Han became, Way Way had to suppress any desire to cough in his presence, no matter how much she wanted to. Seeing his obsessive fear, she began to worry about getting sick. He felt a lot better when her father left, believing that her health was not so jeopardized by proximity to him. He watched over her closely and hovered about her as though she were made of emeralds and gold; it made her feel claustrophobic. She was in a state of perpetual uneasiness about her father, but dared not let it show. Suppressing it made it build up inside her like a ball of fire, continuously burning. She could not allow the slightest gloom or depression to show on her face, so she always appeared cheerful. On days when she did not accompany her husband on trips, when he just went to the office, she would wait till he was out of the door and then sit down at her desk to write her father and Hta Hta. She wrote ten to fifteen pages, covering both sides of the paper with her tiny handwriting. Hta Hta would reply, "I am so busy looking after Daddy, my husband, and the children, I just don't have time to reply properly to your long letters. Sometimes I cannot even read them at one sitting." Way Way would wait patiently for the mail to come from Rangoon, and if she thought a reply was late she became uneasy and sat down to write yet another letter.

Seeing Moulmeingyun in the distance, she took the hat off her head and put it on his. The blue satin scarf she wore around her neck flapped in the breeze, "Hpyut, hpyut." The boat's engine slowed, causing the bow to drop to the water's level. The boat slowly banked to one side and moored. There were watchmen on the wharf all lined up and salaaming them. U Saw Han pulled Way Way up by her hands and led the way, the guards following.

"FIRE, FIRE, BURN! BURN!

Destroy, destroy Imperialist Government.

Reject, reject Constricting Laws!

Our noble cause, MAY IT PROSPER!

MAY IT PROSPER!"

A huge crowd stood on the road chanting in unison with arms and fists outstretched. U Saw Han walked a little distance behind the crowd, quite conspicuously apart.

"I wonder what they are demonstrating against now," said Way Way.

"It's nothing," he replied.

The large crowd was in fact demonstrating in sympathy with the oil strikers of Yenangyaung, the students, and all the various and sundry nationalist strikers that had gone into action all over the country against the colonial British government.

U Saw Han and Way Way saw Ko Nay U in the middle of the crowd, pushing his bicycle with one hand and the other hand extended in a fist, shouting and chanting. "Oh, dear! Ko Nay U is just asking for trouble. It's now just a matter of what day they will come to lock him up," groaned Way Way. U Saw Han had soured on Ko Nay U when he had become "Thakin Nay U," and now pretended not to hear.

They reached home worn out and threw themselves down in the sitting room to relax. Meh Aye took the head scarf and dark glasses from Way Way and went upstairs to put them away. There was the sound of a pop from a soda bottle being opened, and Maung Mya appeared with a tray of alcoholic beverages. He said to Way Way, "Than Than came looking for you. She said there was a telegram."

Way Way's hand holding her orange juice shook as she said, startled, "What telegram?" Maung Mya seeing her shaken, fear written all over her face, averted his eyes while she said to U Saw Han, "He says that a telegram arrived." She turned to Maung Mya and said in a panic-stricken voice, "Go, go tell her we are back."

"When did she come?" asked U Saw Han. Maung Mya stopped in his tracks on his way out and said, "Just a little while ago." He waited until U Saw Han said, with a darkened face, "Well, go on, go on."

Way Way stood up from the sofa and went to the window. Upset at seeing her so uncharacteristically out of control, U Saw Han said in a soothing voice, "Way Way, dear, she'll be here soon. Don't fret so," but he thought darkly to himself, Now they're going to trouble her more.

Way Way saw Than Than, Maung Mya behind her, coming toward the house. She went to the door and lifted the curtain as she looked out at the road. Seeing her as perturbed as before, U Saw Han said, "Way Way, dear, they'll be here, come and sit down and finish your drink." Way Way looked at the approaching Than

111

Than, her heart pounding. She was frightened of the telegram in her hand. She tried to anticipate the news by studying Than Than's face.

When U Saw Han heard Than Than's footsteps, he stood up and came forward to greet her. Way Way said, "What's in the telegram, Ma Ma Than? Oh, I'm so frightened," and grabbed the telegram from her.

"Please come in and sit down, Than Than," said U Saw Han.

Than Than came in slowly and sat on the sofa. U Saw Han went over to Way Way and started reading the telegram over her shoulder. The message was, "DAD DANGEROUSLY ILL." Way Way, tears streaming down her contorted face, came and sat down beside Than Than. "I didn't know you were out, and since Ko Nay U wasn't home, I came over," said Than Than. Seeing the look on Way Way's face, she fell silent and said nothing more. Way Way said to U Saw Han, "Dear, I'll go along with my brother tonight, won't I?"

U Saw Han's face darkened. He could not answer. He knew that he had a duty to send her, but he wondered if it would not be better for her health if he ignored duty. He knew that forbidding her to go would look very bad, but his extreme concern for her health and his fear of contamination was even stronger. He found himself unable to answer.

As he hesitated, Way Way was on the verge of tears. It would be difficult for her to believe that he really loved her if he refused her at this point; on the other hand, it was precisely because he loved her so much that he wanted to refuse.

She could not wait for him to answer so she said again, "I'm going along with my brother on tonight's boat, aren't I?" She managed to control her voice and speak in a normal tone, although her fingers were trembling and she was now crying.

"We'll see, dear," said U Saw Han soothingly, mostly because Than Than was there, but his eyes had the look of a plan in them. "Is Ko Nay U going tonight, Than Than?" he asked. Than Than was in the habit of smiling when she spoke, and her teeth gleamed as she said, "I'm sure he will. He has gone to the Thakin Party office. I don't know whether or not he was in the demonstration, but I've sent word of the telegram on to him."

112

"We saw him earlier on the road among the demonstrators. What about you, Than Than, weren't you there?" U Saw Han joked.

Than Than did not realize it was a joke and said, "I had things to do and wasn't free."

Way Way sat still, brooding, her eyes glazed over. U Saw Han had not answered her question in any real way. She sat quietly like a child being punished. Than Than knew that things were not going well for her sister-in-law and wanted to put in a word about letting her go along with Ko Nay U to Rangoon, but U Saw Han was such an aloof person that any attempt at it was awkward. She had to pretend that she did not know there was any tension between them. It made things more awkward to keep silent, but she could not think of anything to say. Instead she talked about Way Way's father. "He was looking quite well, and even filled out a bit. Of course he had those spells of tiredness, which were alarming. They would not have sent a telegram if it were not something serious. He is the last one to give any trouble to anybody, so the telegram really worries me."

U Saw Han looked at Way Way and thought, There she sits, sulking like a little child. Never mind, I'll coax her out of it later, he decided to himself, and kept an appropriate conversation going with Than Than.

U Saw Han replied, "Then again, he is elderly and gets tired easily and has low resistance. This disease is very exhausting for the patient. Once the germs have gotten into the system, they are very hard to control. Just the other day Way Way started coughing, and my goodness, what a fit it threw me into, what with me constantly worrying about her health."

The conversation then died down for want of anything else to say, but realizing that Way Way was silent and that it wouldn't do to remain silent as well, they both cast around for more conversational topics.

Than Than said, "Ko Nay U has been wanting to go to Rangoon all this time, but he couldn't leave his work. I'm sure he will go tonight."

Silence again. U Saw Han had a cigarette in his mouth, and lighted it. Turning to Way Way, who was sitting by her side, Than Than said encouragingly, "Don't worry, Way, he's sure to get better."

Way Way did not want to talk and just sat with her head bowed, silent. Than Than was uncomfortable with Way Way's silence and was unable to make any more conversation, so she prepared to leave. "I don't know whether Ko Nay U has come back. I'd better go home," she said, standing up. Bending down to Way Way she said, "If you are able to go with Ko Nay U tonight, send Meh Aye over to tell us, won't you?" and went out.

U Saw Han stood up (in the English fashion, as was his wont) and nodded at Than Than as she got up and left. Then he sat down again. Way Way stood up suddenly and moved away. "Where to, Way Way?" he asked as he strode over to her. He held her hands in his and turned her around to face him. Looking intently at her he asked, greatly troubled, "Way Way, are you angry?"

He need not have asked, for her face did not show the slightest trace of anger. She looked as lifeless as if her heart had stopped beating. Her eyes were glazed over, unblinking, without the slightest movement. "Sit down, Way Way," he said as he guided her to a chair. He sat down near her and started stroking her forehead. He said gently, "Oh Way, I don't want you to go. I don't want to send you. To tell you the truth, I don't want you to go near someone who has this disease. I don't want you exposed to the germs in the most critical stage. You'll be tired from just going there. Your eating and sleeping patterns will be disrupted and irregular, and your mind upset and stressed. I just know you will get ill from all this. I don't want anything to happen to you, my dearest Way." In this way, he bared his feelings to her. He was worried that his little Way Way would be hurt, as if she were a delicate piece of porcelain. He told her what was in his heart because he wanted her to know exactly how he felt. Way Way already knew too well, and sat as motionless as a statue.

"It's because I love you, Way Way. Please do not make any other interpretations of it. I care so much."

Way Way faced him suddenly, "So I can't go, can I?" Her voice had no trace of anger and was very faint. It sounded heartsore and weary, as if her strength were ebbing away.

U Saw Han was perspiring. He scratched his head in distress. He did not want it to get to the point of having to force her to stay. He did not have the heart to deliver a "Don't go," nor did he wish to say "I forbid it." He was at a loss as to how to handle her. He no longer stroked her forehead, but sat with his face in his hands, breathing deeply in his distress.

Way Way saw U Saw Han's pain and it went straight to her heart, adding to her suffering. Her face drained of color as she gazed into space, confused and spent, even losing consciousness in flashes.

It was her fate to have happened on a love that demanded submissiveness and renunciation of herself, a love that did not even understand her sacrifices. She thought, If he takes it so hard and is so troubled, I'll just stop myself from wanting to go. Even if I cause more suffering for myself, so be it. Way Way made up her mind. She would simply stifle her feelings and bear it. She got up and walked to the stairs like a sleep walker, unconscious of what she was doing. She threw herself on the bed. She curled up, shut her heavy-lidded eyes, and breathed very faintly. She did not notice when the sun set and when the room grew dark. She could faintly hear the whistle of the boat as it left. Her whole body was stiff and cold. Her neck and shoulders were wet with perspiration.

U Saw Han came into the room, switching on the light. He ran up to her, taking her in his arms. "Way, oh Way," he called, but she could not answer for she could not hear. It was as if her senses had abandoned her. It seemed as if she were drowning without anyone to cling to for support, and that every time she came up for air she was indescribably tired. Then she felt herself sinking into the water again and forced to hold her breath. She had to use all her strength to pull herself out of the water and to the surface. She was suffocating.

Only when U Saw Han, his arms around her, brought her to a sitting position, did her breath come back in big gasps. Her chest rose and fell as she breathed; her lips appeared colorless, and her clothes were wet with perspiration and sticking to her skin.

"What happened, Way Way. How are you? How do you feel?" U Saw Han asked in a soft and tender voice. She became aware that she was in his arms. She was unable to speak, but answered him by nodding her head gently. U Saw Han took a deep breath and then was able to breathe properly. He called out to Meh Aye, who had been listening all the time behind the curtain, her heart beating wildly. But she had slipped away quickly

115

to the back so as not to be seen when Way Way went upstairs. She went to the back yard and looked across the fence toward Than Than. When she caught Than Than's attention, she shook her head negatively. Than Than understood her, nodded, and went back in. Meh Aye then went in and busied herself with her chores, not daring to go up to Way Way until she heard the blast of the steamwhistle from the boat to Rangoon.

When U Saw Han called out for her, she raced upstairs in a flutter, full of apprehension. They changed Way Way's clothing, and doused her forehead and hairline with eau de cologne. She was still propped up and not yet lying on the bed. They fanned her furiously. Then they heard her say faintly, "I got a bit dizzy. I'm better now." Only when they heard her speak did they lay her down to sleep. Way Way dozed off.

That night U Saw Han could not sleep properly. He was apprehensive and filled with foreboding. Every time he heard the sound of a gasp or a sob, he felt around her eyes for signs of tears. He did not feel any, but each time he touched her around the eyes it felt unpleasant to Way Way and was just one more thing for her to cope with.

When morning came, Way Way was better and could move around as usual. There was no change from her normal appearance except that she did not speak much and had a serious look on her face. Since she was not one to bear grudges or speak bitter words, she dressed in the kind of morning outfits he liked to see her in, and went down to breakfast with him. U Saw Han was encouraged by her normal manner, eating and talking as she usually did at the table. He was even happy. He was pleased that she seemed to humor his wishes. He did not hear her usual chitchat, but as she ate and drank he could see no evidence of downcast feelings, and he loved her more than ever. He had been on pins and needles about how to resume the subject of yesterday. Way Way was also apprehensive about his renewing it. Both their prayers were answered as U Saw Han was able to leave without having to mention it, and he was able to kiss her on the forehead with a lighter heart before he set off to work.

As soon as U Saw Han was out of sight, however, the smile disappeared from Way Way's face. She reverted to her broken-hearted state. As the tears flowed down her cheeks, her whole body posture changed. Her body slumped in dejection as, with

116

her head bent, she trod slowly and heavily up the stairs. She went to the shrine room in front, drawing aside the curtain as she entered. She knelt in front of the altar and crouched low, touching her forehead on the floor to pray for her father's recovery. Trembling and shaking, she began to weep. She cried and cried until she was worn out and could cry no more. She raised herself to a sitting position on the floor, her legs tucked under her to one side. With her hands clasped in front, and her eyes closed, she prayed ceaselessly.

She wanted to ask Meh Aye if her brother had left last night, but she could not trust herself not to cry before she was through asking. She was barely able to keep herself under control. Meh Aye, on the other hand, wanted to tell her just that, but since she was not asked she did not offer the news. She hovered around Way Way. Finally, unable to contain herself any longer, she said, "Last night I was sent to tell Ko Nay U that you were not well and could not go along."

Way Way, with her face turned away from her said, "Yes, yes." She turned sadly toward the big house but could scarcely bear to look at it. It seemed as if the house did not want to be seen. Its upstairs windows were closed, as if it were turning its face away. She stood looking at the house, sobbing until she was tired. She looked up at the blue sky and the masses of white billowy clouds. If she took an airplane and flew straight through those clouds, she could get to Rangoon. Way Way went into the bedroom and got onto the bed.

Maung Mya saw his master walking briskly home, his head down. He went to look at the small table clock in the dining room china cabinet. It was only twelve o'clock. U Saw Han usually came at one. Maung Mya figured that his master must be very worried about his wife to have come back so early. He hurried to the back to pass the word along to the Indian cook and to Meh Aye, who was washing clothes in the bathroom. The clothes slapping on the cement made the sound "Hpone, hpone" as she washed. Maung Mya called out, pointing his finger upstairs, "Ssh! Where is your mistress?"

"Upstairs," she replied, jerking her head in that direction.

U Saw Han went upstairs slowly. Way Way sat up with a start, took a towel from the rack, rubbed her face hard, and hurried toward the bedroom door.

117

"Way Way, your father has passed away."

Way Way quickly brushed against U Saw Han's shoulder and stared at his face, her eyes unblinking, her lips quivering. One eyebrow started twitching. Her cheeks and chin started contorting at intervals, her nostrils dilating and contracting. "Daddy!" came out of her with a great gasp as if torn from her constricted chest. The tears flowed as she spread her uncontrollably shaking hands before her, then covered her face and began to weep violently.

U Saw Han could not bear to see her in distress. He opened the telegram and showed it to her. "Here it is, Way." he said. Way Way looked down at the paper, her hands still spread over her face.

"FATHER PASSED AWAY AT 9:45 A.M. KO NAY U."

Way Way cried out, "Oh, my mother!" and ran down the stairs. U Saw Han followed after calling out, "Way, Way, Way!" but she did not hear him. She could not hear anyone, or see anything. She found herself at the old house. Without a word to anybody she ran upstairs.

Than Than, who was sitting down, looked up with startled eyes and called out, "Way Way . . . Way Way!" in a trembling voice as U Saw Han and Meh Aye came to the door. U Saw Han stopped and said, "Than Than, your father-in-law has died." Meh Aye, the servant girl, shrieked and threw herself about like a demented person.

Upstairs Way Way was kneeling by her father's bed, crying inconsolably. Throwing her hands out she sobbed, her face down on the bed. Clearly, above the wailing of Than Than and Meh Aye, she seemed to hear her father's voice saying, "Should I go to Rangoon, daughter?" When their cries subsided, Way Way was still sobbing as though she would never stop. She felt as though her chest would break in half because of so much crying. Let it break, she thought, and kept on until her tears collected in a puddle and she uttered great gasps.

"Please, Way Way, please stop crying. We have to get things ready in order to leave tonight. Let's go home, dear," said U Saw Han. She felt his hands on her shoulder and heard his voice, and the tears subsided. Her heart was broken, and she was completely worn out.

Way Way was disconsolate and filled with burning remorse at not having gone the evening before, when she would have reached him in time. She was filled with regret that her karma was so bad that it had prevented her from going to see her father before he died. She did not blame U Saw Han. He was not at fault. She blamed herself. She had married U Saw Han. Her eyelids swollen and tears flowing ceaselessly, Way Way spent the day curled up while U Saw Han, who had decided to let her go with Than Than, was busy packing her suitcase.

"Way Way, don't forget to take your medicine after you eat, and don't forget to take your tonic before you sleep. Eat at regular times and please don't eat things that aren't good for you," he kept reminding her whenever he thought of something new. He worried that when she was out of sight and with her relatives, she would go to bed too late and eat all the wrong kinds of food. He was worried that the precious little doll he had created would be harmed.

He chose her clothes according to his own preferences. He put blouses, chemises, underwear, longyis, and handkerchiefs into the suitcase. Not knowing how much she needed, he chose more than was required and stuffed them in. Meanwhile, Way Way was curled up on the bed. As U Saw Han packed he worried about her running a temperature and put a thermometer in her mouth. Her heart was beating faster than her pulse. "Well, there is no fever, but you are in a weak state. Don't cry too much when you get there. It will bring on headache and dizziness and the stress will wear you out. Keep inhaling the *zawutha* ammonia.[52] Keep it handy at all times, do you hear?"

Way Way just nodded her head to everything he asked her to do. All she wanted was to go. Into the large suitcase went smelling salts, colognes, medicines for inhaling, medicines for taking orally, and all kinds of medicinal potions. He put in the cod liver oil that he had to coax her to take at home, and worried that when he was not around she would never take it. He went to speak to her about it before putting it in.

"He's already dead, dear, so it really doesn't make any difference anymore. . . don't go too near him and touch him and all that." He had advice and warnings he made in front of others; he had advice and warnings he whispered to her in private. Way Way

---

52. A kind of traditional herbal smelling salts.

just nodded her head in affirmation to whatever he said, as long as she could go. Before she went to the boat, she had to take some painful injections given by the doctor for her nerves. Then she had to get on the scales to see what she weighed before she left Moulmeingyun. Although he did not say so outright, he implied that she had better not lose any weight by the time she returned. To her dying day she would never forget any of it.

❖ 14 ❖

Daw Thet looked out at the car that drove up to the front of the house. Way Way got out, head bowed, with her face partially obscured by a handkerchief she held in her hand, and walked to the house. Than Than and Meh Aye looked up at the house and then started to unload the luggage.

Daw Thet went to the front door and cried out loudly in her grief, "Oh, Maung Po Thein, my brother! You asked for your daughter. 'Where is my daughter? Where is she?' you said. Well, here she is, she has come." Way Way's whole body trembled at the anguish in Daw Thet's voice.

The corpse had been laid out in the vestibule and could be seen from the street. Way Way went up the steps of the house with Daw Thet sobbing behind her. Seeing her father's body, she hastened toward it and pulled the covering away from his face. Clenching her teeth, she forced her eyes to look at him. In death his face had taken on a darkish hue with a blue tinge. She was unable to utter a sound as her heart constricted. The tears fell copiously down her cheeks.

Not far from the bed, Ko Nay U and Ko Thet Hnan sat looking at Way Way, their faces strained from holding in their grief. Hta Hta stood at the foot of the bed gripping one of the bedposts, sobbing. Her face was pinched and drawn, her eyes sunken deep, for she had attended to her father for four or five months without much sleep. Daw Thet stood near Way Way and called out loudly to her brother to awake, though he could not hear. "Wake up and see your daughter," she said. "When Maung Nay U came to your bedside you wanted to know if your daughter had come with him. 'Where is Way Way?' you asked as you gasped for breath. Well, here she is. If you want to see the daughter you longed so much for, just get up and look at her!"

121

On the morning of the day he died, U Po Thein had felt an intense desire to see all of his children. He began to have difficulty in breathing at five o'clock in the morning, and although he was very tired he was conscious. At eight o'clock, Ko Nay U came straight from the boat. On seeing him, U Po Thein had gasped, "Where is my daughter? . . . daughter?" He tried so hard to speak distinctly that he almost passed out with the effort.

Ko Nay U had sat down beside his father and placed his hand on his father's chest. "Way Way was ill and could not come. She will be here tomorrow," he said to soften the truth. U Po Thein nodded as though he heard. Although his eyes widened with fatigue, he still had something to say, but they only saw his lips move and could not catch his words; they did not know what he said before passing on.

It broke Way Way's heart as nothing else could to hear those words, "Where is my daughter?" She cried out with a long strangled sound, "Oh, Daddy, Daddy" and fell on her face beside her father's body, sobbing her heart out. She took hold of her father's cold hand from where it had been placed on his chest and held it tight. Unable to cry anymore, her body shook with long drawn-out sobs, trembling in anguish. Hta Hta came toward her as if to draw her away, but turned to Ko Nay U who said, "Naturally she is taking it badly. She didn't get to see him. Let her cry it out; she needs to," he added, stopping himself from doing the same.

Way Way just wanted to stay near her father. It was as if nothing else would do but to be with him. She wanted to stay for a long time, but a long time cannot be measured in such circumstances. After a while Hta Hta came and coaxed her away. "Come, little sister. Try to control your feelings. One does not always get what one wants. There isn't a single person in this world who gets everything he wants. Come, get up." The people around her could not bear to see her suffering so silently. They thought that if she would scream out and cry and throw herself on the floor in her agony, it would help to relieve her.

By that time, Daw Thet had cried herself out, and since there was the feeding of the monks to attend to, she made her way to the back where she could work. Meh Aye, also having cried hard, followed Daw Thet into the kitchen and, with nobody else around, started telling Daw Thet what had happened since she had left

122

home. "The little mistress wanted to come so badly, but her husband would not let her. Just about the time U Po Thein was breathing his last, she was crying herself sick in the altar room. I peeped in at all this. Even when she was about to leave for the boat, she had to have an injection." The girl was able to tell Daw Thet all that really went on in that household, and it turned sour in Daw Thet's ears.

Daw Thet made a clicking sound with her tongue and said, "If only Hta Hta knew of this . . . ," and then fell silent. Hta Hta did not know how things were with Way Way's marriage, but when she had not come to see her father, Hta Hta's heart grew heavy for her sister. Whatever she sensed about it seemed very near the truth when she saw Way Way's unhappiness and troubled mind. "Way Way, come dear. Get up. Everybody is so upset seeing you this way. If you keep on, it will make everybody even more unhappy."

Way Way moved her head to one side. Her eyes were closed and her face worn and exhausted. Her eyes opened slowly. With a great deal of effort, she tried to rise. Hta Hta saw Way Way's exhausted look and the tears streaming down her cheeks. She slowly took Way Way's hand away from her father's hand, and supported her gently; she was limp and worn.

Way Way was taken into the bedroom, accompanied by her sister-in-law, Than Than. They put Way Way on the bed and talked to her openly, with Hta Hta sitting on the bed beside her. The tears fell from Hta Hta's eyes as she looked at Way Way and saw a troubled invalid, her mental anguish etched on her face.

"I only knew when Ko Nay U told me that U Saw Han would not let you come. There may or may not be a good reason for his decision. You are not to blame for not coming in time to see Father; U Saw Han is to blame for deterring you. Well, it's over. What's done is done, and should be forgotten. For Father's sake, our efforts and thoughts should now be directed towards his merit and welfare in the next existence and what we can do for him in the funeral ceremony. However heartbroken we may feel now, we need to remember that we have a difficult time ahead, and should brace ourselves to meet whatever comes."

Saying this, Hta Hta took in a deep breath and gently let it out. She was quiet, but was thinking about many things. She thought that U Saw Han knew nothing beyond the fact that he loved Way Way. He was not the sort of man to give Way Way peace and happiness. He was not capable of supplying her needs in a simple uncomplicated way. *He* would not forgive, but *Way Way* had to forgive *him.* Hta Hta's mind returned from her thoughts as she looked at her sister's face compassionately. She thought that although Way Way did not talk, she was absorbing what she heard and could think over what was being said to her now.

Actually, however, Way Way's mind was far from receiving the messages. She could neither think nor feel; she was like a person with a wound that hurt so much it was numb.

Hta Hta left her to rest by herself and shut the door behind her. Way Way heard the door closing softly. After a time—she had no idea how long it had been—she heard it open again. Way Way felt unable to move any part of her body. She did not even want to open her eyes or hear a sound. She felt as if she could not bear the weight of a even fly lighting on her. "My daughter!" Hearing the voice, she suddenly felt an unbelievable quaking in her heart. Her face stained with tears, she lifted herself up.

"Mother!" was her anguished cry as she fell into her mother's arms. Her mother held her with great tenderness to her breast and Way Way cried with great hacking sobs. Her mother's eyes glistened; her lovely face was twisted from trying to protect herself from this intense human attachment and thus keep her commitment to the Four Noble Truths.

Hta Hta stood motionless by the bed. She was disquieted, but still stared off into space. The reverend mother looked long and tenderly at Way Way and became very thoughtful. Then, stroking her ever so gently on her shoulder, she said, "My daughter, no one can ever attain peace by struggling for it. No one can ever create it artificially through skill or contriving. Real peace is only within one's own heart." Way Way raised her head, looked into her face and surrendered to her.

Ever mindful of the path she had chosen, the reverend mother's face nevertheless clouded over a small measure as she struggled to hide what was in her heart. She tidied the little strands of hair on Way Way's face. Taking the handkerchief from her daughter's hand, she wiped her tears gently and said, "Yes, this existence is abhorrent. There is no ease or pleasure. As long as there are attachments, there is only trouble." Saying this she reminded herself of the precept. That she drew strength from repeating it showed in her eyes. Thus she was able to compose herself.

Hta Hta's eyes clung tenaciously to her mother's face and watched it come under control. Just observing her mother in this way made her feel as if a whole load of grief was seeping away. It seemed that a certain peace emanated from the brown nun's habit and drove away trouble and sorrow.

Way Way looked at her mother, who turned her eyes to study Way Way's face. It showed several conflicting emotions. The red eyes in the white face showed hurt feelings and distress from continued grief, commingled with thoughts of regret. Large teardrops hovered in those eyes and her lips were pressed together with effort. "Is it true, my daughter, that you did not come in time?" Her bitterness toward U Saw Han, and her sorrow at not arriving in time to see her father alive, burned like hot coals in her breast; she could only cover her face and nod as a great sob escaped her lips. The reverend sister sat at the edge of the bed and continued asking, "Why did you not come with Maung Nay U?" It was like fanning the flames of a fire. Way Way could only answer in sobs and cries.

Hta Hta came closer. Thinking that it was of little use to explain Way Way's plight said, "There were some difficulties. It was not possible for her to join Ko Nay U, Mother." Realizing that a lot of things do not work out in the outside world, the reverend mother did not press her further and was content with the answer. Hta Hta then said accusingly to her mother, who had also not come in time, "Everyone always thought that you were completely estranged from Father, and I always disagreed, but you know, now I think so too." Her mother reddened but collected herself and said softly and peaceably, "Oh no, it was never estrangement. As soon as you sent the telegram saying that he was very ill, of course I wanted to come at once. I had nothing to stop me. I don't deny that. I wanted to come and help the benefactor to whom I am forever indebted. Your father once told me before I became a nun, 'If you ever become a nun and have to wear those clothes, I hope I will never have to see you in them.' I had to decide whether my presence would cause him distress, so however much I wanted to come I had to refrain from distressing him further, and my only recourse was to pray for him from afar." Hearing these words from her mother, Hta Hta's face contorted as she felt the urge to join Way Way's renewed unrestrained crying. The reverend mother arose from beside the bed and left with quiet dignity.

The funeral took place the day after Way Way arrived. Way Way rode in the first car behind the hearse. Her tears flowed ceaselessly, and she could control neither them nor the huge lump in her throat. It was terribly sad for her to think that her father was leaving this world forever, and each moment intensified her pain. Onlookers found it extremely poignant to see the nun in the funeral procession.

They came to the burial ground. Way Way followed behind the slow-moving hearse, step by step, and once briefly she brushed up against it.[53] She stood with the others until the burial was concluded. The sound of earth and stones being thrown on the coffin was unbearable. Hta Hta was on her knees at the grave site sobbing her heart out, while Ko Thet Hnan stood at the head of the grave looking sadly and helplessly at his wife in her distress. Way Way could not utter a sound, but her tears flowed profusely as she held tightly to her mother's hand. They were the last to leave the cemetery. When they got back to the car she turned to face her mother and said, "Please, Mother, take me with you to Sagaing. I don't want to return to Moulmeingyun. I don't want to go back to a place where Daddy isn't there. Please don't let me do that." It all seemed to rush from her.

In the days following the interment and before the offering that was traditionally made to the monks on the occasion of a person's death, the family remained together. Surrounded by the warmth and closeness of the others, Way Way began to feel differently. It seemed as if she were a bird that had escaped from a cage and returned to the family nest. She felt secure. She felt uplifted.

In particular, she felt the comfort of the strength of Hta Hta's husband, Ko Thet Hnan, who emanated good will and affection to all of them under his roof. Modest, soft spoken, unassuming, and decent, he was utterly without vanity, always mindful of the family, and behaved respectfully toward everyone. He was tall, had a noble brow and a refined face, was well-educated, and had a

---

53. To a Burmese this is a very inauspicious thing to happen and is considered a foreboding of death.

sensitive, serious concern for the whole family. Hta Hta was not the only one who was comforted by his love. Way Way absorbed a lot of strength from his presence.

She had been no more than three days in Rangoon and had received two telegrams and a letter from U Saw Han in that short time. The telegram said, "DRINK YOUR MEDICINE REGULARLY. TAKE CARE OF YOUR HEALTH. GO TO BED EARLY." He would send telegrams daily in this manner. His letter told her to return on the first steamer after the memorial service . . . in fact, that very night. "That's all, young lady. I don't want to see you all thin when you come back. Don't get thin." Instead of feeling good about U Saw Han's manifestations of love, she was disturbed to read his letters and telegrams. It seemed to her that she was shrinking from him even at this distance.

In the evenings Ko Nay U was in the habit of coming back late around midnight with fried noodles from Chinatown or *paratas* from Mogul Street, four or five packets dangling from each arm. He would arouse everyone in the house and, setting the packets on the table, would open them up and get everyone to dig in and join the midnight feast. At such times Way Way's mind would turn to her husband, thinking about how he would react to these scenes and knowing how disgusted he would be at the sight.

Ko Nay U would urge Ko Thet Hnan to eat and would not take "No" for an answer. Ko Thet Hnan would oblige in a modest way, joining them hesitatingly, and Ko Nay U would say, "Come on, eat. You are so slow. I can't enjoy myself when I see you holding back in deference to me, so just for my sake, eat so I can enjoy it. Come on, eat up." Saying this, he would pile food up on his brother-in-law's leaf.[54] Then a slow smile would light up on Ko Thet Hnan's face.

Way Way mentally tried to put her husband in Ko Thet Hnan's place. She could not see him mixing in with the family. As hard as she tried, she could not imagine him inside the group. He just stood coldly on the outside. Her heart became heavy, and she had to control her thoughts and not to think of him as it would only upset her. Nothing was as gratifying to her as Ko Thet

---

54. In Burma, take-out food, generally purchased at small shops or roadside stalls, is packaged in banana leaves, which are then used as plates.

Hnan's mixing so warmly with the family and becoming part of it. After all, he was only related because he married Hta Hta, yet his love was for them all, and everyone was made comfortable. She saw him as a shade tree sheltering them in the fierce heat of their sorrow over their father's death.

As unobtrusive and quiet as Ko Thet Hnan was, Way Way's sad face did not escape his eyes and, concerned, he said repeatedly to Hta Hta, "Please, Hta, try to lift up her spirits." When he noted that she was skipping a meal, he would seek her out and say, "Try to eat a little, Way Way," and even though she did not really want to eat, she would feel obliged join the others at the table and have something.

Since coming to Rangoon she had written one letter to U Saw Han. Her tears flowed as she wrote, "I am taking cod liver oil regularly. I am mindful of regularity. I go to bed early. I don't eat snack foods from vendors, but eat bread and butter. I also consume eggs. I single out places with fresh air." So Way Way forced herself to write what the other party wanted to hear, but she was not so successful in compelling her mind to follow, and as a result her writing lagged interminably while her tears flowed unchecked.

Hta Hta quietly watched Way Way as she sat for so long in the lamplight writing. She noticed that her sister gazed into space more than she wrote. Seeing the tears falling made Hta Hta think that Way Way was like someone who had been attracted by a brightly clad doll and desired it tremendously, only to find out when she got it that it was made of straw. But instead of being disappointed in the doll, she blamed herself for having been attracted to it in the first place.

❖ 15 ❖

Way Way climbed up the hill. It was very steep and she struggled along, planting her feet firmly on every step of the brick stairway. She could smell the fragrance of wild mountain flowers. Arriving half way up the hillside, she paused to take her bearings. She noticed the road below, and the monastery on the hill on the other side of it. She looked at her side of the hill and could not see where it led to as it was too steep, so she looked around in all directions of the compass. Wherever she looked, she could see the white dots of pagodas among green trees on every spur and peak of the hills around.

There were tamarind trees at the side of the road. Getting hold of the branches within her reach, she picked some tender green leaves and put them in her mouth, chewing on them until she got a nice taste. Then she spit out the pulp and continued walking.

There was no one to be seen. She was not afraid and felt happy to be by herself. The brick road ended and she had to continue on a jungle footpath. Further up at the top of the hill, she could see a place to rest with a water-pot on a shelf and a bench near by. She hurried up eagerly to sit on it. She looked like a little mushroom or leaf blown by the wind.

She did not realize how tired she was until she reached the top. She panted as she threw herself on the bench. Sitting down and catching her breath, she took the dipper and drew some water from the pot. She raised it high and poured the water down her throat, her lips not touching the rim. The water was lovely and cold and cooled her insides. Throwing some water on her hands, she patted her face and neck with her wet hands.

A monk and a little monastery boy appeared. She had no idea where they had come from. The monk was about fifty years

129

of age. He was thin, tall, and dark-complexioned with deep smallpox marks on his face. He had on gold-rimmed spectacles, and a leather bag hung from his shoulder. The monastery boy was about eight years old and chubby. He was dressed very traditionally, with his hair in a little topknot and silver earrings. His hair was not oiled and looked very dusty. He wore a short-sleeved yellow poplin shirt, and a pink silk longyi made of leftover materials. His perspiring face showed layers of dirt. He walked briskly a few paces behind with his head down, carrying the monk's umbrella on his shoulder. It looked oversized on him.

The monk passed Way Way with grave decorum, looking at her imperceptibly out of the corner of his spectacles as he passed by. The little boy walked along without looking up, but as soon as he had passed by he turned around to look at her. Way Way smiled at him. He started at this, his eyes wide and round with surprise as he turned away with a stern, outraged look. It was too funny for Way Way. She could not contain herself and laughed merrily as she watched the plump little body walk out of sight.

Soon after this diverting encounter, Way Way felt restless. She started to walk again and came to several artificial caves, that is, natural hollows which had been enlarged and shaped by hand. She visited caves numbered thirty and sixty, which she had seen before. After choosing a shade tree, she stopped a while to sit and meditate under it. Then she was up and on the move again. She went to places she did not want to remember she had been to, and tried to go to places she had never been before, but when she got to these places she seemed to think she had been there. She avoided people whenever she heard voices by going down little side roads. She had no desire to see anyone, and wanted to be alone.

Standing on the hill adjacent to the emerald pagoda, she saw the whole vista stretched out as far as the eye could see, with clouds banked over it and, down below the Sagaing Bridge, everything in a blur. A playful breeze started up from the south, blowing against her clothes and through her hair. She turned away, figuring that it came from the direction in which her husband lived in the delta. Then she stood with her hands on her hips, with a sullen expression on her face, and stood eye to eye with "Ko" and said aloud, "You may think what you wish, but I'm not going to explain a thing to you. You can keep on ill-treating me. You are responsible for this. You were not aware that my heart was breaking. Staying with you was to me like being a marionette in a gilded box. This princess doll was not supposed to have a will of her own, but had to be moved by pulling strings. She was not expected to be tired or have any feelings at all. Now the strings are snapped, and she can neither raise a hand nor speak.

"Your desire to do things your way was stronger than any other feelings you had for me. My love for you, on the other hand, made me concede to you and forbear, and I let it bind me up and constrict my world. Here I can go anywhere I want to go. I have freedom. I eat when I want to eat; I don't have to use a knife and fork or put a napkin on my lap. When I'm hungry I can go to the monastery kitchen near the riverbank and sit on the floor and mix the food with my fingers and eat. And if I want to put thanaka paste on my face, I can go to the monastery and use the grind-stone and sandlewood bark, which are always ready for use." She felt her tears fall on her face and, without wiping them away, she began to come down the brick steps.

Within fifteen days of her arrival in Sagaing she had covered every square inch of the hills. If she left the common hall in the morning, she returned at noon, and if she started around noon, she came back when the sun went down in all its glorious flaming colors. When she first came to Sagaing, her mother had been concerned for her and took her around. Her fellow nuns came along to keep her company, and they went to all the different shrines and pagodas, stopping and meditating and then going on. The nuns arose at dawn when the moon was still faint in the sky and cooked an early repast for the monks. Four or five days after she got the hang of it, she went out on her own but stayed fairly close to the nunnery, and later she went further afield. She lived with her mother and five other nuns in the Gunee Chaung rest house. Way Way felt as if a large stone wall separated them from her, so different were their lives from hers. She was the stranger in their midst.

Among the nuns, Ma Thu Kha was about Way Way's age. The others were older women about fifty and sixty years old. Ma Thu Kha had noticed Way Way's depressed mood and wondered if she were weary of the world and was deciding to become a nun. She said, "Miss Way Way, for myself, I never wanted to become a nun,

131

but I had no choice. Nothing really works out in the outside world." Way Way gazed at Ma Thu Kha. Her face registered sadness now, as if simply remembering the unresolved problems of the world had put her in a different mood.

"Ma Thu Kha, has it been long since you donned the robes of a nun?" asked Way Way.

"Not very long. About two years. When my aunt, Thu Ba, came to our village, it was convenient to return with her, so I did, and became a nun."

Ma Thu Kha was silent for quite a while. Way Way had originally thought that she, like Way Way's own mother, had simply tired of the multihued garb of the outside world and so had donned the nun's habit, but now she realized that something had happened outside. She was curious about it but felt too shy to pry further. Ma Thu Kha began telling her without her having to ask.

"The conditions of my life were pretty bad. I had to live with a stepfather who, when my mother was around, was modest and quiet and did not even speak to me. But when she was not there, he looked and acted quite differently. His behavior was not proper, and the way he looked at me and spoke to me was unseemly. It was too unpleasant to think of telling my mother what my stepfather was like, for she trusted him completely, so I thought I'd let her find out for herself. One day he started talking to me and embraced me. I didn't dare mention it to my mother or look her straight in the face. It was so shameful. I didn't want to cause trouble for her and I remained silently desperate until my aunt, the nun, came to our village to collect rice for her nunnery. Shamefacedly I told her everything, so she quietly brought me back with her. When I got here, she told me to become a nun so that I wouldn't have to return."

The tears flowed down Ma Thu Kha's face after she finished. Way Way was saddened to hear the story, and she breathed a deep sigh and averted her face so she would not have to see Ma Thu Kha's bald head.

"So of course you are not happy as a nun, then," said Way Way.

"It's not a question of whether I'm happy here or not. I don't have any other home to go to, besides my mother's place. If I hadn't shaved off my hair my mother would have come and gotten me, and if she knew the whole truth she would be terribly upset. So let's say that in order for my mother's marriage and home to remain intact, I am staying away, far away, and with all my hair shaved off." Ma Thu Kha was smiling. It was a simple story from her heart and it moved Way Way. "In contrast to my life here, my former life was unfortunate. For did not the Lord Buddha say, 'It is our own responsibility to act and no one else's'? What about you, Way Way, will you leave the outside world and choose this one.?"

Way Way looked into Ma Thu Kha's face and said suddenly, "Oh no, I will not."

Ma Thu Kha laughed. Way Way was distressed and felt trapped. Ma Thu Kha said, "Since you left home to come here, your husband must be anxiously awaiting your return." It was difficult to explain things in any depth to the little nun, so Way Way just nodded her head. She then turned her face away from Ma Thu Kha's interested gaze, and the latter did not press her further. After a silence, Way Way got up and left. She started to think of the husband who was waiting for her. His little tender ways, full of concern, seeped into her memory, but then the pain of his disregard for her feelings rose up and overwhelmed them in an instant.

Way Way's mother spent her days and nights in meditation. While her mother was meditating, Way Way went walking in the hills wherever her footsteps led her; there was hardly a single place in the whole range that she had not been. On days her mother was not meditating she still had time to go walking, for her mother was then busy tutoring young novices, day and night, for their examinations. There was indeed very little occasion for them to see each other.

Whenever Way Way returned she answered the nun's questions as to where she had gone that day by saying, "I went to meditate at the pagodas." Instructing her pupils, her mother would throw her a solicitous glance when she saw her return, and then continue with her teaching. She was sure that Way Way, by meditating on the law and doctrine, would find her own way through her difficulties; her grief would abate and she would have peace. She believed that the tranquil surroundings would turn Way Way toward an ordered life and, with increased awareness and delight, her mind would clear itself of its confusion and cloudiness. Because she believed this, she did not deter Way Way from going to meditate in the hills. When she set out from the nunnery, Way Way felt as if she had left the world of nuns behind and was completely on her own in the outside world. So she wandered around by herself wherever she pleased, stopping and gazing whenever she wanted. The mother, watching her daughter's face on her return, was quite unable to tell anything from it and would continue with her teaching. She was in charge of vocabulary, articulation of words, and basic chemical knowledge. She also advised and counselled the young novices. She taught and preached to these first-year students, and her throat was sore from all the exertion.

As Way Way heard the hubbub of voices in the classroom when she came back to the nunnery, she felt again as if she had entered another world. She ate her meal late and alone, sitting on the floor at a little round table. She chewed her food absent-mindedly, not knowing what it tasted like and not being aware of swallowing. After eating, she would lean back against the pillar and see her mother across the hall with the huddled forms of nuns bent over their work. She looked at her mother with respect and admiration.

Her mother's eyes were clear and peaceful and had depth and strength. She put all her energy into presenting the precepts and the law, praying for freedom from the four states of punishment, the futureless worlds of existence and trouble. She quieted her mind with the contemplation of these noble truths and she thought of worldly pleasures as nothing more than saliva, to spit out. As her mother meditated and gained peace, so was Way Way quieted. She felt that although it had already taken a long time to get to this point, she might in time gain control over her mind.

On her arrival in Sagaing, she had received a telegram from "Ko" telling her to come back and to reply immediately by wire as to whether she was going to return or not. U Saw Han had flown into a rage when he received Way Way's letter telling him that she had gone to Sagaing with her mother. First he thought she had no regard for his love for her. Then he imagined that Hta Hta had encouraged her to go, so she came to share the blame. He did not let off the reverend mother, either, for he worried that Way Way would become a nun. The day he received the letter he lost control of himself and was ill-tempered to all around him. Hurt and angry with Way Way, he tossed down drink after drink. What do I care if she doesn't want to come back? he thought as he toughened his mind. But this was only when he was drinking. When he sobered up he could not bear to be without her and felt a great pain and emptiness inside him. He had then sent off the telegram to Way Way, and when she did not reply he got worse. In the evenings he drank himself senseless. Although he wanted to go and get her, his pride would not allow himself to do it. He did not send any more telegrams or write.

He could not hate her. But he could not accept the fact that she could be apart from him and have a separate identity. As he thought of her day after day, he began evaluating her qualities. She was simple and honest. She submitted to his will, gave in to his desires. She respected his likes and dislikes. She never gave him cause for unhappiness. She did not know how to speak hurtful words, she went along with his way of doing things, and behaved according to his rules. How much pleasure she brought him, and peace of mind! Good, good Way, he mused. It's all because her relatives influenced and encouraged her. Little Lotus Flower growing in a pile of manure. U Saw Han wanted to show her relatives that he did not care, that he could and would ignore her, but he was hardly able to stand it. He could not hide what he felt any more than could a monkey sitting on hot coals.

As for Way Way, she was unhappy at the thought of going back home. She was very sad about her father. She felt worst about not being there when her father had asked for her as he lay dying. It still hurt, and the wound would not heal easily. But she also felt sorry for her husband. They would never be happy together again, she could not help thinking, and the rest of the journey of life was going to be joyless. Living apart, on the other hand, required some difficult decisions. She could not make up her mind exactly when she should return. Her husband was not the sort of person who could stand not having his way. Because of the time they had had together, he would never settle for anything less than complete obeisance. She was tired of having to hang on his every word, or watch his every expression to find out how she should act. She knew from his silence that he was angry now. He was one whose pride was easily hurt. She no longer expected any letters.

Way Way received a letter from Hta Hta. She sat where her mother could not see her, and read it carefully.

Way Way, you don't know how much your letter disturbed me. You say that it is a strange life there, yet you don't want to go home. You reveal by this that you do not know your own mind, so you only bring trouble on yourself as a result.

I want to tell you to come back home. It is better for you to return before U Saw Han comes after you. I don't think it is possible to change things at this point, so just try to make the best of it.

It is not as if Dad were alive to make a difference. What has happened can never be undone, so you might as well go back home and make the best of it. That is what I want to say to you.

In this life the good comes with the bad, so just pick out the good. U Saw Han does not mean ill toward you, so don't nurse your hurt so much. His good intentions are not like other people's, but I don't blame him. It is because he is so very much in love with you. How can we blame him for that? Even we, looking at things from a distance, can understand and forgive him. Why can't you, the object of his affections, find it in your heart to understand the man and forgive him?

If mother catches on to what is happening, it would disturb her life, and that would not be good. So for her sake and ours, don't remain so long. Come back. It is not a good idea to leave your hearth and home. I warn you it will come to no good if you drag it out. Consider the other side too, how wretched the man must feel. I don't think he has it in him ever to break up with you. He'll only be ruined, longing for you and pining away. I got a letter today saying that he is drinking himself unconscious every night. Now what good is staying apart doing for either of you, tell me?

Let he who has died rest. Forget what pain has been caused you and with great magnanimity of heart forgive him and come home. Send us a telegram the day you leave. Don't travel alone. Bring Daw Aw Ba or someone with you as far as Rangoon. We'll come and meet you at the station.

136

Way Way read the letter and was lost in thought. She knew that life with her husband would only be miserable for her. She wondered unhappily if she should not shave her head and join Ma Thu Kha.

The reverend mother began to doubt slowly if her daughter's peaked face and problems stemmed from just grief over her father's death. In the time since the telegram came, she had not once referred to it or sent a reply. Her mother was surprised that she never spoke about her husband at all; indeed, she had never seen her son-in-law and had no idea what he looked like or whether he was dark or fair. She found herself thinking about him off and on quite a lot, however. "Daughter, would it not be difficult for him when you are not there?" she asked.

"Oh, it's all right, Mother. Whether I'm there or not, things are taken care of," she replied, which was true.

The reverend mother did not know how this could be, for she did not know the circumstances of Way Way's home life, but she could not get rid of the idea that when a man's wife was not in the house, he would have difficulties with his food and clothes. Way Way did not really want her mother to know about her problems. She felt she should keep them to herself and resolve them in the peace and quiet of the surrounding hills.

The tinkling sound of bells floated down from the many pagodas on the hillsides, wafted on the breeze. She tried to let the sound heal her inner tensions. Sometimes they brought relief. When she climbed the hills, with the yellow blossoms and glossy green leaves of the frangipani trees, and looked at the winding river with its foaming white currents, she did feel some inner relief and peace.

That evening when the river turned a golden color she went down to the bank. She went with a companion, a sixty year old lay brother, U Nyet, who came every evening to Gunee Chaung rest house with the empty containers for the next day's food offerings for the abbot. Her mother served the offering for the clergy every morning. Way Way was always happy to see old U Nyet. He was a refreshing sight.

She said, "Uncle Nyet, let's go down to the river bank," and went along with him. The novice Ma Thu Kha also accompanied them. Old U Nyet talked incessantly as they walked. Although he was sixty, he was in good physical condition and looked ten or twenty years younger. Because he was abstemious, he had all his teeth and they were, moreover, in good condition. His shaven head gleamed and did not reveal whether his hair was white or black. He wore a short-sleeved shirt of homespun. He always carried a bluish-black rosary.

He was deep into the subject of the history and origins of the Sagaing hills, and went on talking enthusiastically. "My grand-child, there are nine sheltered caves, nine ritual halls which serve as assembly halls for ordinations, nine lakes, nine ridges. Nine times nine. Nine departments . . . nine places." Uncle Nyet went on naming the caves, "Taung Hpee Lah Chaung, Shwe Wah Chaung, Pi Tauk Chaung." Then he proceeded to name the ritual halls and the lakes, always with the number nine prominent in his recital.

Way Way walked along, her mind calm and quiet. All was quiet except for Ma Thu Kha's "Lotus Brand" wooden clogs making a scraping sound on the sand. When the old man seemed to stop because he was tired, she asked, "Uncle Nyet, how long have you been a lay brother?"

"Quite long, about ten years or so."

"Why don't you don the robe, Uncle Nyet?"

"It is not possible at this present time. The wife keeps coming and calling me to go back . . . it is not time, yet." Way Way joined Ma Thu Kha's soft laughter, but she really did not feel like laughing.

"And you, my granddaughter, why don't you don the yellow garb? You have a mother herself who is a nun. Don't you want to be one too?"

"I really don't think I do, Uncle."

"Why not?" he asked, studying her.

"Because the "person in the house"[55] will come and get me." The old man laughed heartily at that.

They reached the river bank and Way Way ran down to the water's edge. The water in the river looked like a coverlet of crystals and mirrors. The water flowed gently downstream in one

---

55. A deferential way of referring to one's spouse, as it is considered more polite not to mention the name of one's wife or, especially, husband.

shimmering mass. Further away in midstream the water bubbled up and two large fish jumped and could be seen for an instant, their heads popping up as though in play. They disturbed the otherwise calm expanse of water.

Way Way was watching the moving water and suddenly felt sick. Her head began to spin. She sat down to prevent a fall. She had never experienced this before, and felt so dizzy that she started to be sick.

Ma Thu Kha came and massaged the back of her shoulders. Way Way's eyes blurred and she had to lean on Ma Thu Kha for support. She felt as though she were struggling in the dark, and suddenly everything went blank. She had fainted.

When she opened her eyes again, she did not know where she was. Then she saw that she was on the sand of the river bank. The nuns were all hovering around her. Her mother was kneeling beside her holding an aromatic to her nose. She saw U Nyet standing and staring at her worriedly. The nun Daw Aw Ba, who was pressing down on her chest, seemed indistinct and hazy. Way Way felt very tired. She looked up at the blue sky and found that pleasant.

The reverend sister Daw Aw Ba moved closer to Way Way's mother and whispered, "I don't think it's an illness," and smiled. Then she said to Way Way, "Do you feel any better? You are with child."

Way Way shuddered from head to foot. She tried to get up but her mother's voice said, "Lie still, lie still." She grasped her mother's hand very tightly as though being taken to a place she did not want to go to, and tried to hold back the tears that were streaming down her cheeks.

That night she could not sleep. She was anxious and depressed that she was pregnant. In other words, she thought to herself, I'm going to be subject to being further corrected and improved by my dear husband. Unable to sleep, she got up and went out of the room. In the dark she came face to face with her mother, walking to and fro after her night meditations.

"Daughter, are you all right?" she heard her mother's gentle soft voice. Way Way stood there, confused and dull. Her mother's presence made her quiet and peaceful. Putting a hand on her shoulder, her mother said, "My dear, this is life. Don't be afraid.

Think how happy your husband will be. It is now time to go back
to him. It will be a grievous fault to remain here now." Way Way
went quietly back to the room. Lying face down, she stifled her
sobs.

❖ 16 ❖

He hated the nun most of all. Just because she broke up with her husband, he thought, she wants to break up everybody else. He could see the shiny bald head and the saffron robes right in front of his eyes. To obliterate the sight, he gulped down another mouthful. U Saw Han got wilder as he got drunker.

Yes, Hta Hta is real nice, but thanks for nothing, Hta Hta. She should have stopped Way Way even if it was her mother who was taking her off, and even if she went willingly. She should have known how worried this wretch of a man would be. Who has a right to Way Way anyway? She is married. A woman who left her husband, he though angrily. A woman who doesn't know that husbands are important shouldn't be listened to. He wanted to throw the glass at her face. But the glass was filled with whiskey, so fortunately it was saved.

U Saw Han frowned and gnashed his teeth. His hands began to tremble, but with one of them he clutched the glass tightly. Then he wanted to hit Ko Nay U. Uncouth jungle wallah! Disreputable thakin! This stupid little man who wants to take on the great British Empire and doesn't even know how to make a single sewing needle! He wants to give his sister to those destitute Thakin Party politicians, sends her off with that prevaricating nun, but brings back the old aunt and servant girl. He doesn't even dare come to this part of town with his rabble-rousing slogans and shouts!

U Saw Han's gleaming eyes stared at his glass as he switched off his thoughts. He did not switch off his thoughts about the glass in his hand, however, and downed the contents in one gulp.

"Maung Mya . . . . Whisssskey!" He was very drunk. His loud, deep voice broke the silence and sounded like thunder in Maung Mya's ears. Maung Mya did not want his master to continue drinking. He had not touched his food tonight; in fact, he had not touched his food for a long time. He composed himself during the day and went through the day's work impassively at the office. But at night he drank himself senseless and Maung Mya could hardly stand to watch. He dared not say anything. Like the ideal butler he was, the loyal, faithful servant, he pretended not to see or hear, but crouched low behind the sofa.

"Maung Mya, whiskey!" U Saw Han thundered again. Cold shivers went down Maung Mya's spine as he rose and opened a new bottle of whiskey.

No matter how drunk he got, U Saw Han could not hate Way Way. The more he drank the more he loved her. "My beloved, my love! Way Way, I miss you. I long for you. Don't you miss me? Please come back!" he cried out. The tears gathered in his eyes and fell down his proud face.

Way Way's smile was almost imperceptible on her face; her little voice could be heard faintly. He seemed to see her in the Western-style white sweater and the black crepe longyi with bright red dots clinging to her very attractively. He saw that she was wearing pearls, which suited her special beauty. Each pearl was enhanced next to her skin. Her slender fingers were the color of ivory, but she stood a long way off and would not come closer to him.

U Saw Han looked and looked and gave a great guffaw. He had become even drunker. In his mind he was chasing Way Way, who disappeared right before his eyes. His heart beat rapidly and he could hardly bear it. He had to take deep breaths. After a while he heaved his big body from the sofa. He stood up and was about to pitch forward but caught himself and sat down quietly. Then suddenly, not wanting to sit, he rose and took two or three steps forward, swaying from side to side until he got control of himself. He adjusted his belt and longyi at the waist. His head was down. He looked around the room this way and that with a heart-broken expression.

"Maung Mya," he called in a great voice that did not sound like his own. Maung Mya stood up suddenly from behind the sofa and looked timorously at his master, who was out of control. When U Saw Han's eyes found him, Maung Mya lowered his eyes in deference. He looked out from the sides of his eyes, however. He stood in that posture, quietly waiting to be given his orders.

"Pack up my clothes. I'm going to get my little darlin' tomorrow," he said, using the colloquial English." "She'll only come if I go and get her. Isn't it so?" So saying he staggered towards Maung Mya and clutched at his shirt. Maung Mya nearly fell over and had to hold on to the sofa to keep from falling on his face.

"Yes, sir, you had better go and fetch her. That's the only way she'll come back." U Saw Han's face, all askew, looked up at Maung Mya. He was still clutching at Maung Mya's shirt and the young man had some difficulty breathing. He was not able to breathe properly until U Saw Han let go of him. Maung Mya thought, He's quite different tonight. I wonder what's got into him to change his mind suddenly and want to go and fetch her back? In a way, this is good news; it would never do for him to carry on like this much longer. Lately, Maung Mya had not been able to go to bed until one or two o'clock in the morning because he had to wait up for his master night after night. His work day was longer and his eyes were sunken from lack of sleep.

U Saw Han went clambering up the stairs after pausing to look at Way Way's framed picture. He took it from the writing desk and said, "Good night, darling."

Maung Mya watched this without blinking an eyelash. He watched until U Saw Han was all the way up the stairs, then with a huge yawn he switched off the lights. The living room became dark, but it was almost time for a new day to dawn.

A cool breeze from the south blew in through the window. The drumstick tree at the corner of the house shed its little yellow flowers. They fell softly and persistently to the ground. Maung Mya opened the windows and tidied the room for another day. He drew the curtains aside to let the light in.

The living room was a mess. The ash trays were full of butts and ashes from the cigarettes U Saw Han had smoked spilled around them. They did not present a pretty sight. The day-old gardenias in the little red vase were wilted and yellow. There were English magazines strewn all over the floor. Maung Mya dusted the room and straightened it up. Only when he got to the front door did he realize how wilted he himself was, and gave a long sigh.

Way Way was standing in front of the house, her luggage carried by some coolies behind her. She made a great effort to move her limbs and walk through the front door. Maung Mya was

143

struck speechless and stared at her. He wanted to cry out for joy but could not. In one bound he was at her side. Way Way gave Maung Mya a wistful little smile, her eyelashes fluttering against her pale cheeks.

"Oh, mistress!" he cried. "No telegram. No warning!" he blurted out. Noticing Way Way's worn face, he put on a cheerful expression.

"I didn't telegram on purpose. Where is he?" Her voice sounded feeble to the point of exhaustion. She did not seem to be aware of her surroundings when she looked at the big house next door.

"He's not up yet. He went to sleep only at three o'clock this morning. He will be overjoyed to see you. Last night he said he was going to get you and even asked me to pack his suitcase."

Way Way's eyes filled with tears as she sat down in the nearest chair and slowly leaned back in it. Maung Mya put the luggage inside noiselessly. Although he had had no sleep, he moved briskly. She saw the old familiar objects around her as if from a distance. They seemed cold and impersonal, and she was not touched by them at all. She had distanced herself from those objects that belonged to her so that returning would encourage a certain kind of indifference.

Way Way had her head propped on her hands with her eyes closed. Maung Mya kept watch over her as he went about his duties. He felt reassured as he put two place settings on the table for breakfast. He was so relieved and happy that he did not know whether he wanted to laugh or cry. There was a great smoldering feeling in his chest and he felt quite confused.

The old Indian cook, looking like a large pelican, came into the dining room, crossed the floor and stole a glance at Way Way from behind the curtain. Nodding his head with satisfaction, he smiled contentedly. Striding back in long steps, he left the way he came.

A cough from upstairs shook Maung Mya with fright. He did not know whether he should go upstairs and tell the master or let him come downstairs and discover her himself. Way Way sat on the sofa motionless. He was in a sweat, worrying over what to do. Then he heard another cough. This time he heard footsteps as well, which only deepened his quandary. While he was struggling with it, Way Way got up from her chair with great effort. Propelled

144

by her senses, she walked wearily toward the stairs. Maung Mya stood at attention, eyes straight in front of him, hardly breathing. He felt extremely uncomfortable but forced himself to look. Way Way glanced up when she got to the foot of the stairs, and started up. Way Way's was not agitated, but everything around her was reeling, advancing and receding. She could not see a thing and was like a blind person finding her way in a jungle. Watching her, Maung Mya's heart beat violently.

Way Way moved the bedroom curtain aside and entered the room. U Saw Han saw her. He was utterly unable to leap toward her, but uttered a great cry. Transfixed, he began to tremble and a demented look crept onto his face. At that point, Way Way's knees wobbled and shivers swept over her entire body.

"Way . . . Way . . . Way . . . ," U Saw Han was called out in a cracked voice. He looked at her. He drank in her face, her brow, her cheeks, her chin. He then took in her wan little face with his eyes, drawing strength from the very sight of her. Way Way did not say a word. She showed no signs of feeling. Her face was expressionless and did not move. Indeed, she looked as if she had not seen anything at all, or was blind altogether. "Way, you've returned," he said as he gathered her up in his arms. His voice sounded as if he had difficulty getting it out of his dry throat.

Her ears roared with sound and she felt dizzy. She steadied herself by leaning against him. U Saw Han tightened his grasp with a sigh of emotion, unable to speak. He held her tight. His hands caressed her. He was too moved to say anything, but his silence was more eloquent. Way Way was astonished at the fierceness of his embrace. She had never before seen him as desperately emotional as this; the hug was so tight that she hurt. She realized that he had no hard feelings against her. Afterwards he held her by her shoulders at arm's length and examined her from head to foot.

Her face was drawn and thin, especially around the ears. Her clothes were hanging on her. They were loose and did not seem to belong to her. She looked pale and exhausted. Way Way's tears started to well up as he inspected her, and she felt tight inside her. Her careful control broke as she blurted out, "Ko!" U Saw Han grabbed her once more and, putting his head down on her shoulder, whispered in her ear, "How very thin you have become, my little one."

Way Way was quiet for a moment. Then, gathering her strength and pushing away from him, she said, "I am pregnant." She could not breathe. Her chest was constricted. She fainted dead away in his arms.

❖ **17** ❖

Way Way now had to be very alert and remember all the different medicines that had been prescribed for her. She had to know exactly at what time and in what dosage each liquid or powder was to be taken. As soon as she got up in the morning she had to take a cup of powdered glucose dissolved in water. Half an hour later she had to take a spoonful of a liquid compound. After each meal she had to take a black pill with a cup of hot water. Then in the afternoon she took little, flat, white pills. When she had her four o'clock tea, she had to swallow some sticky, slimy tonic which purportedly contained iron. At dinner time there was the hot water and black pill again. Then before she went to bed, in order to strengthen her blood and her heart, she had to take cod liver oil. Once in a while she had to take a laxative in the form of more small, flat pills.

Way Way's waking hours were filled with thinking about what medicine should be taken next. If she forgot, "Ko" would natter on about it endlessly. Before he left for work he reminded her about her medicines and tonics, and as soon as he returned he would ask her again if she had taken them. She was taking medicine to give her a peaceful night's sleep, to give her strength, to help her digest her food, to improve her blood, to strengthen her heart, and so on. She felt as if she ate as much medicine as she did food.

At the start of her pregnancy she had not eaten very much. She did not like the foods that were supposed to be good for her and craved hot and spicy snacks instead, but because she was supposed to build up her strength she had to eat food she hated. The very sight of eggs and tomatoes made her ill. She was forced to eat eggs and butter, but they made her feel sick. She soon was desperate to sneak next door and eat sour and spicy hot things to satisfy her cravings.

It was not easy for her to go next door anymore. When she first returned from Sagaing she had gone to her brother's house, but when U Saw Han heard about it he was displeased and showed it in his face. To make his feelings clear, he had crossed out the day of her visit on the calendar right in front of her. He was not just afraid of her catching some disease or illness; he was worried that she would pick up all kinds of country ways if she went next door.

Because he had showed his displeasure, she had to refrain from going next door unless it was important. She then had to brave it and put up with his annoyance. Ko Nay U would look at his sister's strained face and try to put her at ease. "If it causes problems to come here, I won't take it amiss if you don't come. Although he doesn't like us, he loves you. We are satisfied on that score. We're not pleased that he keeps you shackled to him, but he does cherish and protect you. We're happy about that. You should at least be grateful for that. You don't realize how much he dotes on you. There are very few men who are so attentive to their wives as he is. It is truly rare. So don't cause trouble for yourself by coming here. Don't worry, I understand."

She found some peace of mind in his consoling explanation of why she had to cut herself off from the closeness of a warm and loving family. As difficult as it was, she reduced the number of her visits.

U Saw Han had put her pregnancy in the hands of a Punjabi doctor trained in Western medicine. He came regularly once a week and administered injections to strengthen her. U Saw Han noticed that she had changed imperceptibly in many ways since going to Sagaing. She seldom spoke. Studying her closely, he saw that her face had a parched look and that she was slowly withdrawing into herself. U Saw Han never questioned her about Sagaing. When the topic cropped up in the conversation, he ignored it and refused to discuss it. He did not blame her for it or hold it against her, but when she talked about it he held up his hand to stop her and said, "Way Way, from now on let us never speak about that again." So she had to be careful not to mention Sagaing in her conversation. In this and other circumstances she

148

was forced to hide the desolation in her heart. She concealed her feelings beneath a protective, matter-of-fact exterior.

U Saw Han was very happy and excited about the baby and took extra care of the mother-to-be. "Tell me, dear, which do you prefer, a girl or a boy? I'm dying to know," he asked her as she sat knitting little baby socks. He watched her nimble fingers stop and her eyelids slowly lift as she looked at him and saw him light up with an intensity of feeling.

She lowered her eyes as though deep in thought and slowly put down her knitting beside her on the carpet. Sitting demurely and looking ahead, she replied, "Whatever the baby is, dear."

U Saw Han seemed dissatisfied with her answer and shook his head, "No, no, Way Way. What do you *want*? A little girl perhaps? A little boy? Tell me!" he pleaded.

Way Way seemed to think about it for a while and U Saw Han waited for an answer. Will she say she wants a girl? he thought as his heart beat heavily, or will she say she wants a boy?

Way Way replied with a calm voice, "Whatever the baby is, dear."

U Saw Han began to get upset. I wonder if maybe she doesn't want a baby at all, he mused. It seemed as if they were miles apart. His questions and her replies were not connecting. He saw her impassivity as indifference, and he wondered whether she had become cold and unfeeling. He looked at her steadily and let out a deep sigh.

Way Way noticed his disturbed expression and thought, Oh dear, he didn't like my honest answer. She became frightened, as she always did when she saw him in a dark mood. She gave him a sweet smile and said, "What about you, dear, do you want a little son or a little daughter?"

Seeing her smile, his fears subsided. "Oh, I guess I want anything we get, either a boy or a girl," he replied returning her smile. He took her soft hands in his and held them tightly.

When she saw his reassured eyes and happy smile return, her heart warmed slowly. She then picked up her knitting and resumed working on it. "The knitting is going to tire you, Way Way. That's quite enough." He stopped her by taking the wool and calling out to Meh Aye to come put it away.

He was in the habit of asking her, "Did you nap this afternoon?" and examining her face closely when he came home every afternoon from the office. Only when he saw a rested face and rested eyes was he assured that she had had her midday rest.

"I tried to sleep, dear, but I couldn't, and since Daw Thet came over, I went downstairs and we had a chat."

His face clouded at once. "What did she have to say?" he asked, alert and apprehensive.

"Oh, she says we should make an ointment to rub the abdomen with after childbirth. She says that it is better to start now and have it ready. She says that we should pound some cloves and camphor and add some rubbing alcohol and put it in an airtight container." She found it difficult to continue when she saw his face grow darker and darker, so she stopped.

"We have a doctor, Way, we don't need all that. And what else did she say?" Way Way could not think of what she should tell him or, for that matter, what she should not tell him, but because it was her nature to be spontaneous she said, "She said I would have to drink some turmeric mixture after the birthing." By this time U Saw Han was really disgusted, but he controlled his anger. He let out a careful "Oh?" and changed his expression.

"Look here, Way Way, only backward village women and Coringee Indians rub turmeric all over their bodies after a child birth. We don't have to do that. We can use talcum powder." He was furious at Daw Thet, whom he considered an interfering old busybody, for undermining him.

Way Way was never allowed to make her own decisions and had to be careful not to oppose U Saw Han. She knew she had to go along with whatever he thought, no matter what. It was as if this were his little kingdom and he was supreme ruler. She had to like whatever he happened to like, and dislike whatever he happened to dislike. He dominated her body and mind, her thinking, her whole existence.

When she was three months pregnant, she could not stand the sight of food and wanted only to eat a little fruit. "Just a little milk. You have to drink just a little milk, Way Way. How can you go on without eating anything? How can you expect to keep up your strength? Just one swallow, one swallow, please. Please drink just a little of this milk." Picking up the glass of milk with extreme distaste, Way Way took a deep breath, closed her eyes, and gulped some down without breathing. She dared not breathe, lest she smell the milk. She stood with her lips tight and

150

her body stiff, her head erect, afraid to move. She was that uncomfortable.[56]

U Saw Han continued coaxing her. "Another swallow, one more swallow. After this one you can stop," he said. Way Way tried to control herself. She stood with her head erect, her lips tightly closed, and tried to push him off with her hands. U Saw Han laughed and brought the glass to her lips quickly. Unable to control herself any longer, Way Way suddenly brought it all up. U Saw Han was extremely disturbed and carried the panting, limp Way Way to an arm chair and lay her down. She lay there, eyes closed and chest heaving. U Saw Han sent for the doctor at once. He was at his wits' end not knowing what to do, imagining all kinds of trouble. I wonder if anything has gone wrong with her insides as a result of her not eating for so long, he worried to himself.

The doctor came and gave her a shot in the arm. Poor Way Way, still tense after vomiting, had to endure another trial of pain. The doctor had to explain at length to reassure U Saw Han that it was natural for her not to be hungry at this stage of the pregnancy. He told him that she would have to exercise and have plenty of fresh air and that she should go for daily walks in the cool of the evening.

So Way Way walked every evening with U Saw Han in the direction of the godown. The walk was very pretty. The red gravel road and the green grass swaying in the breeze made an attractive sight.

"It's nice walking over here, isn't it, Way Way?" said U Saw Han eagerly. Way Way just strolled along slowly at her own pace. "Look, young lady, over there, beside the godown. Do you remember that little stream?" he asked. Her heart beat quickly as

---

56. Burmese, like most other Southeast Asian peoples, generally are not fond of milk or cheese, and these items are not included in the traditional diet. Occasionally, probably as a result of colonial influence, milk is taken for medicinal purposes (as U Po Thein does in an earlier chapter), and in modern times the idea that milk is a healthy addition to the diet has grown. Condensed milk is widely used in tea, as well. But for the most part dairy products are merely considered to taste bad and cause offensive body odors, and they are often vaguely associated negatively with Westerners and invalids.

she recalled the spot where she first felt the pangs of love. In a moment everything turned sad as she remembered that she had learned of her father's illness for the first time that very evening when they returned to the house. As they neared the godown she struggled with her tears. Everything was quiet. They stood under the acacia tree, his arm around her neck. The wind was blowing wildly over the river and the expanse of sky and water were as one. The sun shone on the water and the banks were all asparkle. The sun made a dappled shade under the acacia tree, with bits of light moving about. Little boats bobbed up and down in midstream.

The wind was blowing and Way Way was getting cold. "Let's go home. It's getting late," she said.

He pulled her around and faced her in the glow of the setting sun. He thought she looked rather pale. Her face was pinched and thin, and her complexion was not rosy as it had been before. Her eyes were sunken and ringed with dark, greenish circles. The bones of her forehead her temple protruded. "Oh, Way. You look so thin to me. This pregnancy must be very difficult for you. You keep getting thinner and thinner. When will you ever get nice and fat again?"

Way Way steadied her staggering steps by holding on tight to U Saw Han's arm. She felt heavy and slow. "Than Than says it's like this when you are pregnant, but once you have the baby you regain your weight." Her voice sounded soft and weak.

"Aren't you happy about having a child, Way?" he asked seriously.

She trembled with alarm when she heard him. His question penetrated straight to her core. She had never let U Saw Han know that the only reason she had returned from Sagaing was that she was pregnant, and she wanted to keep it that way.

She said quickly, "Oh, I'm happy to be pregnant." He didn't seem satisfied with the answer, but she did not know what else to say so she gave him a disarming smile. She then asked him his question in return, "How about you, are you happy about having a child?" U Saw Han looked at her steadily and then nodded. He took her hands and held them in his grasp.

"Way Way, your little hands are cold, you must not linger any longer." They took the short cut when they came to the stream. U Saw Han jumped to the other side but returned promptly. "You

can't jump. I forgot that and brought you this way. Come, come."
Way Way looked embarrassed but went along as he pulled her
along with him by the hand.

He went to get a sweater as soon as they reached home, and
brought her the medicine that was to be taken at this time. She
drank it down with her eyes closed and remained quiet, resting
without moving. U Saw Han poured himself a whiskey and relaxed
on the sofa. Yawning, he turned on the radio and listened to the
news in English; he got caught up immediately in the latest war
reports.

U Saw Han started as he heard a groan and a gasp from Way
Way, and went running to her side. She was biting her lips and
pressing her hands to her sides. She had terrible cramping pains
that she could hardly bear. "Dear, I don't know what's happened.
My back and sides ache."

U Saw Han called to Maung Mya, telling him to get the
doctor. He knelt by her side and said, "Don't press your sides,
don't press, Way." He became very distraught because he did not
know what to do. Her breathing was hard and her forehead broke
out in a sweat. He mopped her brow. He heard her moan and
held her hands, kneading them and comforting her. "The doctor
will be here any minute now," he said.

Meh Aye looking at Way Way's pain-distorted face and asked,
"Shall I call Daw Thet?"

Despite her pain, Way Way managed to open her eyes and
look at U Saw Han with an encouraging smile. "Dear, please get
Aunt for me."

"Yes, yes. Go get Aunt, quickly!"

Way Way sat up, holding onto U Saw Han's shoulder, her
head resting against his chest and one hand holding onto her side.
Daw Thet and the doctor and the nurse all hurried into the room
at once. Daw Thet came near Way Way, took one look at her, and
said, "I think she's on the verge of a miscarriage."

The doctor, who had been checking her pulse, nodded in
agreement and said decisively, "Yes, it looks like that to me."

U Saw Han carried Way Way upstairs and put her on the bed.
She perspired profusely and nearly fainted. She rolled in agony,
her lips white with pain. The whole house was in a flurry and
bustle all night long. U Saw Han could hardly breathe properly
hearing her groans. Outside, the night was still. Once in a while

153

the leaves rustled when the wind blew. The night bird called with a jarring sound. Way Way lay limp. She was so tired that she was barely breathing. The night lamp near the head of the bed cast a soft light on part of her face.

Bending over the patient, the doctor looked at her with her hair spread on the pillow, then straightened up and looked at U Saw Han across the room. U Saw Han looked at the doctor anxiously, his heart in his mouth. "It's going to be all right. There is no cause to worry anymore," the doctor said. U Saw Han felt as if a great weight had been rolled away. As he bent over Way Way, his face gradually cleared.

Daw Thet took the nurse downstairs. Pouring water for the nurse as she washed her hands, she said, "It's fortunate that things are better. She has no strength. One has to worry about blood poisoning in these cases of miscarriage." She went on talking.

U Saw Han whispered to Way Way as he bent over her to wipe her forehead gently, "Are you all right?"

Looking up at him she said, "Yes, thank you," but the sound was so faint that he had to put his ear to her mouth in order to hear it.

❖ 18 ❖

The white petals falling to the ground from the rose bushes looked like snow. The green leaves of the bushes glistened, and the breeze blew the blossoms in gentle swirls. Way Way felt cold even with a blazer and a sweater on. She was taking her morning walk behind the house. She had lost weight after her miscarriage and was thin and pinched in the face.

U Saw Han had doubled his concern for her. He wanted her healthy again. He supervised her medication, her sleeping hours, her waking hours, her food, everything concerning her health, in the most rigid manner. She was not allowed to eat any food that was not nourishing or wholesome, and it seemed as if she had consumed more than her own weight in eggs. She had to sleep on time and rise only when the proper allotment of hours had been slept. She had to take her medicine on time, eat on time, bathe on time, and exercise on time. The first thing she did on waking was take her medication. Then she drank eggnog. Then from 7:00 to 8:00 she had to exercise, which meant walking. The back yard was about eighty feet in length and she walked up and down in it.

So great was U Saw Han's desire to get her well that he gave her no freedom at all. She had to submit to his strict regimen, which constricted and ruled her whole life. Half of his salary went into the medicines she had to take orally or by needle. Her afternoon naps were sacrosanct; no one was allowed to visit during this time. He even put a watchman at the front gate to bar anyone from entering during this rest period.

When Way Way came back into the house at six o'clock, which was the hour of sunset, no one was allowed to speak loudly. If there were guests and their voices got loud, U Saw Han would silence them. He would motion with his hand for them to stop and point upstairs. In a whisper he would say, "Way Way has gone to bed." He was not in the least embarrassed at doing this.

As time passed Way Way became increasingly like a wind-up toy and moved only when wound up. All day long she behaved not as she wished but as she was forced to. She came to believe that one's existence was preordained and depended on one's karma.

She was only allowed to write once a week to her mother and Hta Hta. In her narrow and confined existence she would write pages and pages to her sister. U Saw Han would weigh the letter in his hand and say, "You will tire yourself out writing so much. You will strain yourself and get a neckache." So she resorted to writing in a tiny script, filling both sides of the paper to overflowing and leaving Hta Hta nonplussed. Hta Hta wondered why Way Way, whose usual writing was large and round, would write in such a small and crowded hand. Well, she mused, she must have her reasons, and she never questioned her sister about it.

As she walked, she composed in her head the letters she would write to her sister and her mother. She wrote to seek relief from her quiet, narrow existence. Her weekly letters were filled with the minutiae of her life. She would relate the goings-on of the town and neighborhood, report the weather, depict Meh Aye's latest country bumpkin blunder. She would carefully describe the longyi or *eingyi* material that Meh Aye had purchased for her in the bazaar, going into great detail about the colors, design, and price of each piece of fabric. She also wrote copiously about the fruit and vegetables in season in their area. "I think that radishes are now in season where you are, sister. Do you remember how we enjoyed eating *ngape*[57] cooked in broth, and a marvelous ngapi dish prepared with all the trimmings and pickled sour radish as a dip?" "Do you remember this?" she would write, "Do you remember that?"

Subsequently Hta Hta would remember such things as pickled *neem* leaves, pickled bamboo shoots, asparagus, *kimonywet*, and many other leaves and vegetables which were in season when she read Way Way's letters. She also marvelled at her

---

57. A variety of white-fleshed fish.

taking such pains to include all the plants growing around the house in her garden. And because she was so far away from Way Way she would say aloud to herself, "Only she would take such pains to describe them so." Hta Hta could see and smell the rose that just budded and brought so much pleasure to Way Way. She wrote repeatedly about "Ko" and how he looked after her so well, administering medicine according to a precise schedule, so Hta Hta would skip the first part of the letters.

Hta Hta had been very concerned about Way Way after her miscarriage. She had wanted Way Way to have some sort of companionship to revive her, and had believed that a child could solve this problem for her. She could only read between the lines of Way Way's letters since she was so far away and did not know how things really were. Whenever Way Way wrote that she was not feeling too well, Hta Hta would tell her to take better care of herself. Way Way would reply, "You tell me to take better care of myself. I don't know but what I've become delicate because of so much concern over my health. If anything, I'm already getting too much care, so your advice does not apply."

When Way Way received letters from her mother, they were heavy reading, like sermons. When she finished one of her mother's letters she always felt that she had accomplished something if she retained some of the ideas and found herself thinking about them in depth. She availed herself of a collection of ten Jataka stories from her mother's old bookcase next door, but she had to cut down on her reading because whenever she became too engrossed in a book U Saw Han would take it away from her and admonish her saying, "You will get a headache and your eyes will be strained by too much reading." So she then read furtively when he was at work.

She was kept under close surveillance at all times except when he was at the office. He would look her over the first thing in the morning, studying her from head to foot and scrutinizing her face, wondering if she looked rested or if she seemed pale or thin. Thus would he create all kinds of anxiety for himself. If she had not slept well he would say, "Dear, your eyes are sunken; that won't do. Are you feeling queasy? Are you all right?" He would carry on so that whenever he started to ask her these questions she would tremble inside and her heart would beat rapidly.

He was so anxious about her that each day she prayed that she would simply be able to sleep and eat. It was so bad that she never lay in bed when she felt weak or ill, and she behaved like a well person at all times. She was so tired of taking all that medicine and so thoroughly tired of his anxiety over her, that she was afraid to be sick in bed.

Way Way got to the fence and turned around. She looked at her watch. She found that she had twenty minutes left to exercise. When she first came outside, she had been cold and walked briskly to warm up. Now she was tired and walked slowly. She heard the early morning vendors of breakfast foods calling out their wares in the street, and felt a sudden urge to eat a pancake drenched with palm sugar syrup. The fried food vendors were calling the names of all the specialties on the trays they carried on their heads. "*Mohsein baung*! Nice and hot!" cried a hawker. The mere sound of it warmed her insides. She began to remember childhood scenes of her family at breakfast, early in the morning, around a steaming cake of mohsein baung. She remembered it being cut and the portions covered with shredded fresh coconut and pounded roasted sesame seeds. Another vendor called from a way off, "*Kaunghynin baung!*" and that brought back the memory of a big bowl of hot sticky rice with the family sitting around the table, everyone all helping themselves to handfuls of the rice and eating it with great enjoyment. She had not tasted any since her marriage, and it rose clean and fragrant in her mind.

Her mouth watered as she heard each vendor, and then she thought of the bread and butter awaiting her on the table in the house and her appetite left her. She walked over to a pot of chrysanthemums and gazed at the little blossoms. Four little buds were beginning to open up, helped and refreshed by the early drops of dew. Later the sun in its journey across the sky would change them. It would dry them out and make them lose their petals, which would fall onto the ground. She reflected on the impermanence of life as she looked at the flowers.

As she was touching the plants and thinking along these lines, she heard a voice say, "Hey, what are you up to?" Startled, she turned around to see her brother. He had on a hat made of woven bamboo strips, and stood on the other side of the fence in the side lane just coming off the main road.

Way Way ran to the fence and said happily, "What are you doing up so early?"

Ko Nay U came closer to the fence and looked her over. "Is it true that you are not well?" he asked her before replying to her question. The two of them had not seen each other for four or five months. Both were aware of it but kept from mentioning it.

"Oh, nonsense, I'm perfectly alright." said Way Way pursing her mouth. He smiled at her but inwardly felt sad. "Is it true that the English and the Japanese will go to war?" she asked softly and hastily. She was concerned that U Saw Han would be awake and overhear them talking politics.

"There is going to be a war, no doubt about it. Just pray that the Japanese come soon. Only then will we have independence quickly."

Way Way's eyes grew round in amazement, "Now don't you go around talking like that. You'll be arrested! Please stop! Stop it!" she urged.

Ko Nay U threw back his head and roared with laughter, and said, "Where's the Englishman? Isn't he up yet?"

"I don't know if he is up. By the way, have you sent the rice to mother?"

"Yes, I sent her one bag of rice and a tin of oil together with the thirty *kyats* you sent with Meh Aye, in all a total of eighty kyats.

Way Way smiled at him. She felt very sad to be talking across the fence with her own brother, but she pretended to be light-hearted and happy even though she had nothing to be happy about.

"Hta Hta must be busy. She has not written to me. Have you heard from her?" he asked.

"Yes, I've heard from her. I write her once a week. She's well. Her husband is well. He had some sores but he is all right now."

"Well, I've got to go. My dog Letpyu didn't come home last night. Don't know where the bugger's gone off to. Me and my dog troubles." Ko Nay U liked animals and always kept dogs and cats and could not live without them. Laughingly he went on his way. Way Way watched him go out of sight, smiling at first for his benefit, and then the tears started brimming in her eyes. She suddenly felt alone, and a large lump rose in her throat.

As she turned away from the fence she let out a deep sigh and coughed a little. As she cleared her throat and spit, she caught sight of something red out of the corner of her eye. At this she stopped, her heart beating very fast. She realized something was wrong, and everything blurred all at once. She began to get extremely nervous, looking this way and that. She tried to subdue her fears as she took her handkerchief from her coat pocket, cleared her throat again, and put her handkerchief to her mouth. She found it difficult to look, but had to overcome her feelings. She glanced up at the house and went on walking. She looked at her handkerchief and saw a red stain. She rolled up her handkerchief into a ball, and stuffed it into her coat pocket. Her knees were trembling as she sat down on her haunches near the flower pot.

If she had had her way she would have sobbed her heart out, but she did not dare. Her face looked stricken and two tears rolled down her cheeks as she thought, If he knew . . . . Way Way could not think straight. She knew she could not hide her secret. Dreading the time he would discover it, which was inevitable, she sat so rigidly that her whole body ached. She bit her lip until it almost bled. Her head swelled.

She was certain she heard his footsteps coming down the stairs, and her heart pounded. She got up, wiped away her tears, and bent over the flower pot, pretending to examine the flowers. He came up to her. A strong smell of perfume emanated from him that made her throat itch and almost made her cough.

"Pretty, aren't they, Way? They are certainly blooming away. How many lengths did you walk, huh?"

Way Way tried very hard to repress her distress and smiled back at him. U Saw Han saw her smile and thought she looked better than usual.

"I walked for about half an hour and then came over to admire the flowers. They are so pretty. Don't you think they are pretty? Huh? Huh?"

U Saw Han loved her to behave in this manner, with her little voice and her little wiles. Nothing made him happier. It warmed the cockles of his heart. He put an arm around her shoulder and said, "Way, you look absolutely adorable this morning." She smelled his special perfume and felt safe and yearned to lean against his chest and be protected.

160

Although she was laughing, she wanted to cry. She imagined his present cheerfulness changing completely, his smiling face transformed into one distorted with pain. It made her blood run cold to think of it. She smiled brightly as she noticed his eyes brimming over with love for her. She said cheerfully, "Come, dear, let's go and have some breakfast."

With his arm still around her, he guided her into the house. Her heart beat rapidly one minute and slowly the next, skipped a beat here and started thumping there, behaving in as unruly a manner as it wished. When they got to the table, Way Way forgot to sit at her usual place, but it did not seem to affect U Saw Han, who was so pleased with Way Way's happy and cheerful mood that he appeared not to notice. She suddenly realized her lapse and took her usual place opposite him, smiling and laughing, all the while concealing her fear and inner trembling.

Fixing her coffee for her and looking pleased at her bright manner, U Saw Han said, "I think you had a good sleep last night." Her voice would not come out so she nodded her head. "That's why . . . that's why . . . you look so fresh . . . . We must continue with those liver injections and finish the course. Then those little cheeks and lips will regain their color."

Usually Way Way would sit and have her breakfast in a calm and composed manner. Today she seemed different and unsettled, talking a lot. Her voice sounded as though she were crying or laughing or teasing, one could not tell, and her eyes were restless. The only person who noticed this perturbed undercurrent was Maung Mya, who watched her curious behavior as he waited on table. He saw that she acted differently when U Saw Han looked at her and when his look was not on her. My mistress is different today, he thought, confused.

Feigning composure, Way Way was in turmoil within. She was afraid not to tell him about the blood, but even more afraid to bring it up. She could not bear to think of how disturbed he would get when he knew, and could not bring herself to come out with it. She was worried that if she confronted him with it, he would have a stroke from sheer dread of the disease. She was unable to come up with a solution. She was so worried about him that she gave no thought to herself or to what she should do. I won't tell him while he is eating his breakfast, she thought. But

161

then, on the other hand, he'll blame me for not telling him at once.

She did not know how she managed to eat or drink, or how the food went down at all. Her mind swirled with worry and indecision. She had to keep up an outward appearance of calm while everything was going haywire inside.

"You didn't say anything when I mentioned the injections, dear. What's the matter? Is it because they hurt? Aren't they the reason you look so well today? Don't you want to finish out the prescribed course?"

"Oh, no, no. It isn't that, dear," she replied with a half-twisted smile and a voice to match.

"What are you talking about, Way? Tell me." U Saw Han looked steadily at Way Way. She seemed timid and unable to look at his cheerful face. She hung her head down while thinking furiously how to reply.

"I was just calculating how many injections I have left to finish the course. Yes, I will finish it." When she stopped talking, she felt like coughing. She tried her best to suppress it and smile at the same time. She was so afraid that she would not be able to keep this up that she felt as if her hair were sticking on end. Cold shivers went down her spine and her throat itched; she felt a cough coming on. Unable to think of what to do, she quickly picked up her coffee cup, put it to her mouth, and coughed a little behind it. U Saw Han moved his chair back and glancing up suddenly at her face. She quickly swallowed.

"I choked," said Way Way, and U Saw Han's face eased. He came around to her and stroked her back gently. Her heart beat rapidly as she barely managed to keep up appearances. She smiled cheerfully and held on until U Saw Han left for the office with a lighter heart.

She then went up the stairs, heavily, one step at a time, her whole body resisting the exertion. When she reached the top she heaved a sigh, but there was no relief. Her heart felt weak. Her whole body seemed drained of blood and her nerves felt numb. Way Way curled up in bed, sick and miserable. The worst had happened. The tears that flowed were surely not from her eyes but from her heart.

Her eyes were shut but she could see the color of blood. As she recalled the color of her father's blood and compared it with

162

her own, she faced the excruciating truth about what had happened to her. Her choking heart beat on relentlessly. Not only did it not rest, it beat on faster and faster until great drops of perspiration rolled off her brow and mingled with her tears. Shaken to the core, she could not even begin to think of what it would be like to live with her husband in her condition.

She rehearsed over and over again how she would break the news to him. Trying to spare him suffering, she changed her speech again and again; she tried so hard she wanted to die. Between thinking of him and her illness she could find no rest. Finally, she could not think any more. She said to herself, Let whatever happens happen, and then she stopped.

After the commotion in her mind had ended, she felt a sadness so intense and uncontrollable that it was painful. Her mind cast about for relief and attached itself to one thought: that the only way to get any relief at all was to see everything as her karma, as her destiny, and to change her attitude accordingly. As she grew calmer and began to realize the truth of the Buddhist scriptures' analysis of pain and suffering, the trouble she could not face began to recede in importance. She began to get new insights into the nature of suffering in life, and to look at it in perspective. She could see that one went through different existences and that this existence was full of pain and trouble which could be overcome by meditating and avoiding fear.

"Mistress, your medicine."

At the sound of Meh Aye's voice, Way Way moved a little but could not open her eyes for a while. No matter how much medicine she took she had never thought of herself as an invalid, but now she accepted the fact that only sick people take medicine. She turned from her side onto her back and slowly opened her eyes.

Meh Aye noticed her worn out face and blurted out, "Oh, Mistress, don't you feel well?"

"No, no, I don't feel well." She sat up, took the medicine glass from the tray, and gulped down its contents. It occurred to her that now, at long last, she could act and feel like a sick person. She had waited long enough. This medicine was supposed to be taken an hour before meals, so this meant that Ko would be coming home for his lunch in an hour. She rose from her bed in a feeble manner and went down to have her bath. She was late in taking it this morning. In the bathroom, her hands shaking, she washed her stained handkerchief. As she dressed after her bath, she resolved not to spoil his meal, and to tell him only at the end of the day.

All through the afternoon, Way Way waited for the hours to pass. As she waited she tried to look strong. She studied her face for calmness, though inside she was trembling. Seeing her slow movements, U Saw Han assumed that the heat of the day had slowed her down and that she was not feeling as well as she had that morning.

Slowly the day turned to evening and the sky began to fill with bright, twinkling stars. Way Way sat on the sofa and gazed out the window at them, her heart beating insistently. Having eaten dinner, U Saw Han was listening to the radio. Way Way kept glancing at her watch; her bedtime was nine o'clock. U Saw Han bent over the radio as he listened to the news and said, "Way Way, it's nine o'clock, let's go upstairs."

In a reverie, Way Way woke with a start. She made her way slowly out of the room and up the stairs. Meh Aye followed her up with a pitcher of water. Way Way did not get undressed, but sat down on the chair. Meh Aye put the pitcher of water on the bedside table and left. A little later, hearing her husband's footsteps coming up, Way Way steadied herself. Drawing aside the curtain, he moved toward her and said, "Way, are you settling down?"

"Dear, please sit here for a while, I have something to tell you," she said in a trembling voice that did not sound like her. U Saw Han came close and put his arms around her and looked searchingly at her. Way Way turned her face away quickly to avoid his probing eyes.

U Saw Han was immediately alarmed and sat down on the chair, still hanging onto Way Way's hands. Way Way, not looking at him, said, "I didn't want to have to tell you, so I've suppressed it all day long. I coughed some blood today."

"Coughed blood? Coughed blood?" U Saw Han said in a terrified, quavering voice, thoroughly shocked. She drowned herself in that voice, wished that she could drown her body and mind in that voice.

"Oh my word, Way Way, what a thing to happen! We must call the doctor at once. Why didn't you tell me?" he said wringing his hands repeatedly.

Way Way sat in a daze, unable to move, as waves of heat washed over her.

"I've worried that this would happen from the time your father was still here. You must have thought then that I was too worried, too anxious." His voice was a murmur and a moan in her pounding ears. Her chest heaved.

"Way, tell me, . . . was it a lot of blood? Did you vomit blood?" Hearing the heartbreak in his voice, she wanted to cry and had to control her tears.

"Not a lot. Just a little when I coughed this morning, and a little bit when I coughed this evening. Just a very little."

U Saw Han looked at her as she sat with her head bowed. She was calm and steady and he stared at her as though he had never seen her before. Is she just not afraid, or is she very courageous? he marveled to himself. A huge wave of emotion rose within him. "We must not take this lightly, Way. We must send for the doctor," he said in a voice full of alarm as he let go of her hand and left the room.

Way Way was standing in the same spot when he came back up the stairs. Gently he took her by the hand and sat her down saying, "Way, sit down." She glanced once at U Saw Han's face and it seemed that it had aged instantly. She leaned back on the chair and rested her head, closing her eyes. U Saw Han paced the floor, waiting for the doctor. Heaving enormous sighs, he would stop at her side and then start again. The doctor and Maung Mya came hurrying up the stairs. As U Saw Han talked breathlessly and rapidly, the doctor looked with compassion at the quiet form of Way Way. As the needle was administered into the veins of her hand, Way Way made a face and bit her lip.

❖ 19 ❖

Only the vague outline of the river bank could be seen in the dim
light. The wind was cold and stung the flesh. Hta Hta stood
staring at the contours of the indistinct bank through the boat's
cabin. The glare of the electric light flooded the bow. She looked
at the dark silhouettes of the palm trees on the river bank, but her
thoughts were far away.

Since she had heard about Way Way's illness, not a day
passed that she did not worry about her sister. She pitied her with
all her heart. I can imagine how worried U Saw Han must be now,
she thought. He has been worried from the very beginning that
Way Way would catch the disease. He has had Way Way take every
precautionary measure. Now, despite his efforts, she contracted it.
Her luck is just bad, it really is.

She had had to guess from the weekly letters just how Way
Way was coming along. She had asked her to come to Rangoon
for treatment, but because the air was full of the rumors of war, U
Saw Han would not let her go. She was being treated by a local
doctor and was having injections every day. That much she knew.

Hta Hta's husband was being transferred to the Arakan, the
coastal area to the northwest, which would be far away from Way
Way. She had wanted to see her sister so much that she suddenly
decided to come unannounced. She had not been able to decide
with whom to stay when she got to Moulmeingyun. Should she
stay with Way Way or with her brother, Ko Nay U? She was only
going to be there for one night and wanted to spend as much time
as she could with Way Way.

She did not feel at ease with U Saw Han, and besides she felt
constrained by the fact that he had not invited her. Her heart was
heavy at the thought that Way Way's malady was similar to their
father's, with its on again off again character. She could not tell

166

the degree of the disease from the letters. "Today, I did not cough any blood. Yesterday there was a little. I'm better now," was all she would note in her letters. She would then write at length about other things. She often mentioned relatives, close and distant, who lived deeper in the countryside. Some were relatives on their father's side and some on their mother's. Hta Hta had to make an effort to recall who all these people were. Way Way was the only one who knew the branches of the family well. She had always been interested in keeping track of the family tree, and loved all her relatives with a warm and affectionate heart.

Hta Hta thought Way Way wrote about them so as not to forget them, for they never came to visit her now that she was married. It was difficult for them, and Hta Hta thought this was her way of keeping up with them. Hta Hta grieved that this was so. She guessed that Way Way led a lonely life as an invalid, with no visitors or visiting. She was moved to think how happy Way Way would be to see her.

When it was not yet light the boat had stopped at Bogale, and Hta Hta had been happy that Moulmeingyun was quite near. The hazy fog on the river began breaking up. On the horizon above the cleared area on shore a red, ruby-like glow appeared. The river turned crimson from the big red ball that seemed to hang over it. A flock of crows flew over the bank, glorying in the morning.

Hta Hta started getting her things ready, and as she tied up her bedroll the handle of the door turned and a large, heavyset woman appeared and said, "Hta Hta, are you up yet?"

"Come in, Daw Daw Tin. Yes, I've finished packing my things."

Daw Daw Tin was the owner of a cloth shop in Moulmeingyun, a single lady and very well liked by everybody. She had an excellent head of hair, which she wore wrapped around an ivory comb at the back of her head; the bun was a little too large and slanted to one side. Her eyebrows were pencilled black on her powdered face. She wore a freshly laundered blouse made of the best quality muslin and fastened by large buttons of singe topazes, a style that suited her. On one hand was a pair of ribbed gold bangles; the other hand held an ivory rosary. Around her waist was a Zimmai longyi, with the black band showing quite a bit. On

167

her feet were velvet slip-ons from Moulmein. A strong sandalwood fragrance filled the air around her.

"Oh, how happy poor Way Way will be to see you, Hta Hta! As for me, I haven't had a chance to see her since she got married. She doesn't come to the bazaar anymore, and it's difficult to visit her at her house. There is a watchman at the door, and people say that you have to have written permission to be admitted." Hta Hta listened smiling as she saw the disapproval on the speaker's frowning face. "I heard from Than Than and Yin Yin that they saw her once. They met as they were out walking and she was not allowed to talk for very long to them. She had lost a lot of weight since her miscarriage, and is quite, quite thin, they tell me. It doesn't appear to me that she is very happy. And such a restrictive lifestyle!"

"She chose him because she loved him. It's her choice, Daw Daw," Hta Hta retorted.

"Daw Thet comes regularly to the shop and gives me the news. She doesn't see Way Way often, either. She only gets to see her when Way Way is not well. Now it appears that she has your father's affliction. Oh dear, oh dear!"

Hta Hta focussed on thoughts she had already begun. Daw Daw Tin changed the subject to Ko Thet Hnan, and at the mention of her husband, Hta Hta's facial expression cleared. "Oh, you don't know how grateful I am to the doctor, and how much I owe him; I'll never forget him as long as I live. Everybody missed him so much when he left. You are so lucky to have him as your husband! This kind of man makes everybody happy . . . ."

"Oh, don't you believe it! Sometimes I get quite annoyed because he forgets to consider his own welfare and does too much. I really do get upset with him."

Daw Daw Tin listened to her and said, "When they're good, there's always something else the matter," and fell to thinking about the married state.

Hta Hta said, "The best kind of life is one like yours, Daw Daw," at which her companion broke into a peal of laughter.

"I'm not so sure about my blessed single state, Hta Hta. People will say that the best state to be is without a husband, with no worries, no demands, no master. Let me tell you truthfully that it is never good for a woman to be without a husband. It is the proper and fitting thing to have a man. Then why, you ask me, do

168

you choose to be so, and I will tell you that it just didn't turn out that way for me. Oh yes, Hta Hta. I've had my share of suitors. When I passed one up, another appeared, but nothing worked out in the end."

Hta Hta listened to her intently. There was no one else in the cabin, so they could talk frankly. Hta Hta enjoyed the frank and open disclosures of the spinster lady. She listened enthusiastically, and thought her to be most interesting and unusual.

"Then there was another of my suitors," she went on. "He had a great misfortune befall him and entered a monastery for what he thought would be a short while, but he didn't return because he was promoted to the priesthood. He remains there till this day. He is in Pokkoku, where he pursues his vocation, the extensive study of the scriptures." Hta Hta laughed loud and heartily at this story.

Daw Daw Tin smiled wryly, her head bowed. "'What she gets, she don't want, and what she don't get, she wants.' That's me, all right."

Hta Hta thought that even more hilarious. Knowing that she had a great sense of humor, Hta Hta teased, "There'll be another one yet, Daw Daw!"

Daw Daw Tin giggled as if someone had reached out and tickled her. Her large body shook with mirth. "Oh, it's long past time now. If I was not successful in my prime, it's out of the question now. Forget it! Now all my efforts go into fixing up my young nieces. If you know of any suitable young man, junior officer rank, honest and sincere, let me know, please. I'm worried about them and would like to see them properly settled."

As she laughed and wiped her face, Hta Hta's mind shifted to Way Way. She thought of a woman's life and the questions one asks concerning it. It seemed that there was no respite for Way Way. Any way you looked at it, it was unfortunate.

"Oh, we can already see Settway Hill," Daw Daw Tin said, standing up and looking over the prow of the boat.

The corrugated roofs of the godowns and the smokestacks of the rice mills came into view. Hta Hta stood at the window and the warm rays hit her face.

The Irrawaddy River sparkled and rippled with little waves. The boat's steamwhistle blew. Only after the boat had docked and she was climbing up the bank of the river was Hta Hta able to decide: she would stay at the old family house. With her suitcase and bedroll, she got on a rickshaw and headed straight for home. It seemed to her that she could see the big house as they turned off the main road. She looked up at the house next door, which was Way Way's. Just before she got there she had a sudden urge to stop and go in. The windows were open and the curtains down. There was only the watchman in front of the house and no one else was in sight. She passed on with a beating heart and told the rickshaw driver to stop when they came to the big house.

"Oh, Hta Hta!" cried Than Than as she ran out toward her. Hta Hta choked up. "Ko Nay U has gone to the countryside. Daw Thet has gone along to the paddy fields to check on them. Oh, Hta Hta . . . no letter, no warning of your coming! Way Way will be so excited and happy."

When they got inside the house, before she even sat down, Hta Hta asked, "How's Way Way?"

"She looks all right and doesn't stay in bed all the time. Now and then there is a little blood. I get to see her in the morning and in the evening when U Saw Han goes to the office. But she rests in the afternoons and no one is allowed to get in. When we want to know anything we just ask Meh Aye when she comes over."

"Well, Than Than, I think I'll go over now. I don't suppose U Saw Han has left for the office as yet. I'll talk to you at length tonight. When are Daw Thet and Ko Nay U coming back?" Hta Hta was already standing up, ready to leave.

"Are you leaving, Hta Hta? Ko Nay U and the others will be another three or four days. They wouldn't have left if they had known you were coming. And, oh yes, is it true, Hta Hta, that you are going to the Arakan?"

"Yes, we are moving, and that's why I have come to see Way Way. I'll be going now," said Hta Hta, continuing out of the door. "Let's talk about everything when I get back, okay?"

Than Than watched Hta Hta hurry off and groaned to herself, She's in for a shock.

Hta Hta pulled aside the door curtain and called "Way Way!" as she entered the house. There was no one in the sitting room. Way Way was in the dining room. She cried out happily, "Ma Ma Hta!" and came running out to her.

Hta Hta could hardly bear to look at the thin little Way Way she saw. She was down to half her usual size. Hta Hta's heart beat wildly as her spirits sank; she smiled cordially, but her eyes were moist with feelings she could not suppress. Way Way came running and, taking her sister's hand in hers, squeezed it tightly. Hta Hta in turn tried to do the same, but could only feel the boney little fingers covered with skin. They had no warmth in them.

Way Way's eyes glittered and overflowed with joy, but if you looked carefully you could see that they were sunken. Her face looked very pretty as she smiled dazzlingly. "Oh, Hta Hta, I am so happy to see you! You didn't write that you were coming. I dreamed about you just last night. You and I were shopping like mad. It looked like the bazaar in Rangoon."

"Hush little one, you'll tire yourself. Speak slowly," said Hta Hta as she guided her to the sofa. The two of them sat very close together. Way Way did not realize that she was tired, but her voice revealed it.

"Ah yes, since I'm going to be moving to the Arakan and wanted to see you before I left, I made up my mind suddenly and had no time to write. And where is U Saw Han?"

Way Way could not fill her eyes enough with the sight of Hta Hta. She felt a tremendous surge of strength welling up in her. "He's upstairs. He'll be down soon. Meh Aye has filled out and is nice and plump, not like before. Ma Ma Hta, you're looking well too. Did you get to see Ko Nay U? Daw Thet was not well a while ago. Than Than is pregnant." Way Way chattered on incessantly, like a parrot. She enjoyed talking.

While Way Way talked, Hta Hta studied her intently. The pallor of her face showed up against the dark red cardigan she wore. Her neck was thin and her throat looked elongated and moved up and down visibly as she spoke.

"Ko Nay U and Daw Thet have gone to the countryside and won't be back for a day or two. I only saw Than Than. I put down my luggage and came straight here. I didn't even take the time to talk with Than Than. And how about you? How are you? Do you feel all right?"

Way Way looked surprised. "Oh, I didn't even know they had gone." She sat silent for a while. Then, as if remembering something, she said, "I feel fine. It's been a month since there's been any blood." There were sounds of footsteps coming down the stairs and both of them looked in that direction.

"Oh, it's Hta Hta!" said U Saw Han in a bright and cheerful manner and came forward quickly. "I was wondering who was talking to Way Way. And how are you? I hear you are moving to Sandoway."

Hta Hta watched the cheerful, smiling face of U Saw Han as he talked and noticed the lines on his haggard face. She guessed that actually he was a very unhappy man underneath. "We will be moving next month. I wanted to see Way Way, so I came home for a quick visit, just overnight. I'm returning tomorrow."

"Oh, why so soon? Now that you're here, why not stay longer? And have you seen Thakin Nay U yet?" he asked. U Saw Han was smiling and laughing.

Returning his smile, Hta Hta answered, "Thakin Nay U isn't at home. He went to the countryside. Only Than Than is home."

"Way, have you had your milk? Well, come on Hta Hta, let's have some breakfast," said U Saw Han, rising and motioning them to the dining room. Way Way said, "I've finished breakfast," leading her by the hand. U Saw Han noticed that Way Way's little face was all perked up and happy at Hta Hta's being there, and it pleased him very much that she had come. Then he looked at Way Way's place and said, "Way Way, you haven't finished!"

"Oh yes, I have. I've had my milk and eaten my bread. It's just the coffee I haven't finished," and she picked up her cup.

"Sit down, Ma Ma Hta," she said.

Hta Hta sat opposite U Saw Han and Maung Mya brought out plates and cups for her. She noticed something strange, but said nothing.

"Sit down, Way," she said.

Way Way finished drinking what was in the cup and gave it to Maung Mya. She pulled up a chair and sat next to Hta Hta.

U Saw Han seemed as if he did not want to discuss Way Way's health in front of her. He talked about many things, but not about that. Finally he said, "Well, Hta Hta, I've got to go to work. You keep visiting, and stay for lunch. Way Way has to sleep after our meal. So shall we have lunch at, say, 12 o'clock? All right?" He left to go out. Way Way rose and accompanied him to the front door. Hta Hta heard him remind her not to forget her medicine and not to tire herself; then Meh Aye came up to her and said, "Have you come to visit?"

"Yes, just for a short while. My, haven't you put on weight! Way Way is as thin as a rail."

"Oh, of course she's thin. She's not allowed to eat the things she wants to." Meh Aye was speaking her mind. Then fearing that Way Way would overhear her, she looked over her shoulder, lowered her voice, and went on.

Way Way came back into the room. Meh Aye wiped her face and smiled at Hta Hta.

"Meh Aye and the others are all nice and plump," Hta Hta said.

Way Way gave Meh Aye a smile and said to her sister, "Well, Ma Ma Hta, let's go upstairs and have a good chat. We'll have our baths later," and took her upstairs.

Hta Hta had not been upstairs since Way Way was first married. She looked around her as she followed her. Like the altar room, the outside room was neat and tidy. It was furnished with a deck chair and a thick rug; otherwise the floor was bare and polished. There were two bedrooms. Way Way pulled the drape to the one in back and called to her sister over her shoulder. Hta Hta looked upset as she stood outside the room.

"Do you sleep here?" She saw a single bed, a table and a dresser, and some boxes and trunks. Hta Hta pulled the other drape and poked her head into the second bedroom. She saw an elegantly appointed room with a great double bed, a dressing table, wardrobes, and other furnishings that Way Way had brought with her when she married. Hta Hta was very upset but hid her feelings as she let the drape down and went into the smaller back room. Way Way was sitting on the bed. She was at peace with herself and quiet within, innocent and tender.

"I moved over to this room when I became ill. It's really the guest bedroom. I decided to sleep here with Meh Aye."

Hta Hta turned her face away so that Way Way would not see the expression on her face. She went over to sit on the deck chair. At breakfast she had noticed that both she and U Saw Han had the best china with the gold flowers, while Way Way's cup and saucer were plain white, thick, institutional ware, the kind used in hospitals. Again she felt hurt and upset. She could no longer restrain herself and asked Way Way, "Are you eating from separate plates and things?"

Way Way smiled at Hta Hta and nodded her head. Her face was as calm and innocent as before. "The plates I use have to be boiled every time I use them so I purposely chose the thick sturdy kind. The other things are too fragile and will break easily."

Hta Hta controlled herself and listened without emotion. Way Way did not change her manner in the least, so Hta Hta had to carry on as though nothing was wrong. In fact she had to go along with Way Way's acceptance of it and said, "Good. That's the only way to kill the germs. You keep things sterilized and clean that way." Hta Hta knew that the precautions were necessary, but in her heart she felt differently. It wounded her to see her sister treated like a pariah in her own home. Nevertheless, she kept up a good appearance and did not reveal how she felt. She said lightly, "The doctor told you to do all this, of course."

"Oh no. I did it myself. Ko even protested at first, but I thought it was best. Don't you? Isn't it best?" She was asking the question.

Hta Hta went along with her and said, "Yes, of course it is best."

"I dreaded the idea of sleeping alone. But I don't feel I should sleep with anyone while I am sick. I will sleep by myself as long as I'm not well." Way Way explained all this very sweetly and cheerfully, but Hta Hta felt choked with emotion. Way Way's smile was sincere and honest, without a shred of bitterness or self-pity. It was the smile of a person genuinely at peace with herself.

Hta Hta noticed the calm and peace within Way Way and saw that she had been skillful in quieting her mind. Since returning from Sagaing it seemed that she had achieved this inner strength that admitted defeat in the physical part of life, and now accepted her lot calmly. She was impressed beyond words. She marvelled that Way Way was neither afraid of her illness nor, seemingly, feeling depressed.

"So what does the doctor say about the illness? What is his opinion? Does he think you are responding to the treatment? Does he think you are getting better? Wouldn't you like to come down to Rangoon and have X-rays taken? My husband has been trying to get you admitted into the General Hospital in Rangoon. What do you think? Do you want to go?"

174

Way Way thought for a while but didn't seem to consider the matter very long or deeply, for she replied abruptly and very fluently. "The doctor says that the treatment for this illness is the same whether it is here or there or anywhere else. He says that here he can attend to me at any time of day or night, and give me special attention. Now that there is no blood, I take it that I am better. I really don't want to go to a hospital. I'll just settle for the treatment here."

"By this time, the doctor must have worn a trail to your house as deep as a ditch," said Hta Hta.

"Talk about a deep trail! Don't even start! You wouldn't believe how often I see the doctor. When I was first married, I saw the doctor perhaps once a week. Now he comes every day, and the injections are countless. There isn't a spot on my body that isn't punctured, sometimes many times over. I can't bear the thought of needles. I don't even want to look at a sewing needle." She laughed as she said this. Hta Hta felt so sorry for her, and looked at her with deep compassion. As she stopped laughing, Way Way composed herself and said, "This reminds me of what Daddy used to say," and she stopped.

"What did Daddy say?" asked Hta Hta.

"He used to say that this illness is for rich people with enough money to pay by the bushel for a cure. Oh, it's very expensive to say the least," she said.

"Yes, of course, one has to spend money to obtain results and get well again. What about being tired? How are you faring? Are you still getting exhausted easily?"

"Well, I get tired at times, but then at times I don't. I don't keep daily track of it. I just take it as it comes or doesn't come."

"You say you aren't tired, but your voice sounds tired. Come, dear, come and sit on this recliner and I'll sit on the bed."

"Oh no," said Way Way. "I don't want to sit on that recliner. I don't want to look like an invalid. No, no. You stay where you are."

Hta Hta frowned. She said, "It's not important whether you look like an invalid or not. It's just a matter of being more comfortable and get more rest."

Way Way laughed out aloud. Then she was about to say something, but burst out laughing again instead. Hta Hta looked at her. Then Way Way said, "Whenever I sit on that chair, both he

175

and Meh Aye ask me if I don't feel well, and get anxious. They never ask that if they see me on any other chair. So I suppose I look like a rather sick person in that chair."

Hta Hta let out a deep sigh. She was tired and although she did not want to say it, said, "So what's wrong if you do look sick? The important thing is for you to get as much rest as you can."

Way Way did not say a word in reply. She looked at Hta Hta as though she had wanted to say something but thought better of it. She rose from the bed and said, "Well, let's have our baths and get freshened up." She called out for Meh Aye.

After sending Meh Aye to get fresh clothes from her suitcase, Hta Hta went downstairs with Meh Aye to have her bath. She then returned upstairs to see Way Way grinding some sandalwood paste for her. "Oh, don't do that. Let it be," she said to Way Way.

"Oh, it's just a little, for your face, so it will be as fresh as possible. There is enough ground already for your body," she replied. Weak and unwell as she was, she would not have it any other way than to grind some thanaka for her sister who had come to be with her. Hta Hta would rather she rested and not exert herself unduly. Hta Hta finished her preparations, and in return she ground some fresh thanaka for Way Way while she was having her bath.

"Oh, Ma Ma Hta, why did you do this?" said Way Way. Pursing her lips she smeared the paste on her face and chatted merrily all the while. Her range of subjects was wide. She talked about her mother's life being truly peaceful and free of the worries of existence. She talked about how she tried to practice the Law and precepts as her mother did. It had brought her real happiness and she had almost attained the state of mindfulness herself. Then she talked about events in the town and community that she had heard about. Hta Hta stared at Way Way's thin little body and her protruding ribs. She kept averting her eyes in silent distress. Way Way was worrying about Hta Hta. In the Arakan she would not be able to get the food she was used to eating, and Way Way advised her to stock up on ngapi and salted fish to take with her.

Hta Hta had to raise her voice to get Way Way to slow down. Constantly discouraged by U Saw Han from talking, she made up for it when he was not there. "You're so talkative! Rest a while, will you?" After lunch, for which U Saw Han returned, Hta Hta crossed over to the big house and then came back later in the afternoon. She stayed for dinner and went back to the big house to sleep.

In her mind Hta Hta had built up a picture of Way Way's daily routine, the way she ate and drank and sat and moved. She sat at one end of the table with her own plate and spoon, eating her food all by herself. She did everything according to the schedule set by her husband, taking her medicines morning and night. Her appearance was always impeccable, she never complained, and she appeared to maintain a great inner strength. Hta Hta was only able to see things from the sidelines, and it distressed her that she could do nothing about U Saw Han's overly concerned attitude and his excessive care.

"She wouldn't last long like this," she said to Than Than that night, tears rolling down her cheeks. She could not sleep a wink that night, thinking about Way Way and feeling frustrated at not being able to do anything to help her. She kept thinking of solutions, and every time she thought, she choked up and could not breathe.

The next day Way Way did not feel very well. Her cough was bad and U Saw Han said, "I think Way Way talked too much yesterday. Her condition does not allow her to talk too much, Hta Hta." and left for work.

Hta Hta had to keep Way Way from talking, so she chatted to her sister about this and that in order to fill up the time without her talking and to help her be more relaxed and comfortable. She added words of encouragement as she went along, to keep her from feeling discouraged. She convinced Way Way to lie down beside her as she talked.

Later that evening Way Way appeared a little depressed now and then as she sat quietly by and listened to U Saw Han and her sister talk at length.

"Hey, young lady, have you taken your medicine?" U Saw Han would throw out at her, and she would smile and nod her head.

Before it got dark, Hta Hta returned from the big house. Facing Way Way, she said, "I'm going now." Way Way nodded. "Don't exert yourself too much. Rest as much as you can." She nodded again, smiling and looking intently into Hta Hta's eyes.

❖ 20 ❖

Way Way heard the sound of a gong coming from the road. Her heart went faint as she strained to hear better. U Saw Han went to the window and listened, hands on his hips.

"Hear ye, hear ye . . . all men! All paper money of all denominations must be brought to an office of the Burmese Government to be stamped with the seal of the Government of Burma. All paper money—1 kyat, 10 kyats, 100 kyats, 10000 kyats—must be turned in. Anyone using money not stamped with the seal of the Government of Burma will be punished severely for the offense."

His face registering worry, U Saw Han returned to Way Way's side and breathed a loud sigh. Then, changing his expression to one of studied amusement, he said laughingly to Way Way, "Perhaps that was by order of Thakin Nay U."

"I hear that he has not returned form Bassein yet. According to Than Than, he went to Bassein to meet the Burma Independence Army or something."[58]

Thakin Nay U had in fact gone secretly to meet the Burma Independence Army before the British colonial government evacuated, having made clandestine plans beforehand. As soon as the British government withdrew, the Thakin Party immediately took over the town of Moulmeingyun. They seized power and passed all kinds of rules and ordinances, confusing the populace

---

58. The Burma Independence Army (BIA) was founded shortly before the outbreak of the Pacific War by the Japanese and a group of Thakin Party members, headed by Aung San, known as the Thirty Comrades. The occupation government did not fulfill the hopes of the Thakin Party, however, and most BIA supporters abandoned it and the Japanese cause when the BIA was disbanded in July 1942.

no end. In the dislocation that followed the withdrawal of the central colonial government, U Saw Han had been left more or less stranded in Moulmeingyun. As soon as they had taken over, the thakins had gone to U Saw Han's office and demanded all the money belonging to the "white British government." U Saw Han had handed over all of the firm's money in his custody.

After the takeover, U Saw Han just stayed home and hardly ventured out of the house. Because he had no more ties with the outside world, and because of Way Way's illness, he was very troubled about the future. He worried whether the medicine would last and whether new supplies would be available. The doctor had not left with the retreating government, and U Saw Han realized how fortunate that was for them. The doctor was U Saw Han's only real social contact; he was keeping a low profile.

Way Way had heard about the Japanese bombing of Rangoon, and felt relieved that Hta Hta and her family were now far away from the city. When she learned of the loss of lives and the destruction of property in Rangoon, she was very distressed; indeed, the news affected her health and she suffered a relapse. The old Indian cook had left to go with the streams of Indians who were trying to return to India any way they could. She had to make do with Maung Mya, and had to supervise the kitchen and its activities herself.

She used her limited energy to keep the house running according to her husband's Western preferences. She tried to keep the kind of schedule he liked, stocked up on his favorite brands of whiskey and cigarettes, and bought soap, toothpaste, English Tea biscuits, tinned butter, and other items by the case against the day they would be no longer available. U Saw Han would never smoke the local brand of Burmese cheroots or eat sticky rice for breakfast. Knowing that imported goods would stop coming one day soon, she felt very sorry for her husband.

The only way they got any news of the town was when the doctor came each evening. The thakins were in control, sitting in their headquarters with revolvers sticking out at their waists. The townspeople were alarmed and very tense. After giving Way Way her injection, the doctor and U Saw Han would sit with their whiskey glasses, their heads close together whispering to each other. There was no more whiskey available in the shops now. The doctor only got to drink it at U Saw Han's.

179

The Burma Independence Army came to town. Ko Nay U was not with them, which worried poor Way Way. She heard from a different source that he had gone with the main army to Upper Burma. The Japanese flag was flying over the office of the new Burmese government headquarters. They were calling the Japanese "master" . . . in English.

Way Way had only heard that the Japanese were there in town, but had not seen any of them. Then news drifted up from Rangoon that the Japanese were in the habit of slapping the faces of the Burmese. U Saw Han had a clandestine radio. Just thinking of the Japanese sent cold shivers down people's spines.

Meanwhile Than Than had given birth in Ko Nay U's absence. Way Way wanted to go over to see her. She wanted to get news as well. In order to do this, she had to put on the appearance of feeling bright and perky. But presenting a cheerful countenance and brisk ways was exhausting, and she had to hide and rest again. After a great show of hearty behavior, she approached U Saw Han and said, "Dear, I'd like to go and see Than Than and the baby, please."

He immediately looked disapproving and said, "Can you walk all that way? You'll tire yourself out." He looked her up and down searchingly, as though examining her fitness.

Way Way said with great animation, "Oh, it's not far. I can walk there easily."

U Saw Han looked at her doubtfully. She smiled despite her panting heart. U Saw Han shook his head saying, "When you get there you'll have to be climbing stairs. Don't go, Way Way."

"It's not upstairs. Birthing always has to take place downstairs. I'll come back as soon as I've seen them. It will only be a little while," she said brightly, trying to convey lots of energy, her eyes full of eagerness and hope, her heart beating anxiously.

U Saw Han could not but give his consent, against his better judgment.

Way Way's face lit up with joy. Her hands trembled. U Saw Han accompanied her to the gate. He stood looking at her little figure, thin as bamboo, walking slowly along with Meh Aye following behind. He let out a heavy sigh and turned back into the house.

"Oh, here come Way Way and Meh Aye!" cried Daw Thet joyfully as she ran out to meet them.

180

Way Way did not usually leave her house and had not realized how weak she really was. She was extremely exhausted by the walk. She saw Than Than lying on a raised platform-like bed in the dining room. Her body was bright with turmeric, and her head was turbanned with a cloth. Way Way lifted a cloth cover from a four cornered basket and looked at the tiny, red-faced new baby. "Than Than, doesn't the baby look like Ko Nay U?"

Than Than gave her a full smile, exposing all her teeth, and said, very pleased, "He didn't want a little daughter, he wanted a son." Way Way went and sat by her on the bed. Than Than continued, "Oh, Way Way, why did you come tiring yourself out like this. I'm fine." The smell of turmeric was overwhelming and Way Way wanted to cough. Daw Thet was talking about how worried she was about Ko Nay U. They only knew that he had gone off to Upper Burma with the main army, but had no idea where he actually was.

Hearing someone at the front door, Daw Thet went to investigate. "Why, Po Myaing, you've actually come back to us. What a great disappearing trick you did. Wherever have you been all this while?" she exclaimed loudly in her surprise.

Way Way got up quickly from where she was sitting, "Uncle, Uncle! Po Myaing!" she called as she came out of the room towards him.

When Po Myaing saw Way Way, he was wide-eyed with astonishment. "Goodness gracious, Way Way child, what's the matter, what has happened to you, little one?" he asked, his voice showing emotion. Way Way went up close to him. He touched her shoulder and she could not keep the tears from coming to her eyes. "Sit down, sit down child. I didn't know of your marriage until after I returned. I heard of your father's death when I was in Taungdwingyi, just before I left for Popa. I've been all over the country and returned shortly before the country began falling apart. I got back to Kyaikgyi just before the British retreated."

He had given Way Way a chair, and when he finished speaking he sat down opposite her. Uncle Po Myaing was her favorite uncle on her father's side. He was her father's cousin, and about the same age as U Saw Han. Before Way Way married, he had followed a doctor of Burmese indigenous medicine to Upper Burma as an apprentice, and no one had heard from him all this time. Before he left, he had practiced medicine in Kyaikpi, where he had lived with his older sister. He was a bachelor and did not have a wife or children.

"Uncle, how could you stay away so long?" asked Way Way with much feeling.

"I took a long time because I followed my master until I learned all I needed from him. Now tell me about yourself, little one. Goodness, you look terrible. What is your ailment, child?"

"What ailment but Maung Po Thein's of course." put in Daw Thet at this juncture. "She coughs blood, and is taking injections for it." She continued, "Than Than has just given birth, and Ko Nay U is not here. He went with the army and has not come back. It's a little girl. So sweet, . . ." and on she went.

"I see . . . I see . . . ," said the uncle.

Then U Po Myaing's questions were directed toward Way Way and her ailment. His interest was medical, and he saw her through a doctor's eyes. Way Way was the kind of person who, when asked about her health, always said, "I'm fine. I'm all right."

"Oh uncle, the injections don't make me feel any better, but I have to just keep on taking them till I die," she groaned, as what she felt in her heart came out.

Daw Thet's face fell as she looked at Way Way; she was greatly disturbed.

"What nonsense! If they don't help, stop taking them, child. You are all so modern, taking the latest medications. If I were your doctor, I would not even use medicine. I'd cure you with the right nutrition alone. The right diet is all that is needed. How about it, Uncle will take you on. No needles, only proper diet."

Way Way wanted to entrust her life into her beloved uncle's hands. She, more than anybody else, knew how desperately thin she had become and how much more tired she felt every day as she took the injections. They did not help at all and she longed to change the treatment. Some time ago, when her father was still alive, her uncle Po Myaing had once had tuberculosis himself and been cured by diet and nutrition . . . with no injections. So he had first hand experience. U Po Myaing was a physician who prescribed diet without medicine, as opposed to a physician who healed through medicines. He had returned from Taungdwingyi a picture of health, large-limbed, muscular, and healthy. It was very reassuring. The thought that she would never have the chance to have him heal her—would die before that would be allowed—made her ache with quiet desperation.

"Well then, child . . . . How about it? Will you let me cure you? I will take full responsibility."

Daw Thet sat gazing into space with a frown. Uncle Po Myaing looked at Way Way's dejected face and, not getting an answer, said spontaneously, "Child, stop taking those injections . . . I will stay here with you until you are cured. I will not go back to my village until you are well again. How about it? What do you say?"

Way Way shook her head and, not looking at her uncle, said, "It will never do; just leave me to my fate," and got up and left.

His eyes widened with amazement as he stood watching her leave, when Daw Thet came over to him, tapped him on the shoulder, and furtively started whispering in his ear.

"Than Than, I'm leaving now," Way Way said. "When Ko Nay U comes back, let me know through Meh Aye. There's been no letter from Mother, and I don't know how Ma Ma Hta is. I haven't heard from her at all." So Way Way took her leave.

Than Than was aware of the exhaustion in Way Way's voice and looked at her with a heavy heart. "The roads are blocked and the lines of communication have been cut off at the moment. But things will get straightened out soon, then letters will get through. Ko Nay U will come back soon; I'll let you know as soon as he does. Well, go dear, go now."

Way Way turned and left Than Than. She came into the sitting room and saw Daw Thet and U Po Myaing talking softly with their heads together. They stopped abruptly when they saw her. Uncle Po Myaing looked as if he understood her now, having been filled in by Daw Thet. "Are you leaving, child? Yes, yes, go in peace." His voice, subdued and controlled, went straight to her heart. The short time she had had to meet him made it all the more difficult to leave. She thought, He knows about me, and could hardly control the tight feeling in her chest. Daw Thet accompanied her to the door and said, "Keep well, my dear," on parting. She managed to get home without mishap.

U Saw Han noticed her downcast face immediately. Something has upset her. I wonder what it can be, he thought, alarmed. "Is Than Than all right, Way?" he asked.

Way Way went straight to the sofa and sat down. She could not speak at once. After a while, she said, "Yes, she is all right."

"Who else did you see there?"

She glanced at U Saw Han's face and wondered, Should I tell him I saw Uncle Po Myaing, or shouldn't I? She felt like telling him so she said, "I saw Uncle Po Myaing."

"Who's he? Is he the medical man you told me about?"

Way Way nodded. They looked at each other. U Saw Han knew she had something to tell him and wondered what it could be.

"Tell me, what did the physician say?" U Saw Han asked, averting his eyes.

Way Way looked at him and, after thinking for a while, smiled a lopsided smile as though she were about to cry. "The physician said he'd like to cure me, of course."

U Saw Han laughed, "Ha ha ha!" Though she had expected this reaction, she winced as it cut deeply into her. "So what did you tell him, Way?" U Saw Han looked at her and tried to guess her feelings. He studied her to see if by any chance she had reverted to wanting Burmese medicine. He was reassured not to see any signs of elation or expectation on her part. She looked at him coldly and without animation, as though utterly drained. He could not bear this look, and had to turn his eyes elsewhere.

"I told him to leave me to my fate. That's what I told him." Way Way lowered her eyes and listened to the beating of her heart.

U Saw Han heard the edge of sadness in her voice and his face fell. He came and stood before of her. "Way Way, what are you saying? Do you mean you don't like the doctor's treatment?"

"It's not that," she replied pleadingly. He detected the signs of submission in her subdued voice. The sound of her voice welled up like a wave in his heart and he felt wretched.

He had bought up all the medicine he could before the English left. He had cultivated a social relationship with the doctor and dreaded the possibility that he might not come. He acted as if it would be a direct threat to her life if the doctor were not close at hand. So he lived in fear and anxiety. He was convinced that only Western-trained doctors could cure tuberculosis. Certainly, he knew, no Burmese doctor could. Although he had entrusted Way Way to the doctor's hands, he knew the disease was terminal. Day after day there was no improvement, and he saw her deteriorate in front of his very eyes. He had his own thoughts about it. He reasoned that she was not improving because the disease had reached a stage of buildup that made it difficult to expect any improvement, and that the only reason she had been able to hold out this long was the doctor and the injections. However, he could not understand why there was not even a hint of improvement.

He became overwrought largely because he now stayed home all day, with nothing else to do but observe Way Way. She was his sole interest in life at the moment. He sighed a lot as he observed her. She did not behave like a patient, but was always on her feet looking neat and well groomed. She was quiet and peaceful, centered within herself, and his heart ached to see her so. "Who else but the doctor can cure you, Way Way? Burmese medicine is so unhygienic. Their medicines are cheap concoctions made from roots and leaves ground with a mortar and pestle like Indian curry spices. What effect could they possibly have? English medicines are known and used the world over. How cleanly their medicines are made, in labs untouched by human hands! You can see for yourself from the injection vials how reliable, how scientific the process is . . . and it's not cheap, either."

U Saw Han had no faith in indigenous medicine because it was weighed and sold in powder form, and cost next to nothing. He trusted English medicine whether or not it brought results. He trusted it and did not care about the cost. He believed in what he believed in.

Listening to him quietly, Way Way half-believed what he said. He said, "Isn't that so, Way?" and she nodded her head. Then he sat down in a chair facing her.

It was getting dark. Way Way got up and moved slowly toward the dining room. She sat at her place at the dining table at the correct time. Spoonful by spoonful she began on her chicken broth. She broke off a couple of pieces of bread, dipped them into a half-boiled egg, and ate. She then went silently up the stairs.

U Saw Han sat thinking of Way Way as he drank his whiskey. His thoughts stretched out in a long, ragged line. Pictures of Way Way when they were first married appeared before his eyes. Then images of her present condition came crowding in, confusing him. To drown out these later images he drank glass after glass, far into the still hours of night. He got up. Glancing at the dining table, with Maung Mya standing by and waiting for him to eat, he shook his head in the negative and went upstairs. He was careful not to make any noise and went quietly, swaying from side to side. Before entering his room he gently moved aside the curtain hanging over Way Way's door and looked in. Inside the mosquito net he saw his wife's sleeping form dimly in the moonlight, and his heart fluttered. Turning away abruptly, he went into his own room.

❖ 21 ❖

Way Way sat at her dressing table and looked at her reflection in the mirror. Her usually pale complexion was now sallow. Her once rounded cheeks were hollow and her face haggard. Her lips were white. Moving her eyes from her face to her arms, she saw how tiny and bony they had become; one could wrap thumb and forefinger around her wrist with plenty of room to spare. She had just finished her bath and was sitting with her longyi hitched up under her arms. Anxious lest U Saw Han see her, she glanced often at the door as she loosened her longyi and patted freshly ground sandalwood paste on her shoulders and chest. She could not help noticing her prominently protruding ribs. The spaces between the ribs were concave and covered only with skin. Her bony frame reminded her of a skeleton.

Meh Aye stood behind her rubbing the sandalwood paste on her back, hardly daring to raise her eyes toward the mirror in, which she could see Way Way's reflection. She was unable to ignore it altogether, however, and was greatly disturbed by the bony reflection. Meh Aye was the only person who had seen Way Way's body since she had fallen ill.

Way Way slowly pulled the longyi back under her arms. She turned slowly to face Meh Aye and pulled the hem of her longyi up to her knees. Meh Aye rubbed the thanaka paste lightly on Way Way's thin calves. Her legs looked like those of a chicken or duck, with no warmth emanating from them; there was no muscle or flesh. Meh Aye said, "Daw Thet said she would get a piece of sandalwood from the bazaar. May I go over and get it after we've finished here? Would you like me to tell her anything?"

"Yes. Ask her to tell my brother not to listen to the radio."[59] Way Way had heard that Ko Nay U had returned, but she had not yet seen him. He had gone to Upper Burma with the Burma Independence Army and had returned just before the new government under Dr. Ba Maw was formed by the Japanese occupation authorities. Ko Nay U now realized that hoping to attain independence upon the arrival of the Japanese had been a mistake. His political aspirations had been dashed, for he had seen with his own eyes how the Japanese soldiers behaved, and had already started to hate them. There were already people whispering that they would have to fight the Japanese to get them out.

Daw Thet had told Way Way of Ko Nay U's feelings about the Japanese. And though she was not political herself, Way Way would send messages to Ko Nay U by anyone she could. Way Way gave her message to Meh Aye in a whisper, because she was so tired. She had been weakened by the effort of dressing, but the whispering also conveyed a sense of secrecy. She made an effort to talk in a natural-sounding tone only to her husband.

"Mistress, Maung Mya says he could not get a chicken from the market for your supper. He wants to know if he should use some tinned meat from the larder."

Way Way nodded her head to solve the problem quickly. She was so tired of chicken broth, even though it was the only food that kept her alive. Any mention of the word "chicken" made her flesh crawl. She could hardly swallow the soup she daily brought to her reluctant mouth.

She turned to the mirror and brushed her eyebrows with a small brush. She stopped to rest when she was done. She took some deep breaths, timed and regular, and then continued with her usual routine. She took some talcum powder in one cupped hand and applied it under her clothes to her body. She felt refreshed by its fragrance, but she was again tired from the exertion. She moved around as slowly as she could, and was forced to rest often. She dressed with many layers of clothing to make it appear as if she were afraid of catching cold and was

_____

59. Radios were strictly controlled by the Japanese, and listening to them on any but the approved frequencies was strictly forbidden and severely punished.

keeping herself warm. She only felt secure after she had put on a sweater and a jacket. When it was hot, she wore a long-sleeved cotton blouse under her loose, thin muslin jacket. She had also stopped wearing silky longyis that clung to her figure.

Way Way was like a tree in the hot season that had lost its leaves and stood with stark, bare branches. She took great pains every day to look her best; her body grew thinner and thinner. She knew she was dying and she had no fear for herself or of the future life and its consequences. The one thing she tried to do now was to spare her husband's feelings as much as she could and make it less difficult for him.

Meh Aye stood behind her, helping whenever necessary. She held out the sleeves so that Way Way could slip her arms in easily. Way Way stuck out her thin, bone-like arm, but it was really too heavy for her to move. Meh Aye saw this and caught her breath. She appeared so tired from the effort of dressing that Meh Aye's heart pounded to think of it.

When all her efforts at dressing were over, Way Way looked at her watch and found it was four o'clock and almost time for the doctor to come by. She forced herself to stand up and slowly and feebly made her way down the stairs, one step at a time. Without betraying how much effort she was expending, Way Way went toward U Saw Han, who put down the book he was reading and got up from the sofa. Stretching out his hand, he sat her down next to him.

"Way Way, it doesn't look like you have a fever this evening. You look refreshed to me. Did you have a wash?"

Way Way's heart was beating fast and she was too exhausted to reply, so she smiled and nodded and it passed off undetected.

U Saw Han looked at her longyi, which bore a design of white trailing stems and blossoms over a deep red background, and said, "Your longyi becomes you very much, Way Way." As was his habit, he praised and admired what she wore. He looked at her, completely absorbed in her. He saw her beauty and did not see how she actually looked. "How are you today, my Way?"

Way Way exerted herself to say in a normal tone, "Much improved, dear."

He nodded his head gently. If you looked carefully, you would see pain and anxiety in the depths of his eyes.

Casting about to keep up the conversation, Way Way licked her parched lips with her tongue and said, "Dear, it's your bath time."

As U Saw Han rose from his seat, the white-turbanned Punjabi doctor appeared through the curtained doorway. After greeting the doctor, U Saw Han said, "Anything different in the news, doctor?"

"Yes, there is. There is a new government set up in Rangoon, I hear." He spoke half in English and half in Burmese as he recounted the news.

U Saw Han was relieved to hear that a government had been established. The local thakin-run government was too disorganized and its rules too disorderly for U Saw Han's peace of mind. He did not, however, dare to criticize it. He was frightened of the pistols the thakins wore on their hips.

The doctor came up to Way Way and, taking a thin wrist, started feeling her pulse. "Are you feeling any less tired?" he asked.

Way Way smiled and nodded her head. "It's all right." When the doctor released her hand, U Saw Han excused himself and went to take his bath. Way Way and the doctor then went into the dining room. Maung Mya was preparing the hot and cold water as needed. "Doctor, is it to be in my arm or in my buttocks?"

The doctor shook his head and said, "In the buttocks." Way Way went towards the couch that had been moved into the dining room for this purpose.

"Did you send Meh Aye on an errand, mistress?" asked Maung Mya, knowing that Meh Aye had to be present when the injections were taking place. Way Way nodded and said in a weary voice, "Never mind, it isn't necessary." Maung Mya finished the preparations and left the room. Way Way stretched out slowly on the couch and looked at the needle in the doctor's hand. Her muscles always tensed when she was about to have a shot.

The doctor laughed and chatted as he approached. Way Way turned on her side and shut her eyes. This is the most painful moment, she thought as she braced herself for it, but her legs trembled and her mouth twisted. Way Way did not breathe until the needle was withdrawn and then took in one huge gulp of air, contorting her face as she did so. She was so exhausted by it all

190

that she found herself praying this would be her last shot. The doctor massaged the spot with his palm and it hurt so much she felt as though her bones would break. Way Way remained on the couch, numb with pain and exhaustion.

U Saw Han returned from his bath, bent down over her and asked, "Does it still hurt, Way?"

Way Way shook her head, her face looking as if she would either cry or laugh.

"It's just a little while, Way. Come, let's go." Lifting her by the shoulders so as not to hurt, he helped her up. As she leaned on him she had a sudden irresistible desire to be close against his chest and within his encircling arms. She realized that she should not be so close to him, and swallowed hard as she stood apart. It had been a long time since she had been in his arms.

Devoid of sensibility, with feeble steps she followed U Saw Han and the doctor into the front room. Sitting on the sofa and leaning back, she was overwhelmed with a sense of enormous sadness. Large tears formed in her eyes and she took a handkerchief to wipe them. U Saw Han was about to sit near the doctor but he noticed her and came back and said, "What's wrong with your eyes, Way?"

She rubbed them on purpose and said with a muffled voice, "Oh, it's nothing. They're just itchy."

"Oh, don't rub so much, Way," he said, taking the handkerchief away from her. The doctor came over and said that some eyedrops might help. U Saw Han called for Meh Aye, but she did not appear for a long time and Maung Mya came running out from the kitchen saying, "Meh Aye is not here. Is there anything you want?"

"Where's the girl gone to? She must have gone next door. Way, did you send her there for something?"

"She went to get a piece of sandalwood," said Way Way, wondering to herself why Meh Aye was taking so long.

U Saw Han ran upstairs to get the eyedrops and the doctor put a few drops in her eyes.

The dark green curtains hanging over the door flapped a little in the stiff breeze that was blowing. The sun was setting and a crimson light flooded the sky. Way Way looked out of the window past the two men, who were having a drink. From where she sat she could see the window of her old bedroom. Usually it was closed, but today for some odd reason one side was open. Thoughts of the past flashed through her mind. They seemed to come, now clear and now faded, as though hiding a secret. She saw her father's face especially clearly, not as he had looked when he was living but when he had died. It was the face that had been covered with a cloth, which she had lifted. It seemed as though time had ceased to exist, as if she had been whisked away to that past time and could not get back to the present. Only when she heard footsteps behind the drapes did she get up.

"Way, where are you going?" asked U Saw Han, who had suddenly turned to her while talking to the doctor.

"To the toilet."

When Way Way got to the next room, she was startled to see Meh Aye with a swollen face and sunken eyes. She was all the more alarmed when she realized that Meh Aye had tried to change her expression and make it appear to Way Way that nothing was the matter. Way Way stopped. She had had to hide her feelings so much that she could spot it easily in another. Meh Aye's red face showed only too plainly that she had been crying. Way Way went up to her, looked at her searchingly, and whispered, "What's the matter? Tell me."

Hearing her whisper, Meh Aye did not know whether she should tell her or not. But she was unable to keep it in any longer. She came very close to Way Way and said in a low voice, "It's Ko Nay U. The Japanese have arrested him and taken him away. He is on the jetty. The motorboat has not left yet. Ma Ma Than and the others have gone to see him." Way Way gritted her teeth, steadied herself by holding on to Meh Aye's shoulder, and began to tremble. With the greatest effort, she controlled her tears. Her heart beating violently in her chest felt like the waves beating on the shore during a hurricane. Quivering as if possessed, she made her way back into the sitting room and sat down on the sofa.

U Saw Han was startled at her distraught face and cried out in a wild, incoherent manner, "What's the matter, Way, what's the matter?"

"My brother . . . the Japanese . . . have taken him . . . he's on the jetty." she gasped, shaking violently.

U Saw Han, his eyes wide, could only exclaim, "No!" and not another word more.

The doctor said, "Oh," and stood up.

"Please give me permission to go and see him . . . ," she closed her eyes tight and forced herself to say this over and over again with the greatest effort.

Wide-eyed, U Saw Han said with beating heart, "Oh no, Way, dear. How could you manage it? The Japanese would soon be beating on our door, a great long line of them. Besides, it's too far for you to go. It's impossible." U Saw Han's voice was excited and breathless, and he spoke rashly. Way Way felt her chest tighten up as she listened to him. She held his hand as hard as she could, and with tears flowing down her cheeks, lifted her supplicating face, entreating him over and over again and sobbing.

Way Way knew this was the last time she would see her brother. Whether it was her brother who would see her for the last time, or the other way around, was not clear, but it would be the last time. One of them would not survive. She persistently begged U Saw Han. But U Saw Han, though shaken by his wife's distress, could only say, "Oh no, it cannot be."

The doctor put his hand on Way Way's shoulder and said, "Don't go. It won't be good for you. They will interrogate him and send him back."

Finally, summoning all her strength, Way Way confronted U Saw Han and said what she had to say. Looking at him with a frozen stare, she said, "You have no pity for me . . . you do not really love me." Her voice, full of bitterness and resentment, rang painfully in his ears. U Saw Han's throat twisted in agony and he was unable to speak. His heart felt congested.

Way Way looked as though she would go anyway, so overwhelming was her desire, but she was held back by both the doctor and U Saw Han and placed on the sofa. The thought that she would not see her brother one last time broke her heart. In intense pain, she screamed, "Oh, my brother!" as loudly as she could, and fell unconscious.

She was in bed for three whole days. She remained there quietly and only opened her eyes when someone came near her then closed them when they left. She did not speak, simply nodding her head or shaking it when asked a question. Otherwise she did not move. U Saw Han never left her side. He did not speak. He just looked at her and was alone with his thoughts.

At dawn on the fourth day, Way Way stirred in bed. She was trying her best to rise. She managed to sit up after struggling for a while and had to rest after the effort. She then started trying to get out of bed. Close by, Meh Aye was sleeping soundly on the floor. Way Way wanted to go to her dressing table. She wanted to get her diary, which she had hidden in the drawer. She wanted to tear up all the pages she had written since she was married. In her diary she had written down all her thoughts and feelings, all her hurts and disappointments, and all the withdrawals into herself to help her endure her life and get things out of her system. This little book was her secret lake of tears.

"The saddest day of my life."

"I wanted to see my dear daddy's face."

"Little baby . . . of my heart's blood . . . little baby I lost. You have escaped the snares of existence . . . ."

"Ah . . . such is life . . . ."

"Love . . . you hurt so much . . . ."

"Ma Ma Hta and I snuggled close together and slept as we did when we were little girls . . . ."

These were some of the notes she had jotted down in her diary, her most secret possession.

It was just about daybreak and she could see the dim light from the little lamp on the dressing table. Way Way was wondering whether to wake Meh Aye and ask her to get the diary for her, or whether she should do it herself. As she was deciding, she saw that the dressing table was further away from her than Meh Aye was, so she decided to wake her.

When she got out of the bed she felt dizzy and had to cling to the bedpost. She was tired for quite a while. Her head seemed to be buzzing, her throat tight and constricted, and her chest was heaving in waves. She felt faint. Yet she felt she had the strength to do it. She managed to get to Meh Aye by sheer willpower, moving very slowly. When she was almost there, Meh Aye sprang up with a start from her sleeping mat, still half asleep. Way Way and Meh Aye reached out for each other and fell together in a heap on the floor. Meh Aye staggered up immediately, but Way Way fainted away.

Hearing the crash, U Saw Han came running out of his room. He was stunned to see that she had fainted, and just stood there trembling and looking at her. Only when Meh Aye bent down to

194

lift Way Way did he come to his senses and help. Holding Way Way, Meh Aye explained in a hoarse voice, "She was out of bed when she fell," and lifted Way Way onto the bed. U Saw Han, still dazed, held one of Way Way's hands and called "Way Way!" Meh Aye dashed downstairs to wake up Maung Mya to get the doctor.

U Saw Han shook as he felt her hands and feet, thinking that there was no life in her. He noticed the grave expression on the doctor's face when he arrived. He saw the doctor's anxious eyes and nearly went out of his mind. In his distress, he repeated, "Oh, Way Way!"

The doctor listened to her heart with his stethoscope. He listened carefully and heard a faint heartbeat.

"She fainted. How did that happen?" he asked Meh Aye. She hardly knew how to answer him. "She reached out and hugged me," was all she could reply.

Way Way opened her eyes after about an hour and looked around. She recognized Daw Thet vaguely. Daw Thet pushed down the hard ball of fear that she felt inside. Hiding it and managing to smile, she said, "Way Way, are you better?"

Way Way looked across at U Saw Han. She could not see him clearly, but her mind was very lucid.With the doctor's phrase "It's over" in his head, he sat near Way Way, looking at her, deep in thought.

Way Way's life was hanging by a thread. It was not unlike the last leaf of summer left dangling on a bare tree, about to fall.

U Saw Han called, "Way?" She did not seem to hear him. Her eyes moved from one person to another as though searching for someone in particular. When she came to Meh Aye, she knew clearly who she was. As she looked at her, Way Way's expression weakened perceptibly and a bluish tinge came into her face. Her eyes became dimmer and dimmer and slowly closed. They heard a gurgling noise in her throat not long after that, and her chest started to heave.

"Way . . . , Way . . . , oh, Way . . . !" U Saw Han called in a hoarse voice, his fatigued eyes brimming over with tears. He bit his lip as he watched her.

She was extremely tired and the doctor prepared to alleviate her exhaustion with another shot. Everyone looked at the needle and then looked at Way Way, but Way Way did not see the needle.

195

When it was inserted in her vein, her chin jutted out and her mouth twisted. As she resisted, life left her body.

It is summer and time for yellow leaves to drop from the tree, one at a time. The little yellow leaf is detached from the tree and floats down softly and is blown away gently in the breeze.

AFTERWORD

NOT OUT OF HATE AND BURMESE DAYS

Robert E. Vore

The translation of Ma Ma Lay's *Not out of Hate* into English gives scholars working in that language their first extended look at pre-World War II Burmese society as reflected in the fiction of a contemporary Burmese author. One of the benefits of this translation is the opportunity it presents to compare *Not Out of Hate* with George Orwell's *Burmese Days*, until now the only significant fictional account of prewar Burma available in English. Although *Burmese Days* is well known as a source of historical and social information concerning colonial Burma, its perspective, though critical, is nonetheless decidedly a British one. The appearance of an indigenous point of view on this period in Burmese history is therefore especially welcome.

An initial reading of the texts reveals several striking thematic and structural similarities. Both books are, in the most immediate sense, love stories—stories of failed love—in which the central couple consists of a young woman in her late teens or very early twenties and a much older man in his mid-to-late thirties. Plagued by misunderstanding, the relationship between each couple finally disintegrates with the death of one member (suicide in one case,

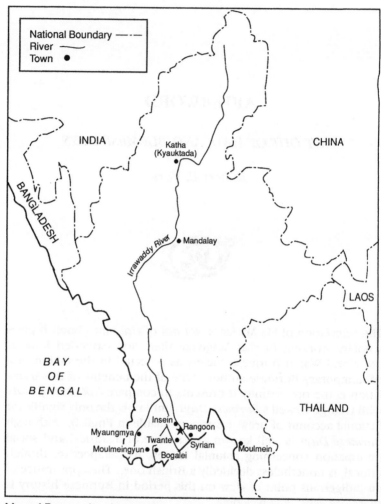

Map of Burma showing selected place names.

GEORGE ORWELL'S STATIONS IN BURMA between 1922 and 1927
were as follows: *Rangoon*, arrived November 1922; *Mandalay*, November
1922 to March 1924 (training); *Myaungmya*, March 1924 to May 1924;
Twante, May 1924 to December 1924; *Syriam*, December 1924 to
September 1925; *Insein*, September 1925 to September 1926; *Moulmein*,
September 1926 to April 1927; *Katha*, April 1927 to July 1927; *Rangoon*,
departed in July 1927.

virtual suicide in the other) who is portrayed throughout as the victim of circumstances which ultimately become intolerable. In a wider and deeper sense, these stories are vivid accounts of cultural confrontation between West and East in which imperialism, nationalism, and social and moral corruption are all important factors. With similar plots and common themes, therefore, the difference in perspective between *Not Out of Hate* (Burmese), and *Burmese Days* (British), becomes particularly intriguing since it clearly suggests that a comparative analysis of the two books would result in a truer and more complete picture of colonial Burma than can be obtained from them separately.

Not Out of Hate, Ma Ma Lay's fifth and perhaps best novel, is set in the real-life town of Moulmeingyun in the Irrawaddy River delta between 1939 and 1942. The story's main character, Way Way, is a young woman seventeen years old who lives at home with her aunt and ailing father, running the household and overseeing the accounts of the family's rice brokerage business. Way Way's mother had left the family five years before to become a Buddhist nun in the Sagaing hills. The book opens as preparations are being made for the arrival of a new rice trader in Moulmeingyun, a trader for a British firm with which U Po Thein, Way Way's father, has business. The person who arrives, however, is not an Englishman, as was expected, but a Burmese by the name of U Saw Han, who is remarkable for his completely Anglicized ways. U Saw Han moves into the house next door, which Ko Nay U, Way Way's brother and a staunch nationalist, had vacated to accommodate him, and soon falls in love with Way Way. When Way Way's elder married sister, Hta Hta, learns during a visit home that Way Way and U Saw Han are meeting secretly at night, she confronts Way Way with the situation and becomes convinced that Way Way and U Saw Han should marry. She easily elicits a proposal from U Saw Han, and the wedding takes place shortly before U Po Thein dies of tuberculosis.

It soon becomes apparent, however, that the marriage is a mistake. Way Way, now living in U Saw Han's house, becomes a virtual prisoner under her husband's sincere but absurdly paternalistic, blind, and suffocating love. U Saw Han dictates when she gets out of bed in the morning, what clothes she wears, when she takes her meals, what foods she eats, and when she goes to bed at night. Oblivious to her real needs, he forbids her to do any cooking or other housework and isolates her from her family. When Way Way suffers a miscarriage and then contracts the tuberculosis that killed her father, U Saw Han becomes even more protective, insisting that she remain in the house, take pills of this and that medicine, and receive daily injections from the doctor of Western medicine whom he has hired. Unable to bear up under such treatment, Way Way eats little, loses weight, and becomes increasingly weak. Out of fear of her husband, she refuses the care of her uncle, a traditional doctor who is said to have cured himself of tuberculosis, and resigns herself to imminent death. Wracked in spirit and overtaken by disease, she finally dies as the doctor administers yet another hated injection.

The title *Not Out of Hate*[1] alludes, of course, to the central irony of the story, for U Saw Han acts as he does not out of hate, but rather out of love, albeit a perverse kind of love which ends with Way Way being reduced to little more than a possession, without a will of her own. From the very beginning, U Saw Han pities Way Way because of the responsibilities she bears for the family's home and business. This pity in turn becomes a deeply felt compassion and finally develops into a messianic obligation to save this "little person carrying such burdens" (*Not Out of Hate* [hereafter, NOH]:91)[2] from her life of hardship. He vows to himself that the "little flower called Way Way will never droop or lose her color, she will always be fresh and fragrant. It has been

---

1. Other renderings of this title (the Burmese is *Monywei Mahu*) in English are *Not That He Hates* (U On Pe, "Modern Burmese Literature," *Atlantic*, February 1958, p. 155) and *Not Because of Hatred* (John Badgley, "Intellectuals and the National Vision: The Burmese Case," in *Literature and Society in Southeast Asia*, edited by Tham Seong Chee (Singapore: Singapore University Press, 1981), p. 51). Allott's earlier suggestion of *Not That I Hate Him* is an interesting twist, but surely mistaken (Anna Allott, "Burmese Literature," in *A Guide to Eastern Literatures*, edited by David M. Lang (New York: Praeger, 1971), p. 394).
2. Page numbers for citation from *Not Out of Hate* refer to the present publication.

pitiful to watch her carrying burdens too great for her years. I am
the only one who can free her and make her happy" (NOH:108).

U Saw Han never fully comprehends that he ultimately makes
life impossible for her. He does not see that Way Way's
"burdens," though real enough, are nevertheless very important
to her; as ties that bind her to the family and home she loves, they
are a source of personal identity and self-worth which she cannot
easily cast off, nor desires to. U Saw Han also does not see that
his own plans for her offer no substitute for the life he has taken
her from. Worse than that, he is an oppressive, negative presence,
providing no opportunity for Way Way to express herself meaning-
fully. It is inconceivable to him that his love for Way Way is doing
her harm, and Way Way's increasing weakness, despondency, and
resignation to death brings him only confusion—a confusion which
never resolves in any real understanding.

The abstract concept of Understanding is, in fact, crucial
throughout the book and may well be taken as the fundamental
moral message underlying all else. The precepts of this message
appear early on at the beginning of chapter 3 in a letter from Thila
Sari, Way Way's mother, in which she explains the Eightfold Path
of Buddhist doctrine, stressing in particular the importance of
"Right Understanding."

> Once you have the right understanding, you will then
> have right intentions, you will say the right words, you
> will perform the right actions, you will live rightly.
> You will put forth the effort to be diligent in the right,
> you will be heedful of the right, and your mind will be
> fixed on what is true.
>
> If you do not understand things rightly, your
> viewpoint will be wrong, your views will be falsified
> and will lead you to wrong action. You will live
> wrongly, your efforts will be for the wrong, and you
> will constantly be fixed in falsehood. (NOH:35)

Subsequent to this exhortation, the story begins to unfold.
Way Way, it turns out, is the victim of poor or mistaken understanding from various quarters. First, she herself does not really
understand her relationship with U Saw Han. Without thinking
about the nature of his feelings for her, she takes comfort in his

attentions and quite naturally responds to them: "'He loves me so much that I love him back, that's all,'" she tells Hta Hta at one point (NOH:94). She lacks the decisiveness and strength of will to assert to Hta Hta and U Saw Han her overriding desire to remain with her father and not get married. Only much later, after returning from the Buddhist monastery at Sagaing (but too late for it to make any difference) does she realize that U Saw Han's motivations are in fact wholly selfish and that he does not, as she at last tells him, really love her (NOH:211).

Hta Hta's understanding, too, must be questioned. Perhaps because, as the elder sister, she feels responsible for facilitating Way Way's marriage, perhaps also because she feels guilty for having gotten married herself and left Way Way to care for their father, she is quick to believe that Way Way and U Saw Han are truly in love and should marry. Although she is no doubt sincerely concerned for her younger sister's welfare and thinks she is doing the right thing by insisting on Way Way's betrothal, her actions nevertheless prove to be tragically mistaken.

But the problem of right understanding is particularly important in the case of U Saw Han, who obviously does not understand Way Way, her family, or, arguably, his own position within Burmese society, and whose life and actions are shown in sharp contrast to those of the other characters who do display right understanding—U Po Thein, Ko Nay U, and especially Hta Hta's husband, Ko Thet Htan, to whom U Saw Han is at one point directly compared (NOH:145). His indifference to everything that is meaningful to Way Way preempts any possibility of mutual understanding, and his persistent attempts to absorb Way Way completely into his world dooms their relationship. The fact that Way Way miscarries their child is physical evidence that their union cannot succeed, and the reason for its failure is at no time more clear than when, just before the miscarriage, U Saw Han forces Way Way to drink milk, thinking that she needs it for her strength.

> "Just a little milk. You have to drink just a little milk, Way Way. How can you go on without eating anything? How can you expect to keep up your strength? Just one swallow, one swallow, please. Please drink just a little of this milk." Picking up the glass of milk with extreme distaste, Way Way took a

deep breath, closed her eyes, and gulped some down without breathing. She dared not breathe, lest she smell the milk. She stood with her lips tight and her body stiff, her head erect, afraid to move. She was that uncomfortable.

U Saw Han continued coaxing her. "Another swallow, one more swallow. After this one you can stop," he said. Way Way tried to control herself. She stood with her head erect, her lips tightly closed, and tried to push him off with her hands. U Saw Han laughed and brought the glass to her lips quickly. Way Way, unable to control herself any longer, suddenly brought it all up. (NOH:167-68)

An aspect of this scene which may escape many Western readers, but would be immediately apparent to Ma Ma Lay's Burmese audience, is the significance of the glass of milk. Drinking raw milk is a characteristically Western habit in Burma. The Burmese do not as a rule drink milk and often suffer the same difficulties digesting milk as other Southeast Asian peoples.[3] Thus, when Way Way vomits, she does so not only in reaction to the manner in which U Saw Han force-feeds her, but also because what she is being fed is foreign to and simply incompatible with her own body. To the extent that the milk represents things Western, therefore, this scene dramatically illustrates the futility and impropriety of U Saw Han's efforts to Anglify Way Way. Culturally, and even biologically, it is against her nature.

This is not to suggest that Way Way is closed-minded to U Saw Han's exotic ways—on the contrary, she is shown at the beginning of the book to be very willing and naturally eager to

---

3. Indigenous Southeast Asians typically suffer from lactose (milk sugar) intolerance, a condition resulting from low levels of the lactase enzyme in the small intestine and characterized by the onset of stomach cramps, nausea and diarrhea approximately sixty to ninety minutes after milk is consumed. For an excellent, although now somewhat dated, review of the research in this area see Frederick J. Simoons, "The Geographic Hypothesis and Lactose Malabsorption: A Weighing of the Evidence," *The American Journal of Digestive Diseases* 23 (November 1978), pp. 963-80.

experience and try them for herself. After she observes the furnishings in U Saw Han's house, for instance, she proceeds to rearrange their own middle and sitting rooms (with new furniture brought from Rangoon by Ko Nay U) to look "sophisticated and Westernized" (NOH:46). She then surprises her father by serving him a typical English breakfast—bread, butter, and fresh fruit. And again that evening, when she accompanies her father and brother to U Saw Han's house for dinner, her willingness to adjust to new customs is evident. When U Saw Han bids them to eat, she is the first one to approach the dinner table, where she proceeds to unfold her dinner napkin and spread it on her lap, despite the hesitation of the U Po Thein and Ko Nay U. She also takes note of the English-style cutlery and observes the details of the table setting so that she can copy it herself later (NOH:57-58).

Nevertheless, the enthusiasm that Way Way demonstrates is only partly attributable to youthful curiosity, for she also has strong feelings of cultural inferiority with respect to U Saw Han that make her feel both self-conscious and threatened. Here the author uses the juxtaposition of the two houses to good effect. Way Way senses, for example, that the windows through which she looks out upon the house next door are also windows which open in upon her own culture and admit critique of it. Thus, ever since the arrival of U Saw Han, she had been "very uneasy" at mealtimes because their kitchen, where they ate, could be seen from the house next door (NOH:45). In another instance, when she first observes U Saw Han at breakfast from the window of Daw Thet's room, she is struck by the difference between U Saw Han's way of life and her own, and suddenly feels "awkward and ill at ease" and "insecure and full of self-doubt" because of the strangeness of what she sees (NOH:26). Only when she retreats from the window, applies sandalwood paste to her face, and then views herself in the mirror, thus reestablishing herself in familiar surroundings, does she again regain her composure. The feeling of insecurity, however, is a portent, for once U Saw Han separates her from her own world, her life becomes a prolonged struggle against an unfamiliar otherworld to which she is given no opportunity to conform, and from which she is given no reprieve.

204

❖

Burmese Days, of course, is much more familiar to the West than Ma Ma Lay's work.[4] The action of this novel takes place in the fictitious town of Kyauktada in Upper Burma (see map) in 1926.[5] John Flory, an expatriate Englishman who has been in

---

4. For discussions of *Burmese Days* included in book-length reviews of Orwell's writing, see the following sources: J. R. Hammond, *A George Orwell Companion: A Guide to the Novels, Documentaries, and Essays* (London: MacMillan, 1982), pp. 89-98; Robert A. Lee, *Orwell's Fiction* (Notre Dame: University of Notre Dame Press, 1969), pp. 1-22; Ian Slater, *Orwell: The Road to Airstrip One* (New York: Norton, 1985), pp. 17-44; Richard Smyer, *Primal Dream and Primal Crime: Orwell's Development as a Psychological Novelist* (Columbia: University of Missouri Press, 1979), pp. 24-40. An excellent biographical treatment of Orwell's time in Burma is included in Peter Stansky and William Abrahams, *The Unknown Orwell* (New York: Alfred A. Knopf, 1972), pp. 145-211.

5. Kyauktada is a fictional name for the real-life town of Katha (Stansky and Abrahams, *The Unknown Orwell*, p. 203). Katha was Orwell's last station in Burma, his only station in Upper Burma, and, like Kyauktada, is both located along the Irrawaddy River and functions as a terminus on the rail line from Mandalay.

In a country as culturally diverse as Burma, the fact that Kyauktada is so far from Moulmeingyun, the setting of *Not Out of Hate*, may raise questions about possible cultural differences between these locations that would affect a comparative interpretation of the two books. The point is worth discussing, if only to show that there are no significant differences, and that, in fact, there is good reason to assume a great deal more similarity between Kyauktada and Moulmeingyun than would at first seem warranted. First of all, although Katha is near to those parts of Burma traditionally inhabited by the Shan and Kachin peoples, the town itself is nevertheless in an area predominantly inhabited by Burmans, the same cultural group that is dominant in the delta area where Moulmeingyun is located. Second, Orwell spent only three months in Katha (part of which time he was ill), too little time, certainly, to acquire the deep and subtle impressions which he obviously called on to describe such scenes as the pwe dance in chapter eight or the visit to the bazaar in chapter nine). It is more likely that the inspirations for these and other scenes came from elsewhere—that, as

Burma for fifteen years, works for a teak logging company, spending part of his time at his logging camp in the forest and the remainder of his time in Kyauktada. When in town, his activities are largely divided between the English Club, whose other members he nonetheless despises for their bigotry, his Burmese mistress, Ma Hla May, and his Indian friend, Dr. Veraswami, to whom he repeatedly and hatefully declaims the immorality and hypocrisy of British imperialism. When Elizabeth Lackersteen arrives from England and she and Flory meet, she immediately becomes for Flory the solution to the loneliness that has long plagued him and which now becomes particularly acute. He abruptly evicts Ma Hla May from his house and thereafter wants nothing more to do with her. Meanwhile, he begins paying court to Elizabeth, inviting her to watch a native *pwe* dance, visit the local bazaar, and share in some tea with one of his Chinese friends—most of whom, however, she finds disgusting. The only times they communicate at all well are on walks in the jungle or, especially, while hunting, and it is after having shared in the killing of a leopard that Flory becomes convinced their betrothal is assured. His proposal of marriage that evening, however, is interrupted by an earthquake and then becomes out of the question with the arrival the next day of Lieutenant Verrall, who, as an aristocrat of sorts, is regarded by both Elizabeth and her aunt as an infinitely better candidate for marriage than Flory. An affair immediately ensues, but Verrall, never intending to marry Elizabeth, steals out of Kyauktada when the intentions of the Lackersteens become too obvious. With his rival gone, Flory again comes into favor, especially after helping disperse a crowd of local Burmese who attack the Club in response to the beating of a young Burman by one of the Englishmen. As before, however, his

---

Stansky and Abrahams claim, "if *Burmese Days* is a *roman à clef*, the key to its characters is not to be found in Katha, but in all the stations leading up to it, from Myaungmya to Moulmein, where Blair [Orwell's real family name; George Orwell is a pseudonym] had stopped and suffered and, as it were, made notes en route" (p. 203). These other posts, where Orwell collectively served more than three years, are all in Lower Burma, four out of the five of them in the Irawaddy River delta very near Rangoon and Moulmeingyun, the settings for *Not Out of Hate*, and very near also to Bogalei, where Ma Ma Lay was born and raised.

hopes are dashed, this time when Ma Hla May thoroughly disgraces him by entering church on a Sunday morning and, in front of the entire congregation, demanding the money which she claims he has promised to her. Elizabeth, utterly appalled at what to her is an unforgivable outrage, denounces Flory and, despite his entreaties for understanding, declares that she will never marry him. Completely crushed, he returns to his house and kills himself with a pistol, after first killing his pariah dog.

What most strikes the reader about Flory and Elizabeth is, as with U Saw Han and Way Way, their total incompatibility. The only way they are able to enjoy any kind of a relationship at all is by seriously deluding themselves as to the kind of person the other really is. This is particularly true of Flory. For his part, Flory sees in Elizabeth nothing less than his own salvation (a reversal of U Saw Han's perspective on Way Way). He feels that, with her, it would be as if he "was delivered forever from the sub-life of the past decade—the debaucheries, the lies, the pain of exile and solitude, the dealings with whores and moneylenders and pukka sahibs"[6]; it would mean he could begin over again "as though those grimy years had never touched him" (*Burmese Days* [hereafter, BD]:283).[7] His attitude towards her, however, is naive and simplistic. He wants to "interest her in things Oriental" (BD:121) and have her "love Burma as he loved it" (BD:121), but in his passionate effort to save himself, he greatly misunderstands her, somehow thinking that she is different from all the other "bloody fools" (BD:37) at the Club. This misjudgment, obvious as it is to the reader, causes him genuine confusion: he invites her to the pwe dance, telling her, "It'll interest you, I think" (BD:104) and then, when she leaves in disgust, has "no inkling of the real reason why she was angry with him" (BD:110); he later asks her to come along to the bazaar because "it would amuse her to see it" (BD:129) and then, after a second disagreement, is "too miserable even to ask himself how it was that he offended her" (BD:136-37).

---

6. George Orwell, *The Complete Works of George Orwell*, vol. 2: *Burmese Days: A Novel* (London: Secker & Warburg, 1986), p. 284.
7. Page references for *Burmese Days* are keyed to the edition cited in the previous note.

The truth is, of course, that she is not different from the others, and he could just as well have invited Colonel Bodger to join him in viewing the dance, because for Elizabeth, as no doubt for the stereotypic colonial colonel,

> it was not the *pwe*-girl's behavior, in itself, that had offended her; it had only brought things to a head. But the whole expedition—the very notion of wanting to rub shoulders with all those smelly natives had impressed her badly. She was perfectly certain that that was not how white men ought to behave. (BD:110)[8]

Even while hunting—when they are happy together—it is still painfully obvious that they are at spiritual odds, Elizabeth drawn only by the power to take life, and Flory fascinated with its beauty. This is clear, for instance, from the passage in which Flory shows Elizabeth a pigeon he has just shot (granted the irony that it was he who shot the bird):

> "Look at it. Aren't they lovely things? The most beautiful bird in Asia."

---

8. Elizabeth's allegiances are clearly indicated in a symbolic way by the fact that Orwell has her wearing tortoise-shell spectacles. As the Maung Htin Aung points out, the Burmese word for "tortoise" (*leik*) sounds very similar to the Burmese word for "English" (*Ingeleik*). The similarity, Htin Aung explains, was often played on to make anti-colonial statements: Burmese girls, for instance, in expressing distaste for things British, could be seen "throwing away their tortoise-shell combs with contemptuous gestures" (Maung Htin Aung, "George Orwell and Burma," in Miriam Gross [ed.], *The World of George Orwell*, [London: Weidenfeld and Nicolson, 1971], p. 21). Orwell, who knew the Burmese language well, must have been aware of this implicit meaning of *leik* and purposefully used the English equivalent in his novel. With her tortoise-shell eyeglasses, therefore, Elizabeth quite literally sees with the eyes of imperialism. Her marriage to Mr. Macgregor at the end of the book promises to be agreeable, since he bears the appearance of a turtle and has been nicknamed the tortoise by the Burmese (BD:25).

Elizabeth touched its smooth feathers with her finger tip. It filled her with bitter envy, because she had not shot it. And yet it was curious, but she felt almost an adoration for Flory now that she had seen how he could shoot.

"Just look at its breast-feathers; like a jewel. It's murder to shoot them. . . ."

"Are they good to eat?"

"Very. Even so, I always feel it's a shame to kill them."

"I wish I could do it like you do!" she said enviously. (BD:170-71)

Such opposing sentiments are indications of the gulf that lies between them and makes it impossible for them to be truly united. Their one accomplishment together—the killing of the leopard—is grossly annulled when the leopard's skin is ruined in the tanning, a miscarriage which, like Way Way's dead child, symbolizes the utter failure of their relationship.

In the final analysis, Flory is hopelessly caught between, on the one hand, his undeniable Britishness and dependency on colonialism, and on the other hand, his conviction that the British colonial life in Burma is nothing but a "life of lies" in which "every white man is a cog in the wheels of despotism" (BD:69). Lacking the will to openly reject the "pukka sahibs' code" (BD:69), his only recourse is to either go along with it—to "dance the *danse du pukka sahib*" (BD:156)—or learn to "live inwardly, secretly, in books and secret thoughts that could not be uttered" (BD:70). Unable to reconcile himself to the part of pukka sahib, he must choose the other, hidden life. But this life, too, becomes unbearable. As the reader is told,

it is a corrupting thing to live one's real life in secret. One should live with the stream of life, not against it. It would be better to be the thickest-skulled pukka sahib who ever hiccuped over 'Forty years on' than to live silent, alone, consoling oneself in secret, sterile worlds. (BD:70)

His one hope, of course, is for someone to "halve his loneliness" (BD:57), to share the beauty of the place with him. That this is impossible, that Elizabeth is after all just another burra memsahib, condemns Flory to his life of bitter despair.

As analogous protagonists, Flory and Way Way share several important characteristics. First, in their respective environments they each suffer the almost complete loss of individual free will. Flory likens himself to a dancer, mindlessly playing the part of the pukka sahib, while Way Way is likened to "a wind-up toy [that] moves only when wound" (BD:173). Second, this lack of free will is linked, at least in part, to the character's own inability to be assertive in the face of opposing opinions. Way Way, wanting to resist and put off marriage, is simply not able to speak her thoughts and feelings in the face of Hta Hta's and U Saw Han's overbearing demands on her. Similarly, Flory curses himself repeatedly for not having the courage to stand up and confront the club mentality which so disgusts him. Third, both Flory and Way Way are portrayed as outcasts. For Flory this is in part inherent—the hideous birthmark he bears on his face brands him physically as an outsider—but the social conditions in Burma exacerbate his differences from his fellow countrymen and make of him (as the connection between Flory and Flo, his stray dog, suggests) a true pariah. Way Way's alienation begins with her marriage, which makes her an outsider to her own family, and is then made worse when she contracts tuberculosis, a contagious disease that forces her to become even more isolated from those around her. In the end she is relegated to living by herself in the poorly accommodated guest room and is also, like Flory, a "pariah," a term her sister uses (NOH:191).

Beyond the immediate level of character, there is in addition a broader range of meaning to these books which encompasses the cultural and political conditions existing in Burma during the period in which the stories are set. In *Not Out of Hate*, despite the fact that no Englishmen actually appear, the British presence is implied through the character of U Saw Han, who is English in almost every way possible, from the kind and arrangement of furniture in his house to his too-formal and too-direct (according to Burmese custom) ways of dealing with other people. Moreover, U Saw Han, as judged from his domineering and possessive nature, seems to personify (as does Elizabeth in *Burmese Days*, although not in the same way) the very essence of imperialism. At one point in the text, for instance, he is seen dictating the affairs of the household "as if this were his little kingdom and he was supreme ruler" (NOH:167).

If U Saw Han is thus taken to symbolize British imperialism, then *Not Out of Hate* becomes richly allegorical: U Saw Han's house is the setting within which he (the British) oppresses Way Way (the Burmese), making her a virtual prisoner (a colonized people), all of which is rendered ludicrous by the fact that the house (Burma) is not his anyway, but hers (the house is owned by Way Way's family).[9] The greatest irony in this approach to the book is that, if the allegory is carried to its conclusion, the motivating force behind imperialism is seen as a sincere concern for the welfare of the colonized people (in the same sense that U Saw Han loves Way Way), and any "wrong action" on the part of the imperialist power is the result of a lack of "right understanding" concerning those over whom it has assumed control. This suggests that *Not Out of Hate* both vindicates and blames the British. On the one hand it implies that the British sincerely believed in their message of "white man's burden" to uplift the Burmese; on the other hand it holds that the Burmese did not need uplifting in the first place and, as it turned out, suffered great hardship and injustice at the hands of well-intentioned colonial rulers who were blind to reality.

---

9. In exploring the possibility of a symbolic meaning in the fictional character of U Saw Han, one may be tempted to see a connection with the Burmese politician U Saw (1900-?). Not only are the names similar, but U Saw had, like U Saw Han, strong affiliations with the British, and rose to prominence (when the political party of which he was the major figure came into power) in 1939, the same year that U Saw Han comes to Moulmeingyun and the action of *Not Out of Hate* begins. The similarity, however, ends there. Cunning, ruthless and self-serving in his political dealings, U Saw's personality type was very different from and even opposite to that of U Saw Han, whose blundering ignorance invites pity. With such disparate motivations, therefore, a symbolic connection between U Saw Han and U Saw seems unworkable.

The critique of imperialism given in *Burmese Days* is similar in some respects to that arrived at by the allegorical interpretation of *Not Out of Hate*, but different in others. The main spokes-person on the issue, and clearly the mouthpiece for Orwell's own views, is of course Flory, who in his discussions with Doctor Veraswami speaks of imperialism with open hatred. As in the Burmese novel, Flory objects to the notion that Burma benefits from British rule, pointing out that, to the contrary, the country has and will continue to be ravaged by the English.

> "Of course I don't deny [he tells the doctor] that we modernise this country in certain ways. We can't help doing so. In fact, before we've finished we'll have wrecked the whole Burmese national culture. But we're not civilising them, we're only rubbing our dirt on to them." (BD:40)

And, taking the case of India, he asks,

> "Where are the Indian muslins now? Back in the 'forties or thereabouts they were building sea-going ships in India, and manning them as well. Now you couldn't build a seaworthy fishing boat there. In the eighteenth century the Indians cast guns that were at any rate up to the European standard. Now, after we've been in India a hundred and fifty years, you can't make so much as a brass cartridge case in the whole continent." (BD:39)

But the two novels differ in their interpretations of the motives behind English rule. Not a believer in British good will towards the native populace, Flory proclaims the raison d'etre of imperialism to be, plainly spoken, thievery. "'How can you make out that we are in this country for any purpose except to steal? [he asks the doctor] It's so simple. The official holds the Burman down while the business man goes through his pockets'" (BD:38). As for the "slimy white man's burden humbug," as he calls it (BD:37), it is in his view only a ploy to make the thieving look meritorious and respectable, a necessary pose, in other words, in the danse du pukka sahib. But even more than that, it is also a lie

212

whose consequences are ultimately suffered by the British themselves. "I suppose it's a natural lie enough," he says,

"but it corrupts us, it corrupts us in ways you can't imagine. There's an everlasting sense of being a sneak and a liar that torments us and drives us to justify ourselves night and day. It's at the bottom of half our beastliness to the natives. We Anglo-Indians could be almost bearable if we'd only admit that we're thieves and go on thieving without any humbug." (BD:37)

The conclusion that imperialism turns back on its practitioners, corrupts them, and eventually imprisons them in their own charade is the central statement in *Burmese Days*. The "beastliness to the natives" is recognized, but the point is that the colonials too—the Macgregors, the Lackersteens, the Westfields, the Maxwells, and Flory himself—are victims of their own (fundamentally evil) enterprise. As the critic Francis Odle has commented, Burma is "the place where the white man had no resting-point between being a god and being a joke,[10] or, one might add, between being a god and a criminal, a god and a pariah.

There is something of this in *Not Out of Hate* as well, for if U Saw Han is examined further, he too is a kind of victim of the danse. He sincerely plays his role as modernizer and protector, but the part nevertheless extracts from him its price. In particular, he seems to have lost all regard for Family, a very non-Burmese attitude. The familial bonds which so enrich Way Way's life, for instance, are nowhere present in his character: his own family is never mentioned, he is not close with Way Way's family, and even with Way Way herself his attitude is that of a detached, beneficent guardian rather than of a husband. And this detachment, this setting himself above others and not wishing to share with them their life and value that life accordingly, leaves him empty inside. It seems true, as Hta Hta guesses at one point, "that he [is] actually a very unhappy man underneath" (NOH:189). With

___

10. Francis Odle, "Orwell in Burma," *Twentieth Century* 179.1048 (1972), pp. 38-39.

nowhere to turn for emotional support and gratification, he is, like Flory, extremely vulnerable. It is no mere coincidence that both of these characters resort to drunkenness to face their personal hardships, and it would have been no surprise if U Saw Han, like Flory, had committed violent suicide in the end. As it is, his attraction to Way Way is really little other than a misguided attempt to find self-worth. Underlying his desire to protect her is a selfish, almost psychopathic need (which he himself, of course, does not comprehend) to make her totally dependent upon him. This is the only means available to him of trying to bring about a meaningful relationship between them. Way Way's understanding of this later in the book partly explains her fatalistic resignation in the closing chapters. She knows by then that it is not really she who deserves pity, but him. He is, like the British colonials in *Burmese Days*, a man caught in a folly of his own making.

In shifting to our final topic—nationalism—the discussion turns to other parts of both *Not Out of Hate* and *Burmese Days*. In *Not Out of Hate* this means stepping outside of the Way Way-U Saw Han allegorical microcosm and looking instead at the character of Ko Nay U (Way Way's elder brother) and the activities associated with him. In *Burmese Days* it means focusing on the peasant "uprising" instigated by U Po Kyin at Thongwa and the attack on the Club depicted in chapter 22.

Looking at Ko Nay U, it is evident that there is between him and Way Way a sharp contrast in character types which is perhaps relevant to the picture of Burmese society that Ma Ma Lay is presenting in *Not Out of Hate*. Whereas Way Way is a "soft and quiet" person (NOH:69), Ko Nay U is opinionated, candid, and outspoken. Way Way, for instance, passively submits to domination by U Saw Han, but Ko Nay U, although understanding and respectful of his sister's feelings, openly declares his dislike of the Anglophile, referring to him derogatorily as "the Englishman" (NOH:119) and even "Master Chicken-Shit" (NOH:50), and opposes Way Way's marriage to him. If Way Way, in other words, symbolizes a Burmese populace submissive to foreign rule, Ko Nay U's role is to motivate that populace to assert its cultural integrity and political independence.

It is evident that Ko Nay U's nationalistic convictions have developed over a considerable period of time, apparently beginning during his schooling at the University of Rangoon where, the reader is told, he graduated in 1935 (NOH:51). Saya Chit, the Burmese literature instructor in Moulmeingyun, comments that Ko Nay U was "disillusioned by the colonial education system ever since he went to college" (NOH:70). That he was so disillusioned is not surprising; the University of Rangoon was riddled with student discontent virtually since its opening in 1920. A student strike in that year had protested against what the students perceived to be anti-Burmese policies regarding admission and the curriculum, and from that time forward the campus was a center for nationalist activism. The situation encountered by Ko Nay U would have been very much like that described by Htin Aung, who was a student at the University in the 1920s.

> If the English professors (there were no Burmese) had been dedicated teachers, they could have moulded their students in such a way that they would become less hostile to the English, without making them less nationalistic in outlook. Unfortunately the professors belonged to the Imperial Educational Service, and considered themselves officials rather than teachers. They stayed aloof from their students, and behaved as if they were avenging the [student] strike of 1920.[11]

---

11. Maung Htin Aung, "George Orwell and Burma," p. 25. It is interesting to compare this impression of the Imperial Education Service teachers with an anecdote that Orwell relates in another work: "I remember a night I spent on the train with a man in the Educational Service, a stranger to myself whose name I never discovered. It was too hot to sleep and we spent the night in talking. Half an hour's cautious questioning decided each of us that the other was 'safe'; and then for hours, while the train jolted slowly through the pitch-black night, sitting up in our bunks with bottles of beer handy, we damned the British Empire—damned it from the inside, intelligently and intimately. It did us both good. But we had been speaking forbidden things, and in the haggard morning light when the train crawled into Mandalay, we parted as guiltily as any adulterous couple." (George Orwell, *The Road to Wigan Pier* [New York: Harcourt Brace, 1958], p. 177.)

From this glimpse it is no wonder that Ko Nay U's animosity toward the university became deeply rooted and was to remain with him long after graduating.

Back in Moulmeingyun four years later, Ko Nay U becomes directly involved in nationalist politics. He joins the Dobama Asiayone, a political organization aimed at motivating young Burmese to support the nationalist cause, and then establishes a chapter of the Dobama Asiayone himself in Moulmeingyun.[12] In addition, he opens a reading library "in remembrance and honor those many writers and artists who have kept the historical heritage of our country alive for us" (NOH:70), demonstrates in support of the strikers from Yenangyaung who are protesting against the British-owned Burma Oil Company, and eventually joins the Burma Independence Army to take up arms against the British.

All of these later movements and events in which Ko Nay U takes part reflect the general fact that by the 1930s and early 1940s, nationalism in Burma had become both well formulated ideologically and well organized politically. The Dobama Asiayone of which he becomes a member was organized in 1935 when the previously existing Dobama Society (originally established in 1930) merged with the All Burma Youth League (established in 1931). It was this organization which adopted for its members the honorific title Thakin (as Ko Nay U does) in a symbolic gesture to defy the British, for whom the title up until then had most often been

---

12. For a thorough and very recent study of the Dobama Asiayone, see Khin Yi, *The Dobama Movement in Burma (1930-1938)*, Southeast Asia Program Monograph (Ithaca, New York: Cornell Southeast Asia Program, 1988). For additional information on the nationalist movement in Burma, see B. K. Drake, *Burma: Nationalist Movements and Independence* (Kuala Lumpur: Longman, 1979) and Albert D. Moscotti, *British Policy and the Nationalist Movement in Burma, 1917-1937*, Asian Studies at Hawaii, No. 11 (Honolulu: University Press of Hawaii, 1974). For a comprehensive treatment of this period in the colonial history of Burma see John F. Cady, *The History of Modern Burma* (Ithaca, New York: Cornell University Press, 1958). Other general discussions can be found in F. S. V. Donnison, *Burma* (London: Ernest Benn, 1970), pp. 93-139, and Maung Htin Aung, *A History of Burma* (New York: Columbia University Press, 1967), pp. 266-308.

reserved. Aside from the Dobama Asiayone there were many other nationalist groups politically active during this period—the Young Men's Buddhist Association (originally formed in 1906), the All Burma Student Movement (1930), the All Burma Peasants' Organization (1938), the All Burma Cultivators' League (1938), and the All Burma Trade Union Congress (1940), to mention only the most prominent. Clearly, Ko Nay U's environment is one in which Burmese independence is a major concern across many sectors of Burmese society.

The issue of nationalism is less integral to the story of *Burmese Days* than *Not Out of Hate*. This is not surprising, since Orwell's point of reference is a British one, and Burmese nationalism, although recognized as a critical part of the cultural and political milieu of the time, is not central to the book's message. Thus, when Flory is at his logging camp in the forest in chapter 20, he hears about the unrest in Thongwa only at third-hand, through a letter from Dr. Veraswami, who himself only reported the news as he heard it in Kyauktada. The goings-on among the peasants themselves are never entered into. The same is true of the confrontation between the local Burmese and the English at the Club after Ellis, one of the Englishmen, had beaten a young Burmese boy. The point of view is from inside the Club looking out, and nothing is revealed of the developments among the Burmese between the time of Ellis' brutality and the time the confrontation occurs.

Nevertheless, even as portrayed these events reflect the general feeling of the Burmese during the 1920s, a decade particularly rife with Burmese-British tensions. For their part, the Burmese peasants had protested British rule ever since 1886 when administrative and legal changes decreed by the colonial government caused many traditional village institutions to be eliminated. But in 1919 this residual animosity was greatly aggravated with the passage of the Government of India Act, which made Burma a province of India virtually without representation in colonial government, rather than an independent colony as many Burmese nationalists had both desired and expected. This, followed by the 1920 student strike at the University of Rangoon and the controversy over dyarchy reforms in 1923, meant that by the mid-1920s

nationalist sentiment was at a high pitch.[13]   Orwell himself
testifies to this in another writing when he says that in Moulmein,
where he was stationed in 1926 and 1927, "anti-European feeling
was very bitter" and that he was "hated by large numbers of
people."[14] Against so volatile a background, it is easy to understand how U Po Kyin could with such facility incite the peasants at
Thongwa to stage a revolt (though it was hardly that), and why the
very thought of revolt caused such alarm among the British. It is
also easy to see why the Burmese in Kyauktada united so spontaneously and angrily to confront the Club with their demands that
Ellis be justly punished, and why the refusal of their demands was
enough to trigger physical violence. It was out of events such as
these that the calculated, powerful nationalism of the 1930s grew.

The manner in which the subjects of nationalism and
imperialism are differently treated in these novels suggests much
about the similar sensibilities of the two authors. In both books,
imperialism is dealt with in a questioning, ideological way. It is
approached as an ethical problem as well as a social tragedy, and
the central issues raised—U Saw Han's ignorance, Way Way's initial
fascination with the West and her later self-doubt, Flory's
psychosis, and the bigotry of the Club members—are all abstract

---

13. Whereas before 1922 the colonial government was under almost
complete British control, under the dyarchy reforms certain powers
were transferred to elected Burmese ministers of the newly formed
Legislative Council. Among the powers transferred were control over
agriculture, excise, health, public works (except irrigation), forests and
education. The powers maintained under the Governor's Executive
Council concerned law and order, land revenue, finance, and labor.
Although the reforms were ostensibly instituted to decentralize control
in the government, many Burmese were suspicious of the intentions of
the British. A similar dyarchy system in India had come under much
criticism, and in Burma there was great skepticism as to just how much
control the Legislative Council would have. The dissatisfaction of the
Burmese was illustrated by a boycott of the first elections in December
1922; only 6.9 percent of the eligible Burmese actually voted. The
reforms, however, remained in effect. See Cady, *The History of Modern
Burma*, pp. 242-46 and Htin Aung, *A History of Burma*, pp. 285-87.
14. George Orwell, *Shooting an Elephant and Other Essays* (New York:
Harcourt Brace, 1950), p. 3.

and subjective. In these cases, both Orwell and Ma Ma Lay are obviously using their art to make moral statements.

They both address nationalism very differently, however. Here, the picture is much more objective, even historical. In *Not Out of Hate*, Ko Nay U and the nationalist movement appear as a distinct subplot, free of any literary device aside from straight-forward narrative. There are no hidden or unrecognized motives, no misunderstandings, no plays of symbolism, and no subtleties of imagery. The reader is not given to question the legitimacy of nationalism, but only to recognize its existence and force. Much the same is true in *Burmese Days*. The nationalists operate quite outside of Flory's psychological quagmire, and the laconic and superficial account of the Burmese dissidents suggests that Orwell has no quarrel in that quarter (he in fact recognizes and even sympathizes with their cause). Despite the fact, therefore, that nationalism is an issue in both of these works, the outstanding questions remaining in the reader's mind—as, no doubt, the authors intended—primarily concern the British and their imperialistic venture.

In keeping with the epigraph of this Afterword, I have tried in the foregoing discussions to show how the artist—really two artists in this case—can make a sympathetic connection between two cultures in the midst of what is in other ways a destructive confrontation. In these two books, George Orwell and Ma Ma Lay express very similar philosophies regarding the colonial situation in Burma: they both sympathize with the tragic victims—Way Way, Flory, even U Saw Han—and call for a greater understanding from the oppressors.

That the course of events in the books in fact betrays connection—that the heroes both die—does not indicate a pessi-mistic fatalism. Ma Ma Lay wrote *Not Out of Hate* in 1955, after Burma had become independent—and she no doubt shared the optimism of the time concerning her country's part in the post-colonial world of equal nations (although she later became disillusioned with the oppressive socialist government in Burma). And although it is true that Orwell, writing from 1930 to 1932, did not foresee Burmese independence (he in fact believed Burma could not defend itself as an independent nation), he still hoped for fair and mutually agreeable relations between England and Burma, and remained very active in the affairs of both Burma and

India in his later years.[15] Clearly, then, the social ills which both of these authors expose in their fiction are problems which they either knew or believed to be correctable.

In another sense the two books themselves constitute a connection, the specific nexus of which is the four major characters: Way Way and U Saw Han; Flory and Elizabeth. Enough similarities have been explored between these couples to show that they can indeed be seen as direct points of union between the books. Way Way and Flory, as counterpart characters, are very much alike both in terms of the circumstances they face and in their reactions to those circumstances. The reader, knowing one, finds the other also familiar. U Saw Han and Elizabeth, in their absolute British mentalities, are likewise counterpart characters. In other respects, U Saw Han and Flory resemble one another. Although Flory is the more aware of the two, the dilemmas they each face have many common features. And finally, the dynamics of the relationships themselves are the same in the sense that what U Saw Han is ultimately seeking in Way Way is very close to what Flory seeks in Elizabeth, and that in both cases the characters involved share no real understanding.

Taken together, these connections form a definite link between the books, a sort of bridge across which the reader can, with remarkably little shifting of gears, enter both the world of Burmese family life and vibrant nationalism in *Not Out of Hate* and the desperate, corrupt, psychotic life of the colonials in *Burmese Days*. One might expect novels such as these, coming from very different cultures, to conflict and perhaps to be incompatible; these do not conflict and are not incompatible. They are, rather, complementary works which together offer us a more complete view of Burma in the prewar era than we could gain from each taken by itself.

---

15. During World War II, Orwell worked for the British Broadcast Corporation for two years as a broadcaster to India and Burma. Reportedly he had planned to return to Asia after the war to take up a post with a newspaper in Lucknow, India, a plan which he was forced to abandon when he became ill with tuberculosis (John Gross, "Imperial Attitudes," in Miriam Gross [ed.], *The World of George Orwell*, [London: Weidenfeld and Nicolson, 1971], p. 36).

Additional Bibliography

Allott, Anna. "Burmese Literature." In Leonard S. Klein (ed.), *Far Eastern Literature in the 20th Century: A Guide* (England: Old Castle Books, 1988) pp. 1-9.

————. "Prose Writing and Publishing in Burma Today—Government Policy and Popular Practice." In Tham Seong Chee (ed.), *Literature and Society in Southeast Asia* (Singapore: Singapore University Press, 1981) pp. 1-35.

Amirthanayagam, Guy and Harrex, S. C. *Only Connect: Literary Perspectives East and West*. Adelaide: Centre for Research in the New Literatures in English; Honolulu: East-West Center, 1981.

Eagleton, Terry. "Orwell and the Lower-Middle-Class Novel." In Bernard Oldsey and Joseph Brown (eds.), *Critical Essays on George Orwell*, (Boston: G. K. Hall, 1986) pp. 111-129. Originally published in *Exiles and Emigres: Studies in Modern Literature* (London: Chatto & Windus; New York: Schocken Books, 1970) pp. 78-108.

Knapp, John V. "Dance to a Creepy Minuet: Orwell's *Burmese Days*, Precursor of *Animal Farm*." *Modern Fiction Studies* 21 (Spring 1975) pp. 11-29.

Kubal, David L. "George Orwell: The Early Novelist." *Arizona Quarterly* 27 (Spring 1971) pp. 59-73.

Lee, Robert A. "Symbol and Structure in *Burmese Days*: A Revaluation." *Texas Studies in Literature and Language* 11 (Spring 1969) pp. 820-35.

Matthews, Brian. "'Living With the Stream': George Orwell's *Burmese Days*." In Guy Amirthanayagam and S. C. Harrex (eds.), *Only Connect: Literary Perspectives East and West* (Adelaide: Centre for Research in the New Literatures in English; Honolulu: East-West Center, 1981) pp. 93-106.

Meyers, Jeffrey. "The Ethics of Responsibility: Orwell." *The University Review* 35 (December 1968) pp. 83-87.

Minn Latt. "Mainstreams in Burmese Literature." *New Orient Bimonthly* 1:1, 3, 6 (1960); 2:6 (1961); 3:6 (1962). Series of five articles.

Muggeridge, Malcolm. "Burmese Days." In Harold Bloom (ed.), *George Orwell* (New York: Chelsea House, 1987), pp. 21-24. Originally published in *World Review* 16 (June 1950) pp. 45-48.

Mya Sein. "The Women of Burma." *Atlantic*, February 1958, pp. 122-25.

Orwell, George. *The Road to Wigan Pier*. Forward by Victor Gollancz. New York: Harcourt Brace, 1958.

Rai, Alok. "Colonial Fictions: Orwell's *Burmese Days*." *Economic and Political Weekly* 18, no. 5 (29 January 1983) pp. PE47-PE52.

Stevens, A Wilber. "George Orwell and Southeast Asia." *Yearbook of Comparative and General Literature* 11 (1962) pp. 133-41.

Wadsworth, Frank. "Orwell as a Novelist: The Early Work." *The University of Kansas City Review* 22 (December 1955) pp. 93-99.

This series of publications on Africa, Latin America, and Southeast Asia is designed to present significant research, translation, and opinion to area specialists and to a wide community of persons interested in world aVairs. The editor seeks manuscripts of quality on any subject and can generally make a decision regarding publication within three months of receipt of the original work. Production methods generally permit a work to appear within one year of acceptance. The editor works closely with authors to produce a high quality book. The series appears in a paperback format and is distributed worldwide. For more information, contact the executive editor at Ohio University Press, Scott Quadrangle, University Terrace, Athens, Ohio 45701.

Executive editor: Gillian Berchowitz
AREA CONSULTANTS
Africa: Diane Ciekawy
Latin America: Thomas Walker
Southeast Asia: William H. Frederick

The Ohio University Research in International Studies series is published for the Center for International Studies by the Ohio University Press. The views expressed in individual volumes are those of the authors and should not be considered to represent the policies or beliefs of the Center for International Studies, the Ohio University Press, or Ohio University.

Printed and bound by CPI Group (UK) Ltd, Croydon, CR0 4YY

09/06/2025

14685965-0003